THIRST

Books by Karen E. Taylor

Hunger

Crave

Thirst

Published by Kensington Publishing Corp.

THIRST

the vampire legacy

KAREN E. TAYLOR

KENSINGTON BOOKS
www.kensingtonbooks.com

KENSINGTON BOOKS are published by

Kensington Publishing Corp.
119 West 40th Street
New York, NY 10018

All Kensington titles, imprints, and distributed lines are available at special quantity discounts for bulk purchases for sales promotion, premiums, fund-raising, educational or institutional use.

Special book excerpts or customized printings can also be created to fit specific needs. For details, write or phone the office of the Kensington Special Sales Manager: Kensington Publishing Corp., 119 West 40th Street, New York, NY 10018. Attn. Special Sales Department. Phone: 1-800-221-2647.

Kensington and the K logo Reg. U.S. Pat. & TM Off.

ISBN-13: 978-0-7582-7487-8
ISBN-10: 0-7582-7487-4

First Kensington Trade Paperback Printing: October 2012
10 9 8 7 6 5 4 3 2 1

Printed in the United States of America

Contents

THE
VAMPIRE
VIVIENNE

For Brian and Geoff—
the best sons a mother could ever have

Acknowledgments

Big thanks as always are due to my husband, Pete, and to my sons, Brian and Geoff, for being willing to forego home-cooked meals and clean laundry during the writing process. Thank you also to Mary and Dave for their help with the French phrases; to John for his last-minute tidbits of advice; to John Scognamiglio, my wonderful editor; to Cheryl Weiner, my fabulous agent; to Laura, just because; and to all the folks on sff.net who listened to IRC sessions, most especially Lena, who put up with more of my private wailing than anyone else. Take a bow, folks. Viv wouldn't have existed without your help and support.

Prologue

The shimmering figure in the mirror is little more than a girl. Sitting before the reflection, she brushes her lustrous blond hair and studies her pouting image. Finally, satisfied with the results, she rises from the vanity stool and, with a flirtatious shrug, drops the white satin robe from her shoulders. The girl's skin is almost as white as the clothes she sheds; perfect and unblemished, it glows in the flicker of many candles.

She runs long, delicate fingers over breasts and thighs, giving a high-pitched, tingling laugh at the shivery sensations the touch brings. The mirror reveals her as young and succulent, a girl only beginning to wake to the mysteries of life, lips yet unkissed and a body still only dreaming of the passion that awaits her.

Deeper in the reflection lies a huddled mass of bedclothes, underneath which rests the young lover chosen for this special evening; chosen for his strength, the curl of his dark hair, and the blue of his eyes. It was the eyes that had decided her on this man; the way they watched her over a glass of wine, the way they burned into hers. It is time, she knows, long past time, and he will be the one.

The girl smiles at herself in the mirror one last time, knowing she should not, knowing there are reasons to shun her reflection. Mirrors, she has learned, should never be trusted. Still, she looks on herself and smiles.

But you must know, *mon ami,* the mirror lies, for the girl's reflection changes and a demon grins back at her. The lips curl and snarl, the teeth sharpen to fangs, the eyes glow with lust and hunger.

The mirror lies and the mirror will always lie; I know, for I am she in the mirror. My name is Vivienne Courbet and I am no girl.

Like countless others before him, my youthful lover is deceived by an innocence lost over three hundred years ago, yet still perfectly preserved in my face and body. And although he will not have the virginal conquest he expected, rest assured he will be more than compensated for the blood he gives to sustain my evil, unnatural, and wonderful life.

Part 1

Chapter 1

Paris: the House of the Swan, 1719

I was not always the demon in the mirror. Once I was human. Born in the usual manner, I grew, I played, I matured. Attending church with Maman, I prayed, crossing myself in name of the Trinity, believing in that sweet salvation promised us by the priests. When Maman died, I stopped praying, stopped believing. And when I was old enough to be bartered and married, I rebelled, setting my feet on an irrevocable path, one that I would not now undo even if I could.

Such a familiar story was my life to that point that I need not tell it further than mentioning the rebellious girl, the unrelenting father, the late-night escape, and the long walk to the opportunities of the big city; in short, nothing that hadn't been done thousands of times before and since. In time I found my way to one of the few places a young lady of my ilk could exist without the interference of father or husband.

The House of the Swan beckoned to me, the name seeming a good omen. Had I not been called Mademoiselle Cygnette by my nurse from a young age? Here, then, I thought, was a place for me to stay. To be honest, I had almost reached the end of my endurance; any place willing to take me in would have done.

The proprietress met me at the door, saw to it that I was bathed, clothed, and fed, explaining to me that such kindness must be repaid with work. I agreed to work in her house for a place to sleep and meals, but after two weeks of backbreaking labor, I discovered there was another job here, one for which a girl was clothed in fine garments and had her meals served to her, a job in which such a girl was courted by rich and elegant gentlemen. Not entirely innocent as to the nature of Madame's business and aware enough to recognize the cunningness of her recruitment, I nevertheless knocked on her bedroom door one evening, looking for a way out of the kitchen.

"Entrez vous," she called and I dropped her a curtsy in the doorway. She smiled when she saw me and clapped her hands together as if in amusement of joy. "Why, if it isn't our newest little swan. Come in, my dear, and tell me how you are enjoying the work to which I put you."

"If you please, Madame, the work is fine. And I am very grateful for your allowing me to stay in your house, but some of the other girls have been talking and I wondered if I might . . ."

She threw her head back and laughed. "I wondered how long it would take such a precious princess to tire of manual labor. But do you know what you ask? Tell me, Vivienne." She rose from her chair and walked toward me, grasping my chin in her hand and turning my face up to her. "Are you a virgin?"

Now I was not, but she had no way to know that, nor was it in her best interests to prove that I was not. So I dropped my eyes and managed a blush and she clapped her hands together again. "Marvelous," she said, with a wry chuckle, "never say more than you need to, my dear, and always let that blush answer for you." She nodded her head and rang the bell at the door. "You'll do just fine, my little swan."

"Madame?" Chloe appeared at the door in answer to the bell.

"Take Vivienne to the empty room, Chloe, and set her up with some nice clothes." She looked at me intently, then nodded again. "Yes, I think that some of Marie's dresses will do, but none of the darker colors. White would be best." Cocking her head to one side, she thought. "Yes, white. And pink. Something youthful, with lots of frills and ribbons."

So before I became a creature of the night, I became a lady of the night. I should be ashamed to admit that the life suited me, but so it did, perfectly. The other women pampered me, dressing me as if I were a doll, brushing my hair and exclaiming over its natural curls. Madame was well pleased with me; she contrived to sell my virginity several times, until rumor of my existence became fact. Odd, how the fact really made little difference to the men; it was not virginity they craved, but rather the feel and look of innocence, the sweet blush of first love, something that I was able to provide them time after time. In this, they proved easy to please and so long as they were pleased, my position remained secure.

And life was good. Madame discovered that I had a passable singing voice and added me to the roster of the girls who could entertain the guests in public as well as in private. With girlish pride I looked forward to performing in the tableaus and dramas, loving the applause and the adulation. It was during this period that I learned how to read and write and speak a smattering of other languages. I was well fed and elegantly clothed, warm and secure.

As the days and weeks turned into months and seasons, though, I grew restless.

"Chloe?"

"Hmmm?" She gripped a brush in her teeth while she was dressing my hair, combing it with her fingers and forming it into long spiraling curls.

"Where were you before you came here?"

She took the brush out of her mouth and held up a mirror for me to see the results of her work. "*Très bon,* Vivienne. But it is easy when one works with natural youth and beauty. As for where I was? What does it matter? I am here now."

I shrugged. "I am curious, that is all. It seems to me that I have seen nothing of the world. First I was at home and now I am here. And"—I got up from my chair, walked over to the window, and leaned my elbows on the sill, watching the people walking by—"it is good here and life is wonderful. But there must be something more, something wondrous. I know that the world is waiting for me and only me to come by and claim the prize."

"And what would that prize be?"

I laughed. "I have no idea, Chloe. Which makes it all the more wondrous, don't you agree?"

She gave a disgusted snort. "You have read entirely too many of Madame's books. Chivalry and romance? There will be no white knight riding in to save you from the ogre. The best you can hope for is to save a little money against the time you will not be young and beautiful. It is true that now you are much loved, and men praise you for the softness of your cheek and the whiteness of your breasts. But do you think this life lasts forever?"

I sighed. "It should, Chloe."

Chapter 2

Then, one evening, almost one year after I had arrived at the House of the Swan, the owners paid us a call. Madame herself came to get me so that I could be introduced. I could detect her nervousness and her fear from the minute she opened my door.

"Vivienne," she said, glancing around in the room to see, I presumed, if I was alone, "you have been summoned. Messieurs Leupold and Esteban have come and would like to meet you." She fussed with my hair and fluffed up the frills at the neckline of my dress; her hands trembled and her voice sounded tight and nervous.

"Madame?" Never before had I seen her this flustered over the arrival of two men. "Who are these men?"

"Oh, my dear, they own this house. I merely run it for them. And oh, they never send word that they are planning to visit. No, sometimes the door just opens up and they are there. Voilà!" She gave a little humorless laugh.

"But why do they wish to see me?"

"They have heard of you, Princess. The men talk and the

women talk and you are very much sought after. Apparently"—
and she gave another little laugh—"you have acquired quite a
reputation in a short time. But come, we have no time for small
talk. They are waiting."

With that she rushed me down the hallway and practically
pushed me into her private bedchamber. There, surrounded by
the heavy brocade and velvet of Madame's accoutrements, in
front of a roaring fire, stood two men, the likes of which I had
never seen before.

They were not particularly tall, not particularly handsome.
Dressed sedately, their hair was dark, their skin pale. One might
have taken them for brothers, not so much because of their
looks, but because of the similarity of their demeanor. They
seemed to me more like men of religion than the sort who
would traffic in this business. Nothing would ever distinguish
them from any other man one might meet. Or so I thought, until
they both turned away from the warmth of the flames and fastened their eyes on me. I took one tiny breath, overcome with
terror and delight, amazed at the depth of those eyes and the
worlds they promised me. In short, before a single word was
spoken, I was lost.

"Go." That word was not directed at me. Madame murmured a quick acquiescence, the door opened, closed. And we
three were alone.

"Your name is Vivienne, is that correct?" The older of the
two spoke and smiled at me.

"*Oui,* Monsieur."

"I am Victor," he said with a small flourish and bow, "and
my friend here is Maximillian. Or Max for short."

"Monsieur Victor, Monsieur Maximillian." I gave them both
my best curtsy, the one I had been taught to use before royalty.

The gesture was not wasted on them. Victor threw his head
back and laughed. His laughter should have put me at ease; instead I felt a cold sweat trickle down my back. "No, girl," he
said, grown serious again, "we are not royalty, in any sense of
the word. Just Victor and Max will do. What did that interfering old harpy tell you about us?"

"She said nothing, sirs, nothing that could be considered de-meaning. But she seemed"—I hesitated a second, then contin-ued—"frightened. Perhaps because you own the house and hold the power . . ."

At this the one I was to call Max shook his head. "Perhaps, but I doubt it, little one. She is frightened of us because she knows it is safer that way. Humans have such a good instinct for furthering their own lives. But you"—and he gave me what I supposed he thought was a kindly smile—"you aren't fright-ened."

I laughed, a high-pitched and ringing laugh men often called enchanting. "No, Max, I am not. I have been afraid of so few things in my life. My nurse always said as I was growing up that I had the temperament of a man. That I would come to no good end as a result. And, well, here I am." I laughed again. "So she is proven right. But still I am not frightened. Life is too short for fear or worry."

"Is it, Vivienne?"

Something in the way Max said those three words made me shiver in anticipation, as if he knew a secret I did not.

I smiled at the both of them, wondering what exactly was ex-pected of me. Was I to seduce them both? Together? Separately? A soft knock at the door brought me out of my speculations and I crossed the room to answer. Madame came in without a word and set down a tray containing tempting little morsels of food, fruit and cheese and bits of bread together with a fine vintage red wine and three of her best crystal glasses.

She patted my arm as she walked back out of the room. It seemed as if she was crossing herself, but that was silly. Mad-ame was hardly a religious individual. I shrugged, closed the door after her, and, on impulse, reached over and drew the bolt shut. "There," I said, moving over to the tray and pouring wine, "that is much cozier. No interruptions."

We raised our glasses and drank a toast. "To long life," I pro-posed; Victor and Max exchanged a curious glance, then pressed me to sit down on the couch while they fed me and fussed over me. When half of the food was gone and all of the wine, they asked me to stand in front of them.

"Turn around," Victor ordered, motioning with his hand, his voice growing stern.

I did so and when I faced them again, their expressions had become more alive, more animated. I felt a flush of excitement, as warming as the fire.

"Take off your clothes."

I had heard that phrase hundreds of times since coming to the Swan, and obeyed it each and every time. At times I would undress slowly, playfully, drawing excitement from each little movement; other times I would be hurried and frantic. The outcome, of course, was always the same. Never had the action been fraught with peril or fear; it had always felt as natural as the sun setting and the moon rising. But to stand naked in the presence of these two men seemed somehow an irrevocable step, final and forever. And I had lied to Max, for I was frightened, more than I had ever been in my meager years, more because I did not know why.

I wanted to run and I wanted to stay. I wanted these men to leave and never return, while at the same time I knew I would regret that parting for all of my life. Poised on the brink of the unknown, I froze, unable to move, unable to speak. Caught in the gaze of their eyes, I could barely breathe. The room grew unbearably hot, the flicker of the candles distorted my vision so that it seemed that Max and Victor hovered over me like two large and merciless birds of prey, I took one step backward and crumpled to the floor.

When I awoke, I was lying on the couch, my dress had been loosened, and the room felt lighter. Holding a glass of wine to my lips, Max knelt next to me. I smiled at him, rather shyly. "I am sorry," I said, "I'm not sure what happened. It was very strange, it seemed that the two of you were . . ." I couldn't finish the thought. Instead I craned my head up and looked around the room. Victor was gone.

"He left," Max said, easily reading my thoughts. "I asked

him to. I suspect that the two of us were a bit much for you. We are not your typical gentlemen."

I laughed at that and reached over to caress his face. He jumped slightly at the touch, but then leaned into my hand. His skin was smooth, cool to the touch, and although his eyes reflected the flames of the fire, they were also cold. So deep and fathomless and yet, so dead. I lifted my other hand and cradled his face, mesmerized by his eyes, wanting to do nothing but stare into them forever.

"What are you?" The whisper escaped my lips before I could think.

"Do you really want to know?"

"Oh, yes." I breathed as his mouth came down on mine. "Oh, yes, please."

Whatever I may have thought of Max afterward, that night he was, for me, the perfect being. He seemed at once an angel, a man, and a demon. He possessed me in ways even I had never known possible. Bringing me to the brink of ecstasy over and over again, he tested my limits, my strength, my passion. The feelings I felt were not love, not for either of us, but I was captivated, nonetheless. Watching the light from the fire sculpt the fine lines on his ageless face, I saw his canines grow and sharpen in his pleasure, felt them graze my skin as he kissed me. I knew his true nature then and reveled in the knowledge, welcomed his bite, wanted the opportunity to give everything I had.

Before he bent to drink fully at my neck, though, he stopped and pulled away from me. I gave a moan of disappointment and reached my arms up to bring him back to me.

"No." He stood up and towered over me where I lay, gasping for air. "Do not tempt me, Vivienne. I am very hungry, but I have dallied here too long and it is close to dawn. If you feed me now, I will take too much and you will surely die. I don't have the time to replenish you, nor do we have the time to prepare a place for you. And I would not force you into this decision so soon."

He began to put his clothes back on and silent tears flowed down my cheeks. My entire body felt emptied, as if he had drained me of the will to live. I heard myself saying, over and over, "Come back to me. Oh, please, come back to me."

He laughed as he headed for the door. "Enjoy the dawn, Vivienne, for if I return for you tomorrow evening, it will be your last."

He did return. He drained me to the point of death, brought me back to life with his own blood, wrapped me up in blankets, and carried me away to my new existence.

I was nineteen years old; I would never age, never have to sicken and die. The entire world stretched out at my feet and worshiped me; life was an adoring servant willing to give me everything I could ask. Made forever beautiful and forever young, I never once regretted that evening.

Chapter 3

Toledo: the House of Esteban, 1768

"I do not care whether it's Christmas Eve or not, Max. I'm hungry. I'm bored, and I'm going down to the village." Even knowing that I sounded like a petulant child didn't stop me from voicing my complaints. "This place is as quiet as a tomb and it's driving me mad."

For the first fifty years, Max and I had traveled extensively, sometimes just the two of us and sometimes with Victor. That life had been nomadic and exciting. There had always been new experiences, new people, and exotic foreign cities to explore.

But when a year ago Max had decided to acquire and live in his ancestral home, the thrill faded. I felt trapped in this huge drafty house, I was always cold and always bored.

"Vivienne, we've been through this a hundred times. You are too noticeable, too memorable. Must I remind you that the last time you went into the village unattended, three bachelors presented themselves the next day to ask my permission to court you? You make entirely too much of an impression on the local boys. They've never seen your like before."

I gave a dry laugh. "They have barely seen my like now. I can't have spent more than ten hours out of this house since we came here. I'm weary, Max, and so filled up with ennui I could scream. And let's be honest, I am not your daughter, nor your wife that you can order me about or keep me prisoner here."

"You are not a prisoner, Vivienne, but I worry about you—"

I cleared my throat, interrupting him. "Must *I* remind *you*," I said, echoing his tone and words, "that I am seventy years old and more than capable of survival all on my own? I have already learned everything you were willing to teach me, years ago. Let me out, Max. Or let me go."

"And where exactly would you go?"

"Back to Paris." I sighed. "And haven't we had this conversation before?"

He laughed. "Yes, so many times that I can't number them." Then he shrugged. "Fine, go into the village. Find yourself a nice young man to feed on. But try not to be seen by any others. They ask questions, they are capable of drawing the obvious conclusions. This is my family home; I do not wish to be driven out of it."

"I understand." I jumped out of my chair and got my cloak. "Thank you, *mon cher*. I know that you are concerned for me and that you do your best to keep me out of trouble. But what you do not understand is that I thrive on that same trouble you try to avoid. You are happy here, hidden away, with your library and your cellar full of mice and wine. I need excitement and singing and dancing. And every so often"—I kissed him on the cheek—"just a little hit of trouble."

I heard him laugh as I headed for the door. "Vivienne?"
"Yes?"

"Be careful. And have Frederick ready the coach for you and
drive you into the village. That way you can stay until the crack
of dawn and still make it back here safely."

Christmas Eve and I was free at last. It didn't matter that
Frederick would be staying quite close to me or that he was
likely to take back a full report to Max on our return. I wouldn't
expect anything else of him—he was Max's servant after all. I
could ask him to leave, I could get angry with him, but it would
do no good. He could not help obeying his orders and had been
told, no doubt, to keep a tight rein on me.

So I ignored him as best I could and walked to the church.
Services were just starting and I knew that I would find Diego
there. Sliding into one of the pews in the back, I searched out
the crowd until I saw him, seated toward the front, with his
mother and father and an entire pew full of his brothers and sisters. Señor Perez was the second richest man in the village and
Diego was his first-born. Young, handsome, and strong, his
blood had the sweetest taste, honey tinged with cinnamon and
cloves.

He felt my stare, turned in his seat, giving me a nod and a
slow, lazy smile. My heart beat just a little faster with that smile;
my gums tingled with anticipation. "Happy Christmas, indeed,"
I whispered as I slid back out of the pew and quietly exited the
church. Diego would know where to find me.

Back in the far corner of the churchyard was a cemetery, lined
with huge old trees. I walked through the graves for a while,
pausing to read some of the names and dates. Most of them had
lived fewer years than I now possessed and that fact made me
sad. And pleased me all at the same time. If life was good and
something in which to rejoice, why shouldn't I be pleased with
my seemingly endless years? I laughed softly and spread my
arms, curtsying to the assembled dead. "Pardon, Messieurs et
Mesdames, that laugh was not at your expense."

I heard the service ending and knew that Diego would arrive

soon. "Where shall I hide?" I asked of the closest gravestone. "Behind a tree? No, that is too simple. How about up a tree?" I inclined my head as if I could hear the answer from the grave and laughed again. "Yes, that will do. Thank you for the suggestion."

I climbed the nearest tree and sat on one of the lower branches, my legs swinging back and forth, waiting for Diego.

"Vivienne?"

I kept quiet and watched him move through the paths. Finally he stood almost directly underneath where I sat. I waited until he turned his back to me, then dropped down silently and came up behind him, putting my hands over his eyes.

"Surprise, *mon chou*. And a *joyeux Noel*."

He picked me up and swung me around. "Where have you been? I have been walking here almost every night looking for you. Why can't I call at the house for you? Not being able to see you is driving me crazy."

I made a face, probably lost on him in the darkness. "It is Max again. He thinks because he likes to live as a hermit that I should too."

Diego shook his head. "He keeps you as a prisoner in that horrible place, not even letting you out on market days."

"That does not matter. Max has his reasons and there is no arguing with him. Let's not waste our time by talking about it."

Diego kissed me then, his lips soft against mine, his tongue darting into my mouth. Oh, but he was sweet. And when I was with him, I felt young again, although I was older than his grandmother. I wrapped my arms around his neck and returned his kiss, pressing myself up against his warm muscled body.

He pulled me down to the ground, still kissing me. Then pushed away abruptly. "I almost forgot. I have a present for you."

I smiled, deep enough to bring out my dimples. "A present? For me?" I clapped my hands together. "I love presents."

He laughed indulgently. "I know you do, Vivienne. And so I bought you this."

He handed me a small parcel, wrapped in a silk handkerchief and tied with a ribbon. I unfolded the cloth and saw a tiny but ornate silver cross with a delicate chain. "Oh, it's lovely, Diego. Thank you."

I unfastened my cloak, letting it fall to the ground, and handed the necklace back to him. "Here, put it on me," I said, turning around and holding up my hair. He fastened the clasp and I turned back to him. The cross nestled in the notch of my neck and I put my hand up to it.

"Thank you," I said again, "I will treasure it forever."

He smiled and kissed the tip of my nose. "I am glad you like it. Alejandro said that you wouldn't. He said that you couldn't possibly wear it."

"Why would he say that?"

Diego looked away. "He says that since I only meet you at night and since I come back from seeing you pale and tired, that you must be one of the walking dead. But no, that is nothing but nonsense. And what does it matter what Alejandro thinks?"

I laughed, perhaps a bit higher pitched than normal. "Yes, it is nonsense. But you must tell him that I meet you at night because that is the only time I can get away from Max. And"—I gave him a wicked smile—"you are pale and tired for the best of reasons. Because you have been making love to me for most of the night."

"I can't tell him that."

"No?"

"No, I would not tarnish your reputation. I love you, Vivienne. I wish to marry you. And tomorrow, regardless of what Max thinks, I will call and ask for your hand."

"No, you mustn't. Promise me you won't, Diego."

"But I don't see what the problem is. . . ."

"No," I said, perfectly serious now and feeling all of my seventy years. "You do not see. Nor do I wish you to see." I gripped his shirtfront and pulled him close to me so that he could see into my eyes. "You must not ask to marry me. I cannot marry you, cannot marry anyone. Do not speak of it again."

He moved back from me and I felt the fabric of his shirt tear under my fingers. "Vivienne? What is wrong? You do not sound like yourself. Why can't you marry?"

I sighed. "I am sorry, Diego, I just can't. And that is all I can say. Please do not ask me again."

"But—"

I put my hand to his mouth. "Hush, *mon chou,* not another word. Don't you want to know what present I brought for you?"

He kissed my hand. "You didn't need to buy me a present."

I laughed, happy to see that he had dropped the subject of marriage. "I did not buy your present. I brought it with me, and hid it. Somewhere underneath all these clothes."

He put his hands on me and began to explore. "I don't see any presents," he said, unfastening the ties on my blouse. "I will have to keep looking."

"Please." I breathed the word, loving the feel of his hands, needing his warmth and his weight. "Oh, please. Find it quickly, Diego."

And he did. We made love there in the cemetery for hours, testing each other's endurance and strength. And when it was all over, I nipped at his neck and drank just a little, not to feed, but to hold the taste of him in reserve, to savor as I lay in my lonely box in Max's cold house.

Chapter 4

Toledo: the House of Esteban, 1769

"There must be a way."

Diego and I had managed to meet almost every week since Christmas. Max had given up on trying to keep me at the house; perhaps he feared I might really return to Paris, leaving him alone. Why he feared this, I had no idea. It was not as if I provided him comfort or companionship; quite the contrary, we had begun to have bitter fights, when we spoke at all. It was much like being tied to an unloved marriage partner, without even the dubious comfort of the phrase " 'Til death do you part."

As a result, Diego became the one joy in my life. I, who had always lived for pleasure, who had always looked forward to the setting of the sun with relish and anticipation, was reduced to relying on a human man.

"There must be a way," he said again, "a way we can stay together always without Max interfering."

I gave him a long discerning look. He had grown accustomed to my strange life, accepting that I could only be with him at night, welcoming the taking of his blood that occurred every time we made love. There was a way, I knew. If I were to transform him into a vampire, Max would have to accept him into the house. There would be no danger of exposure to the outside world; Diego would no longer be a stranger to be feared and guarded against; instead he would become a trusted member of the family.

"There is a way, Diego, *mon cher*. It will be difficult, but well worth it. And we can stay together forever."

He kissed me. "I would walk any path to be with you, I would face the devil himself for you, I would die for you."

Such noble and endearing words, they were exactly what I had wanted to hear, making me ignore the voices that urged me to hold back, wait. I would not wait.

Seventy years of living had not necessarily made me wise; rather I was as foolish and headstrong as I had been at eighteen, always making impetuous decisions when I should have stood back and considered my actions. And I knew this about me, even at that time, so I had no excuse for what I did.

At first, it seemed that everything would be fine. Max was not particularly pleased when I presented him with his newborn vampire son, but grew quickly accustomed to the situation.

After all, here was somebody new for him to intimidate and frighten and teach in all things vampiric.

And Diego changed in more than physical ways. He looked to Max now for direction and guidance, readily embracing the bloodthirstier aspects of his new life. I forgave him this little betrayal; Max was undoubtedly the better teacher of the two of us, and I still had Diego to myself in the long daytime hours when he slept with me in my coffin.

When he advanced to the stage of being able to hunt alone, Diego changed completely. Demanding his own coffin, he grew withdrawn and surly, never speaking to me, and rarely to Max. Every so often a body of one of the villagers would be found, dead and drained, brutally savaged. Since there were wolves in the forests and it was a particularly bad winter, the blame was laid there. At first.

Max reassured me. "The boy is young and it is all new and exciting to him. He's playing right now with his powers; he will settle down, no doubt, and begin to exercise discretion about his feedings." Then he ruffled my hair. "We are not all as civilized as you, my dear. You seemed born to the life, knowing instinctually those things you must do to survive. Even when they seem the wrong things. I did well in choosing you."

I laughed. "It was not much of a choice, Max. One night we met and the next, voilà! And I certainly don't know why you did it."

He gave me a sharp look. "Do you not indeed? Why did you change Diego?"

I sighed. "I wanted a companion, someone with whom to share the life. You and I were not exactly amiable at that time and I was lonely. It did not turn out the way I had hoped."

"No." He favored me with one of his twisted smiles. "It rarely does. But your reasons are close enough to mine. And perhaps your choice was just as good. He has certainly taken to the hunt quite well."

"Too well. I miss the man he used to be."

"Sometimes, the change is subtle, as in your case. And for others it is a life-defining event and the person they were before dies."

"What were you like, Max, before the change?"

He said nothing and looked away, but not quickly enough for me to miss the beginning of tears. Max? Crying? Anathema. I did not question him further, suspecting that I really did not want to know what tragedies lay buried in his heart next to the man he once was.

But despite Max's reassurances, Diego didn't settle down. With each sunset he grew wilder and more violent; the dead bodies appeared more frequently now, most with their throats ripped out, and ugly rumors began to circulate through the village. Rosa, one of our new servants, brought in and carefully subdued by Max to act as my maid, would bring the gossip back with her and tell me, as she brushed my hair and dressed me.

"There is talk," she said, "of bringing the white horse to the cemetery."

"The white horse?"

"To detect the grave of a vampire. How could you not know?"

I shook my head. "But there are no vampires in the cemetery."

"Popular superstition has it that those who die by the bite of the vampire come back to life as one."

I threw my head back and laughed. "That is one of the silliest things I have ever heard. If that were true, then the whole world would be vampires."

She gave me a smile and then sobered instantly. "True, Miss Vivienne, but that doesn't stop the villagers from talking. They say that they will kill the monster."

I sighed. *Ah, Diego,* I thought, *my sweet-faced friend, I have done a terrible thing. And now I shall have to correct my mistake.*

"Diego?" I touched his sleeve as I passed him in the hallway. "Come and speak with me for a while."

For once, he didn't shake off my hand and he smiled, his eyes almost the eyes I knew. "That would be nice, Vivienne, I have not spent much time with you lately."

We sat on one of the sofas in the music room. "You must stop killing, Diego. Death is not necessary, you know this. Even you do not need to take that much blood to survive."

"Why do you assume that I am to blame for the deaths?" His voice was soft and sincere. "They could just as easily be his." He nodded toward the piano. "He was, after all, my teacher in all things."

"Max is not a killer," I said with certainty.

"No? Can you be sure? So sure that you would think it of me and not him? You know me well. Just how much do you know of Max?"

"Max is not a killer, Diego." My voice lost a little of its conviction. "I would have known before now."

"Would you truly? If he hid it from you?"

"Yes, I think I would still know."

"But you are not sure, Vivienne. I know this by the look in your eyes. Max is a dangerous monster, much more powerful than we could ever imagine. And who knows the sorts of games he plans?"

"Nonsense," I said, but he changed the subject, taking my hand and kissing it slowly.

"I have been neglecting you, my love, but now that I have learned all I can learn to make you proud of me, to prove that I am worthy, perhaps we can we share the night again?"

He sounded so like the Diego I knew. "It is good to have you back, *mon chou*." I took him by the hand and led him to my room. By the time the dawn was near, I was sure that I was wrong about him. And almost as sure that I was wrong about Max. It was unthinkable that this lovely creature who rested at my side could be a killer.

"Still," Diego said, returning to the subject when we were sated with the touch and taste of each other, "I fear Max. As you should."

"We could go away, Diego. To Paris." I smiled and ran my nails down his perfect skin. "You will like Paris, I promise."

"Yes," he agreed, giving me a kiss and getting up from the bed, "we will go to Paris together, you and I. And then you will see that it is not I doing the killing."

* * *

The next evening when I awoke I was alone in my coffin. Only the faint scent of him held the reminder that we had been together. But I smiled as Rosa dressed me, thinking of the plans we had made. Paris. I held the name in my mind like a prayer.

Rosa seemed happy, she even hummed a little song as she brushed my hair. "Good news, Rosa?" I asked, thinking perhaps she had a lover in the village.

"Oh, yes, Miss Vivienne. The monster is dead."

"What monster?" I felt a small chill crawl up my spine and shivered.

"The one who was killing the villagers. So now there will be no need for the white horse, no need for a vampire hunt, and we can all live safely again."

"How did this happen? Do you know?"

"Master Esteban did the honorable thing."

"Max? Did he surrender to the villagers?" I could hardly believe what she was telling me. "How do you know?"

She laughed and shook her head. "Master did not surrender to anyone. What a silly notion. He was the one who killed the monster."

"Diego?" I whispered the name, still feeling the touch of his breath on my skin. "Diego?"

She spat. "He does not deserve his Christian name; that man was the devil himself. One of his victims was my sister. May he burn in hell forever."

"Diego!" I jumped up from my chair and ran down the hallway to Max's room. "What have you done to him, Max?"

"Vivienne, it is over. He challenged me and I won. I will have the remains taken down to the villagers with our apologies for harboring the monster."

"You killed him."

"An understatement, my dear, but yes, I did. He left me no choice."

"Where is he? May I see him?"

"I would not advise it, but if you wish." He pointed to a second coffin in the room that I hadn't noticed before.

I opened the lid. And screamed.

Diego's head rested on top of his chest. The wound was ragged. Max had torn him apart, it seemed, with his bare hands.

"How did you do this?" I asked, not really wanting to know.

He gave a bitter laugh. "I had not actually known it was possible. But I remembered Victor describing the technique." He held his hands up, parallel with the floor and fingers fully tensed and extended. "You drive both hands through each side of the neck, like so"—and he brought his fingers together in a quick, violent motion. "And when they meet, you push them up."

I closed my eyes for a second and wished I hadn't, since I could easily visualize the action. Somewhere in the back of my mind, I heard a voice asking, "Did the head fly far?" It was my voice and Max laughed fully now.

"You are amazing, Vivienne. I present you with the decapitated head of your recent lover and convert and this is all you can ask? I have underestimated you, perhaps."

I ignored him. "Diego said that it was you doing the killings, that he was innocent."

"And you believed him?"

I looked at him and dropped the lid of the coffin down. The echo of the noise sounded hollow and cold. "I do not know what to believe, Max. Except that I wish to be gone from here and from you. I am weary of all of this and do not wish to play your games. You will give me ownership of the House of the Swan, I will go back to Paris, and I do not care if I ever see you again."

Chapter 5

Paris: the House of the Swan, 1792

Monique showed up on my doorstep one rainy spring evening over two hundred years ago, drenched, underfed, and disheveled. It was certain that she had no knowledge of whom she was asking succor. I doubt even that she knew what sort of establishment she had entered.

I had long since quit working and retired to the background, appearing very infrequently and always veiled, to disguise my youth as best I could. If any of the women employed at the Swan knew what I was, they kept my secret in exchange for the safe haven I offered them. The money they earned was theirs to keep, with only a pittance held out for expenses of the house. It was an equitable arrangement for all of us.

That night I was alone and sitting in my bedroom in front of a warming fire when Monique was brought to me for my approval. She curtsied to me from the doorway. "Mademoiselle," she said with a slight shiver in her voice, "I wish to thank you."

I nodded at the woman who had brought her. "Thank you, Rosa. Leave her here, but bring us some food." I took another look at the bedraggled creature shivering in my doorway. "And some brandy."

"Yes, Mademoiselle Courbet." Rosa hurried off. I sighed as she moved away. How had she grown so old? She'd been as young as I when first we met, and now she was stooped and crippled with age. Years ago I had offered her the chance at immortality, but she chose to remain as she was. I often wondered if she regretted the decision. Still, Max had always insisted that one needed at least one human servant to safeguard the long daytime sleep. And Rosa was mine, totally devoted to me.

Hearing a slight whimper from the doorway, I turned in my chair and beckoned to the girl. "Come in, child." I pitched my voice lower than normal, putting a slight quaver in it. I had learned the role of the aging Madame well by this time. Only the youth of my hands betrayed me, and those I hid with gloves. "And warm yourself by the fire."

As she walked past, I noticed that she moved slowly and gingerly as if in pain, detected a faint smell of blood permeating the air around her. I caught my breath. "Are you hurt, girl?"

She turned her face up to me, her cheeks flushed with the warmth of the fire, her eyes huge and haunted. "It will heal, Mademoiselle." She attempted a curtsy again, but instead gave a gasp of pain and crumpled up, dropping to the floor.

Until that moment, I had not realized that I still possessed human feelings. *In fact,* I thought with a dry laugh as I knelt over her, *I am not so sure I ever possessed them.* Perhaps something special in her brought out these emotions, perhaps I had merely gone too long without someone to love. Whatever the reasons, her arrival gave me a gift: the ability to care.

She moaned softly and her eyelids flickered.

"Poor little lamb," I whispered as I picked her up and carried her to my bed, settling her into the pillows as gently as a mother might, brushing a strand of black hair away from her pale face. "Let's get you clean and dry."

I stripped away her sodden clothing, shocked by the bruises revealed, marks of very recent violence. She had been beaten with a stick or some other blunt weapon, the blows seemingly concentrated on her abdomen. As I bent lower to wrap her in one of my own robes, I was assailed by a strong odor of stale blood and rot. Peeling away the putrid rags wadded between her legs, I found more, stuffed within her to stem the flow. But this was not her normal monthly occurrence, it was far worse and more serious.

Looking around the room to see that I was not observed, I dabbed my finger in the now freely flowing blood trickling down her thigh, held it up to my nose, then touched my tongue to it. The taste was bitter, tinged with poison and death. I shuddered, glancing down at her again, examining the bruises, the blood, the distension of her abdomen, understanding at last what had been done to this girl.

"*Mon Dieu.* And they would call me a monster." I shook my head, growing angrier with every second. "But this, this is truly monstrous."

The girl started to shiver and I wrapped her up tightly in the blankets. "Who did this to you?" I whispered to her, knowing she couldn't comprehend, much less answer me. "Who did this? Your father? Your lover? Who would be so inhuman as to beat the baby out of you and then leave you to die? Monstrous!"

I heard a step in the doorway and spun around to see Rosa in the doorway, a tray in her hands. "Rosa"—I gestured to her— "put the food down, but bring the brandy here. Then send someone to fetch the midwife and bring me some hot water to wash her. I fear this poor little waif may be dying on us."

Staring down at the pale figure, Rosa set the tray down on the bed table. She crossed herself and mumbled something under her breath. I gave her a push in the small of her back. "No time for prayers, woman. Now hurry!"

As she scurried out of the room, I poured a glass of brandy and sat next to the shivering girl, holding her up around the shoulders and coaxing her to drink. She sputtered a bit, but then drank, long-pulled and hard-swallowed sips until the glass was empty. I poured her another and she drained that as well, giving a drawn-out sigh as I laid her back on the pillows. Rosa reappeared with a basin of hot water, lavender scented, and a large assortment of washing and drying cloths. Between the two of us we had the girl cleaned and dried by the time the midwife arrived.

"One of your girls, Vivienne?" Marie slipped out of her wet cloak and walked toward the bed. She had long dealt with the House of the Swan and so her familiarity was permitted.

I shook my head. "*Mon Dieu, no!* I would not treat even an animal like this. She came in off the streets."

"Not a good place to be these days." She tossed the covers away from the girl and clicked her tongue. "Bad," she said, "but I have seen worse. With enough rest and care, she should survive." Marie spread the girl's legs open and gently examined her, shaking her head when she had finished. She dipped her reddened hands into the basin of lavender water. "The after-birth, at least, is gone. I had feared from the odor that it hadn't passed, but fortunately I was wrong. And now that her blood is flowing steadily, well, that should cleanse her. What happened to the baby?"

I handed her a cloth to dry her hands and shrugged. "I do not know, Marie, she did not have it when she came. I would guess that whoever did this to her would have disposed of the child as well." I felt myself growing angrier than I had been in a very long time. "*Immonde!* And God forbid whoever did this should ever show his face around here; I will rip him to shreds."

Rosa shivered, but Marie gave a grim laugh and nodded. "Just so, Vivienne. I believe you would. Now, you must keep her warm and clean; after an hour or so, you can probably wad up some cloths between her legs to catch the blood. Your bed, of course, is ruined." She gave me a glance from the corner of her eyes. "Not, I suppose, that such a thing would bother you." I tensed, then relaxed when she finished her thought. "You have plenty of beds here."

I paid her and escorted her through the hallways and down the stairs to our back entrance. "Thank you, Marie, for coming so quickly."

She nodded and smiled. "You might want to assign someone else to watch her during the day tomorrow."

I had gotten so involved in the drama of the sick girl, I'd not even thought about arrangements. Of course I could not stand watch over her during the day or I would die, but Marie would not know that. "Yes." I nodded as if in consideration. "I can get Rosa to watch, so that I can attend to business."

"Or rest." She laid a warm hand on my cheek. "You look very pale, Vivienne. Be careful of yourself, my dear, these are be-coming dangerous times. And I would hate to lose my most steady source of income."

She opened the door and I watched her walk out into the rainy streets, wondering at her warning. But she was right about these being dangerous times; I could scent the blood fury in the air.

Chapter 6

Closing and locking the door, as if to keep the trouble outside, I turned my veil down and moved into the entertainment room. Here the men would meet the girls and make their choices for the night. Since it was still early in the evening, the room was crowded and noisy, but fell quiet when I walked in, save for a whisper or two explaining who I was.

"Mademoiselle Courbet," one of the revelers called. "Perhaps you would sing us a song? The one about the earl and the milkmaid has always been one of my favorites."

I cleared my throat and smiled at him through my veil. "I fear, young man"—and I deliberately made my voice hoarse and harsh—"that I am past the singing of such a song. However, I thank you for asking. It is good to be remembered. Now, since you have been so kind and since I feel like celebrating this evening, good Messieurs, tonight the wine is free."

"How about the girls?" a man called out. "Are they free too?"

I looked over at him; he was quite young and obviously a nobleman as well as extraordinarily drunk. I crooked my finger at him and he walked rather unsteadily across the floor to face me.

"What is your name, young man?"

"Michael Leroux, at your service, Madame."

"Ah. I shall keep your service in mind, Michael. But I must tell you that there is only one girl, as you say, here who is free. And I daresay you may not be man enough for her."

He looked around the room with a simpering grin on his

dandy's face. "I am man enough for any woman in this room. Which of these ladies is to be mine tonight?"

I laughed and pulled him closer to me by the lace of his jabot, so close that I could smell the scent of bitter wine on his lips. "I fear, Monsieur, that you are slightly addled, perhaps by the grandeur of this company, perhaps by the fine wine we serve. No matter, for none of these women will be yours tonight. Rather"— I stared into his eyes through the veil, giving him the full force of my power and my smile—"*you* will be mine. Come."

I walked out of the room, never turning around to see if he followed. I knew that he would, he had no choice. As I started up the stairs, listening to his footsteps falling behind me, the room we'd just left became noisy once more with laughter and ribald jokes at Michael's expense. "Poor fellow," I could hear them say, "forced to make love to an old lady."

Pulling a key out of my pocket, I unlocked the door to the room I used for my assignations. Michael walked in behind me and hesitated at the door. "Sit down," I ordered and he settled in on one of the ornate brocade lounges as I closed and bolted the door.

I pulled off the veil that covered my face. "Look at me, Michael," I said.

"Perhaps it would be best, Mademoiselle, if I did not. I will just keep my eyes closed and—"

"Fool. Open your eyes, Michael, and you will have a surprise."

His fists clenched, but he turned and as his eyes fastened on me, he smiled. "You're not old, Mademoiselle Courbet," he said, blushing slightly. "I had always heard that you were old. But, no. You are young and beautiful. And I love you."

"Silly boy." I laughed, enjoying the obvious shiver this caused him and moved slowly toward him, unfastening the hooks on my bodice as I did so. "Beautiful, yes, and thank you, Monsieur. But I am old, older than you can imagine."

He shook his head when I finally stood before him. He put his hands out, touching my waist, then moved them up until he reached my breasts. "But your skin is so perfect, cool and smooth, like the marble of a sculpture." He touched me gently, almost reverently. And I sighed, loving the feel of his warmth against my cold flesh.

I leaned down and took his face into my hands, lightly kissing his lips, staring deep into his widening eyes. "And you, *mon cher gamin,* are so warm and so human. We could be the perfect match, you and I." He nodded and I smiled, letting him see my fangs. "Too bad you will not remember."

The skin on his neck punctured easily, his blood tasted rich and dark. He didn't fight. His hands at first still rested lightly on my breasts; then they moved around behind my head to hold my mouth to him. I pulled on him slowly savoring each mouthful of his essence, imagining as I did so that I could see into his soul, that I could select and keep a piece of him.

I was hungrier than I'd thought, no doubt due to the earlier activities with the injured girl and the overwhelming sight of her blood. So when his grip loosened and his hands fell away from me, dropping limply to his sides, I knew that I had taken just a bit too much. My hunger was satisfied and I felt no need to drain him to his death; so with an effort of will, I pulled my mouth off of him and wiped my lower lip with the palm of my hand.

Michael's eyes were still open and his breath came in low gasps, but when I put my head to his chest, I could hear his heart was beating normally. He would live. But not to tell the tale.

"Michael." I knelt in front of him and grasped his face again, not gently, but purposefully. "Can you hear me?"

He nodded. "*Oui,* Mademoiselle. You have the mouth and the voice of an angel."

"Hardly an angel, *mon cher,* but I thank you for your sweetness and that portion of your life which now dwells with me. As a reward, you will find that you remember nothing of our evening. Do you understand?"

He twisted his brow as he looked up at me. "But I do remember—"

"No." Meeting his eyes firmly. I pitched my voice to be its most commanding. "You remember nothing. You came to my room with me and then you fell asleep. Too much wine, Michael, is not good for a young man with an amorous intent. You fell asleep and we did nothing."

"Nothing." He nodded, still dazed. "I had too much to drink and fell asleep. We did not—"

"No, we did not. In fact, you do not even remember my face. It is all a blur, as if washed away in the wine." I reached over and lightly brushed his eyelids so that they would close. "Sleep now."

I walked out of the room, refastening my bodice and leaving the door slightly open. One of the girls would find him at closing time and see that he found his way back to his friends. Or his friends would come seeking him out. It did not matter to me.

Rosa still held watch over the girl in my room. I sent her to sleep with the instructions that I would wake her before dawn so that I could take my daily rest. She nodded, knowing my ways, and smiled shyly at me. "She will live, won't she?"

"I will do my best, Rosa, to see that she does."

I changed into my dressing gown and sat for a while, sipping brandy and watching the flames of the fire. Michael's blood still warmed me, filling every inch of my body with life and vitality. By now certain aspects of my life had become boring. Most particularly I dreaded the daytime confinements, but the taking of blood was always exciting, always new. Such a lovely experience, leaving me full of energy and joy, enabling me to continue forever. And the varying tastes of the victims were so entrancing. I sipped again at my brandy and laughed. "Like the difference between fine wines," I said softly. "Michael, *mon gamin*, my, you were a young vintage, impertinent but sweet. *Merci.*"

My speaking disturbed the girl in the bed and she began to thrash around and moan. I took off my dressing gown and lay down next to her, covering us both with a heavy blanket. I whispered to her of sleep and peace and healing, glad that I had fed and was not tempted to weaken her further. Holding her like this, brushing back her hair and whispering, I was almost overwhelmed with affection and love. The question of why I should react to her in such a way did not cross my mind. I had never suspected the existence of one who could inspire such emotions in a creature such as I and did not bother to wonder why; instead I reveled in feelings as wondrous and delicious as the first taste of blood.

My acceptance of her was complete and eternal. She would be my daughter, my sister, my friend, and my love; anything else was unthinkable.

She rolled over to me and wrapped her arms around my neck, nestling close to my breasts. I could feel her warm breath tickling my skin. I smiled. Life was good.

"You will be fine, little lamb. I will take care of you, forever."

Chapter 7

Monique recuperated quickly, surprising all of us with her strength and tenacity. After a week, she was out of bed, walking slowly but getting around. After two weeks, she managed to take over most of the duties Rosa would ordinarily do. It seemed a natural enough transition; Rosa was aging, after all, and would continue to age. Growing feeble as of late, she seemed to be withering before my eyes and I knew that I would need to replace her soon, regardless. So within a month of her arrival, Monique acted as my new personal maid and guard; she took my strange requests and requirements as if they were nothing out of the ordinary. I counted myself fortunate to find another like Rosa, suspecting Monique was so grateful to me for saving her life that she'd have served me even if I were the devil herself.

Of course she was more than a servant. She was my friend and confidant, perhaps even closer than that since she had been sleeping in my bed from that first night. We were not lovers, not exactly, but in her eyes, I'm not sure she knew the difference. After my first taste of her blood, she belonged to me. The experience of feeding held her in thrall; something I had done to make sure of her loyalty all the while thinking it was unnecessary in this case. She loved me as much as I loved her. I had made such an instant connection with her; how could it be different for her?

A timid knock on the door interrupted my thoughts. "Mademoiselle Courbet?"

"Damn it, Monique, have I not told you time and time again to call me Vivienne?"

"*Oui,* Mademoiselle. I shall try. But for now there are two things that require your attention. Rosa is very sick and a gentleman by the name of Maximillian Esteban is here to see you."

"Max? Here? Tonight? *Merde.* And Rosa? What is wrong with her?"

Monique shrugged. "I am not sure, Mademoiselle . . ."

I gave a small cough.

". . . Vivienne." She gave me one of her rare smiles, pleased, I thought, at being able to use my given name. "Rosa has been vomiting most of the day. Cook thinks that some of the meat has been tainted."

"Well, tell Cook to toss the meat out into the street and fetch the midwife for Rosa."

"And Monsieur Esteban?" She whispered the name as if it were a prayer, and a warning went off in my head.

I shot her a harsh look; her eyes were bright and her cheeks flushed. "You are to stay away from Monsieur Esteban, Monique. Do not disobey me in this. I will see to him myself."

She dropped a small curtsy and hurried back out the door. I sighed. *You cannot have it both ways,* I thought. *Give her orders and she is a servant. And if she is not a servant, then you have no right to command her.*

"A new swan for the house, Vivienne?" Max's voice laughed from the hallway. "She's lovely. Nothing like a little new blood to liven up the place."

"Good evening, Max." I said, ignoring his laughter. "To what do I owe the honor of this visit?"

He crossed the room, picked me up, and kissed both of my cheeks before setting me down again. "Nothing special, Vivienne. Just wondering how my little French flower has been doing."

I glared at him. "She is doing fine although she has grown stronger thorns since last we met. I want no interference from you this time."

He sat down on the couch in front of the fire and stretched his hands out to the warmth. "Are you still angry?"

I gave a small puff of breath. "Do you even need to ask me that, Max?"

"No, I suppose I do not. But he was not right for you, you know that. He was too weak to control his actions and wouldn't have lasted more than a month on his own."

"But Diego was mine. And you hadn't the right."

Max nodded. "Yes, that is true. But you must see I was trying to protect you; you were younger then and weaker. An inferior transformation would have threatened your existence, our existence. He was rash and violent and would soon have brought trouble down on all of us. You did not know that at the time and I did not take the time to explain. I now give you my most heartfelt apologies. So do not stay angry with me and do not think badly of me. It will not happen again."

I stared at him for a while trying to read his expression and failing miserably. Finally I threw my hands up in the air and laughed. "I'd hardly think my thoughts mattered to you, dearest Max. However, that was a pretty enough apology and I see no need for us to be at war."

"Good." He patted the side of the couch; I walked over and sat next to him. He took my hand, kissed it softly, and then crooked it around his arm.

For a long time we sat together silently, watching the flames. He had fed recently—I could scent the blood on him—and as a result he was calmer than normal. For the first time since we met, I found his presence relaxing; had anyone walked in and seen us, we'd have appeared an old married couple, secure in each other and needing no talk, no touch. How wrong such appearances could be.

Then I felt him tense and shift in his seat. "And now, although I hate to bring up the subject, let us speak of the war here. I have heard of Monsieur Guillotine's new device, new at least to this city, and I wanted to remind you that beheading is one way to kill our kind. There seems to exist strange influence in this city; one that turns normal humans' minds to thoughts of blood and destruction. Be careful, Vivienne, that you do not incite the mob."

"Nonsense. What use would they have for my head? I am not royalty, not nobility. I am just a simple working girl. I do not get involved with politics."

"Even so, my dear, it might be best for you to leave this place until things settle down again. There is no logic to mob rule and that is where this city is headed. Let the others stand in the squares and howl for blood. You have no need to be involved. I remain safely ensconced in my ancestral home; you and whosoever you might chose to bring along would be welcome there."

I turned to him and smiled, laying a hand along his cheek. "You came all this way to warn me, *mon cher?* To offer me safe haven? I find that touching"—and I laughed, knowing that I should not—"but unnecessary, and we shall do just fine without your help."

His eyes grew cold and he brushed away my hand. "I should have known you would refuse my offer. But keep it in your mind, Vivienne. It may be that you are right, or you may still have need of a place to run to."

"I will remember."

He stood up. "I'll be here for the next month or so, my dear. And I will contact you before I go back to Spain in case you have changed your mind. Other than that, I will leave you alone. You have matured and grown well." He smiled down at me. "Even with the thorns." He began to move toward the door, but turned around halfway. "Do you hate me?"

"Hate you?" I thought for a second or two. "Except for the incident with Diego, I have no reason to hate you. You have given me eternal life and I am grateful." I studied the fire for a minute. "And you are right about Diego. I should have known that your instincts are better than mine; but do not tell Victor I said that or I swear I will tear out *your* throat."

He laughed, bowed, and turned to leave.

"Oh, Max!" Jumping up from the sofa, I ran to the door and called after him. "Next week we are having a masque; I'd be happy if you could attend. I assume you are staying in the old place. Shall I have someone bring you an invitation?"

"Yes." He nodded, then laughed. "Vivienne, I believe you would celebrate the birthday of Torquemada. What is the occasion for this fete?"

I smiled, feeling my dimples emerge. "It is true, Max. I do love a celebration. So this is my 'I am weary of this revolution' party, but do not give that away. No need to tempt the mob."

He bowed again and exited. I heard his footsteps in the hallway, the pause at the top of the stairs. the whispered "pardon, Monsieur."

"Ah, but you are lovely, my dear," he said, "so no pardon is needed. What is your name?"

My hearing was acute enough to catch the faint answer and recognize the voice. I felt every muscle in my body tense.

"And a lovely name, Monique." Max spoke again. "You are an intriguing young lady and I hope we shall meet at a later date. I would like to know more of you." She gave a short gasp and I heard him walk down the stairs.

"Not this one, Max," I said through clenched teeth.

"Mademoiselle?"

I spun around and looked at her. "Nothing, Monique."

"I could hardly avoid speaking to him, Vivienne, it would have been rude."

I nodded. To repeat my earlier warning might only make him more fascinating to her. So I shrugged and smiled.

"And how is Rosa? Did you get Marie?"

Monique shook her head. "She was out. Babies have notoriously bad timing. But I was fortunate enough to meet a doctor who heard me inquiring about Marie as he was passing by. He came with me and is seeing to Rosa now."

"Quite the fortunate encounter, Monique."

"*Oui*. And he is quite the gentleman, physician to royalty, he told me."

I laughed. "Every doctor in this city used to claim that title. But now? This doctor must be a foolish man."

Monique's eyes grew round. "Oh, no, Vivienne. He seems very wise and very concerned. I have never seen a man with such gentle hands." Her eyes darted away from mine and rested on the floor.

Poor little lamb, I thought, remembering not for the first time the bruises she'd sustained before coming to us, *I am quite sure you have never met a man with gentle hands.*

I nodded. "If you say so, Monique, it must be true."

"*Oui*, it is true. And he said he would like to speak with you."

Chapter 8

I would not have been able to count the number of men I had met by this time in my life. There had been so many, in so many different capacities. None of them were able to resist me; with only one word, one look, they would come to me and feed my needs as lovers or as prey. Even considering the warmth of affection I felt for Monique, I had thought myself unmovable and untouchable in the area of *l'amour*.

Apparently, Eduard DeRouchard had been born to prove me wrong.

He was quite simply the most handsome man I had ever seen. A perfect example of humanity, he had a classic beauty: long golden hair, strong broad shoulders, and a porcelain complexion that would make other men seem feminine. For him, though, it was the perfect finish; stripped bare, he could be mistaken for a statue of Adonis. My first thought upon seeing him was that I must possess this man. And my second thought was that I never really could.

Eduard straightened up from where he stood over Rosa's bed and looked at me with deep green eyes. He then shook his head and turned back to her, laying a hand on her face, closing her eyes. "I am sorry; I couldn't save her. The poison in her system was too strong."

"Poison?" Stunned, not just with the death of a valued servant, but with the presence of this man, I struggled to understand. "Who would poison Rosa?"

"You mistake my words; it needn't have been a deliberate attempt. Tainted food could easily cause the same ailment."

"Ah, I see. Nonetheless, I thank you, Doctor . . ."

"DeRouchard. Eduard DeRouchard." He gave an elegant bow, reached over to take my hand, and brought it to his lips. I felt myself blush.

"Vivienne Courbet." I stated my name, pulled my hand out of his grasp, and stifled the desire to curtsy. Beautiful though he was, and intimidating in that beauty, he was in my house and I was the mistress here. "*Merci,* Dr. DeRouchard, for your attempt. Poor Rosa. She was a good woman and I will miss her." I moved past him, laid a hand on her cheek, kissed her lightly on the forehead, and pulled the blanket up over her head.

Only then did I notice the great stench in the room; the odors of vomit, sweat, and blood permeated the air, a hideous assault on the senses that made me feel dizzy and sick.

"Perhaps, Doctor"—I motioned to the door—"you would like to clean up and partake of refreshments before you leave?"

"With a hostess of such great beauty offering such wonderful hospitality, I may never leave."

I laughed. "That, *mon cher,* can certainly be arranged."

Eduard followed me to my room under the watchful eyes of Monique. She trailed along behind us, hesitating as we entered the room, looking as if she were going to burst into tears or explode into anger. I smiled at her to forestall either outburst and gave her a kiss on the cheek.

"Monique, my lamb, be a dear and get the good doctor some food and wine. That's a good girl."

She glanced at me and then at Eduard.

He smiled at her. "Go on, girl, you should listen to your mistress." She dropped him a curtsy and left the room.

"I am not really her mistress, you know. I am also her friend."

"That is fortunate for the girl. You are, no doubt, less demanding because of that friendship. How long have you known her?"

I thought for a moment. "She came to us a little over a month ago."

"And now she is your maid?"

"I have been training her in that capacity, yes, since I did not think Rosa was as capable as she had been."

"And now Rosa is dead."

I sighed. "Yes. Poor woman. She had served me for so very many years."

He put his head back and laughed. "Cannot be all that much, Mademoiselle, for you can't have seen many more than twenty years."

"Very many years," I repeated, enjoying his look of disbelief. "And"—I glanced at him, smiling—"I am perhaps not so young as you think me."

I saw a glint of curiosity enter his eyes, saw questions beginning to form there in his mind. But a knock on the door distracted him and when Monique entered, the subject of age was forgotten.

"Food," she said sullenly and with less grace than usual, slamming down the tray filled with bread and fruit and cheese. Then she set a carafe heavily on the table next to the food. "And wine. As ordered."

"Thank you, Monique." Eduard got up from his seat on the lounge and walked over to her. "Are you happy here?"

"Why yes, Monsieur."

"And is this position preferable to your former one?"

She dropped her eyes. "I do not wish to speak of the past, Monsieur. You can rest assured that I am satisfied here."

"That is good. You must be sure to treat Mademoiselle Courbet with great care and courtesy and obey her. Do you understand?"

"*Oui,* Monsieur. I should know that without your saying so."

"Monique gives perfect satisfaction." I interrupted, wondering why Eduard should care for my domestic arrangements. "We were lucky to find her when we did."

"Good," Eduard said.

Monique looked over to me. "If that will be all, Mademoiselle Courbet, I think I shall retire now."

"By all means, Monique my lamb. Sleep well."

When she left the room, I turned to Eduard. "Dr. DeRouchard," I started.

"Eduard," he said with a smile. "You must call me Eduard."

I nodded. "Eduard, then, I fail to see why Monique's service should be of concern to you."

He shrugged. "It is not my concern, really, and I hope you forgive my impertinence. But she seemed rather sulky and I wanted to remind her of her duties. Girls like her often forget things in the heat of the moment. And that would not do."

I poured him a glass of wine and another for myself.

"Enough of the talk of servants, dead or otherwise," he said. "That is not the conversation one should have with a beautiful lady." He picked up one of the glasses and handed the other to me.

"And what shall we drink to?" I said. The touch of his hand over the glass was like lightning in the night sky and suddenly I felt unable to breathe.

"Let us drink," he said, his eyes staring into mine, "to the magic of the night."

And the night was magic. Or perhaps it was only Eduard. Not since Max had I met a man so capable of moving me.

And I was not thinking of Max.

From his first touch, I could only think of Eduard, with his firm hands and eyes that glowed with passion like torches at the palace. Seemingly insatiable, his body enfolded mine, enclosing me tightly in its heat. Never had I felt so warmed, never had just the touch of hand and mouth alone been enough to carry me past the brinks of passion, past the puny ecstasies I had known before. This was new. This was heaven and hell and all the good and bad things I had ever known—no, it was better than all of it. Better than feeding, better than blood, better than life.

And when he joined himself to me, I cried out and my voice was savage and loud, echoing off the walls in the room, the houses in the street. An inhuman call, something wild, something frightening, it was the roar of the lioness within.

Eduard looked down at me lying naked beneath him, straining upward to pull more of him within me, holding him there, crying and convulsing around him. As I climaxed, I saw the buildup of his release tighten his body. The muscles in his arms tensed and glistened with sweat, his eyes shone like molten glass reflecting the candle flames. He shook and cried out, as loudly as I had, the lion satisfying the heated call of his mate. And then as he reached his climax and filled me with his seed, Eduard laughed. Long and low and full of pleasure and joy.

As he rolled from me, I gave a small giggle and a loud sigh. "Oh," I said and that was all.

"Yes," Eduard said. "I feel the same."

I ran lazy fingers down the side of his face, grazing him lightly with my nails, and he shivered. I kissed the trails that my fingers made and worked my way down to his neck, licking the skin gently, enjoying the taste of him. But my sensitive tongue felt a notch there, a hardened patch of skin. I opened my eyes and looked closely.

"But you have been hurt," I said, shocked at the ugly scar that traveled half of the entire width of his neck. "Eduard?" I said in amazement. "This cannot be what it appears to be. It looks as if someone had slit your throat, but then how would you be alive?"

He laughed. "Vivienne, my love, how can you doubt that I live? Have I not spent the entire evening showing you that I was, most certainly?"

I traced the mark with the tip of my fingernail and he shivered. "Of course you are alive, Eduard, and I am glad of that. But this scar . . ."

"I was a baby. My nurse was careless with a knife as she carved an apple by my cradle. It was not as deep a cut as would kill me. So rest assured, my dear, I am fully human and fully alive. And more than willing"—he pulled me into his arms again and deposited small tickling kisses on my face and neck—"oh, yes, more than willing and able to prove it."

I murmured something as he continued to kiss me, harder now, his mouth moving down to my breasts and my stomach, searching and tasting and taking me back to the heights of earlier passion. I curled my fingers into his hair and held his head to me and murmured something that may have been "love."

And so on that night, when death walked inside the house and bloody-handed revolution prowled the streets without, I made my second deadly mistake. Perhaps the first mistake of taking Monique in and nurturing her triggered this error. I had been warned, by both Max and Victor, that certain human emotions should be avoided. Pity, despair, and guilt undermined the instincts of a vampire; complacency fostered an unhealthy recklessness. I had at some time in the past fallen into these traps, but had managed to avoid the major pitfall. Even with Diego I had not fallen. I knew now that I could not have forgiven Max for his murder so readily if I had loved.

No, love, I had been told over and over, was the worst of them all, for it demanded a surrender of self both physically and spiritually that was difficult enough for a human to manage. For a vampire to fall in love with a human meant death.

Death be damned, I thought as I lay in Eduard's arms, sated with our lovemaking, drunk on his presence, his scent, and the singing of his blood in his veins and in mine. "Death be damned," I whispered, fully willing to stay with this man until the rising of the sun.

Chapter 9

Monique saved me from that fiery death by knocking on the door about an hour before dawn. "Mademoiselle Courbet?" she called from the hallway, "it's almost dawn."

Eduard rolled over and lazily kissed both of my nipples, then got up from the bed and began to dress. "I had not meant to stay so long, my dear, I will need to hurry away. It was a wonderful night, was it not?"

I smiled and sighed. "*Oui,* it was. Perhaps . . ." I bit back my reply. I did not need to beg a man to return. And although I did not understand the attraction Eduard held for me, I knew that it was an improper impulse. The best thing for me would be to show him the door and never see him again.

Fully dressed now, he leaned over the bed and kissed the tip of my nose. "I will call again, of course, dear Vivienne. And I can only hope that you will continue to receive me."

In response I shrugged and stretched. "We shall have to wait for that moment to see, Monsieur le Docteur."

Monique knocked again, her voice acquiring a note of panic. "Vivienne? Vivienne, did you hear me? Are you in there? Are you all right? Open the door, Mademoiselle, it is almost dawn."

Eduard opened the door and smiled at her. "Your mistress is quite safe, girl, I have not murdered her in her bed. Adieu."

Yawning, I rose from my bed and stretched again, enjoying the feel of my body and the play of muscles overused in the night of passion. Monique stared at me, shook her head, and began to prepare the room for my daily sleep. She fastened the shutters at the one lone and narrow window, pulled the three sets of heavy velvet drapes across. Watching her as I put on my silken nightgown, I could see that her shoulders were tense and trembling.

"What is it, Monique?"

"Nothing."

I walked over to her and set my hand on her shoulder. She jumped. "Nonsense. Do you think I cannot tell? You are upset about something, dear one. Tell me."

"It is nothing, Mademoiselle." She pushed the words out through clenched teeth, twisted away from me, and threw open the lid of my coffin, to shake out the cushions and sheets as she did every night. But her anger made her careless and the lid bounced against the bedposts and slammed back down, catching one of her fingers in the process.

Monique cried out and stood up, holding her finger before her eyes. Small drops of blood fell on the carpet, blending in with the dark red pattern. Tears welled up in her eyes and a low rumble of obscenities began deep in her throat like a growl. I could not catch the words, she spoke them so quietly, so hurriedly. At first I found her vehemence surprising, then shocking, and finally humorous. It was, after all, only a cut finger and she was using words not spoken in even impolite company.

She glared at me as I started to giggle, but I couldn't help my reaction. Her anger only made me laugh harder until finally she burst into tears.

"I want to go home," she wailed. "I hate you. You're cruel and terrible."

Home? I thought, getting my laughter under control. *I didn't know she had a home.* Then, I felt a rush of panic. *No, she mustn't go home. Rosa is dead and I need her.* Anxious to salvage the moment, I crossed the room and took her in my arms, comforting her as I remembered my nurse comforting me. "Ah, *ma belle petite,* it is only a cut finger. I win fix it for you."

Pulling back away from her, I took her hand and stared into her eyes, putting her finger to my mouth and licking away the blood. It was a small gash and had already stopped bleeding.

"See?" I said, laying her hand on top of mine and patting it. "It is already healed."

She shook her head. "No, it is not healed."

"But . . ."

She backed away from me. "Don't you understand? It's not the cut or the finger or even your laughter. It is he."

"He? Eduard?"

"Yes. And you."

"I? And Eduard?" I shook my head. I could feel the approaching sunrise like a heavy weight in the center of my being; the dawn affected my ability to think and to function. I didn't need this argument, I needed to sleep. But I knew that I had to calm whatever fears and insecurities Monique had to ensure the safety of that sleep. "What about Eduard and me?"

She sighed. "If I needed any further convincing, this would do it. You must indeed be what you say you are, Vivienne. You certainly aren't human."

I gave a low laugh. "I have never led you to believe otherwise, *mon chou*. I may be a monster, but I am an honorable one. There have been no lies between us."

She thought about that for a moment. "No, you have been always truthful with me. And so that makes my anger harder to understand. You saved my life, you gave me friendship and companionship. I am bound to you, with gratitude and with blood. And yet . . ." She walked over to the bed and pulled the blankets and the sheets off, throwing them to the floor.

"And yet? So tell me, little lamb. How can I know what has hurt you and how can I make it better again, if you won't tell me?"

Her face crumpled up and once more tears flowed down her face. "You made love to him. In our bed." She kicked at the bed linens. "Pah. I can smell him in here even now. You locked me out and took pleasure with that man. In our bed."

I stood watching her for a minute as she gathered up the soiled linens and took fresh ones from the armoire. "You're jealous? That's what this is all about?"

Monique held the sheets up to her face, her body jerking with little sobs. When she finally looked at me her face was blotchy, her eyes red. "I know that none of this means anything to you. I know I mean nothing to you." She gave a twisted smile. "I know that ultimately even he can mean nothing to you. You are incapable of feeling emotion. I know this." She stomped her foot and set the linens onto the bed, sitting herself beside them. "All you care about is a living body to warm you and protect you, a bellyful of blood, and a safe haven from the sun."

"But that is not true."

"No lies between us, Vivienne. Remember?"

I nodded and gave her a wan smile. "I never forget. And you are wrong, I do care for you, Monique. As if you were my sister or my daughter. But if you wish to go home, I will send you home, pay you well for the services you have given."

"Home?" She spat the word at me. "I have no other home than here. Not now, not from the night I came to your door and you brought me in under your roof. Do not taunt me, Mademoiselle Cygnette. The action is beneath you."

"Monique," I started but she glared at me.

"And how am I to be reassured that you do care for me?" She tossed her head. "How much do you care? As much as for Rosa? She served you faithfully for how many years, Vivienne? And seconds after she died and her body was still warm, you turned your back on her and dallied with a man you'd only just set eyes on. She deserved better notice from you. Did you give her a second thought? Would you give me a second thought?"

I sighed and sat down next to her on the stripped bed. "I cannot help what I am, Monique. Nor do I want to. I am more than content with my life. That, however, does not mean that your well-being and happiness are unimportant. I understand I can't make you believe me."

"But you can. You can make me do anything you want; you have that power. And I have seen you use it, on everyone here but me. Am I so unworthy of your attentions? You should have left me on your doorstep to die."

I jumped from the bed and threw my hands up into the air. "You must be the most exasperating woman in this city. What on earth do you want from me, Monique? Tell me and I will try to oblige. Otherwise, I need my rest."

To my surprise she smiled, moved toward me, grasped my hands in hers, and kissed them. "I want to be like you. I want to live forever, to stay young and vibrant."

I laughed. "Is that all?"

"So you'll do it?"

I nodded. "At some point, yes, I'm sure of it. But not this morning, *ma chere*, and not until I can train someone to replace you. The both of us will need protection. And I would feel more secure once this horrible revolution is settled. But I promise I will do what you ask." I moved to the large wooden box at the foot of the bed. "May I sleep now?"

"Yes, sleep, my lovely mistress. And I will stand guard."

I climbed into the coffin, pulled the lid down, and settled in, waiting until I heard the sounds of her moving around the room to draw the bolts shut. No need to let her think I didn't trust her.

"But it is true, I do not trust you, Monique, not yet." I whispered the words as my body acknowledged the rising of the sun with a shiver and a sharp bite of pain.

But I did not fall asleep immediately, as was my wont. Instead, I replayed the previous evening over in my head, trying to remember each touch of his hand, each word from his mouth. I closed my eyes and felt the texture of his hair and skin on my fingers; I licked my lips and caught the wild, strange taste of him.

Eduard, I thought, *how strange you should come to me when you did. And how strange that I could love you.* Perhaps, though, the care and affection I felt for Monique carved a way for him into my heart. Had he come years ago, could I have made love with him, but not felt it for him?

"No." I whispered the word as I felt sleep overcome me. "I would have loved you at any time we met. I had no choice."

Chapter 10

The next evening came and it seemed as if the argument between Monique and me had never happened. Even when Eduard called for me and we spent the rest of the night as we had the previous one, she was content and happy, even to the point of humming a little song as she brought him food. My promise that she would one day be transformed was apparently all that was needed to ensure continued peace.

As the days passed, though, I felt rather uncomfortable with that promise. I still remembered the look of Diego's body after Max had finished beheading him. I imagined Max's fingers piercing Monique's delicate neck, pushing their way through the soft flesh, and flicking off her head as if he were doing nothing more than plucking an apple from a tree.

I shivered at the thought and Eduard looked over at me, one eyebrow raised. He had been painting me, a skill I hadn't realized he had, and I had been standing naked for this pose, looking out the window. He set his brush down. "I am finished in any event. And you will take a chill standing there naked with the night air blowing over you."

I laughed and turned back to the window. "I was not shivering from the night air, Eduard."

"Then what?" He came to stand behind me and wrapped himself around me. I put my arm back and patted him on the cheek. "Shivering from nothing more terrible than having to stand still halfway across the room from you. But now you are here and I am warm."

He grasped my fingers. "No, you're not. You're cold," he said. "Cold as snow, cold as death. In fact, you are the coldest woman I have ever met, Vivienne." He laughed. "As well as the most passionate. A miraculous combination of fire and ice. Quite a fascinating subject."

"Subject?" I turned in his arms to smile at him and trailed a long fingernail down the muscles of his arm. "Is that what I am, your subject? Be careful, Dr. DeRouchard, those who have subjects are under close scrutiny. Monsieur Guillotine's device is growing more popular these days."

He sobered immediately and pushed away from me. "You should take this all more seriously, Vivienne. People, good people, are dying for less."

"I mean no harm, Eduard. And it is only you and I here now."

He laughed. "Yes, and we know each other so very well, do we not? I could be your worst enemy. You know nothing about me and yet you let me into your most intimate embrace. Monique had the right idea that first morning. I could have meant you harm. You are entirely too trusting, and . . ." He stopped and looked at me, giving me a huge grin. "Well, if it weren't so ridiculous I would say that you are innocent. There is a war going on outside your very door, Vivienne. It may indeed pass you over like the angel of death. Or it may come looking for you."

I picked up my dressing gown from where I had dropped it on the floor when I posed, and put it on, walking across the room to the bottle of wine Monique had brought in earlier. "Why is everyone so determined these days to rule my thinking? First Max. Then Monique. And now you. I am capable of coming to my own conclusions and I am more than capable of living my life as I choose."

"Max?"

I poured two glasses of wine and offered him one. "Max is an old friend of mine. You will, perhaps, get a chance to meet him at the masque next week."

He made a noise of disgust. "And that's another thing. This fete of yours is ill timed. When there are children starving in the streets with no shoes to cover their feet, you should not be calling attention to your affluence. Won't you reconsider?"

"Tell me, Eduard, why should I reconsider? Because of vague fears? Veiled threats? It is not my fault the children are starving in the streets. Not my fault they have no shoes. I am nothing and no one. Why should anyone bother with me?"

"Because you call attention to yourself. You are affluent and obviously enjoy it. You are beautiful and flaunt it. And you are simple to think that you can avoid being remembered in the same thought as the aristocratic gentlemen who frequent the House of the Swan."

"Now I am simple? Eduard, take care you do not go too far and anger me."

"Come, my love, why should that anger you? You are simple; it is one of your best qualities." He laughed a bit, and came over to me, touching my arm.

I jerked away from him, spilling the wine I held all over the front of my gown. "Damn it, Eduard, look now what you've made me do."

It was silly for me to be angry, but that realization only made me worse. I was powerful, I was beautiful, and I would live forever. How dare he imply that I was stupid?

"How can you care for the state of your clothing and not care for what is happening right outside your door?"

"Eduard, my darling man, I know the danger of these times as well as you. And I choose to live my life in spite of them. So let us not fight over this."

"And if there are riots in the streets the evening of your party? What then? If innocents are killed, you can console yourself with the knowledge that you are living your life as you choose?"

I shook my head, bit my tongue, and held out the glass to him again. "Drink, Eduard. We need not fight."

"No, I should be going. And I think it might be best if I do not return. You are just a bit too careless of your fate and the fate of those who depend on you to make your company comfortable."

"Go then, you bastard!" I screamed at him and smashed the glass I had been offering against the hearth of the fireplace. "Run and hide like a rat on the street. But remember, being timid will not keep the mob away. Have a care to your own head."

He bowed to me. "You may regret those words someday, Vivienne. I can only pray that you manage to live that long."

I watched as he walked out the door. I regretted the words already.

"I think that's all of it, Vivienne." Monique had rushed into the room after hearing the sounds of the broken glass and my screaming. She got up from the floor where she had been picking up the shards and put them into the refuse basket.

I thanked her. "If I were being melodramatic, I would tell you that, should you find them, any remaining portions of my broken heart can be thrown into the fire."

Monique laughed. "But you would never be melodramatic. Nor"—she gave me a sly glance out of the corner of her eyes— "do you have a heart."

Giving a small chuckle, I wrapped my arms around myself. "No heart. You are right there. I keep giving it away to bastards."

"I saw his face as he went down the stairs, Vivienne. It must have been a good fight. Would it help if I said I was sorry?"

"No."

"Then . . ." She paused a bit. "It probably wouldn't be a good idea for me to say I warned you."

I flopped down onto the couch with a sigh. "You can say it, you should say it. And then you should keep saying it until I listen. Love? What was I thinking?"

She came over behind me and rested her head on my shoulder. "You were thinking you were lonely and that you wanted to love and to be loved. No crime in that. And maybe you couldn't help yourself. Sometimes attraction is intense, and he has more than his share of magnetism."

"Just so." I sighed. "He is perfect, though. I should not have lost my temper."

"You are entitled to lose your temper, Vivienne. And he is not perfect, he just looks so."

"And acts perfect. And his hands are perfect and his mouth and the taste of him, his eyes, his voice, his soul. Everything about Eduard is perfect." I sighed and got up from the couch. I glanced at the painting he had been working on and wanted to cry. "Oh, Monique, I miss him already. He is my only and my perfect love."

A wicked smiled crossed her face. "No, Vivienne, he is not. But I have thought in what way he would meet your description. And decided that what he is, is the perfect bastard."

"Monique!"

"You know it is true, Mademoiselle. Eduard is a bastard, like all men. But being Eduard DeRouchard, he must do it much better than the normal man."

I shook my head and smiled. "It is true, Monique, he does do everything better than the normal man. Were he just a common bastard, I could not have given myself as I did."

She walked over to the dressing table, picked up my hair brush and walked back. "And that is your problem, Vivienne. You give yourself where you should not. I am surprised that you have lived as long as you have. On what?"

"Instincts, my lamb, I live on my instincts. And while I may have been fool enough to fall in love with the man, I never did trust him. At least not as much as you seem to think I did." It was a lie, of course. I trusted him completely and unreservedly, though I would not admit to the fact.

Instead, I leaned into her as she brushed my hair and let out a low purr of contentment. "Instincts," I said again, "are all I have."

"Then," Monique said dryly, "your instincts must be very good. Will you train me as well?"

I laughed. "Better, I hope."

"So when shall we start?"

I hesitated. "Let me speak with Max first."

"Max? Monsieur Esteban? What has he to do with it?"

"Everything and nothing, Monique. Please let it rest until then. One of the first things you must learn is to consider consequences."

"A lesson in which you, no doubt, excelled."

I slapped her gently on the arm. "Hush. You are getting entirely too sassy for a servant."

She took my hand, kissed it, and held it against her cheek. "We are more than servant and mistress. We are two halves of a whole, light and dark. Come to the mirror and I will show you."

She led me to the mirror and eased the dressing gown from my body. And then she stripped off her clothes and we both stood naked, side by side, staring at our reflections.

My skin glowed white in the flicker of the candles; her olive skin seemed to absorb the light. My hair shone yellow, like the sun I now shunned, and her head was as dark as a moonless sky. The bruises on her abdomen were faint now, barely visible, but I remembered how she had been mistreated before she had found her way to this house.

I reached over to gently stroke her stomach, feeling again the rush of anger I had felt on her arrival. "Do you still hurt, *ma chere?*"

She put her hand over top of mine and smiled. "I ache sometimes, but it is fine."

"I have asked you many times, Monique, who it was that beat you. And you have never answered. I can see that they suffer the same fate, if only you tell me."

She shrugged. "It doesn't matter. That was in the past and I am here now. And there are compensations."

"Compensations?"

"Oh, yes." She turned to me in the near darkness and touched my naked shoulder. "There are compensations. I have you now. And you are beautiful." She kissed the shoulder she'd touched. "And kind." She kissed my neck and ran her tongue up to my ear. "And passionate." She breathed the word into my ear and I laughed softly.

"That tickles, Monique."

"Shall I stop, Mademoiselle?"

She continued kissing my ear and her hand reached up and caressed my breast, teasing the nipple into erectness. "If you want me to stop," she said again, "you only need to say so. But I think you should let yourself go. And trust the one person who loves you the most."

I sighed. She was not Eduard, but her hands felt so good on my body, her breath was sweet and soft, and I gave myself over to her passions.

Chapter 11

Shortly before dawn, I crawled out of bed, away from Monique's entwining limbs and hair, and went to the window. The only light inside the room came from the now dying fire, so, still naked, I pulled the curtains aside, opened the shutters, and stared out into the narrow, dirty streets. Somewhere, not all that far away, stood the guillotine, both beloved and hated by the people of my country.

I wondered, and not for the first time, about this strange preoccupation the city seemed to have with death; how many lives had been taken by that cool and gleaming blade, how many of the necks sacrificed on that bloody altar had once been touched by my lips and teeth? I closed my eyes and stretched my own neck out, imagining the terror experienced. Once again I pondered the nature of human beings; they would consider me a monster for the life I led, for the small amount of blood I stole. And yet they inflicted far more horrible crimes on each other and called it justice.

I shook my head and gave a low laugh as I refastened the shutters and closed the draperies. Just as they would never understand my kind, I would never fathom them. "Fair enough," I whispered and walked over to the bed, staring for a while at the sleeping girl. Then I leaned over her, pulling the blankets up around her shoulders. "You may scoff, little lamb," I said quietly, "at my inability to care. And yet, you live only because I can and do love."

She rolled over and smiled in her sleep, whispering a name I couldn't hear. I longed to climb back into bed with her, to warm my cold body against hers, but the sun was rising and the coffin awaited.

I was not so foolish and headstrong as to completely ignore the wise warnings of both Max and Eduard about my planned masque. It was undoubtedly a bad time to celebrate anything at all. And yet, to my mind, that was one of the best reasons to proceed. Besides, I'd already had my costume made and the girls seemed to be looking forward to the change.

With a thought to the starving children Eduard had alluded to, as well as a hope to avoid giving offense to the mob, I gave orders to the kitchen staff that they prepare four times as much food as the number of party guests warranted. They were to hold the extra victuals in the kitchen and distribute to anyone who happened to call at the back door, whether begging or demanding.

"Even if they come back for more," I told Cook, "give them food until we run out. We do not need any trouble, especially not with so many people here that evening."

She nodded. I knew that some of the food would find its way into her baskets for distribution to her friends later on. It did not matter; the whole situation was a token appeasement at best. I hoped only that I would be considered a small target, hardly worth bothering when one had nobility and royalty to condemn and centuries of injustices for which to be recompensed.

To be honest, I had a difficult time understanding the conflict; there was plenty of everything to go around. Simple redistribution should not have to be so painful. So the sympathies I had rested with both sides. And with neither.

Now the guillotine, that was a different matter entirely. It seemed to me like so many human advancements—a total waste of energy and time and, in this case, blood.

Not that I was likely to knock on the palace doors and complain. I laughed to myself as the image of this crossed my mind. *Excuse me, Your Majesties,* and of course I would do my most practiced curtsy, keeping my eyes down in respect and humility, *did you know that gallons and gallons of blood are being wasted every day in the square? And did you know that this very blood could feed so many hungry vampires?*

And the king would be courteous and gallant. *Oh, my dear Mademoiselle Courbet,* he would say, *this is a travesty and an outrage. We would stop such cruelty if we could. But since we cannot, we shall at least send someone over to collect the waste, just for you.*

Perhaps I should attempt to take the castle in the dead of night and transform the both of them into monsters like myself. The queen would then refrain from exciting riot by her suggestions of the choice of solid food for the peasants. Or would she still persist in her innocent folly, saying, "Let them drink blood"?

I shook my head, laughing out loud as I opened the door to my room. I supposed that everyone was right; I did not take the current political situation seriously enough. But I was what I was and this very human battle meant nothing to me.

My room was dark and I noticed that the shutters were open; a light mist had curled in, filling the corners of the room, visible only by the faint light of the embers of the unbanked fire. "Monique should not have left these open," I said as I crossed the floor and closed the window against the night. "Anything or anyone could come in." Then I thought again of the queen and how those words I had given her would sound so delightful. I laughed at it once more.

"It must be a good jest, Vivienne. It does my lonely heart good to hear your laughter. And do not chide Monique for the open windows; that was my doing."

I jumped and turned. A lone figure was standing by the bed, elegantly dressed in a black velvet coat and breeches. "Victor!"

I ran over to him and gave him a light kiss on each cheek. "But Max did not tell me you were here."

"Because, most likely, when Max called last, I was not here. I think"—and he lowered his voice somewhat, as if imparting a secret wisdom—"there are many of us gathered in this city now, more than you know, more than even I do. It is, perhaps, the scent of blood that draws us; like carrion crows we are called to scenes of war and death."

I twisted my mouth, trying to stop the giggle that threatened to escape. It was no good.

"Ever lighthearted, Vivienne?" He sounded offended. "I had hoped that the years would have begun to take their toll on your high spirits. But still you laugh."

"As often and as well as possible, Victor. It is usually the only answer that serves."

He shrugged. "Maybe you are right, my dear. But don't you worry about your welfare and safety?"

"*Sacre bleu!* Why is everyone so damnably concerned with my well-being all of a sudden? I have managed thus far and managed well. I am careful of those things that matter. As for the rest, it is nonsense. Why should I care why you have been drawn to the city? You are more than welcome to lap up the co-pious blood being spilt here."

"Even if that blood is yours?"

I narrowed my eyes and approached him. "Is that a threat, Victor? Yes, I have kept my sense of humor over the years, and I am truly sorry if that offends your vampiric sensibilities. How-ever, I assure you that my instincts are just as finely honed as yours and I am as prepared to defend my existence as you are."

It was Victor's turn to laugh now. "Good. No, my dear, it was not a threat. Just a concern. I enjoy your presence too much to want to see your life end so soon. And certainly not by my hands or teeth." He walked over to the small serving table and pulled the top off of the carafe of wine. "May I?"

"Oh, certainly. Your unexpected arrival put all thoughts of hospitality out of my mind. Please, be my guest and help your-self."

He poured one for both of us and handed me a glass, clicking his up against mine and nodding. "And now, I must say something about that unfortunate occurrence that caused you and Max to part company."

"No. You must do nothing of the sort. I have spoken with Max about it."

"And you have forgiven him?"

"No."

"But surely after all this time—"

"No."

"I merely thought—"

"No! What Max did is unforgivable. That he did it with the best of intentions makes no difference. That he was right about Diego makes no difference. Diego was mine, to make or unmake."

"Ah." He drained his glass and poured another. "So it was not the act of killing that was reprehensible to you, but rather an issue of who was responsible?"

I shook my head. "It hardly matters, Victor. Diego is dead and that is that. I know better now than to trust Max." *And,* I thought, *you—since you have come here to plead his case.* "It's not as if I had any rights under law; I could hardly bring this before a human court."

"But what if we, as vampires, had a court? A group of us bound together with our shared needs and goals? We could prevent these sorts of unfortunate incidents from occurring, we could ensure the continuation of our species, eliminate the risk of human intervention in our affairs."

I laughed. "A cadre of vampires? And this is why you have come here at this time? To get support?"

He nodded. "As I have said, many of the others are here at the moment. Drawn to the turmoil and death. Or perhaps causing it. However, this seems like a perfect opportunity to find agreements and alliances. To govern those that need governing."

"But why involve me, Victor? I have no interest, no concerns that I can't handle myself. And I certainly have no great desire to govern. I have seen what happens to those who try to rule the world and it is not a pretty sight."

"But you will not oppose me?"

I gave a little shrug of my shoulders. "Provided you are not stepping on my toes, Victor, you may do what you like. I am, quite frankly, surprised that you would even take the time to ask; what possible difference could my support or lack thereof make? I am just a girl, getting by the best that I can."

He smiled. "You are more than you know, my dear, but we shall save that discussion for later. Except for me to say that I am pleased you have done so well. Most of our kind don't make it past the first fifty or so years. They get careless or suicidal."

"I can assure you, *mon gars,* that I am neither."

"Good." He poured himself another glass of my wine and drained it. "Now tell me about this little celebration you are planning."

I shrugged. "There is nothing to tell. It is a masquerade and it will be held tomorrow evening, regardless of the damned revolution, and"—I gave him a warning look—"regardless of what everyone thinks of it being ill-advised."

Victor stood up and shook his head. "I would not presume to advise you, my dear." He paused, but ignored my slight snicker. "I was merely hoping to gain an invitation."

"Done."

He bowed. "Then, until tomorrow evening, I bid you farewell."

Chapter 12

The night of the party arrived without any of the predictions of the doomsayers coming true. We were not mobbed and no one was dragged from the house to be set up on the guillotine platform. The first of the guests arrived while I was still dressing; no easy feat, this, since my costume was quite elaborate and Monique kept fussing over how the feathers would not lie properly, how my headdress would slide from one side to the other with my slightest motion.

"Enough," I said as she shifted the swan's head for the hundredth time, "we will just say that I am a drunken swan and leave it at that." Giving her a slight push, I held the white feathered mask up to my face and looked over my mirrored image. "Mademoiselle Cygnette," I said, curtsying and giggling. "If only my old nurse could see me now."

"Vivienne?"

"Ah, when I was young, I spent an extraordinary amount of time splashing in puddles and pools on my father's estate. That habit, plus the fact that I was very slim with a very long neck, is what earned me the nickname. It has nothing whatsoever to do with the name of this house. That, you see, was a pleasant coincidence."

She smiled. "For whatever reason the name was given, it certainly suits you."

"And you, my lamb? Are you going to get into costume soon? Or will you be spending the night watching the fete from the top of the stairs?"

"I only need a short time to prepare. You should go downstairs without me, though. I do not want to spoil your entrance."

I nodded and the swan's beak bobbed down in front of my eyes. I tugged at the back of the wig on which it rested to straighten it out. "I should have dressed as something simple, like a monk. This is much too top-heavy; I feel as if I might topple down the stairs if I move too quickly."

Monique gave me one of her rare laughs. "Imagine, you as a monk. Just don't make any sudden movements"—she adjusted the hat again—"and you should be fine."

I gave her a doubtful look and started to nod, but thought better of it. Instead I turned and slowly glided out of the door, my neck held high and stiff. I took the stairs carefully, holding up the costume's skirts and enormous train with one hand, gripping the banister with the other. A man dressed as a harlequin, replete in red and black and trimmed with golden bells, waited for me at the bottom of the stairs, holding out his arm to me as I approached.

Even with the number of people already in attendance, their human aromas mingling with the nauseating odors of food, I could discern his own unique scent. "Eduard." His name escaped my lips like a sigh, my heart jumped, and I felt breathless. I cleared my throat to disguise the fact that his appearance moved me as it did. *Damn this man,* I thought, *I should not react this way, like a young girl in the flush of first love. This is my world and I am mistress here. How can he affect me so?*

"My dear Vivienne," he said, his deep voice pitched so that only I could hear, "I tried, but I could not stay away. Do you forgive me?"

"Forgive you? For not being able to stay away?" Finally reaching the bottom of the stairs, I laughed and kissed him. "I am the one who should apologize; having ordered you out for nothing more than concern for me, knowing all the while that I would regret my actions."

"And did you?"

My mouth twisted up into a wry grin. "You know very well I did, Eduard. Half of Paris must have heard me screaming at you that evening."

He laughed, as I intended him to. "No, you silly goose, do you regret your actions?"

I turned my head slowly and gave him a long, cool look. "I suppose that depends entirely upon yours. And if you persist in calling me a goose, when any fool can see that I am a swan, I will throw you out again."

"But I am not just any fool, Vivienne. I am your fool."

"Are you, Eduard?" I looked at him closely, searching for signs of sarcasm and finding none. "Are you really?"

"Yes, of course. And now, Mademoiselle Cygnette, kindly do me the honor of granting me the next dance."

I should have expected that he would excel at dancing as he did at everything else. Was there nothing he couldn't do and do well? *Damn the man,* I thought again, *why does he have to be so perfect?* He put his hand to my waist and I trembled, feeling I could dance with him forever, feeling that I could spread my artificial swan's wings and fly, deep into the night sky, far away from the hunger and the blood, to be nourished only by his touch and his smile.

Apparently Eduard was not the only fool present.

As we moved around the room, swaying and spinning to the music, I caught glimpses of people I knew; the gaudy colors and fabrics of their garb blended with their faces as we whirled past. The room grew strangely distorted, almost unreal, as if my emotions had become visible, generating waves of heat. Only Eduard and I existed; the rest was mirage.

Monique stood up against the wall, dressed as a shepherdess, all ribbons and bows and lace. She had her arms crossed, mask in one hand and crook in the other. I thought for a moment that she was glaring at me in hatred, but no, I must have been mistaken, for as we danced closer, her face lit up and she smiled at me, blowing me a kiss. Then she nodded to Eduard and moved off to another area of the room, joining in conversation with a monk and a grim reaper.

When the song ended, the dancers stopped in their places and applauded the musicians. Eduard leaned over and kissed my hand, his breath warming my skin. I blushed and turned away, murmuring something about not neglecting the guests.

I mingled for a while with the crowd, speaking to those whom I recognized beneath their finery and welcoming those whom I did not know, complimenting the girls on their varied costumes. The masque was a raging success, if such success could be based on the sound of laughter, the countless plates of food and glasses of wine consumed. As for me, I cared for none of it now, wishing only that they would all disappear and leave me alone with my love. I could feel him, circling the room as I did, and his presence seemed to fill the house, covering me with warmth.

The mention of my name and a burst of laughter caught my attention and I walked over to the corner where Monique was still deep in conversation with two of the guests. I wrapped my arm around her waist and gave her a kiss. "Having a good time, little lamb?"

"Max," I said, nodding to the monk, and "Victor," to the death's head, "I see you have managed to entertain Monique in my absence."

"Quite the contrary, Vivienne," Victor said, "she was entertaining us. I see that some of your, ah, charm, has worn off on her. She is a delighlful companion."

I nodded. "I am glad you approve, Victor. And, Max?" I gave him a warning look. "What do you have to say?"

He laughed. "Well, she is a vast improvement over your last pick. You will get no interference from me at this point, but I think you may be moving too quickly."

I laughed back at him and rolled my eyes. This from the man who had given me only one last sunrise? "What little patience I have, Max, I learned from the master. But I am as sure of her as I can be."

Monique looked back and forth at the three of us while we spoke, her dark eyes searching mine, trying to gather some meaning out of our cryptic conversation. "Vivienne? I don't understand. Have I done something wrong? Offended anyone?"

"No, of course not, little lamb. Do not let these gentlemen intimidate you, Monique. You are wonderful and will continue to be so."

"Good. I see that Eduard is here."

I ducked my head to hide my smile of pure pleasure; instinct told me that my romance with Eduard should be kept hidden from both Max and Victor. "Yes, of course he is here. Are we not the most fashionable house in all of Paris?"

"But you have left him alone. Shall I go and keep him company?"

"I am sure he would enjoy your company, Monique. Tell him I will be along presently."

She nodded, curtsied prettily to Max and Victor, picked up two glasses of red wine from the closest tray, and moved across the room. I watched her navigate her way through the crowd to reach him, looked at the two of them standing close together, his blond head bending close to her dark one. Holding my breath and biting my lip, I tried to hide the violent flash of jealousy I felt as he brought her hand up to his mouth. Monique smiled up into his face and I clenched my jaws and fists.

"I presume that this Eduard is a special friend of yours, Vivienne. I would like to meet him." In the time I had been watching the dancers, Victor seemed to have vanished, but Max had remained by my side. His voice was a strange mix of concern, curiosity, and suspicion. When he offered me a glass of wine, I relaxed my hand, smiled my thanks, and took a sip. "He seems familiar to me, somehow. Perhaps he and I have met before?"

"I would not think so, Max. *Mon chou,* he is just a man, nothing remarkable or memorable."

"Ah. A regular of the house then?"

"No, not exactly." I took another sip of the wine to cover my nervousness. "He is a doctor, you see. Monique brought him here to tend to Rosa the night she died."

"Wait! Rosa is dead? When did this happen and why didn't you tell me?"

I shrugged, my eyes darting back over to where they stood talking. Monique was laughing and Eduard was touching her elbow and leading her out to the dance floor.

"Vivienne?"

"Hmmm?" I could almost feel the weight of his hand on her waist.

"We were speaking of Rosa. And how she came to be dead."

"Yes, we were." She looked happy and dizzy, much the same, I imagine, as I looked when dancing with the man.

Max reached over and gave my shoulder a shake. "Wake up, girl, what is wrong with you this evening?"

With great effort, I turned my back on the dancers and poured my full attention into the conversation. "Rosa got sick one day a while ago. Monique went to fetch the midwife; she's quite skilled, you know, even with situations other than childbirth. But Marie was out on another call. And Eduard happened to be walking by, heard Monique inquire after her, and volunteered his services."

"How fortunate for Monique." His voice acquired an edge and I shivered. "But he didn't seem to do much to help Rosa, did he?"

"He did the best he could, Max. He explained to me that the poison was too firmly entrenched in her system and that he could not do anything to check it."

"Poison?" His voice rose over the noise of the room and several people nearby turned and stared. Max glared at them, then smiled an evil grimace and motioned with his finger that they were to turn around. Not surprisingly, they obeyed his unspoken command. He lowered his voice. "What do you mean? Rosa was poisoned?"

I gave a small humorless laugh. "That is exactly what I said at the time. But he did not mean that she was poisoned as in someone trying to kill her, just that there was poison in her system. His best theory was that she had eaten some tainted meat or other food. And, well, the food supply has been rather unreliable lately, or so I have heard. There seems to be no shortage of blood, at least."

"True."

"I am sure he was right about the food, Max. Why would he lie to me?"

"Why, indeed." He took a drink of his wine and watched the dance floor. "The tainted food theory seems rather likely, as much as I hate to admit it. And Rosa was not immortal and was getting old. Still, I don't like the thoughts of you being unprotected."

"But Monique protects me now."

"I see. And so Monique is now filling Rosa's position? Once again, how fortunate for her."

I knew what he was implying and I grew angry. He had started out this way with Diego and I was determined that not happen again. "Listen to me, Max, you black-hearted bastard." I stared deeply into his eyes and did not relent. "This one has nothing to do with you, do you understand? Diego and I were living under your roof and your protection when you murdered him, so perhaps your actions were proper. But this house is my territory; it has nothing to do with you and you will not inter-fere. Do you hear me? You will not interfere; I will not allow it."

Max looked away first and I counted that a victory. "Very well, Vivienne," he said, sounding penitent, although not one bit less arrogant. "Let us call a truce and discuss it no more."

I smiled, placated by his tone; he couldn't help his arrogance any more than I could. It was part and parcel of what we were. The knowledge of our superiority over humans carried into every one of our interactions. "Yes, let us change the topic. How are you enjoying the party?"

He gave a grunt. "Like any large gathering of humans, it makes me nervous. And hungry. But I have to say"—and he got a mischievous glint in his eye—"this hat object you are wearing is making me crazy."

I giggled. "You are right, Max, as always." Reaching up, I slid the headdress and the wig off, setting it down on the table as if it were a platter of food. Pulling the pins out of my hair, I tossed my head and combed out the tangles with my fingers. "Ah, that feels so much better. And if the truth be known, Max, that headdress is one of the worst mistakes I have ever made."

His eyes strayed to the dance floor; the music had ended and Monique and Eduard were making their way over to us. "I doubt that, my dear, but I think it would be wise of me to leave now. I will perhaps get to meet the inestimable Eduard another night. In fact, I will make an effort to do exactly that." He bowed to me and quickly slipped away into the crowd, before I could comment or even say good night.

No matter. Eduard was back. And once again the rest of the guests seemed to disappear. I took his hand.

"I see," he said, "that Mademoiselle Cygnette has lost her head."

"Hush," I said to him, "that is not a good thing to say out loud. And it is not my head that I have lost."

"What then?"

I put a finger to his lips. "Hush," I said again and started to lead him out of the room, "and come with me. I grow weary of this celebration."

He smiled at me and I lost myself in his eyes. "Bored with your own masquerade, Vivienne? What shall we do to remedy that?"

"I am not sure, Monsieur le Docteur, but I feel confident we will find something to do."

Chapter 13

" I have always meant to ask you," Eduard said as we entered the door to my room, "about this wooden chest at the foot of your bed."

"What is there to know?" I laughed and came up behind him, putting my arms around his waist and resting my head on his shoulder. "It is a chest. It is wooden. And"—I flung my hand out—"voilà! It is at the foot of my bed."

"But what purpose does it serve? It has no lock on it, so you must not use it for valuables. I have never seen you put anything into it. Or take anything out of it, for that matter." He reached over and lifted the lid before I could stop him.

"We store linens in it," I said, darting around and slamming the lid. I sat down on top of it and kicked my legs back and forth.

"But," he said, reaching down and picking me up, "not very many linens, as far as I could see. The lid felt so heavy, it must be made of something more than just wood. And why is the lock on the inside?"

"Because, my dearest Eduard, that is where the lock is. Why ask me? I did not make the silly box. It is, if you must know, a family heirloom. And"—I twisted in his arms, wrapped my feathered wings tightly around him, and looked deep into his eyes—"I do not wish to discuss it. Now, make love to me, *mon cher*, so that I do not regret missing my own celebration."

He smiled at me and kissed my forehead. "We would not want you to regret a thing, Vivienne. It would age you. And even you must beware of the passages of time."

"Even I?" I smiled as he carried me to the bed and laid me down gently, as if I were made of porcelain.

"Foo." I snapped my fingers. "I will never grow old." Then I pulled him down to me. "At least as long as you are here."

His mouth fell on mine and once again I lost myself in his embrace. Like the first time, I thought that moments like these were ones for which I would gladly die.

And then I ceased to think. And gave myself over to emotion and touch.

"Vivienne?"

"Hmmm?"

"Although you seem to plan on living forever, I fear I may not be here all that much longer."

"Nonsense, my sweet man." I ran my nails down his arm and laughed at his shivers. "The night is still young."

Eduard sighed. "No, you do not understand. I have reason to believe that I will soon be a prisoner of the revolution. As physician to some of the royal family I have been rather too outspoken in my dislike of the unruly mob that now rules Paris."

"What?" I sat straight up in bed and stared down at him. "And you have been so careful to warn me away from just such a situation. How do you know?"

He nodded. "I know. It is one of the reasons I tried to stay away from you. I would not want to lead the mob here to your house."

"I do not care one bit for the mob. But if you feel you are in danger, we must make arrangements for you to leave the city. No, leave the country entirely. I have friends who . . ."

My voice trailed off. I had exactly two friends who were in the position to offer succor, and somehow I did not think either one of them would welcome me if accompanied by my current paramour.

Nor did I wish to put Eduard in danger. Diego had been miles and even decades away from a guillotine and still he had lost his head.

"No." He pulled *me* back down to him. "I should not even have mentioned it. I hadn't meant to. But," and he sighed again and whispered his words into my neck, "I did not want to go without saying good-bye. You have made such a difference to my life in such a short time and I hope you will remember me fondly after I am . . ."

I silenced him with a kiss. "No talk of death, Eduard. Here, in my room, in my house, there is no death for you. I will not allow it. And what if there were a way to hold death at bay? Would you take immortality if it were offered?"

"Perhaps," he said, his voice growing distant, "that is what I am doing. You are right, though, we should not be talking of this." He looked into my eyes and stroked my hair. "You are to forget that I have said anything, my dear. I am being morose, as I am wont to be at times. It means nothing; I have had premonitions all my life and I am still here, still alive."

I curled up next to him, running my nails lazily down his chest and to his groin. I giggled at his instant reaction to my touch. "Wonderfully alive, I would say. No." I continued to caress him. "Gloriously alive. And you will stay that way if I have the slightest say in the matter."

Eduard laughed and gave me a long, slow, and passionate kiss. "How could I not, now that you have ordered it? Now, let us ring for a bottle of wine and we shall toast our immortality."

Getting out of bed, I wrapped my dressing gown around me. "There will be no answer to the ring, Eduard, not this evening. Let me get the wine."

I was surprised to find the masque still going on when I arrived at the bottom of the stairs. The musicians had long since departed, but the guests were still drinking and singing and talking and dancing. Many couples could be seen in various stages of lovemaking—most of them guests, as the girls hardly considered this activity recreational. Looking around the room, my only thought was how grateful I was that I had others who would clean up the mess. And that when I awoke the next evening and climbed out of my coffin, life would be back to normal.

No one paid any attention to me as I moved through the room and took one of the few unopened bottles of wine from the table. I noticed my headdress still sitting there on display, still attached to the wig, but someone had gotten a cleaver from the kitchen and cut off the swan's head.

What an odd thing to do, I thought. Then I surveyed the room and watched the guests for a second or two. They were behaving in the most decadent fashion, many in complete deshabille, flagrantly displaying breasts and organs probably best kept clothed. I gave a low laugh and shook my head. A decapitated swan, and not even a real one at that, was mild compared to what they could be capable of. It wasn't as if I was planning on wearing the silly thing ever again; in fact, if I'd thought of it first, I might have done the same thing.

Even so, it looked so pitiful and it seemed such a mean-spirited thing to do. I thought then of tossing them all out into the street. But no, Eduard was waiting.

I paused outside of Monique's room to make sure that she was asleep; not entirely an altruistic gesture. I didn't want her to have another attack of jealousy because Eduard was in our bed. It sounded as if I hadn't needed to worry. She had someone in there with her, a man. They were talking and I went to move on, having seen enough flagrant displays downstairs. But three steps away I stopped, recognizing the male voice, droning, deep. And her voice carried a degree of fear I had never heard in it before.

"No!" I slammed the bottle I carried to the floor, unmindful of the shattering glass and sticky red wine that showered my feet and legs. The door was locked when I turned the handle, so I gripped it harder and turned it again. This time the knob crumbled in my hand as if it had been made of clay.

Max raised his head away from Monique's neck as I burst

into the room. His eyes glowed with an unholy pleasure I knew all too well. Blood dripped from his fangs and he growled at me. "Get out, Vivienne. This has nothing to do with you."

I flew at him, nails extended, putting all of my strength into the leap. "She is not yours," I hissed as I knocked him to the ground and raked his face. "She is not yours and I will not permit you to touch her again."

I held him down, nails at his throat now, and turned my head. "Monique, little lamb, go to my room, stay there, and lock the door. Eduard is there, he will protect you. And Max will threaten you no more."

He couldn't have taken much of her blood since she was able to run from the room. I heard her bare feet slapping against the floor, and her gasp of pain as she hit the remains of the bottle. But still she hurried down the hall and soon I heard the door to my room open, then heard it slam shut.

"Are you quite done?" Max pushed away from me as if I weighed nothing, wiped his hands over his already-healing face.

I shook my head in disgust. "All of Paris to feed on, Max, and you had to choose the one forbidden. Why must you be so perverse? So inhuman? I should never have let you in this house. I would kill you if I knew how."

He laughed and got to his feet, adjusting the monk's robe, tightening the belt about his waist. "You couldn't kill me even if you knew how. You quite simply don't have the nerve for it."

I bared my teeth at him. "Touch her again and we will see just how much nerve I have."

"Be fair, Vivienne. You were busy with the exquisite Eduard; and I thought 'what difference would it make to her if I claimed Monique?' "

"But there was no need for it to be her. Any woman at the masquerade would have gone with you and fed whatever appetites you wanted fulfilled."

"It is not a matter of appetites, my dear. I don't trust her, not one bit, and neither should you. She was skulking outside your door earlier, did you know that? Nasty little habit, staring in at keyholes."

"I don't believe you."

He laughed. "Of course you don't. You are as enchanted with the lovely Monique as you are with the good doctor. And I wish I knew why. It worries me; neither of these humans"—he spat the word—"should be able to exert such power over someone like you."

"You are welcome to your worries, Max, but do not inflict them upon me. And perhaps what is happening is not what you think. Could it not be possible that the great Maximillian Esteban is wrong?"

"Sarcasm does not become you, my dear. It makes you quite unattractive."

"*Je m'en fous!* I think that the influence Eduard and Monique have over me has nothing at all to do with power."

"Then what, Vivienne?" He smiled and I wanted to tear into his face again. Instead, I looked away from him.

"Perhaps, Max, this power is love. The truth is that I truly care for the both of them, something a cold bastard like you could never understand."

He threw his head back and laughed. "Love? Now I am even more worried. Did you never listen? What have Victor and I told you time and time again about the false emotion of love?"

I folded my arms and glared at him stubbornly. "It is love, Max, no matter what you think."

He shook his head. "Mark my words, Vivienne, between the two of them, they will have you dead yet. Take care who you give your heart to, lest they tear it out and devour it." He reached over and patted my cheek; I pulled away with a growl. "I have invested a goodly amount of money, time, and blood in you and I do not wish to see it all go for naught."

"I am not your child anymore, Max. And I am not your wife, nor your servant. As far as your investment?" I threw my hands up into the air in exasperation. "I care nothing for that. And if the truth be told, neither do you. All you wish is to have total control over me and mine. And that will not happen. I do not wish to see you ever again. Please do not return."

He shrugged. "As you wish. But my offer for safe haven still applies. I would welcome you should you need a place to go. Blood binds us together more thoroughly than ever love would."

"I will seek sanctuary with you, Max, when I'm dead and buried."

He laughed. "Technically, of course, you already are dead, but we won't argue over semantics now." He nodded, bowed with a flourish, and walked out the door, his boots crunching on broken glass.

Chapter 14

When I got back to my room, I knocked softly on the door. Eduard flung it open with a questioning look. "What exactly is happening here, Vivienne? She's been bitten, not by any sort of animal I am familiar with. And her feet are all bloody."

I sighed and glanced over to where Monique lay, sobbing and gasping for breath on the lounge, holding a red-stained cloth to the open wound on her neck. The air was full of the tang of blood; I caught my breath and walked over to her, kneeling down and brushing her hair back from her pale face.

"Did she tell you what happened?" I asked, giving Eduard a quick glance out of the corner of my eyes, before turning my attention back to Monique. I moved her hand away from the cloth and tucked it down at her side, peering underneath to see the damage. Max had not just bitten her, he'd worried at the wound like a mad dog. "Bastard," I whispered under my breath. "I should have killed him where he stood."

She smiled up at me weakly. "I am all right, Vivienne. You saved me. Again. Thank you."

"Poor little lamb, I am so sorry. This should not have happened."

"What should not have happened? What exactly is going on here?" Eduard raised his voice and both Monique and I jumped.

"Oh, hush," I said, "you are upsetting her more. Bring me some of the brandy on the night table and a glass."

He nodded and did as I asked.

I laughed as I put the glass up to her lips and she choked a bit on the bitter drink. "I seemed destined to force brandy on you, my lamb. Drink it all up, yes, that's a good girl." I filled another one. "One more and then we will have the doctor look at your feet."

After the second brandy, she fell asleep and Eduard was able to pick out the bits of glass that had imbedded themselves in the soles of her feet. He washed them and bandaged them; left her to sleep on the lounge with one of the blankets from my bed to cover her. Eduard fussed a bit more over the wound on her neck, but I knew it would heal well.

"Thank you," I said. "I could have managed, but you were much gentler and thorough than I would have been."

"Of course," he said, "but now will you please tell me what happened?"

"One of our guests got a little carried away in his merriment. I have seen to it that he will not return."

"And her feet? What happened there? They were cut to ribbons. She won't be able to walk for weeks."

"That, I fear, is my doing. I dropped the bottle of wine I'd been bringing back for us and she ran through it on her way here. Nothing more hideous than that."

"Ah." He gave me a smile. "I didn't mean to yell at you or blame you. I was merely worried for the girl. I am sorry, though, that my request for wine ended this way."

I gave him a wan smile. "Actually, if you hadn't sent me out for drink, it might have been worse." I shivered slightly. Would Max have drained her dry? Torn her apart? Left her dead body for me to find or tossed her into the streets? "But it was not the worst and she'll be fine in a day or two. Thank you again."

He shook his head. "I can't help but think that there is more to the situation than you are telling me. But as no lasting harm was done, I will trust your explanations. And your assurance that this will not happen again."

"I will do everything I can to protect her, as I have since she arrived here."

"Good."

An awkward silence fell on us. For me, I was ever aware of the impending sunrise and Eduard was distant, distracted.

"I do think that I should be—"

"It has been wonderful—"

We both spoke at the same time and laughed nervously.

"Ladies first," he finally said.

"I am glad you came back." It was as close as I could get to saying what I really wanted to say. The words of love, the words that told how empty I felt in his absence, how much I missed his voice, his touch when he was gone—these words froze up in my throat. All I could do was smile. And say it again. "So very glad, Eduard."

"As am I."

He gathered me up into his arms and held me, swaying slightly. I turned my head to draw in the delicious scent of him and moved my mouth onto his neck, not to feed, not to bite, but to savor his taste. And as I nuzzled, he kept me close, stroking my hair, rocking us both gently back and forth. Tears began to stream down my face; I hadn't cried a tear since the night Max transformed me. I turned my face away and wiped my eyes on my dressing gown sleeve, sniffed once, and pulled out of his arms.

Nothing more needed to be said. He picked up his fool's cap from the bedpost, kissed me once on the forehead, and walked out the door. I smiled, even as I continued to cry, listening to the jangling sound of his costume's bells until he was gone.

Eduard never returned. For a few weeks he sent letters daily, tied with red satin ribbons onto bundles of violets and lavender. Monique reported that she would sometimes see him in passing on the streets when she ventured out. He never spoke to her, she said, never even looked her in the eye. "Perhaps he didn't see me. I could follow him the next time if you'd like."

"No, Monique. He knows where I am, knows that I am waiting. Do not seek him out. There is no need."

But there was a need, and it was my need, one stronger than I ever would have believed. The tears I had cried that last evening were a response to the truth—somehow I had known, even without his talk of fate and death, that he would leave and I would never see him again.

I grew moody and temperamental, withdrawing more into the shell I had occupied before he arrived. I rarely left my room, and when I did come out I remained veiled and did not speak to anyone. Monique faithfully escorted a patron of the house to my room every few nights and I would feed halfheartedly.

These feedings involved no real contact—no touch, no love-play, not even the delicious rush of power I often felt flowing through me with the blood. I would take what little I needed, impart the suggestion that the victim should forget, and send him on his way.

During the day, I would lie in my wooden box, surrounded by the dying flowers he had sent, grasping his letters in my hands as if they alone kept me alive. I tried not to sleep, since dreams of him were torture, so vivid and real I often felt that all I needed to do was roll over and open my eyes and there he would be. In those dreams, he was with me and I could reach over and feel him next to me, taste his blood, touch the silklike texture of his skin, thrill to the brush of his lips on mine.

At night I had taken to standing, naked and in total darkness, in front of an open window, curtains pulled back and shutters thrown wide open. I searched the face of everyone who passed below my window, hoping beyond hope that this one would be Eduard. It never was. But as their footsteps receded, I would close my eyes to wait for the approaching steps of another, praying to the God I had abandoned with my mother's death, praying for the return of love. Each time I looked I found only strangers, and in truth I did not expect different, yet I could not help myself.

I was empty now, without him. Emptier than I had been before we met, because I knew now what I lacked. I knew that he was out in the city, somewhere; I perceived his presence as tangibly as the kiss of the night breeze on my naked skin.

Night after night I stood thus, searching, hoping, and praying until dawn threatened. Then Monique would take me by the hand and pull me away from the window, closing it tightly against the sun. Clothing me in a white satin nightdress, she would brush my hair and wash my face and hands, leading me eventually to the wooden chest at the foot of the bed so that I could once again spend the day with his letters and his flowers.

Had it not been for Monique, I'd have ended as one of the fatalities of which Max and Victor had spoken. My life rested in her hands during these days and nights and she more than repaid my trust in her as she had more than disproved Max's suspicions.

Max's suspicions did not matter now, for Max had disappeared as completely as Eduard had, taking Victor with him, I presumed. All I had left in the world was Monique.

I felt sorry for myself for a little over a month. Then, one evening, as I came out of my coffin, I noticed a difference in my emotions, a lightening of my spirits. And any discomforting dreams I might have experienced must have faded upon wakening exactly as dreams should, for they left no pieces of themselves behind.

I stretched and yawned; my sleep had been deep and nourishing. Why should it not have been? Hadn't it always been so? For a long moment I could not remember why I had been unhappy, only that I had been. And now, I was not. Something had changed.

Thinking, I stretched again and realized, with a girlish laugh— the *hurt is gone*. It was not that I had stopped loving Eduard; I did still and feared that love would be with me always. But the sharp ache of missing him wasn't there. I sat on a little chair in front of the mirror and brushed my hair, humming a song I'd heard someone singing outside my window years ago. Smiling at my image, I leaned over and kissed it. "I am back," I said with a giggle, "and I am very hungry. But oh, I feel wonderful."

"You do?" The mirror reflected the occupant of the bed as she poked her head out from underneath the covers.

"Yes, I do, *mon chou*. And why shouldn't I?"

Monique got up and stood behind me, taking the brush from my hand. "And that was my thought always. I am glad you've come around. I was worried."

I peered at her reflection in the mirror as she brushed my hair. She did indeed look worried. Her skin was sallow and lifeless and her eyes were rimmed by dark circles, as if she too had been unable to sleep. As I looked closer I saw that she had been crying.

I pulled her hand down to my mouth and kissed it. "You are a sweet little lamb, Monique. And I will always be grateful to you. Just remember." I gave her hand a little playful nip. "Next time you swear you hate me and wish me dead, remember that you could have destroyed me at any time this past month and I would not have been able to stop you."

She smiled. "I am already regretting it."

"Foo," I said with another laugh, "you love me and you know it. Just as I love you."

"What about Eduard? We have to talk about him, Vivienne."

I made a face in the mirror and stuck my tongue out at her. "Nothing to talk of. Eduard is gone." I felt her tremble. Had she disliked him so much? "And whatever enchantment he held over me is gone with him."

She continued brushing my hair, smoothing and stroking. It felt so good to have her do this; it felt so good not to hurt as I had. I gave a long, low hum of pleasure and Monique smiled and kissed the top of my head.

"And so, Monique, you have been pretty much cooped up in this room with me for over a month. Shall I give you the night off?"

She started to protest, but I continued.

"Or would you like to come hunting with me? You have asked for me to give you this gift of immortality and yet you have no idea what it entails. Coming out with me would be good preparation for your soon-to-be new life."

She clapped her hands together. "That is certainly an easy

choice, Vivienne. Hunting, of course! What should I wear? Where
will we be going?"

"Let's just walk for a while. Wear something dark, so that we
are not so obvious, and I will show you a side of Paris you have
never seen before."

We set off, arm in arm, looking nothing more than two ladies
taking a leisurely stroll. In a low voice, I began explaining to
Monique what to look for in a victim. "Never choose one too
old or too young."

"The blood isn't as good?"

I laughed, drawing a curious look from a few passersby. "Not
at all. Blood is blood. Even the blood of animals will sustain us
for a while. And while it is true that everyone's blood carries a
different taste, a different feel, I have never tasted any that was
bad. But taking from the very old and the very young is risky
since they are most likely to suffer ill effects from our feeding.
They could sicken. Or die."

"And what difference does that make? You are superior to
humans in every way. Why should you care? And when I am
like you, why should I care?"

I stopped and pulled back from her so that I could look her in
the face. "It makes all the difference in the world, my lamb. A
vampire who kills repeatedly is one who eventually will be discovered and killed herself. You take what you need, no more.
Survival. It is the first lesson Max taught me. And perhaps the
most important. Never call attention to what you are, never let
them know you are there, waiting. And never let them remember."

"You call attention to yourself. Most of Paris knows who
you are."

"Ah, that may be true. But do they know what I am?"

She thought for a moment as we walked on. "No, I don't believe they do. And if they did, what then?"

I sighed. "I would be hunted down and killed. Have no
doubts on that count. Superstitions still rule the common peo-

ple. I am, as you may have noticed, an evil creature, a minion of Satan himself, if you would believe the priests."

"The priests are wrong." She smiled. "You have many faults, it is true, but you are not evil."

We turned down the next street and walked along the river for a time, all the while moving slowly and certainly toward Place du Carroussel.

"The priests may be wrong, but that does not stop their followers from listening. Wrong is not always visible from outside appearances. You know this, we all know this." I made a sound of disgust and spat on the ground. "Pah! We would live in a better world without the priests and the leaders telling us what we should do and how we should live."

We continued walking in silence for a while. The streets seemed ominously empty; most respectable people would be home with family. And the reprobates would undoubtedly avoid this square like the plague. But I was neither and there was something on display here I wanted to see. Something that defined this time and this city. I should have come before and I would have, despite my confessions of disinterest, had I not been distracted by Eduard.

"But I don't understand," Monique said, "you may scoff all you like, but you *could* make it better. With all your powers, all your strength, you could rule the world."

I laughed even harder, and my high-pitched voice echoed down the narrow streets, sounding furtive and guilty. No doubt it was the first laughter this spot in Paris had heard for some time.

Monique looked angry at my laughter. "You could rule the world," she repeated like a child. "You should rule the world."

"Rule the world? Why would anyone want such a task? You, my lamb, are living in times that prove such ambitions vain. And deadly."

She noticed, at last, where we were standing. Even in the darkness, I could tell that she'd gone paler. The wooden platform smelled of newly hewn wood. And fear. And blood.

"Here, Monique, this is the fate of those who wish to rule. For me, I wish no part of it. Nor would I wish it on any."

She shivered next to me as we stood looking at the handiwork of mankind.

Chapter 15

"**W**hy are we here?" Monique whispered.

"A good question, my pretty ladies." A guard came out of the shadows of one of the walls. "There is nothing to see here right now. Just wood and steel, and"—he took a long look at us and made an effort to stand taller in his uniform—"myself." He stepped closer and smiled, stroking his mustache and beard. "And I am, of course, your obedient servant."

I glanced at Monique, nodding my head ever so slightly in the guard's direction. "Watch me." I mouthed the words and she flashed a quick understanding smile.

"Good evening, *mon Capitaine*. And just how obedient a servant are you, I wonder?"

He picked up on the sexual invitation my voice offered and smirked, putting his hand over his heart and bowing. "Obedient enough, pretty one, and more than willing to serve your every need."

I laughed and slowly moved closer to him, so close that I could smell the cheap wine he had been drinking. Looking into his eyes, I lowered the pitch of my voice. "You sound so sure of yourself. I like that in a man. But how shall I test your sincerity?"

"Give me a task, lady, so that I can prove myself worthy of your attentions."

I nodded and paused, as if thinking of a task, while he stood expectantly in front of me awaiting my command. *So very easy,* I thought, *there is no challenge here. He is already mine.*

"Would you, perhaps, explain to me how this machine works? I have heard so much about it, but alas, have not been able to see it demonstrated."

"It is quite simple, lady. The traitor mounts the stairs and lays his head on the platform, the lunette. The executioner pulls the lever, the *declic,* and whoosh!" He made a chopping motion with his hand against his other wrist. "It is done. The leather bag that had held the heads has now been replaced with a basket of sorts." He laughed and shot me a sly smile. "Although not the sort of thing a pretty mademoiselle would want to take to market."

"Have you done this? Have you pulled the lever and watched the blade fall?"

"Me? No. We have Sanson for the task. He is quite skilled. In fact, he was here today for the newest list. You should have come to witness the event—many of the city's fine ladies do. Today the list was long. And still the number of traitors to our glorious revolution grows."

"No doubt. And who was on this list? Can you tell me that?"

I really didn't care to know, I was not even sure why I had asked. And I knew what his answer would be.

"No, I fear I could not tell you that, even if I remembered. "

"Then, perhaps, you are not as obedient as you promised."

He shook his head and put his arms out in a supplicating gesture. "But surely, lady, you can find a more appropriate task for me. Why do you care for the names of the traitors?"

"I do not, that is true." I looked over at Monique where she had sat down on the steps of the platform. She was staring at the steel blade fixed in its upright position, holding her arms to herself and shivering despite the warmth of the night. "What do you think," I asked her, "shall we forgive this good soldier and give him a kiss good night?"

She stood up and came over to us. "Yes," she said, "and then let us go. I don't like it here."

The guard looked back and forth at the two of us. "Kisses

from two such beautiful ladies would make this night duty a pleasure. Who shall be first: the raven-haired one who is hauntingly familiar in her beauty or the blond goddess?"

I laughed. "Save me for last, *mon Capitaine,* I am likely to leave you too exhausted for kissing anyone else afterward."

He turned to Monique and kissed her, a perfunctory gesture. She stood stiffly and accepted his attentions. *We will have to work on that,* I thought, *she must not be unwelcoming. But there is time and she is not yet a vampire.*

"My turn." I opened my arms and the guard fell into them, his lips on mine before I could move. Although his obedience was in question, his aggression certainly made up for the lack. I pushed away from him. "Slowly, lover, you needn't be in such a hurry."

"Ah," he said, groaning, his hands grasping at my waist and pulling me to him, "but you taste so good I need more than one kiss."

I laughed softly. "Here? In front of this damnable machine? I think not, my good Captain."

"No?"

"No. We bargained for kisses and kisses are all you will get. But I promise you will not regret them."

And now I turned the aggressor. I kissed his mouth, hard and hurried, pulling at his lower lip with my teeth, grazing him for that first delicious taste of blood. He lifted me toward him and I wrapped my legs around his waist, still kissing him, nuzzling the skin of his cheeks, giving a low purr of delight. "Perhaps," I whispered huskily, "for such a strong and handsome soldier I can give a little more than kisses."

I felt him throb up against me in response and as his hands traveled under my skirts and up to my thighs, I took advantage of his distraction and fastened my mouth on his neck.

How fortunate that he was so strong and so hungry for a woman. When I bit him, he didn't drop me, nor did he flinch or fight. Instead he leaned farther into me, holding me tightly, letting my teeth sink deep into his flesh. I drew on him, enjoying the hot rush of his blood on my tongue and in my throat. Each swallow burned into my body, filling me, burning in its wake all fears and aches and thoughts of lost love. None of that mattered; all that remained was my mouth and my hunger and the satisfaction of blood.

As always, when I drank of my victims' physical substance, I concentrated on their spiritual aspects as well, capturing a bit of their personality and essence to carry with me into eternity, my way of paying them back for their sacrifice. I found in his mind the image of a girl he had loved who had died giving birth to his first child. I saw the child too, dying of a fever in his arms. His mind and his life were opened to me in the feeding and I kept what I could to hold for him.

The grasp he had on my waist began to falter, so I slid my legs down and stood on the ground, still drinking at his neck, but more slowly now, like the gentle, weary touch after the frenzy of love. Then, with a sigh from both of us, I pulled away.

"Forget," I whispered in his ear. "This never happened. I do not exist, except in your dreams. You have fallen asleep while on duty again." Leading him back to the post he had been standing when we arrived, I kissed his cheek. "Thank you, *mon Capitaine*. Sleep now. And wake up with no memory of me." He lay down, curled up, and was softly snoring even before I could turn away.

I wiped my mouth with the back of my hand and looked for Monique. She was standing on the platform now, staring up at the *mouton*. The blade shimmered faintly in the moonlight, blood tinged, although that may have just been a reflection from the red painted wood surrounding it. She caressed the wooden framework, running her fingers over it as if it were a lover's skin, her lips moving as if in prayer. Then she leaned over and kissed what the guard had called the lunette.

"Monique?"

Although I said her name softly she reacted as if I had screamed it across the square. She jumped and shivered, turning unfocused eyes on me.

"Monique?" I said it again, this time with more command. "Come down from there, lamb, I would not want the rope to shift."

She shook herself slightly as if awakening and looked around her in confusion. "What am I doing up here?"

"A good question. And one I was just about to ask."

"I don't know; it was like a dream. I felt something pulling me to this spot." She shivered and hurried down the platform stairs. "Are you finished with the guard already? I fear I wasn't watching all that closely."

I shrugged. "Do not fret about it, my lamb. There will be other feedings and other nights. You have many years in which to learn the art."

"So, did he finally tell you who was executed today?"

"No. It does not matter."

"But I want to see if you can make him tell you. He must know the names and you should be able to drag them out of him. Try. Please. Show me how this control of one's victims is done."

I nodded. "Fine, if you wish." I walked back over to the guard and knelt down next to him. "Listen to me, *mon cher,* while you still sleep, I want you to tell me the names of those executed today."

He muttered something.

"Louder, *mon Capitaine,* so that I can hear."

He began to rattle off a list of names, meaningless to me since this was merely a demonstration of my power. I barely listened as he gave names, professions. I motioned to Monique. "Let's go now, while he is still reciting . . ."

As I started to go, I heard a name that chilled me and I turned back to him. "Stop. Say that last name again, if you please."

He paused, trying to remember what that last name was. Then, without emotion, without remorse, he said what I had dreaded to hear.

"Eduard DeRouchard, Physician to the Royal Family."

Chapter 16

"**Y**ou knew!"

We had walked back to the House of the Swan in silence. Each step I took fed my rage, so that by the time I closed and locked the door to my room my temper was totally out of control.

She said nothing in reply, had no defenses, no prepared alibi to stave off my wrath.

"You knew, you lying bitch!" I screamed the words, totally uncaring of who heard. "You had to have known, otherwise you'd not have had me ask the guard for the names. Is that true?"

Still silent, she met my eyes and I found that I could read nothing in them. Saw nothing but the reflection of my anger. She should have been frightened. *Why isn't she frightened?* I wondered. *Does she not know I hold her life in my hands?*

"Monique? Answer me."

She studied the carpet at her feet. "I don't know what I should say, Mademoiselle. If I say that I am innocent of the foreknowledge of Eduard's death, you would find me guilty anyway."

"So." I walked over to her, grabbed her chin, and forced her head up so that I could see her eyes, placing the nails of my other hand at her neck, reopening the wound Max had given her. Small trickles of blood began to form and still her eyes held no fear. "Admit it and I will let you live. You did know."

"As you wish."

"That is not an answer, Monique."

"I am sorry, then, for it is the best I can do."

Another thought occurred to me then, with the remembrance of Max's suspicions. She seemed to have hated Eduard. Could it have been possible that she had turned him over to the executioner? And on what charges?

"And perhaps"—my voice grew quiet now, almost a whisper,

my nails digging deep gouges into her skin—"perhaps it is more than just the foreknowledge of his death you cannot admit to. Perhaps you had a hand in it."

"No," she wailed, reacting now with a little more vehemence, "whatever you may think of me, Vivienne, do not think that. I loved him too."

Silent tears began to stream down her face, matching the rivulets of blood that flowed down her neck.

"You loved him?"

"Yes, I did." She wiped the tears off her face with her sleeve in an angry gesture. "I did not love him for him. But for your sake."

Suddenly all of my anger rushed out of me. Dropping both of my hands, I pulled her into my embrace and let her cry.

As if the tears had opened a gate, she spoke. "I saw him die, Vivienne. Word was brought here early this morning as you slept that he would be executed."

"You should have woken me."

"With what end? For you to rush out into the broad daylight and die also? No, I could not do that. But I could be a witness for you, so that you would know what happened. He died well, showed no fear of the crowd or the blade." She moved away from me and sat down on the lounge, wiping her tears on her sleeve.

"They were like dogs, that crowd. Howling like dogs for blood. But Eduard faced them, he looked them in the eyes and they backed off like the animals they are." She continued to sob as she talked, sniffling and wiping.

"Did he have anything to say? Somehow I cannot imagine Eduard going without some fine words to be remembered by."

She nodded. "He did, he said 'Good citizens of France, beware the passages of time.' And then as Sanson released the blade, 'I will return.' "

I shook my head. "Good last words, Eduard," I said with a soft laugh at the irony, "but I do not see how you can keep your promise."

"Nevertheless," Monique said, "those were his words." She

paused a bit and put her hand up to her neck, noticing in confusion the blood there.

"Ah, let me tend to that for you, *mon chou*. I was angry, but I should not have hurt you like this. You have been hurt enough for one short lifetime." Soaking a handkerchief in the water basin by the bed, I dabbed at the drying blood.

She accepted my ministrations passively, hardly flinching as I cleaned the new and the old wounds.

"I claimed his body." She gulped a bit and sniffed. "And his head."

"What?"

"It did not seem right, to let him lie there with the others. So I told them I was his wife and they let me take him away."

"Why would you do such a thing, Monique? And what did you do with him?"

"I washed him and dressed him in some clean clothes I found here. I"—she gulped again—"I sewed his head back on the best I could. One can hardly tell . . ."

"Where is he?"

"I had them put him in Rosa's room. So that we could have a coffin prepared to bury him properly."

I looked at her in disbelief. "And you did all of this today while I was sleeping? Why did you not tell me when I awoke?"

"I—" She hesitated, pulling in a short breath. "I could not bring myself to say the words, Vivienne. You were so much improved, so much like your old self. I did not want you to go back down into that darkness in which you have been dwelling."

"I understand. And I thank you for your kindness and your care. But can you tell me why you did any of this at all? Why claim his body? Why wash him and dress him and"—I shuddered slightly—"sew him back together?"

She glanced away from me, not meeting my eyes. "So that you could say good-bye."

Monique took me by the hand and led me to Rosa's room as if I did not know the way. It was as she said. Eduard lay there, still and pale. I pulled aside his shirt collar and jabot, peering at the jagged cut and her careful stitching. I still was not sure why she had done this, but I could not deny the truth.

I sighed and leaned over to kiss his cold lips. They held no warmth, no attraction. This was not my Eduard, but rather a husk that he had shed.

I wondered where he had gone, where his charm and determination were now. "Poor Eduard," I said to him, "death has turned you into a liar. You will never return. And I will always miss you."

Somewhere out on the street a dog barked and a baby cried. Monique shivered and hugged her arms to herself. "I asked around and found out that his family has a crypt. His brothers will come for him tomorrow and he will be laid to rest there."

I nodded. "Thank you. It's good that I was able to see him; I'd never have been able to imagine him dead otherwise."

"After everything you have done for me, Vivienne, it's a small thing."

I shrugged. "Quite to the contrary, my lamb, I'd say it was a Herculean task you've accomplished. I doubt that I shall ever be able to repay you."

We stood in silence for a while and all I could think about was the futility of human life. This man had been gifted when alive; he saved lives, he changed lives, he created objects of beauty, he loved. He was capable of giving a creature like me, damned and unnatural, a chance to love. And now he was gone, taking with him all those unique things that made him who he was.

"Such a waste. The fool man. He did not need to die. I would have saved him from this fate; he had only to ask."

"*Oui.*"

This was why one didn't fall in love, I thought. Eventually they die. Eduard's death happened sooner than I would have expected and under more violent circumstances, but even at that his years had always been limited. I looked over at Monique. *And here is another I love who will die, as certainly as the sun rising.*

"Unless," I said softly, "unless I hold back the dawn for her forever."

"Pardon?"

"Prepare yourself, Monique. I have lost enough loved ones to last me through eternity. I will not lose you. And I will not wait another day. Come."

Chapter 17

It was fortunate that I had fed well earlier in the evening. Creating a new vampire was an energy-draining process, as I knew from the one time I had attempted the task. At least this time, I could do what I needed to do without having to worry about the interference of Max.

Monique seemed nervous about the change, which was more than understandable. It was a big step, even for someone who wanted the transformation as much as she seemed to.

"You needn't go through with this, little lamb, if you don't want to. I won't force you. It must be something entered into of your own free will."

"It is," she said. "This is what I want. But"—she gave a little smile—"I can still be frightened, can't I?"

I laughed. "You have no need to be frightened of me, Monique. And I will be gentle, my girl, much more so than Max was with me. You may even find it enjoyable. It is a little like falling asleep and waking up in a wonderful new dream that will never end. And you will never be sick and you will never die."

"How is it done?"

"It is a simple transfer of blood. I take most of yours and replace it with about half of mine. Which leaves us both a little weak for a day or two, until we can feed enough to replenish what we've lost. Within a day or two, you will be completely adjusted to the change."

She smiled wanly. "I do not know, Vivienne. I give you all of my blood and you only give me half back? It sounds like you get the better of the deal."

"Perhaps. I hadn't ever thought of it in that way."

I began to undress. As well as being tiring, creating a new vampire often caused a mess and I didn't want to ruin my dress with bloodstains. She came up behind me and undid the back of my bodice.

"Now," I said as I slid out of the dress and out of the corset and petticoats, "are you sure you really want to go through with this? I feel like I am rushing you. There needn't be a hurry, you are still young and healthy. Rosa hesitated too long; in fact she was still deliberating when she died. But you have years and years before you reach her age."

She gave a choked laugh. "I do not want to reach her age. And besides, that was Rosa. I'm not Rosa and I am sure. What, after all, is there not to like? You love your life, you say so all the time. And you have no regrets."

"True. Then if you have made up your mind, there is no reason to wait. Let's get on with it, we are quickly running out of night."

I sat down on the bed and patted the surface next to me, smiling. "Take off your clothes, my lamb, then come and"—I gave a small chuckle—"lie down with the lion."

She obeyed and stripped quickly, climbing in and lying down. For a while, we just lay side by side with me stroking her hair and her face, whispering soothing words until I could feel the tenseness of her body relax. I pulled her in closer to me and positioned her with her back facing me. Her body was warm, so soft and alive next to mine, something that I would miss when this night was finished.

I sighed and brushed her hair aside, wrapping an arm tightly about her waist.

"Try not to fight, Monique, if you can. No matter how close to death you feel you are coming, do not fight. And do not fear, I will not let you go."

She nodded. "I will try."

I began kissing her, starting with the corner of her mouth that I could reach, whispering sweet nonsense to keep her calm. I ran my mouth across her cheek and to her ear, then nuzzled my way down to her neck, pulling just a bit on the skin, nipping, testing. The arm that was around her waist I moved up so that my hand cupped her left breast. Her nipple hardened at my touch, a touch that served a triple purpose, to both comfort and distract her and, more importantly, to monitor the beating of her heart.

Still mouthing and licking her soft spice-scented skin, I tightened my grip on her just a bit. She moaned and pressed herself back against me and in one sudden movement, I sank my fangs into her.

Monique tensed against the sharp pain, then relaxed as I drew on her, quicker than I would for a normal feed. I opened my eyes as I drank, watching the color of her skin lighten and pale. The warmth of her body began to transfer to mine as I swallowed more and more of her blood.

She began to shiver and still I drank, pulling almost every available drop out of her. Her heart slowed under my hand, faltered, then restarted, although beating slower with every second. We were past the point of no return now; if I did not replenish her with my blood she would die.

I pulled my mouth away from her neck, shifted my position so that I was kneeling next to her on the bed. Then with one sharpened nail I cut a vertical slash on my wrist. Precious blood spurted out before I could get my arm to her mouth. "Drink, little lamb, drink as much as you can hold."

Max had once told me that this was the critical factor in transformation. There were some, he said, that simply refused to drink. And so they died.

"Drink." I said the word with more command. I would not allow her to die. Not now. Not Monique. I pushed my wrist hard against her mouth. "Drink!"

There was a curious tickling sensation at first as she merely lapped at the flow and I laughed, reaching underneath her now cool body and sitting her up, supporting her back and head. Her lapping grew into hungry swallows and soon she was pulling on me with strength and determination. "That is good, my lamb, keep drinking."

Eventually, I felt myself weaken and pulled my wrist away from her. Her eyes were squeezed shut like a newborn baby's and she gave a low growl, reaching out greedy hands for me. "No," I said, leaning over to lick a few beads of blood from her lips, "that is enough for now. There will be more later, much more and many laters."

She whimpered a little and I kissed her again. Slowly and deliberately she opened her eyes and looked at me. After studying my face for a long time, she smiled. "Thank you," she said, her voice hoarse and soft. "I feel so alive, and—" She stopped and took a deep breath as she looked all around the room. "Vibrant. And real. It is as if everything were new, and everything were a gift, especially for me." She sprang up from the bed and moved from place to place, pausing first to look out the window, then dashing to the fire to study the flames.

I listened to her exclaim about her heightened awareness, how she could see and hear better than she'd ever thought possible. And how the colors were so very bright and the scents on the night air so fascinating.

"I can smell the flowers in the market stalls, Vivienne." She had run back to the window, thrown open the shutters, and leaned out. "I can smell the flowers," she yelled out into the night and her voice echoed off the surrounding walls. Then she turned around, grinning. "It is as if they are growing right here under our window. Wonderful."

I gave her an indulgent smile and got up from the bed, sliding into my dressing gown and sorting through my armoire for a garment for her. Then I sat back down on the bed and waited. We had, I estimated, only a small amount of time, perhaps only minutes, before dawn. Her euphoria would quickly dissolve in that first encounter with the sun. But I let her have her exuberance knowing there was nothing I could do or say to prepare her for the next shock of her new existence: the object that had once brought light and joy into her young life, as it had to all of us, was an enemy now, to be shunned and avoided at the risk of pain and death.

A harsh lesson, to be sure, but a necessary one. I remembered Max telling me about those new ones who did take the blood, but could not make the adjustment; if left alone they would run out into the sunlight on their very first dawn and thus end both their human life and their vampiric one.

"Oh," Monique said, pulling me out of my thoughts, "you never told me it was like this, Vivienne. Or I'd have begged you sooner to change me." She was standing in front of the mirror, running her hands over her naked body, examining the places where she used to be scarred. Now her skin was like cool porcelain, still a little darker than mine, given her natural complexion. "And I can feel the blood moving through my veins, feeding me, changing me, completing me."

"Wait, little lamb." I walked over to her and handed her a dressing gown. "Put this on. For now, you must dress or you will grow cold in your sleep. There will be plenty of time for you to explore your new body tomorrow evening." I fastened the shutters on the window and pulled the heavy curtains closed. Then I crossed the room and double-bolted the door. "This will have to do, I suppose. But we will need to acquire some human help soon, for guarding and watching and daylight errands."

She nodded, losing some of her elation in the knowledge of what she had become, what she had given up.

"I assume you do not mind sharing my coffin." I opened the lid, shook out the blankets, and fluffed up the cushion, grabbing another from the bed for her. "There's really enough room for two, if we cuddle together. And it is all we have—tomorrow evening we can see about getting you a coffin of your own. But this will be fine for tonight. It will be more than fine. And it is not so bad." I was talking now just to reassure her. Her eyes began to glaze over as the sun moved closer to the horizon. "Yes, tomorrow we will get you your own coffin. But for now, come in with me."

She shivered as my words took effect, watched in silence as I extinguished the candles and climbed into the box. "Come, lamb, it is not so horrible. Trust me when I tell you when the sun rises, you do not wish to be out in the open, no matter how well protected. Come now, it is time. This is the price we pay."

She crawled in next to me and we both lay down. I threw the bolts on the lid, arranged a few blankets over the both of us, and held my breath. Waiting for the dawn.

"This will be a shock to your system, Monique. And there is nothing one can do to prepare for it or prevent it. The rising of the sun is a deadly time for us and our bodies recognize the danger even though our minds know that we are safe. Instinctual reactions, you see. And we have to take the good with the bad."

When dawn came, Monique opened her mouth and a squeaky little gasp escaped her lips. I felt the same shock run through my body, but it was an old sensation for me. For her it was new and frightening and very painful.

"Hush, little one." I pulled her in close to me and whispered into her ear as she sobbed. "It will be all right, you'll see. It does not last long."

Chapter 18

Monique slept in my arms that day locked away from the destructive sun, experiencing the first sleep of a vampire—a deep and boneless thing that so closely resembled death that even I, who had experienced it for almost a century, feared that she might have actually died. But no, I could hear the beat of her heart, the rush of her newly transformed blood flowing through her veins. It was a strangely reassuring sound, almost a lullaby, soothing and comforting.

Much more so than the sounds from without.

First there was the knock on the front door, something rare in a house of this nature. Deliveries were made in the back, of course, and most of the working girls would be asleep. No one called during the day. Yet, there was the knock. And someone answered.

I heard deep male voices.

"We are looking for Mademoiselle Courbet. Is she here?"

"She is sleeping, Messieurs, and we all have orders not to disturb her sleep." It was Cecile who had answered the door and I breathed a sigh of relief. She must have been a light sleeper, a fact for which I was grateful now; I felt her capable of handling whatever situation arose.

"I care nothing for your orders," said the man. "I have been told that this house"—the word came out as a sneer—"holds the body of our brother, Eduard DeRouchard."

There was a long pause. I could picture Cecile giving this man her coolest look behind her heavily lidded eyes, assessing not only his worth as a human being but also for his potential as a source of francs. I always pitied the ones who failed either of her tests; they would often mope around for weeks.

This one must have done well, for when Cecile answered there was more of a welcome in her voice than normal. "Yes, Monsieur, he is here. He was your brother? Such a shame, Dr. DeRouchard was a favorite here. Monique had him laid out in Rosa's room."

There was a short barked laugh. "Rosa must be a devoted employee, to entertain a corpse in her room."

"No, Monsieur, you misunderstand me. Rosa is dead also and so—"

He laughed again, interrupting her explanation. "Is this house a mortuary or a brothel?"

"A good question, Monsieur, and one some of us have come to ask."

I tensed. Hopefully she was referring to the number of dead bodies that had been here in the past months and not to the fact that the mistress of the house spent her days sleeping in a coffin. I had no doubts now, this evening I would need to find a watcher for us. And make plans to leave Paris immediately. My hands began to slide the bolts open, should I need to quickly exit and crawl into the bed. I lay quietly, waiting for the sound of them at my door.

"But if you will follow me, I will show you to Rosa's room. Monique said yesterday that she would prepare the body. I did not know what that entailed, nor did I want to ask. This way, Messieurs."

I heard them mount the stairs and come down the hallway, but they stopped at Rosa's room and entered there.

"Ah, Eduard," the man said. "How glad I am that Mother is not still alive to witness this. It would have broken her heart." He lowered his voice and I thought he was praying, joined by a few of the others. Then his voice grew louder when he, I presumed, addressed the other men in the room. "Go and get the coffin from the cart and bring it up here."

More footsteps down the hall and the stairs and the sound of the door opening.

Cecile gave a little yawn. "Is there anything else you require, Monsieur?"

"No, thank you. You have been quite kind. But we have woken you, have we not? I do apologize for interrupting your rest."

I heard her laugh and thought from the coquettish tone of her voice that Eduard's brother must have been handsome.

"It is no problem, Monsieur, I can sleep when you leave. May I offer you refreshments? I'm not sure what there is in the kitchen, but I would be happy to see."

"No. But thank you. Your name?"

"Cecile."

"A lovely name. I will remember you. Now, my dear, where is this Monique person? I'd like to thank her for the wonderful job she has done. Eduard looks only as if he were sleeping. You have to look closely to see that he is not breathing."

"Yes, he does look quite alive. It will be a comfort for us all to think of him like that."

"Can you get her for me?"

"Who? Monique? She is sleeping in Mademoiselle's room, most likely. Shall I wake her?"

"No."

There was another pause and the sound of feet moving. Cecile giggled. I assumed that he had kissed her or tried to. That he was Eduard's brother there could be no doubt, however inappropriate and irreverent his actions seemed, carrying on a flirtation over the decapitated body of his brother. And for Cecile to giggle as she did, it appeared that not all the charm in the DeRouchard family had been wasted on my dear, dead love. "I seem to have woken enough lovely ladies for the day. Besides, I have an unpleasant task ahead of me. Let the esteemed Monique sleep."

"As you wish, Monsieur."

The other men arrived with much scuffling of feet and a bit of groaning. There was a quiet consultation over how best to get the body into the coffin and then I heard them close the cover.

"Thank you, Cecile. You have been most helpful."

"My pleasure, Monsieur. As I said, Dr. DeRouchard was a favorite of the house. God rest his soul."

There was a low rumble of laughter again. "Yes, well, I suppose that is in God's hands. I couldn't say. Good day."

I heard Cecile sigh and heard them struggle with the coffin on the stairway. The front door opened, then shut. And Eduard, my Eduard, the only man I had ever loved, was gone forever.

I began to cry, silently, holding on to Monique as if she were my only salvation. I cried for Eduard, his life ending like this, abruptly and uselessly. Had I listened to his premonition, had I believed him, I could have stopped this event. We could have gone away, we could have spent eternity together. But I hadn't taken him seriously and so now he was dead.

I cried for Monique, poor little lamb that she was, picturing her claiming the body of a man she hated for the sake of a woman she loved, picturing her washing him and stitching him back together, as if he were a poppet to be mended. I gave a small bitter laugh at the irony of Monique doing all of this for someone such as I. That she loved me did not matter. Of course she did; I had fostered the emotion, mesmerized her with my powers. She had no choice in the matter.

And, in a rare bout of self-pity, I cried for myself, wrapping my limbs about Monique and holding her so closely I could feel her heart beating against mine. I cried for the opportunities of a normal life that I had carelessly and frivolously abandoned. For babies that would never suckle at my breasts. For the joy of growing old with ones that I love. For the sun that I was forever denied.

Then I opened my eyes and wiped away the tears. Ridiculous, that I had been reduced to lying in my coffin crying about situations over which I had no control, grasping for comfort from a wayward girl. This was not the way I usually acted and was certainly not the way I should act.

I needed to remind myself that a creature such as I had no desire for love or for friends; the emotions I experienced with Eduard were nothing but an aberration. It only took the memory of how I had reacted to his desertion to tell me that my love for him was impossible.

And what I had let happen with Monique was more than unfortunate. Now was too soon for her to make the change. She needed months of preparation and guidance, such as I had never received. But I had allowed the desolation and guilt at Eduard's death to make the decision. And there would be repercussions, I knew. As there had been with Diego.

But I would not let Max hurt her. I would not let Max know of her existence. "Don't worry, little one," I whispered to her, "we will go away, away from this horrible city of death. We will hide from those who wish us harm. And I will take care of you as long as you need me to."

Chapter 19

" I feel as if I have been starving for years. Hurry. Please."
Monique had awoken very hungry and anxious to try out her newly born powers and senses. I remembered well that excitement and knew that I couldn't really curb it.

"The night is young, little lamb, and we have plenty of time. For now, we need to speak of certain things."

"There is one thing that needs to go," she said, dressing and examining her sharpening teeth in the mirror. "You will have to stop calling me a lamb. Look at my fangs." And she turned and gave me a wicked smile. "Have you ever seen a lamb with such teeth? No, I am a tiger now."

I laughed. "I suppose you are right. But you are not yet a full-grown tiger and you will need to listen to your maman if you wish to survive."

While I dressed, I described to her what I had overheard during the day and outlined the plans I had made. "First thing we must do is find someone to act as our guard. I do not wish to lie awake every day waiting for someone to break down the door. There are enough dangers in this life; and that is one that can be easily avoided. Had I been thinking clearly, I'd have done this task before transforming you."

"Did someone try to break down the door today?"

"No, but it was too close, I thought. I will not permit that to happen again."

"So what sort of person should we choose as our guard? I'd not have been much help to you in any sort of serious confrontation. And neither would Rosa have. Perhaps we should try to find someone more suitable, someone more capable of defending us."

I nodded. "I had never intended for Rosa to serve as my guard as long as she had. But the years piled upon each other and I grew accustomed to the routine we'd established. I have been too careless in the past, counting on the courtesy of those around me. But Cecile showed me how false that courtesy can be. I propose we go back to Place du Carroussel and recruit that guard into a new service. He will do quite well, especially since he is already tied to me."

She nodded. "He will do quite well. But I must ask about this bond. How does that happen? That the connection exists, I know, since I felt the pull of it in my own blood. But I have wondered even as I experienced it. Does everyone you feed on develop a bond with you?"

"Yes. And no. The bond is there, certainly, but one must exploit it, and that is something I ordinarily do not do. Unless there is a need. And tonight we have the need. Let us go and claim our guard, our brave and daring captain who likes nothing better than kisses from strange ladies."

We were fortunate in that he was on duty again this evening. Once again he emerged out of the shadows and began to explain to us the workings of the device. But when I moved closer to him and looked him dead in the eye, he stopped in midsentence and stared.

"Yes," I said, walking up to him and running my hand down his arm. "I have returned for you, *mon Capitaine.*" I stretched up on my toes and kissed him full on the lips, still maintaining eye contact.

"But, but," he stammered a bit, "that was only a dream. Wasn't it?"

I laughed. "Perhaps it was a dream. And perhaps it was not. But for now, I wish you to remember me again."

His eyes widened and his hand went to his neck. "I remember your kisses, lady. Do you want more? Everything I have is at your disposal."

"What is your name?"

"Raoul Mountaigne."

"Ah, a nice strong name for a nice strong man. Do you like the service you give here, Raoul?"

He glanced around. "The nights get lonely and cold some-

times. And I have been having the strangest feelings, even"—
and he gave a wan smile—"before that dream of you. As I stand
and watch I think I see the souls of those who have died here rising up out of the ground. And while I know in my head that it is
only fog and mist, my heart thinks differently."

"And so you do not like your post?"

"In short, no. But a duty is a duty and I have been assigned
this one." He inclined his head toward the guillotine. "I would
not dare to leave it. Watching this device at work has a not so
strange way of warning one off the thoughts of shirking."

I laughed and after a second he joined me. "No doubt, Raoul.
And your sense of duty is to be greatly admired. But if you had
another alternative? Serving two beautiful ladies perhaps? With
an opportunity to travel and see the wonders of the world?"

He laughed. "If I left my post, I'd need to travel and travel
quickly. And yet, it is tempting. Especially if I am to assume that
the two beautiful ladies are standing in front of me."

I nodded. "What time do you get off duty, Raoul?"

"Midnight, Mademoiselle."

"Good. Come to the House of the Swan no later than half
past twelve and ask for Mademoiselle Courbet. You know
where the house is?"

"Most certainly."

I took his face between my hands and pulled it down to me,
so that I could kiss him again. "Do not fail me, Raoul, and you
will be well rewarded."

He bowed. "I will be there, Mademoiselle."

Monique pulled me aside and whispered in my ear, "Is that
all there is to it?"

Nodding, I linked my arm into hers and began to lead her
away. "For the moment, yes. But he is only intrigued now. Later
we will make sure that he is enraptured."

"And so now I can feed?"

"Yes, of course, my little lamb, er, tiger." I gave an amused
snort. "It will take some getting used to you as a tiger. Now, do
you want an easy conquest? Or do you want a full-fledged
hunt?"

She thought for a minute. "I am tempted to want the hunt and yet perhaps it would be best the first time to take the easy way."

"Fine, *mon chou,* it is your choice, there is no difference between the two so far as your stomach is concerned."

Once we returned to the house, I made my way up the stairs but told her to go to the main room, choose her victim, and bring him back to me. I changed from my outdoor dress to a pink silk dressing gown, brushed my hair in front of the mirror, then began to pull the cork on a bottle of wine, setting out three glasses.

The knock on the door coming as soon as it did surprised me; It would have taken a much longer time had it been I doing the choosing. But she was hungry and inexperienced and had, I saw when they entered the room, picked a man who closely resembled Eduard. As I thought about it, though, I realized that I was not particularly surprised by this, her choice, considering the mixed feelings she had expressed about Eduard. I myself had chosen for my first victim a man who could have been my father—in appearance, in age, and in social standing.

Max had not been surprised either, when I told him why I had selected that one out of the many I could have chosen. "It is the way it is, at first. We look for someone familiar, someone who makes us angry and yet comfortable at the same time." In his always infuriating manner, he had refused to tell me who his first victim resembled. "Bastard."

"Mademoiselle?" Monique's young man seemed confused by the word and I laughed.

"Not you, good Monsieur, I assure you. Please come in and make yourself comfortable."

As I poured the three glasses of wine, I realized with a touch of laughter that this situation was much like my first evening with Max and Victor. I wondered if this young man would faint dead away in front of the fire as I did. But no, I was not like Max or Victor—their main goals always seemed to be intimidation and fear. My only wish was to be left alone so that I could feed in safety. And if there was a little bit of fun to be had in the bargain, so much the better.

Letting Monique take the lead, I sat down in front of the hearth and stared at the fire, watching it dance and twist, imagining that I saw a face in the flames. Like Raoul I could see the ghosts and still would not believe. Strange, given the sort of creature that I was, that I was so skeptical. But, if you had asked up until the moment I'd met Max, I'd have said that the existence of vampires was nothing more than a myth.

Perhaps then I would believe in ghosts only when I was one. Laughing, I picked up a small chip of wood that had fallen from the basket and tossed it onto the fire, thinking *If I must be dead to believe, I can easily do without belief.*

Monique cleared her throat and I turned my attention back to the situation at hand; she'd managed to peel back the young man's shirt collar and jabot, but had stopped there, unsure of how to proceed. She shot me a pleading look and I got up from the hearth and went over to them where they sat together on the lounge.

"And what is your name, young man?"

"Jean-Paul."

"Well then, Jean-Paul, tell me something. Have you ever had a woman?"

He smiled. "But of course, Mademoiselle. Many women."

"Ah." Reaching down and taking his hand, I brought it to my mouth and licked his fingers. "And have you ever had two women? At one time?"

His eyes darted back and forth between us and his breathing grew noticeably heavier. "No, not exactly, Mademoiselle, but I am sure I can oblige if that is what you want."

I smiled. "It is indeed what we want. Come to the bed, Jean, and we will show you how one strong man can satisfy the appetites of two hungry ladies."

Monique giggled and followed us, joined me in laying him down and stripping him naked, then stripping ourselves and settling in one on either side of him. That he was intrigued by the situation was obvious and Monique gave a low whistle of appreciation. "Very impressive, Jean, certainly there is enough of you for both of us."

"I would hope so." Proud of his manhood and intoxicated with our attentions, Jean put his arms around us and pulled us both in close, so that each of our heads rested on his shoulders. I glanced over his chest at Monique and gave a slight nod.

She smiled back at me and I saw that her fangs had lengthened, but she seemed uncertain about their placement. I nodded to her again.

"Close your eyes, Jean." I brushed my hand over his face, "And keep them closed. We have a little surprise for you. You do like surprises, do you not?"

He laughed. "Surprises from two such as you are always welcome."

I gave him a playful little slap across the cheek. "Then close your eyes or there will be no surprise."

"Yes, Mademoiselle," he said meekly and obeyed.

I opened my mouth wider than I would ordinarily have, curling my upper lip back and pulling my lower jaw in, exaggerating the position and the motion so that Monique could see and learn.

She did the same and when I nodded, she lowered her mouth to his neck.

It was a clumsy bite, of course, being her first. And it must have been painful; his eyes flew open in panic and he jumped, trying to push her away. Quickly, I moved over top of him and impaled myself on him, rising and falling slowly at first and then with more urgency, until he closed his eyes again and moaned in pleasure.

After he reached his orgasm, I motioned for her to take her mouth away. She peered up at me, gave a low growl, but withdrew her fangs. At the same time, I slid myself off of Jean.

And it was over. She licked her lips and gave me a triumphant smile. I snuggled up next to a tired Jean. "Sleep for a while, *mon cher*," I told him, "and when you awaken you will remember none of what happened here. Do you understand?"

He nodded and mumbled his assent.

"Good. Now sleep."

We dressed him again and woke him up, sending him on his way a tired but sated man. Although he would have no remembrance of how he came to be that way, still he would look back on this night and smile without knowing why.

"Always give something back, Monique," I said after he walked out the door. "Never steal what you must take; let them think they are giving it freely and they will forget more easily."

"So how did the tiger cub do, Maman?"

I leaned over and kissed her on the lips, flicking my tongue inside her mouth for a taste of Jean's blood. "You did well, Monique. He was young and strong and eager. You did not take too much and you did not take too little. And you did not choke or cough; often the first taste is bitter and sour."

"It did not taste bitter or sour to me, Vivienne. It was as sweet and as thick as honey." She smiled. "When can I do it again?"

Chapter 20

It proved to be as busy a night as the previous was, and although the tasks involved were more pleasant, they were no less grueling. No sooner had we sent Jean-Paul on his way than Raoul appeared as ordered.

As she had with Jean-Paul, Monique escorted Raoul to our room, gave him a glass of wine, and encouraged him to get comfortable. This time, though, it was I who sat on the lounge with him while Monique watched.

Holding his hands and looking into his eyes, I spoke to him for a while, explaining the tasks expected of him. As duties went, none of them were particularly onerous, but I wanted to make sure that he understood completely what it was he needed to learn to do.

After he was questioned and found correct on all counts we moved on.

"What do you think I am, Raoul?"

He shrugged. "To be honest, Mademoiselle, I am not sure. It would seem that you are one of the old myths come to life, if such a thing in our enlightened age is possible. My mother's mother would tell stories of the dead or the undead rising from their graves to suck the life from the living. But I always assumed they were stories told to frighten the children. And I always assumed they were like dead creatures, bloated and ugly and incapable of human speech, not beautiful and full of life like you."

I smiled. "Thank you, Raoul."

"If you had wings, I would think you an angel. Not one of the undead."

I laughed, the high-pitched peals echoing off the walls. "If I am an angel, *mon Capitaine,* then I am one of the fallen. But for that matter, I do have wings. I shall show you." I slipped out of my dressing gown and stood naked in front of him. "Watch."

I closed my eyes for a second, gathering my thoughts and my strength. Then I folded my arms around me and dropped to a crouch. I shifted awareness of my humanlike form into another familiar one. Shadows grew up from the floor and began to engulf my body, spreading darkness over every available bit of skin. Feathers began to emerge from the shadows, feathers soft yet piercing, covering me completely. I stretched my neck up and felt it grow, felt my face shrink back in on itself and my nose grow into a long graceful beak. Within seconds the transformation was complete and I was now a giant black swan. Monique gave a small gasp as I spread my wings wide. She had not known this was possible. And Raoul was entranced.

In an instant, I banished the feathers and my skin grew tawny and furred. The wings disappeared, my neck shrank, and my body elongated, growing sturdy and well muscled. I felt vicious claws emerge from what had been my hands and feet and were now the deadly paws of an African lioness. Putting my head back, I gave a loud roar. Monique laughed in delight and Raoul flinched.

In another instant, I banished the fur and the claws, along with all the other attributes of a physical body. For one short moment, I was no longer perceivable by the human eye and both of them looked around the room in dismay. Quickly I pulled to me the mists of the night, curled the wisps around to approximate the size and shape of my human form. And then with one great effort of thought, I was back in my human form, standing naked in front of them.

"And that, Raoul," I said, putting on my dressing gown once more, "that is the sort of creature you have been called to serve. Will you stay?"

If he refused, I would have to kill him here and now. That was ever the risk one took when revealing the truth. Fortunately, he smiled shyly and dropped to his knees in front of me. "Gladly, lady. I would give you my life if you asked."

"Good. I hope that giving of your life will never be necessary. Now get up off the floor, Raoul, and let me seal this deal with a kiss."

He came to me and I enfolded him in the pink silk sleeves of my gown. Then I bent him over my arm as if in a dance and drank from him, just a token swallow or two. His blood tasted fresh and clean and I sighed softly as I released him from my grasp.

"One more thing, Raoul, and you will be free to go and arrange that which you need to arrange to make it possible for you to serve us."

"Whatever you ask, Mademoiselle."

"First, you are to call me Vivienne. I do not care for the for-' mality of titles. And second." I went to my dressing table and opened up a jewel box, finding an ornate cloak pin. I pricked my finger with the tip and walked over to him. "Open your mouth."

He did so, putting his head back and his tongue out, a gesture most often seen at church. But this was no holy communion, it was not the blood of Christ, it was my blood. I squeezed my finger over his opened mouth, forcing three drops of that precious fluid to fall upon his tongue. More than that and he might, over time, transform into a vampire. And I wished him to remain human and under my control.

He swallowed and choked. The taste was bitter no doubt, but after his initial reaction, his face softened into a smile and his skin seemed to glow. I kissed his cheek and smiled back at him.

"Now go, Raoul, and make your arrangements. I wish you to be back here an hour before dawn and I will tell you then your tasks for the day."

"Until then, Vivienne," and he bowed and left the room.

"Do you think he'll be back?" Monique spoke from the corner of the room where she'd observed the ritual.

"He could not stay away now for any reason in the world; he would desert the deathbed of his mother to come to me. A good choice, Monique, he will serve us quite well. Tomorrow we will have him make all the necessary arrangements for us to leave Paris."

She gave a short little surprised squeak. "We're leaving Paris? Why?"

"Why not? Eduard is gone. Running the House of the Swan has become wearisome, especially now. Some of the women have approached me about taking over the ownership and management of the business; I believe they have earned that chance. Plus, I have become just a bit too visible, too accessible here to all too many people. I wish to travel in secrecy for a while."

"But," she stammered, "but I had no idea. I do not wish to leave Paris."

"I have been thinking about this for a while now, Monique. Long before you showed up on my doorstep. I have purchased a small chateau in the mountains; I assure you it is at least as plush as this house, perhaps more so. And there is a good-sized village nearby so that we will not suffer for lack of food. What is there for us here that we cannot have in greater safety elsewhere?"

I walked over to her and gave her a hug. "I know, change is

frightening and you have lived your whole life in this one city. But the world is a wonderful place and it is time to move on. I have had more than enough of this revolution and wish to be as far away as possible. And perhaps in another place, the memories of the recent events will be less painful."

What I did not voice to her was that my chateau had been acquired in secrecy. Neither Max nor Victor knew that it existed and I would not have to fear her death at their hands. Their promises not to interfere meant nothing, I knew. And Max already had taken a dislike to Monique much as he had to Diego.

"I see," she said, "you miss Eduard and wish to be away from all of it. And of course, you are right. It will be an exciting adventure for us. I just had never considered the possibility; I was born here in Paris and I thought I would live out my life here and then die. But now." She clapped her hands together like a child receiving a gift. "Now the entire world is open to me. And it is frightening and exhilarating at the same time."

"Exactly as life should be."

She smiled then and all was well.

I kept Raoul quite busy over the next few days. His first order of business was to acquire Monique her own coffin. I found that I could not sleep when she was with me, so unaccustomed was I to having another of my kind present. After that, she and I busied ourselves with packing and he acquired a team of horses and a large enough coach to accommodate both our coffins and our personal articles.

Cecile and some of the other women took over the management of the house. My absence would make no difference; we had acquired a good reputation over the years, if such a thing is at all possible for a brothel. Men knew that the House was fair and clean and relatively sedate and discreet. The customers would continue to come and I needn't fear that my desire for escape would affect anyone else.

Monique alternated between bouts of pouting and rushes of excitement about our departure. She showed great agility, though, in learning the life of the vampire quickly and well. Her hunts were extremely successful. She could subdue the largest man with just a touch and a glance; the amount of blood she drew was never too much or too little, and her victims always forgot.

"And for tonight, Vivienne," she said on our last night in Paris, "I would like to hunt alone. I feel that I am ready and that this is something that will further my learning."

I was delighted. "Yes, *ma chere,* that is a wonderful idea. Just do not miss the time."

She laughed and gave me a hug and a kiss on the cheek. "Yes, Maman, I will be back home before dawn. Thank you."

"For what?"

"Everything," she said, waving as she went out the door. "Everything and nothing."

I watched from the window until she moved out of my sight. "Hunt well, my little lamb. Walk softly and safely this night until you come back to me."

But dawn came without Monique. I should have suspected that she would run away from me; that her love for the city of her birth was greater than her love for me. But I had not realized how strong the ties had been. I didn't fear that she was dead; the bonds between us would let me know if that had occurred. There existed still that little nagging presence of her, even after Raoul gave up the daytime search and I abandoned the night one.

Finally I grew angry at her ungrateful desertion and yelled out the window. "The city is now yours, you little bitch, and I hope it treats you as you deserve." A childish gesture, I knew, but I was hurt. She could at least have said good-bye.

As I climbed into my coffin I looked over at Raoul, drowsing by the fire. "Make the necessary preparations, *mon Capitaine,* we leave tomorrow."

It is always amazing to me how quickly the time passes. For one such as I the years seem to run together. I'd had so many lovers, so many servants, so many victims, and all of their faces blend into one in my mind. It is almost as if there is no time;

every moment is the same moment, every taste of blood is the same taste.

In the two centuries that followed my self-imposed exile from Paris, I did not attempt to transform a vampire companion for myself. Nor did I attempt to contact any of the others of my kind. The experience with Diego and Max was too saddening and the desertion of Monique too much of a betrayal for me to have the heart and desire to go forward. I had once again become incapable of love.

So I lived as a solitary creature, a vampire alone, seeking out humans only for food and for satisfaction of my sexual desire. At first I had employed a series of protecting servants. Raoul served me loyally for many years, his human system fortified and the ravages of time slowed for him by small doses of my blood. But even he grew old and died, and subsequent protectors lived even fewer years, until eventually the apathy and disbelief of human beings made their positions unnecessary and I found I could survive quite well without them.

And the years fell around me, like blossoms shaken off a tree in the wind. I watched the world change around me while I, alone and unknown, remained unchanged. The demon in the mirror smiled and lied and continued without end, without a companion and without love.

And that is the way I thought I always wanted it to be.

Part 2

Chapter 21

"*Je t'emmerde, espece de porc a la manque!*" I hung up the phone, and swept the entire contents of the damned desk on the floor.

Monique, now my personal assistant, came into the office at my outburst, looking over at me with a tolerant smile on her face. She had grown used to my tirades. "So, who is the worthless pig you were talking to this time?"

"Does it matter?" I stood up and paced around the room, flinging my arms up in the air in frustration. "This having to deal with humans all the time is making me crazy. Had I known this job entailed diplomacy I would have turned it down."

"As I remember, Vivienne . . ." She began to pick up the items from the carpet and set them back on the desk surface. "You really had no choice."

Ignoring her response, I continued my ranting. "Humans! It is all well and good when one chooses to seek them out for food. Or even sex, for that matter. But now? Now I must flatter this one. And threaten another. Keep the balance and keep the peace." I shook my head. "And is that not enough for one vampire to handle?"

From the corner of the room where she was crawling on hands and knees gathering paper clips, Monique gave an absent response. "Is it?"

"No, but of course it is not enough. Now all the Cadre members with more than a hundred years under their belts are petitioning to become house leaders. I ask you, Monique, how many leaders can we possibly need? And then there are all these requests to install new vampires. How long will it be before this whole damned city is filled with nothing but bloodsuckers? Where will we all be then?"

Monique stood up from the floor, paper clips clutched in her fists. She dropped them into a crystal bowl that miraculously had escaped breaking. Then, with a twisted smile, she repositioned the telephone and picked up the receiver, putting it to her ear for a second, holding it out to me with a nod. "Not broken yet, *mon chou*, perhaps you'd like to try again."

"No. It won't help." I flopped back down into my chair, like a petulant child, resting my elbows on the desk and my chin in my hands. "They'll just bring in a new one."

She came up behind me and wrapped her arms around my neck, placing a kiss on the top of my head. "My dear Vivienne, I can't believe you are taking this so seriously. It's not like you."

I reached up and ran my fingers over the top of her short black hair. "I can scarcely believe it myself. Perhaps I will outgrow it."

She laughed softly and walked over to the door, checking the clock on the wall "If you don't need anything else, Vivienne, I'd like to go now. I want to get out before all the good ones are taken."

"Hunting tonight?"

"Yes." Her voice dropped to a husky whisper. "Come with me. It would be fun—just like the good old days."

I met her eyes, saw the weight of her years, and for just a second I wondered who she was and why she was here. Ten years ago she had reappeared in my life abruptly and without warning or explanation. And I had taken her back into my world with no recriminations or accusations; *truly,* I rationalized, *all she had done to me was run away, not much harm in that.* I had wished to leave Paris and she had wished to stay. Such a very small betrayal in the overall scheme of things.

And yet, those years spent apart were hidden from me and she did not speak of them. *Fair enough,* I thought, *we all have our own personal demons of which we do not talk.* She was still Monique and I loved her, in my way, remembering the poor little lost lamb she had been. But her eyes were those of a stranger, until they filled with flames of lust and hunger. And at times like that I knew her, knew that the bond of her making still held us together. Her eyes were like my own and what they offered me was so very tempting. We had spent countless nights together after her return, hunting and feeding and making love to so many in so many different ways. And the games she devised were intriguing and amusing.

I sighed. Although I was hungry, I had no time for the games. "No." I shook my head reluctantly and sighed again. "I'm expecting more phone calls."

"Suit yourself." She leaned over the desk and kissed me lightly on the cheek. "Maybe some other night."

"Monique?"

She stopped in the doorway and turned to me expectantly. "Yes, *mon amie?*"

"Turn the lights out when you leave."

I do not know how long I sat there behind my desk in the darkness. Vampires do not measure time as humans do. A second, a decade, a century—all seemed much the same to those who have an endless span of years. I preferred not to think of it most of the time, having known perfectly sane creatures who drove themselves to madness with the contemplation of eternity. I enjoyed my life too much to want to spend it insane. And why should I not enjoy my life? What else could there be for one such as I? Love was a nightmare, an emotion best kept under lock and key. As a being incapable of love, I had no spouse, no child, nothing to burden me in the way my one and only blood sister was burdened. The only responsibility I carried was my position as leader of the Cadre, a dubious distinction at best. What did it matter the sort of leadership this clan of ancient vampires received? We knew we were the superior beings; humankind had no knowledge of us and therefore had no fear. Without fear there can be no hate and without hate, no violence capable of threatening our existence. Safe and secure, locked away in our underground warren, we were guarded by the disbelief of the rest of the world. Our anonymity kept us alive; even as we moved among them, fed upon them, interacted with them, we remained invisible. All in all, not a bad deal. Life was good.

Except that I was trapped here taking care of Cadre business. I sat for a while longer, tapping my long, white-lacquered nails on the desk in boredom, glaring at the phone, daring it to ring, hoping it would not.

Finally, I jumped up. "Monique is right, I shouldn't care about any of this. And so"—I reached over and turned on the answering machine—"I am now finished."

I wound my way through the empty hallways, pushed the button for the elevator when I reached it. When Victor was still in town and still in charge, it seemed that this place was a hotbed of activity. But now it was dead. *As dead as its inhabitants,* I thought and gave a low laugh. Deader, actually, since the inhabitants here had at least a semblance of life. I heard the phone ring in my office, echoing once off the walls, followed by the phone greeting, short and sweet: "Name, number, message. At the beep," then Monique's throaty laugh and the actual beep of the machine. There was a pause, a cough, and another pause, until a faint, almost familiar voice said, "Monique? Vivienne?"

"Forget it, Monsieur, whoever the hell you are," I said as the elevator door opened and I got on, giggling, "we have all gone fishing." The doors closed and I noticed someone had left the key in the lock that opened the panel allowing one access to the business quarters and the sleeping quarters. I used the key, so I wouldn't have to rummage around in my bag for mine, and pushed the button for my floor. Then I closed the panel and locked it, taking the key with me, making a mental note to issue a warning on Monday. People around here were getting sloppy and complacent.

I understood that tendency. In fact, I was guilty of it more than once, even during the most recent crisis that had left several of our members dead, a crisis now that most of the Cadre referred to as the Martin fiasco. Fortunately I had not been in charge then—Victor had abdicated his rule in favor of Mitchell

Greer, the husband of my sister. Mitch had governed well, much better than I ever had or would. *If only,* I thought for probably the hundredth time, *if only he would take it again.* I gave a low laugh; that was a vain hope. He would do it but only if *she* asked, and of course she would not. And I couldn't blame her for that; if he were mine, I'd guard him too. So I was back to it again; the governing of the Cadre rested in my hands.

But not now, I reminded myself as I opened the door to my room. "Even the queen gets a day off now and then." I winked at my image in the large wardrobe mirror.

I put on a pair of faded jeans, skintight and torn in the appropriate places. Topped off with a cropped pink mohair sweater, I looked even younger than normal. I accentuated this youthful appearance by putting my hair into two pigtails at the top of my head, elastic bands with little pink beads holding them in place. Looking in the mirror, I bobbed my head to make sure the hair had the appropriate bounce, checked out the back of my jeans to admire the curve of my ass and the small bits of white flesh shining through.

"Cool," I said, practicing the dialect I would need to speak, and with a giggle I shook my head, as if in time to some music. "Man, this band is unfuckingbelievable!" Although most of the places I hunted were too noisy for my voice to be heard, still I prided myself on the ability to blend. My normal accent would be too distinctive and I did not like leaving clues behind me. If something went wrong, if fragments of memories remained with my victim, I did not want trouble following me back. Vivienne's first rule—protect the place you sleep.

The place at which I slept was Cadre headquarters, located levels below one of the city's most upscale restaurants. The Imperial had existed in one form or another for almost as long as I remembered. Victor Leupold Lange owned it, but he was currently away in New Orleans playing house with the daughter of my sister. An odd relationship; he being the oldest of us and she just newly transformed. But since my personal war had always been waged against Max and Max alone, I couldn't begrudge Victor what little bit of comfort he had found with the girl. And she, at least, would get the training her mother had not received. Victor had turned over the management of the restaurant and the Cadre several years prior. In fact, he had abdicated his positions so abruptly and had withdrawn from life so completely that many of us feared he would commit suicide. The girl, Lily, saved his life. It was my fondest hope that someday he would want control of this organization again and I would be free.

I caught the elevator up from my room and moved down the hallway toward the employee entrance. One of the largest men I had ever encountered stood there, guarding one of the few ways into the place. I had met him about a year ago, playing piano in a blues club in New Orleans. He had been a great find and proved to be quite loyal to his maker. I smiled at him as I passed. "Claude, how are you this evening?"

"Well, Miss Courbet. And if I may say so, you're looking fantastic as usual."

"Thank you, Claude. If anyone is looking for me, I'll be out for a bit. Or a bite."

He gave a small laugh. "It's a fine evening for a hunt."

"*Oui,* but then when isn't it? Has Monique left?"

"Some time ago."

"Ah." I stood looking up at him for a second. He really was huge. Then I patted him on the arm. "I suppose I will be going then. Good night."

"Good night and good hunting, Miss Courbet."

Chapter 22

Once on the street I walked for several blocks before hailing a cab to take me to the place I chose for this evening, an under-twenty-one dance club. Sweeter meat than my normal fare, I thought with a giggle as I paid the cab driver and got out to stand in line with the rest of the young people, observing their interactions and eventually, before gaining access, making the acquaintance of another girl who had come by herself.

Her name was Heather, her hair was purple, and she was dressed all in black. "Vivvi," I said with a calculatedly shy smile. "Have you been here before?"

"Vinnie?" she asked, or rather yelled, since we were standing right outside the open door and the band had already started.

"No, Vivvi. Lots of Vs. It looks cool when I sign my name."

Heather laughed. "Yeah, I guess it would. My name is so ordinary, it's like everyone is called Heather these days. I want to change it, but my mom freaks whenever I mention it."

"Yeah." I rolled my eyes and nodded my head in appreciation of the vileness of some parents. "My dad's like that too. What an asshole he is. I mean you just want to say, 'Go away and leave me alone,' you know?"

Heather laughed and I knew we had bonded. A little early in the evening, perhaps, but I'd found my target. It was always easy to find suitable prey; so many lonely, desperate people in this city, anxious to make contact, to reach out to someone else, seeking comfort, seeking approval, seeking love. This girl was no different, but she was strong and healthy and would hardly miss what I would take. Some vampires only preyed on the same type of person over and over again. I craved variety and even if I did not, blood was blood, male, female, young or old: each served their purpose admirably. And I saw no need to leave a discernable pattern.

"Nothing to trace," I said.

"What?"

We had moved into the main room of the club by now. The band was deafening and the sea of bodies intoxicating. I didn't need liquor to get my high. "Nothing," I screamed back at her. "Wanna dance?"

An older woman would have taken offense at the suggestion, but Heather was young enough so that dancing with other

women, provided it wasn't slow dancing, was perfectly acceptable.

We joined the other dancers on the floor, what seemed like
hundreds of human bodies crowded together, with their scent of
blood and sweat and the perfume of arousal. The entire experience was so intense that it hurt, generating a physical craving
and longing that made me ache deep inside. Oh, how I longed to
drink them all, to hold them all tightly in my arms, to capture
their sweet essences and keep them with me forever.

But I could not have them all. Instead I intensified my efforts
with the one I had chosen and smiled at Heather. She smiled
back, lost in the dancing almost as much as I was lost in the
flood of sensations. Her small breasts jiggled against her black
T-shirt, circles of perspiration grew under her arms, and still we
danced, until she was breathless and laughing.

I leaned over to her after three or four numbers by the band.
"I need to go to the girls' room. You want to come?"

"Might as well," she shouted back, "it'll be less crowded
now than when the band takes a break."

The line for the ladies' room stretched almost to the dance
floor, and I laughed. "If this is less crowded, I don't think I want
to see it any other time."

"Yeah," Heather agreed, "do you need to go really bad?"

"Yes, I do. Think they'll let me cut ahead?"

Heather shook her head. "This crowd? No way. But you
know, I know another place, just down the street. Small little
neighborhood type bar, we could go there, it's not usually too
crowded and"—she gave me a sly look—"the bartender likes
me. He'll give us something a little stronger to drink than soda if
we ask him nice."

"Sounds good to me." I wrapped an arm around her waist
and we left the club, trying to keep in step with each other, giggling as we walked the two blocks to the bar she spoke of.

Charlie's Place was perfect. Dark and seedy, with a clientele
interested only in getting drunker. Two obviously underage girls
arriving made little impact on their plans. After gesturing me
into a back booth, Heather stopped off at the bar and got us

both a beer. Then she slid into the seat next to me so that both of us were facing away from the bar and slid one of the mugs in my direction.

"If I sit looking at him," she whispered to me, her breath tickling the hairs on my neck, "it gives me the creeps. He's a nice guy, yeah, but he's so old."

"Yeah." Old? The bartender was a child, probably no more than twenty-eight or -nine. I turned my head to look at him again and she nudged my arm.

"Oh, no, don't look. Don't encourage him, he'll come over if you show too much interest."

Still, as he kept the beer flowing, she softened toward him. Not quite the effect I was hoping for. I needed to get her alone, not to get her all dewy-eyed over him. No doubt I could persuade her, but I preferred it when they came with me of their own free will; it didn't seem sporting the other way. And yet, I was very hungry.

"He's not all that bad," she was saying, "he's sort of cute, really. Just older enough to make it feel weird, you know?"

I looked into her eyes and laid my hand on her arm. Her skin was so warm, so vibrant. "You can do better than him," I said.

"Do you think so?" Her eyes widened, but she didn't pull away from me.

"Oh, definitely." My voice sounded lower, expectant. "You're beautiful, Heather. I can't believe you don't know that."

I kept my eyes on her; she blushed, then smiled. "Think so?" She repeated the question.

I nodded. "Of course. I would never lie to you, *mon amie.*" Then I giggled, trying to drop back into my role. "Anyway, I really need to pee right now. Where is the bathroom?"

She slid over and got up from the bench, swaying just a bit. "I'll show you, I need to go too."

I was glad to see that it was a bathroom with several stalls, even gladder that it was completely empty. Heather rushed into one of the stalls and I took the one next to her, not needing it, of course, but pretending. She talked to me the whole time and when her flow stopped, I rustled the paper a bit, flushed my toilet, and went to the sink, taking the elastic bands out of my hair and combing through it with my fingers.

I heard the rasping sound of the zipper of her jeans. Her door flew open and she came out with a giggle. "Man, I really needed to go." She washed her hands, and stood at the mirror next to me. The dim light of the bathroom made her hair look almost black and I realized why I'd felt so drawn to her. She reminded me of Monique when I had first met her. Poor little waif.

I reached over and pulled back Heather's hair, fastening it with one of the bands I'd taken out of my own hair. "See?" I said, standing behind her and whispering in her ear while maintaining eye contact in the mirror. "Your face has classical lines, your cheekbones are exquisite, and your eyes? They are magnificent. You are a beauty."

It really wasn't fair, I didn't have to play with her this way. She would have done anything that I asked of her at any time, but I needed this contact, the reassurance that, despite being a monster underneath, I could be and still was desirable. It wasn't really sex I was looking for; instead I wanted a willing surrender.

She turned around and reached a trembling hand out to touch my face. Her eyes were distant and glazed over. A willing surrender? I laughed inwardly at my conceit. *Not this time, Vivienne*, I thought, *this girl is not Monique*. But still I hungered for her. Without saying another word, I pulled her to me and fastened my mouth to her neck.

The taste of her was worth all of the time I had spent seducing her. Each sip brought her closer to me; as I drank her blood, I also absorbed some of her spirit, her youth, her beauty. And in a hundred years when she would be dead, I would still hold a part of her, a feel of the girl she was this evening, a photograph etched in memory.

She moaned in my arms and I took my mouth away, licking the small puncture wounds there. Then I pulled her hair free of the elastic and brushed it down over her neck. "Such a sweet girl," I whispered to her. "You will not remember this, you will not remember me for what I am. I am just a girl you met, not important, easily forgettable. But I will carry you with me forever."

I kissed her on the lips then and left her standing in the bathroom, swaying slightly and holding on to the sink. Her bartender friend would make sure that she got home.

I slowly made my way back to Cadre headquarters, avoiding further contact with humans, wanting to hold her sweetness in my mouth as long as I could.

I have heard that some of my kind do not sleep in coffins, there being no scientific necessity for such an arrangement. I have been told that a simple bed can suffice; as long as the room was not accessible to sunlight one would be completely safe. That may be true in modern days, and I have at times slept so, but my instincts have always called out for the safety of an enclosed area. My own particular coffin had been custom made; lined with steel plates, equipped with three heavy bolts for added protection, and fitted with a pink satin-covered mattress and pillows. Ostentatious, perhaps, and possibly unnecessary, but it was comfortable and secure.

Shortly before dawn then, I changed into a white silk nightgown and crawled into my haven, pulling the inner locks shut, settling into the pillows, anticipating with delight the day's sleep, the sweet dreamless void. I smiled; it had been a good hunt.

Chapter 23

The next evening fell, much like the previous evening and the one before that. Once again I was trapped in my office in Cadre headquarters, deep within the bowels of the Imperial. But at least I had only a short amount of time to spend here, since tonight was the Masquerade at Dangerous Crossings. I chuckled to myself about the club. I'd purchased it from Deirdre who'd inherited it from Max in the days it had been called the Ballroom of Romance.

I'd had no patience for romance for many many years and so immediately after acquiring the place, I gutted it and converted into a borderline S&M club. It had turned out to be a huge success. People would wait in line for hours to gain admittance and many would pay a fairly exorbitant amount of money for the privilege of hanging in my dungeon rooms, in the hopes that I might choose one of them and feed. Perhaps it seemed foolhardy to expose my nature so blatantly, but no one believed that I could be a true vampire.

And so Dangerous Crossing was born and opened to rave reviews from the magazine critics. It all came as no surprise to me. If my years had taught me anything, it was that the human heart had the capacity to seek out and embrace pain with uncanny accuracy.

And not just the human heart. The planned masquerade brought memories of other times. Of how Eduard and I had danced and laughed and made love. That it was love, I had no doubt. Never before and never since had I experienced the emotion. And although I knew him for only a short amount of time, and lost him, I could close my eyes and catch the scent of him in the air, the touch of him on my skin. I allowed my thoughts to form into fantasies of Paris and a time that never existed, one during which Eduard was not executed. We would walk the nighttime streets arm in arm and in silence, the fullness of our hearts needing no words. We would stroll past the Place du Carroussel and see nothing more threatening than our own shadows on the sides of the buildings, hear nothing more horrible than the steady patter of rain on the roofs and the cobblestones. Here the guillotine never existed and citizens of France did not kill their own. And I would laugh and tell him the story of the dream I had, of the revolution and how he had been killed. "But I am not dead," he would say, "I am here, with you. And will always be."

When the phone rang again, I jumped, having lost myself chasing ghosts down the rain-drenched streets of Paris's yesterdays. I glared at the phone wondering which city government buffoon was calling, wondering what petty problem would soon become the Cadre's problem and, by extension, mine. I even played with the idea of not answering. But with the sixth ring I picked it up, making a silent note to set the answering machine when this call was over.

"Yes?"

"Vivienne?" The voice was low-pitched and distant.

"Yes?"

"Vivienne Courbet?"

"Yes. That is I. What is it you want?"

There was a pause on the other end of the line, followed by a deep exhalation of breath that might have been a sigh. "This is a private line, Monsieur." I gave a small laugh. "And I am not one to entertain anonymous obscenities. State your business and your name. Or I will hang up."

"No, you misunderstand." The caller sighed again. "Do not hang up. I have a message far you."

"Well?"

"Prenez garde à la fuite du temps."

The line went dead and as I set the receiver down, I noticed that my hand was shaking. Beware the passage of time, he had said.

It was not a good message. And I had too many years behind me of which to beware. A chill shivered up my spine. Then I stood up and hugged my arms to myself. "Foo, it is stupid to be frightened. They are only words. And"—I reached over and turned on the desk lamp, foolishly searching the corners of the room for the shadows of yesterdays—"words cannot hurt me."

"I should hope not, Vivienne." The deep voice was shaded with laughter and I jumped, startled, then looked up to see the smiling face of Dr. John Samuels. "But you do know that it's not healthy to be talking to yourself, don't you?"

"Sam, *mon cher,* do not attempt to analyze me. You are not my psychiatrist. And do not tease me. I have had a bad day and an even worse night."

He walked across the room and deposited a light kiss on my

cheek, correctly gauging my mood and sensing that I wished no prolonged demonstrations. I sighed. *Ah, Sam,* I thought, *how can you be so right for me and yet so wrong all at the same time?* I knew better than to get involved in a serious relationship with a human. Over three hundred years of experience taught me that it just wouldn't work. And yet, here I was again, walking the tightrope, balancing needs and emotions, hoping to forestall or avoid the fall. I sighed again and shook my head slightly, forcing my face into a brilliant grin and stretching up on my toes to give him a kiss back.

"So, how was your day? Did you manage to get Mitch and Deirdre on the phone? Did you get them to come to my party?"

"No such luck," Sam said. "Deirdre was determined that they stay where they are for now, to spend some time alone. And they both sounded like they were enjoying living in England again." He shrugged and then smiled. "I don't believe I ever met a more stubborn couple. It's a bit of a miracle to even have them back together again. She was so adamant after he left and he was so guilt-ridden that he had been tricked into leaving."

I laughed. "If you ask me, Sam my sweet, the two of them need to relax; all that thinking and questioning can make one crazy. They should let it all go, learn how to have fun, and just exist."

"In short, they should become more like you?"

"Exactly, *mon cher.* For am I not the perfect being?"

Sam did not laugh as I meant him to. Instead he shook his head and gave me a questioning look. "A perfect being should not be frightened when a friend appears in her doorway. Don't try to fool me, Vivienne, what's wrong?"

"Nothing is wrong," I began to insist, but the phone rang and I reacted with a small sudden intake of breath.

"Nothing? Is it nothing that you can be frightened at the sound of the phone ringing?"

I glared at him, then glared at the phone as it continued to ring. I reached my hand out to pick it up, but pulled it back to my side when I saw that it was shaking.

"I am not going to answer that. I've had enough of business to last me an eternity. Therefore, I declare this workday over." As if to punctuate my words, the phone abruptly stopped ringing. I gave one nod of my head and then tucked my arm in his, noticing for the first time that he was wearing something other than his stolid, professional suit. "*Trés bon,* Sam. That tuxedo fits you perfectly, just as I knew it would. But haven't you forgotten your disguise?"

He laughed at me. "As if everyone there won't know who is on your arm for the evening. Regardless." He reached into his inner coat pocket and pulled out a small black half mask. "I didn't forget. I didn't want to put in on just yet."

"Yes, I know, you think my masquerade a frivolous thing. But it will be fun, I promise. Now let's go find the party."

Chapter 24

The Masque at Dangerous Crossings was already under way by the time Sam and I arrived. Like last year's party, it was supposed to be invitation only, but that idea only worked in theory. All of the public officials I dealt with on a daily basis needed to be invited; likewise, all Cadre members and the regular Crossings clientele. Adding in guests and friends of friends who'd managed to get their names on the list at the last minute, it was hardly an exclusive crowd.

Sam and I entered through the employee entrance; it wouldn't do for the hostess to be seen out of costume. Jules met us at the door looking rather uncomfortable in his pirate costume.

"Good evening, Miss Courbet, Dr. Samuels." He nodded and the golden earring looped into his left earlobe jiggled.

"You look wonderful, Jules," I said, reaching over and adjusting the bandanna that covered his curly brown hair.

He shrugged at my comment. "I feel silly."

I laughed. "But of course you do. That is the point of masquerades. Everyone feels silly, everyone looks silly, and so we can relax and let down our inhibitions. And women find pirates almost as devastatingly attractive as vampires, is that not right, Sam?"

Sam nodded. "It's the element of danger, the unpredictability of an unknown."

"See?" I said with a smile. "You cannot lose, *mon chou*. Now, how is the crowd tonight?"

"Restless," Jules said, "and anxious for the hostess to arrive."

"No doubt. I shall be ready soon. Has Monique come in?"

"Just a few minutes ago."

"Ask her if she will come back to Max's office and help me dress."

Jules walked away while Sam and I headed in the direction of the office. Max had been dead for years and still we all thought of this place as his. In truth, I found it hard to believe that he was dead; he had been a constant in my life for almost three hundred years, omnipresent, and at times I thought omnipotent. Max possessed so much power, lived for so many years. How could he allow it to end here, at the hands of one of his converts? It still made no sense to me. But for all of that, I was not sorry that he died. Quite the contrary, actually, I thought as I touched the brass plaque on the outside of the door. It hadn't happened soon enough. My only regret was that it had not been my hand to do the deed.

"May you rot in hell, you evil bastard."

"Excuse me?"

I started out of my reverie and smiled at Sam. "Nothing, my darling. Just an old lady's memories."

He laughed, his eyes running over my body like a caress. "As if you could ever be old, Vivienne. No matter how many years you have lived."

"*Merci,* Monsieur Samuels." I inclined my head to him and entered the office. Once it had been furnished entirely in black leather and chrome, but I had redecorated the interior when my sister came into ownership. I had even gone as far to renovate the small secret room behind the wardrobe mirror. Max had used it, I assumed, as a safe and secret haven. There had originally been two coffins stored there, one with his name on it and one with the name of Dorothy Grey. Max's had been put, finally, to its proper use and he had been buried in it. Deirdre's was still in her room in Cadre headquarters. Last I had looked, she was using it to store clothing. I felt a sudden rush of affection for her, irritating though she was at times.

"I wish, Sam, that you had managed to get Mitch and Deirdre to stay. At least for this night so that they could come to my party."

I opened the wardrobe door and pulled out my costume, neatly sealed in plastic wrappings. Sam craned his head to see and I put it back and closed the door again. "No," I said, giving him a little tap on the wrist, "you must not see it beforehand. It would be bad luck."

Sam laughed. "I think that is only for weddings, Vivienne."

"Oh, you are right, of course." I walked over to the bar. "Would you like a drink, *mon cher?* Fortification before we greet the crowd?"

"That would be good, thank you."

I busied myself, opening a bottle of wine and pouring two glasses. There was a rustle of paper and when I turned I saw that my desk now contained a few brightly wrapped presents. "And it needed only this, Sam, to make me feel an old lady. Who told?"

Monique spoke from the doorway. "I did, Vivienne. You didn't think that you could escape the birthday celebrations again this year, did you?"

I sighed. "It is not really my birthday, you both know that."

Sam gave me a kiss on the cheek. "It's as good a day as any to celebrate it, though, especially with the party already being prepared. Besides, Vivienne, I know how much you adore presents."

"True." I sat down and looked at the packages. "Which one shall I start with?"

Sam walked over and pushed the smallest box in my direction. "Open this one first. Deirdre gave it to me when I drove them to the airport last month. And I have been keeping it secret ever since."

"Ah, my dear little sister." I pulled off the paper and opened the box, laughing when I peered inside at the necklace of bats and red stones. "Priceless." I held it up to show the others. "Where on earth did she get it?"

"I don't know," Sam said, "but she told me to tell you that they are 'creatures of the night. They fly.' "

Giggling, I clasped the necklace around my throat, then turned my attention to the other three presents. "Which one now?"

Sam handed me a small square packet. "Claude gave this to me earlier."

I smiled. "I am sure I know what this is." And when I opened it, I found that I was right. A New Orleans blues collection. "Very nice," I said, "I will have to thank him for this later. Where is he?"

"He's been watching the door," Monique said. "There were a great many people trying to get in without invitation and Jules thought he'd be a good doorman."

I laughed. "Now which one is next?"

Sam handed me the largest package this time. "This one is from me."

Savagely, I attacked the paper. "Ooh," I said as I saw what was inside. "A laptop computer? Thank you."

I read the box; it might as well have been written in Greek. Although since I did speak some Greek that would have been more comprehensble than the phrases that were printed there. "I love it," I said with a grin. "There is something so unconventional about giving a three-hundred-year-old vampire a computer for her birthday."

He looked a bit disappointed at my response.

"Oh, no, Sam. Do not pout, *mon cher.* I love it," I said again. "It was very sweet and thoughtful of you. Not to mention, modern. But whatever shall I do with it?"

"You'll learn how to use it, that's what. It's archaic, the way you've been running an organization and a business without one. Trust me, Viv, you'll like this as much or more than VCRs and vampire movies."

"I am sure I will." I got up from the desk and gave him a long, passionate kiss, to make up for my somewhat lukewarm reception of his gift. He leaned into me and returned the kiss, running his hands up my back and holding me close.

I practically purred with the pleasure of his warm touch. "I will thank you better later, *mon cher,*" I whispered to him, "when we are alone."

Monique cleared her throat and we separated. "There's one more, Vivienne," she said, holding the last box out to me. "This one's from me. But perhaps, Sam, you could leave us alone, so that after it is opened, we can dress for the party?"

"No problem." He gave me a quick kiss and went to the door. "I'll go tell them to start the music."

After the door closed behind him, I smiled at Monique. "Thank you for remembering."

She shrugged. "It was nothing." Then she gestured with the box. "Do you want to open this?"

"Absolutely." I tore the wrappings from it eagerly, then stopped in amazement when I saw the contents: a small oil painting of a blond-haired girl standing naked by an open window, moonlight pouring over her pale skin and illuminating that which she was studying outside. I knew the scene well, having stood at the same window, although the artist had taken liberties with the location. Place du Carroussel had never been visible from my window in the House of the Swan. But still, it was a legitimate conclusion. The girl of course was I and the painter was . . .

"Eduard." The name escaped my lips in a whisper; it was a name I hadn't allowed myself to speak aloud for centuries, no matter how often I thought it. Running my fingers gently over

142 Karen E. Taylor

the paint, I closed my eyes and pictured his strong hands gripping the brush, remembered also the touch of those hands on my body. I sighed, not meaning to. "Ah, dear Eduard."

Monique smiled, the tips of her canines peeking over her lower lip. "Yes, it is one of his. As soon as I saw it, I knew you had to have it."

"But where on earth did you find it?"

She shrugged. "Our last trip to Paris, remember? There was an antique dealer right outside of the hotel."

"And that is where you kept disappearing to? Your big secret?"

Monique nodded.

"And here all along I thought you had a lover stashed away somewhere." I set the picture on the desk and moved toward her, giving her a hug and a kiss almost as passionate as the one I'd given Sam. "Thank you, *mon amie*. There is nothing to compare to this. But it must have cost you a pretty penny."

"Actually." She pulled out of my arms. "It didn't cost me all that much. The antique dealer"—Monique gave me one of her devilish smiles—"proved very cooperative. So you weren't too far wrong with the lover theory. Anyway, I thought you'd like it. Now let's get dressed for the party."

Monique was ready much sooner than I, having picked a simple Egyptian tunic and headdress to wear. It suited her well, I thought, her tall, lithe body almost glowing through the sheer gauze material of the dress. With the addition of a little bit of gold jewelry and a gold half mask she was done while I had hardly donned the first of my voluminous petticoats.

"Whatever was I thinking," I said as I twisted around to fasten the ribbons at my waist, "when I chose this costume?"

"You were thinking about the past. And that is always a mistake." With a laugh, Monique came up behind me and began to help me dress, fastening the tight bodice and smoothing the outer skirt down over the many layers of net, lace, and wire hoops.

"It is strange," I said, wiggling my shoulders about, trying to get comfortable in the tight sleeves, "that we once wore all these clothes and never gave them a second thought."

"Hold still," Monique murmured, her hands twisting my hair up onto the top of my head and fitting the feathered hood around my face. "And voila, you have once again become *Mademoiselle Cygnette.*"

I picked up my mask from where it had fallen to the floor of the wardrobe. It too was adorned with white feathers, and the handle was covered in white velvet and trailed satin ribbons. Standing in front of the mirror I appraised my appearance.

Staring back at me was a pale girl seemingly covered in feathers. My gray eyes looked enormous and almost black in the sea of whiteness. I turned my head from side to side, then looked over to Monique. "Some rouge, do you think?"

"No, I don't think. You look glorious just the way you are. I just hope you aren't planning on feeding in that getup. A drop of blood would ruin it."

I threw my head back and laughed. "Oh, Monique, you know as well as I do that nothing can be ruined by blood. But I fed well last evening, so you need not worry." I turned around and craned my head about to see the back. "It is very like that other one, isn't it?"

"Almost exact, I'd say. Except, of course, for that silly headdress. Although why you'd choose to wear it again . . ."

I shivered slightly. Why had I chosen this costume again? Not that it carried such horrible memories; no, I had worn such clothing on one of the happiest nights of my life. And yet I had always made such an effort not to dwell in the past, not to try to regain days and years long lost.

"*Prenez garde à la fuite du temps,*" I whispered too quietly for her to hear. "Just lately, Monique, I feel that the past is stalking me; that I am the prey and others, unknown, are the hunters. I feel that all of my years blend in with each other so that I hardly know what is the present and what is the past. It is frightening and I do not know how to fight this feeling."

Monique shrugged. "You are under pressure, *mon chou,* that is all."

"Is it? I wonder. . . ." I made a concerted effort to swallow the past, to bury it deep within so that it could not reemerge.

Then taking a deep breath, I lifted my mask to my face and smiled, making a small curtsy to the mirror and to Monique. "The past be damned, we are here now. It makes no difference how we arrived at this moment." I giggled a bit as I moved toward the door. "Let's party."

Chapter 25

Dangerous Crossings looked festive for once, less like a dungeon and more like a ballroom. Perhaps it was the bright colors of the costumes, perhaps it was the electric candelabra I'd found in storage in the basement and had hung on the walls, although they in themselves were rather ominous, being hands holding the electric candles. Still, the extra bit of light helped brighten the atmosphere as did the hundreds of balloons floating above the dance floor, dangling glittering streamers.

Sam had met me at the door to the club; Monique gave my hand a brief squeeze. "You don't need to have me ruining your entrance; after all, it's your party," she said and quickly disappeared in the sea of bodies.

Sam cleared his throat, watching her leave. "That's quite a costume she's almost wearing. But you, Vivienne, you look radiant. Like an angel."

"A swan, actually," and I raised my arms to show him the wings.

"Of course, a swan." He pulled away from me briefly, inadvertently, then tucked my hand back into the crook of his elbow. I doubt that he was even aware of his reaction, that he realized the reminder of my alternate shapes was disturbing to him. A man of science, Dr. John Samuels could believe in vampires only because he could not deny the evidence. Vampirism was viewed and accepted by him as a disease, either of the body or the mind. It little mattered which since both could be easily adopted into his philosophy. But to accept and deal with the shape-shifting of which we were capable? No, he had not acted the same toward me since I'd exhibited the talent, treating me with just a little more wariness than before. It was not a good sign for our relationship.

Nor, I thought as we proceeded through the crowd to my special table, did I want it to be a relationship. I was not my sister and he was not Mitch.

No, what Sam and I had was convenient for both of us. Gone were the days when I needed a watchdog as Raoul or Rosa had been. Now I simply needed an escort, someone with whom I could make a memorable entrance. I had heard that he'd once referred to himself as "arm candy" and perhaps that wasn't too far off the truth. He was one of the most handsome men I knew in this most recent century, but it was more than that. I liked the man, I cared for him—he was a wonderful lover, he made me laugh, and he made me feel beautiful when I knew that the mirror lied.

I gave him a sidelong glance as we moved through the crowd and took our positions at my private table. And what did he get from me? Besides the vicarious thrill of escorting one of the most dangerous women he'd ever meet? I met his eyes and he smiled.

I had once asked him that very question. We had just made love and I was dressing to return back to my room before dawn. He lay on his side and watched me, his elbow resting on the pillow and his head propped up on his raised hand.

"Sam? *Mon cher?*"

"Hmm?"

"Why do you waste your time and your precious few years on a creature who can ultimately only mean heartbreak for you? As hard as I try, I am afraid I cannot see that we have any future with each other. You should leave me and find a nice human woman." He made a snorting sound at that comment, but I continued. "You should settle down and have children. And every year at Halloween, you can tell them about the vampire you once kept company with."

He laughed just a bit and gave me a sad smile. "They wouldn't believe me. Besides, I don't want a nice human woman. I'm happy with you."

"But why?"

He rolled over onto his back and stared up at the ceiling for a second before answering. "It's simple, Viv. And it's all about re-search, of course. How else will I be able to publish my study on the hemoglobinly impaired? You can't possibly think it has any-thing to do with you. You are just a guinea pig for my studies. I hope you don't mind."

I had kissed him then and walked back to Cadre head-quarters, shaking my head. *Research, indeed,* I'd thought, *there's more to it than that, my man.*

But I took his answer at face value. It didn't do to think too far ahead in a relationship with a human.

So I pretended my reasons and his reasons were all of the truth. That way we both received what we said we wanted. A perfect relationship that took us nowhere. In a hurry.

Jules came by and filled our glasses with champagne, bring-ing a plate of hors d'oeuvres for Sam to eat. From the platform on which our table sat, I watched the dancers, enjoying as al-ways the closeness of so many humans. And for this one night, at least, the clothes were enjoyable as well. Ordinarily the clien-tele dressed in black almost entirely; it didn't matter what the garment was made of—silk or leather or vinyl or spandex—the color was always the same. Finding such conformity depressing, I took great delight in being different and breaking the chain by wearing something in pastel shades.

Tonight, though, I did not stand out in the crowd. I could mingle with them and not be recognized. And neither could any-one else; one of the thrills of a masquerade, I thought, was the complete anonymity it granted everyone.

I finished my glass of champagne and took Sam by the hand.

"Dance with me," I said and we found a place on the dance floor. To my great delight, the band, chosen for their eclectic style and repertoire, began to play a waltz.

"Now this is dancing." I smiled up at him as we twirled around. "Nothing like the half-crazed jiggling they do today."

He nodded indulgently.

"It's not fair, you know."

"What?"

"That you should be handsome, intelligent, sexy, and a good dancer."

"A plethora of riches?"

"Oh, yes."

I closed my eyes and let the music carry me along. The song ended all too soon, and as we turned toward the band, applauding them, Monique stepped up on the stage and took the microphone.

"Good evening," she said, "and welcome to the second annual Dangerous Crossings Masquerade. Some of you may know me as the shadow of our esteemed hostess, the vivacious Vivienne Courbet, a woman who needs no introduction. Except that I am going to give her one regardless. Vivienne?"

I shook my head and she laughed. "Can you believe it? She's suddenly shy, a personality trait no one would suspect." There was a small bit of laughter at this, including Sam's. "But I happen to know of another of her aspects that no one else does."

"What is she doing?" Sam leaned over and whispered. "What is she going to say? Is she drunk? Do you want me to get her out of there?"

"She isn't drunk, but don't worry. I think I know what she's going to say. And I'm going to kill her."

"I was at the band auditions," Monique continued, "and there I've discovered the one thing I had forgotten about Mademoiselle Courbet. She is an accomplished and talented chanteuse." She paused and looked straight at me. "Vivienne? Would you, please?"

"Only one," I said as I mounted the stage. There was a moderate amount of applause, not overwhelming, not even particularly encouraging. And I couldn't blame them for being skeptical; they had come for the open bar and the free food, not to hear me sing.

I looked at the band leader. "Do the one we did at the auditions."

I took the microphone from Monique and stuck my tongue out at her. "Thank you," I said as she moved off the stage. "You will pay for this later."

"But"—I addressed the crowd—"since I am here and you are here and we've all got to do something, I will sing my favorite song. Written by Monsieur Willie Nelson and with apologies to Mademoiselle Patsy Cline who is really the only one who can do this song justice. Although since she is dead, I'm sure she won't object too much."

The band began the short introduction, just keyboards and drums. And I sang. After the first few lines, people began dancing again and as they moved past the stage I recognized some of the couples. Monique danced with Sam, and Jules, with one of our waitresses. Even Claude was present; dressed as an impressive Cardinal Richelieu and amazingly light on his feet, he seemed to engulf an unidentified and tiny young woman dressed as a cat. When the song ended, the applause sounded more than polite. "It is a wonderful song, is it not?" I said and curtsied to my audience. *"Merci."* I put the microphone back into its stand. "Enjoy the party."

At first I thought the noise from the back of the room was an overenthusiastic fan of my singing. But no, the voice sounded angry and harsh. Then I discerned the words.

"Death to the vampires of the Cadre."

From my vantage point on the stage I had a clear view of the club. The guests who knew what those words meant tensed and spun around to face whatever threat approached. A woman in a French maid costume screamed. A flash of black and red darted out the exit with the faint jingling of bells. "Give him room," someone else said. "Is there a doctor here?"

"Why bother?" said another woman, a note of choked hysteria in her voice. "He's got to be dead right now."

"Lock the doors!" I heard Claude's steady voice and was thankful he was here. "Do not let anyone leave. And yes, young lady, that means you. As well as your friend and the twenty people standing behind you. I have called the police and the paramedics and they will be here soon. Until then, everyone stay put and stay calm."

I stepped off the stage and the crowd parted for me, closing back in behind me.

Jules lay on the floor, a three-foot wooden stake protruding from his heart. My nostrils flared from the overwhelming scent of his blood. I heard one woman sobbing uncontrollably and someone else was vomiting in the corner. At least I was right about one thing; this would be a night to remember.

This made no sense. Why would anyone want to kill Jules? He had no enemies, he had been charming and well liked by club employees and Cadre members alike.

I knelt down next to him, not caring that the pool of his blood was being absorbed into the feathers of my costume. His eyes were wide-open in shock, his hands twisted around the stake as if he had attempted to pull it out before he died. I shivered, reaching over to close his staring eyes and smoothing back a lock of black hair that had escaped his once-jaunty pirate bandanna. "I am so sorry, *mon ami*. You will be avenged."

Chapter 26

"No," I said for what must have been the hudredth time that night, sitting behind my huge desk in Max's office. "I do not have a clue who might have done this. Jules had, to the best of my knowledge, no enemies and there was no good reason for him to have died like this. Why would you ask me to determine the purpose behind a madman's actions?"

The police had arrived shortly after the paramedics. Neither of them could have arrived soon enough to be of help to Jules, but the medics were wonderful at calming a hysterical crowd. The police were being less than helpful, I thought, spending entirely too much time questioning me and not near enough time trying to track down the murderer.

"Once again, Miss Courbet, do you know what the phrase"— and he consulted his notebook for the exact words—"death to the vampires of the Cadre' means?"

I stood up from my chair and leaned over my desk, glaring at him. "Of course I know what it means. I speak English easily as well as you. But as for why such a thing would be said? There are no vampires here, they are creatures who do not exist. So I can only surmise that the murderer is crazy."

"And the Cadre? What is that?"

The existence of the Cadre was not necessarily a secret. On paper we were a group of rich entrepreneurs; only one or two within the city government knew we were more than that. And I was determined to keep it that way.

I shrugged. "We have been over this, Officer, many times. Perhaps he was speaking metaphorically. Perhaps he saw all the costumes and really thought there were vampires within. Perhaps he had a pointed stick he wanted to try out. But I"—I walked over to the window and pulled the curtains open just a bit to check on the night sky—"I have no idea what he was thinking."

Dawn was a little more than an hour away, I estimated. And I could not stay here answering mindless questions until it arrived. Turning away from the window, I faked a yawn. "Now, if you don't mind, it is very late and I am very tired. I have lost an employee and a friend tonight, in a horribly gruesome manner. I suggest you leave me to my rest and attempt to make sure this does not happen again."

What could they do? There was absolutely no way I could be charged with this murder; the entire club was witness to my innocence. And there was no reason why I should be charged. Why they had lingered as long as they had here in my office asking questions I'd already answered was almost a bigger mystery than the crime itself.

Except that if they weren't stupid, and I didn't believe they were, these men could certainly tell that I wasn't being entirely honest with them. It did not matter, I knew, especially when Sam came back into the room and nodded to me. The phone rang and I picked it up.

"Hello?"

"Vivienne? Do you have any idea what time it is, woman? And what the hell is going on?"

Every city government has at least one individual who, from his seemingly innocuous position, holds all the power and pulls all the strings. In New York City at this time it was James Christensen.

"Jim," I said, "I'm so sorry to have woken you, but I need your assistance. Perhaps you would like to explain to some of your officers that I am not a murderer."

"Oh, dear. I had heard about that, Vivienne, and you have my condolences. But why are they accusing you?" He made an exasperated noise. "Never mind, just let me talk to one of them."

I held the receiver out, waving it in the direction of the officers. "Mr. Christensen would like to speak with you."

The two officers exchanged a quick glance and seemed to stand a little straighter. "Yes, sir," the one who took the phone from me answered. "This is Sergeant DeMarco."

I could hear Jim on the other end of the line. "What the hell are you doing harassing Miss Courbet? I can assure you she didn't instigate this event. Get off your asses, get the hell out of there, and catch the bastard who did it."

"Yes, sir."

"And put her back on the line. Now!"

Sergeant DeMarco gave me a sheepish grin and handed the phone back to me.

"Merci, Jim," I said, "and aren't you sorry you missed the party?"

He gave a sleepy laugh. "Not at all, as a matter of fact. Is there anything else I can do for you?"

"No, thank you. Sleep well."

"You too, my dear."

I hung up the phone and looked over at the officers standing there. "Are there any other questions I can answer for you?"

"No, I'm afraid we've already taken up too much of your time. Thank you for your courtesy."

I waited until they were well out of earshot before I started to giggle. "Amazing what you can do with a phone call to the appropriate person. Thank you, Sam."

"My pleasure, Viv, as always. I rather enjoy riding to your rescue."

I walked across the room to him and gave him a warm kiss. "I feel rather guilty about it, though. They were only doing their jobs. And they knew I knew something I wasn't telling."

He shrugged. "You'd no other choice, Vivienne. It serves no good purpose for the general population to know what the Cadre is. Half of them wouldn't believe it and the other half would be sharpening stakes."

I shivered. "I can't believe this happened, Sam. What does it mean? And why Jules? Why not me? If you were privy to the secret of the Cadre, I would be the obvious choice to kill. Jules was a little fish."

Sam thought for a while. "Maybe the death wasn't the primary reason. It could be that Jules just happened to be in the wrong place at the wrong time. Maybe it was a message."

"But from whom? And why? So few people know we exist and we harm no one."

He smiled at that comment and I grew just a bit angry at him. "Damn it, Sam, you know that's true. We take so very little and we give back a lot. Look at all the Cadre money that's been given to charities—day care centers, housing for the homeless, soup kitchens—you name it, and we have supported it." I gave a bitter laugh. "Although it is true we do not do this for the most noble of reasons, we do do it. And that is what matters."

Sam nodded and looked at his watch. "Are you going back to

Cadre headquarters tonight? If so, we'd better grab you a cab and get you there soon."

"No, I think I'll stay here for the day. Care to stay with me?"

He smiled. "And sleep with you in your coffin? I think not, sweetness. But thanks for asking."

"Oh, Sam. I wish you would stay." I ran my fingers up his cheek and through his hair, kissing the corners of his mouth. "There's a bed in there," I whispered persuasively, "as you well know."

He pushed me away. "I can't. As tempting as the offer is, I have some things I need to take care of tomorrow."

I pouted. "But I thought you said you didn't have to work tomorrow. Stay with me, Sam. Please."

He started to refuse again, but something changed in his expression. "What's wrong, Vivienne? I know that what happened with Jules was horrible for you and everyone else. But I have the feeling it is more than that with you. Talk to me. I'm a good listener, you know. It is, after all, how I make my living."

"If I knew, Sam, I would tell you. I have this haunted feeling and I'm not sure I can explain it. I have tried to live all my years without ever once looking back in regret or sadness or anger." I laughed, picked up the painting on my desk, and set it back down. "And it has always worked for me. No worries, no responsibilities, no tears—just me and *la joie de vivre.*"

"But in this last week it is as if . . ." I paused. "Oh, I don't know. I am no good at this self-examination, I fear. But that phone call this afternoon and this painting Monique gave me"—I ran my fingers over the frame—"the flash of a red and black costume on the dance floor, singing for the crowd, seeing Jules dead—all of it adds up to something and I do not know what it is."

His eyes searched my face. "Maybe it's stress. You've hardly taken any time off since you returned from Paris; you had this party to arrange, Cadre business, Dangerous Crossings business. All of that is more than one person can handle."

"That is what Monique said. But I've been in worse situations before and never felt this way."

"Maybe it'll go away. You're upset right now about Jules's death, which is perfectly understandable. You wouldn't be normal if you weren't."

Choking back the beginning of tears, I gave him a wan smile. "But I am not normal, Sam, and I am afraid. Something terrible is waiting. I do not know what it is, do not even know why it is there. But I can sense it on the edge of my senses, pacing back and forth, stalking me, mocking me."

I moved to where my costume hung over the wardrobe door—Jules's blood had been absorbed by the feathers, turning the skirt a dirty red almost to the waist. I plucked one of the feathers and held it to my nose, then laid it down on the desktop as if it were one of my birthday presents.

"Sam," I said, trying and failing to disguise the tremor in my voice, "do you believe in ghosts?"

He walked over and kissed me on the forehead. "No, sweetness, I don't." Then he stepped back, holding my arms. "And I don't think you do either. Get some rest, okay?"

Chapter 27

I laughed as I showed him to the door. He was right, of course, I didn't believe in ghosts. And I was stressed and weary. No doubt things would look differently after a good day's sleep.

At the desk I pulled a ring of keys out of the top drawer, collected my presents, and unlocked the door behind the wardrobe. When Max had been alive, this room was no more than a concrete block cell, unlit, unfurnished, cold, and dank. I'd had the room wired and brought in decorators, so that it was now a serviceable area, comfortable and welcoming. I chuckled to myself; when telling this story to others of my kind, I always liked to elaborate and tell them that, of course, the workmen had to be killed after the job was done and that I had walled the dead bodies in behind the floral wallpaper. In reality, they had taken their money and left. I imagined they'd seen stranger sights.

In addition to my spare coffin the room also held a small bed, covered in a floral chintz that matched the decor of the office outside. I kept an assortment of clothes in the chest of drawers in one corner, and the built-in shelves at the end of the outside wall held a stereo system and CDs, a television, a VCR, and an assortment of tapes. I would rarely admit it, but I was hopelessly addicted to vampire movies. It didn't matter if they were good or bad or howlingly funny, I loved them all and watching them over and over was one of my secret narcissistic pleasures.

A large set of bookshelves held an assortment of titles, classics and contemporaries, most written in French. It was the first language I had struggled to read and despite all the years away from my country it was still my language of choice.

I took off the clothes I'd put on after stripping away my blood-soaked costume and pulled a pink silk nightgown from one of the drawers. As I slid it on, I wished that the room had been big enough to allow for a small bath. The smell of Jules's blood lingered sour on my skin and I longed for hot water to wash it away.

Instead I sprayed myself with some of my cologne, a special blend I had made in France, expressly for me: cloves and orange blossoms.

I locked the door then, scolding myself for not having done it sooner, then walked over and pulled the spread back on the bed, crawling in and flipping on the television with the remote control.

The morning news was on. And last night's events at Dangerous Crossings were the lead story. I sighed. My little masquerade party had turned into a nightmare.

I turned up the volume on the set. ". . . Miss Courbet, owner of the club and one of the city's most mysterious and eligible bachelorettes, was not available for comment."

"Damned straight," I said. "Nor will I be. And what is this nonsense? Bachelorette?"

It would have been the end of the story, but the anchorman turned to the newswoman. "So, Terri." He had an avid look in his eyes and I was surprised he wasn't drooling; it was such a juicy story. "This is not the first bizarre killing to happen at the site, is it?"

"No, Bob, you're right about that." She shuffled her papers a bit and straightened them out against the desk. "Before it became Dangerous Crossings, this particular club was called the Ballroom of Romance. And two people died in that club during that incarnation. Both of them by the hands of a NYC police officer in the line of duty."

"One of the deaths was a simple shooting, right?"

She nodded. "Yes, very cut-and-dried. A young man by the name of Larry Martin. He was apprehended while in the process of attempting to kill noted clothing designer Deirdre Griffin. Although"—she gave a smug smile, revealing perfectly straight white teeth—"Martin's choice of a murder weapon was, coincidently, a pointed stake."

"And the other killing?"

"The owner of the club at that time, Max Hunter, had been impaled on the door of his office."

"Yet another wooden stake, Terri?"

"It was actually the broken-off leg of a bar stool, Bob, but certainly close enough to a wooden stake to count."

"So what does this all mean to us now?"

She laughed. "It means that Halloween is over and has been over for a month. So put away your plastic fangs and your cape, or you may be next."

"*Merde*, such funny people." I clicked the OFF button on the remote with a violent flick. "Put *this* away, Terri," I said with a sneer.

I suppose it could have been worse. Regardless of the misfortune of the deaths they reported, the events were meaningless enough to them to relegate them to a joke. At least no speculations were being made about why, of all places, this club had such a history. No conjectures about why the method of killing was so archaic and reminiscent of bad horror movies. No headlines from the *New York Times* screaming VAMPIRES LIVE AMONG US! In truth, the Cadre paid big money in bribes to avoid this sort of publicity.

But they had gotten close this time—they were dancing around issues, pointing at coincidences one in the know could recognize as false. I took some consolation from the fact that this was a city in which all sorts of outrageous crimes were committed daily and today's hot news story often ended up as back page filler tomorrow. Yet, with enough hints and speculations, anything was possible; this story was filled with all the elements the public loved: blood, lust, and death. Not to mention the potential for hating those different. And I had learned over the years never to underestimate the depth of human prejudice for anything that deviated from the norm.

My hands went to the new necklace I wore, and, stroking the bats as if they were worry stones, I sighed. I missed Deirdre. And Mitch. Either of them would have known what to do; together they'd know what steps to take to avoid disaster. I missed Victor and his "listen to me or die" leadership that had always managed to sidestep complications like the one that threatened now to arise. Even Max might have had some good advice for me.

Then again, I thought, sitting up in bed and looking over at the bookshelves, *I do have advice from Max.* On the bottom shelf of the large bookcase was an entire set of black leatherbound journals authored over the hundreds of years of Max's vampiric existence.

I got out of bed, put in the new blues CD Claude had given me, and sat cross-legged on the floor, pulling out journals one by one and reading the first several pages.

It was fascinating reading. An incredible true story told by an incredible man. For while I disliked Max almost to the point of hatred, I could still acknowledge what he had been: a powerful and magnetic creature capable of so much I'd never have thought possible when I was human. Or even when I was a young vampire. I still could not understand how he had let himself be killed. Perhaps the answer lay in his journals.

The pages were brittle with age and the handwriting had faded. That, plus the fact that at least the earliest ones were written in archaic Spanish, made them difficult reading. If there existed an answer here, I was going to have to work for it.

"Typical Max," I said as I pulled out the next volume. "Never make it easy." I turned the pages slowly, giving each a perfunctory glance before moving on, until I caught a glimpse of my name, along with references to Victor and a group Max simply called the Others.

> *Paris, December 1792*
> *We arrived in good time, with hours before sunrise. Victor went to prepare our normal quarters and I, to escape his company, went to walk the streets. I passed the House of the Swan but did not go in. I would save that visit for tomorrow evening when there was more time. Plus, I must admit that I fear meeting Vivienne again. Does she still hate me, I wonder, for the death of Diego? Or is she willing to let the past remained buried?*
>
> *I find it strange that I should care. What difference could her low opinion of me make? I detest Victor and yet we are still together despite that fact. The ties between maker and created are very strong.*
>
> *The atmosphere of the streets is tense, fear hovering over the buildings and the people like dark storm clouds. And I feel that presence Victor has come looking for. The Others, as he calls them, are here, manipulating the existence of all who dwell in this city. There is indeed a curious crackle in the air, like lightning making ready to strike, a certain bone-chilling excitement, akin to that felt while transforming to another physical shape. If I can believe Victor's as-*

sessment that this is proof of their existence, then they must exist.

He would like to recruit them, to join our powers with theirs. I would prefer to leave them to their own devices. What they do to humans makes little difference to me; even should the frenzy of the revolution the Others have purportedly stirred and incited cut off every other head in France, it will not affect me or my life.

No, I am not here for a cause, not here to support Victor's move to unite vampires under a common goal. I have more power surging in my blood than I ever wanted to have, I have no wish to associate for all eternity with those of my own kind.

No, I did not come with Victor for any of those reasons. I came to make peace with Vivienne, if it is possible. And to remove her from the potential danger of this revolution if she will allow me.

I smiled. "That is very sweet of you, Max." Then I laughed. "Although I remember at the time I thought you were being an interfering bastard." I paged forward. Much of what was written were descriptions of Paris and the rooms in which he and Victor always stayed. And the many feedings he had made. His hunger must have been greater than mine, he seemed to need the blood every night. Or perhaps it was a desire.

Paris, December 1792
I must admit after seeing Vivienne again that she is a magnificent creature, a fact I manage to forget when not confronted by her. She has agreed to let the issue of Diego lie buried with his remains. But now I find that I do not like her current choice of companions. Perhaps I am just a jealous old man, a father for whom no person can be found acceptable for a much beloved daughter. But it is more than that. Monique

*does not ring true. And this Eduard that I keep hear-
ing of? I dislike him already, intensely. Both of them
seem to have some hold over my perfect little swan.
Oh, how she would laugh if she knew that is how I
think of her. Even before we attempted her change to
her winged form, I knew that a swan was what she
would be.*

*So I shall attend her masque and meet this Eduard.
And then I will decide what is to be done.*

"What is to be done?" I said the words aloud, not liking what
they implied. Could Max have had something to do with Eduard's death?

I shook my head. Even if it were true, there was nothing I
could do. Both of them were dead, buried, and out of my life.

I am not entirely sure that I wished it otherwise.

I put away Max's journals and turned out the light. The enclosed space of my coffin was a comfort; the lavender-scented
satin sheets were soothing. I slept.

Chapter 28

And I woke. Better rested, but none the wiser. As always my
sleep had been deathlike: deep and dreamless. If I had hoped
that reading Max's journals would trigger a response, help filter
those cryptic messages from my subconscious, and subsequently
solve all my problems on wakening, I was a fool. A fool who
never dreamed.

I'd asked Sam about this once.

"I do not dream anymore, Sam. In fact I can hardly remember what it is like to dream, it has been so long."

He looked at me in disbelief. "That's not possible, Vivienne. Everyone dreams. You just don't remember them, that's all."

"I remember everything else in my life, Sam. Can my dreams be so terrible that they must stay buried deep inside me?"

He laughed. "Or maybe they're so good, your mind doesn't want to ruin your waking life."

I rolled my eyes. "How could anything be that good when I love every part of my waking life? Unless, of course," I hinted with a twisted smile, "they were dreams of you and me and . . ."

"Forget it, sweetness. I have to take a shower and get to work; I'm on the night shift tonight."

I followed him into his bathroom and watched as he undressed and got into the shower. He turned on the water, stepped into the tub, then looked over at me, holding the curtain open. "Do you want to come in?"

"No, *mon chou,* you like the water too cold."

"Good." He pulled the curtain shut. "You like the water entirely too hot."

I gave a soft laugh. "So what does it mean if I don't dream?"

"What?"

I raised my voice so he could hear me over the rush of the water. "What does it say about me if I don't dream?"

"It says you're one crazy lady, Vivienne. But I already knew that. And I love you anyway."

"No," I had whispered as I walked out of the room, "do not love me, Sam. That is the one dream I do not want. And cannot have."

I opened the coffin lid and peered out. The bedside clock indicated that it was about fifteen minutes or so past sundown. Stretching, I climbed over the side of my box and went to the dresser, from which I pulled out a pale blue sweater, a pair of panties, and a pair of black jeans. With the clothes tucked under my arm, I unlocked the door that led to my office, and from there walked out into the hallway, toward the employees' lounge. I knew that I would meet no customers and precious few staff members after the announcement last night that Dangerous Crossings would be closed until further notice due to the police investigation in progress.

"I really must have a bath installed down in my office," I said, entering the female employees' area so that I could finally take a shower.

Sam was right about the water temperature. I turned it up just as high as I could, in the hopes that it would warm my cold blood for a while, and as I soaped and shampooed and rinsed, I hummed the song I had sung for everyone last night. It was still one of my favorites, although now every time I heard it I would think of Jules.

And there's nothing wrong with that, I thought, *it is as good a memorial as anyone could get.*

Turning off the water, I reached for a towel on the nearby set of hooks and dried off. I pulled my sweater over my head, then wrapped another towel, turban style, around my wet hair and finished dressing.

On my way back to the office, I detoured to take a look at the main room of the club. It had been cleaned since the party, and there was nothing out of the ordinary left to illustrate the extraordinary events, except for the festive streamers still hanging down from the few balloons the cleaning staff had missed and the small area cordoned off by yellow emergency tape. *An interesting juxtaposition,* I thought as I watched one of the balloons descend slowly from the ceiling and bounce once against the floor. I wondered again why this had happened.

". . . A message," Sam had suggested, and perhaps that was true. And if so, would there be another such message? And would they keep getting delivered until we were all dead?

And why should anyone bother?

"What the hell do you want?" My voice filled the quiet room and was answered only by a high-pitched screech coming from the farthest corner of the bar.

"Who's there?" Two voices said the words in unison and I tensed. Another messenger?

"Show yourself," I said and again another voice spoke over mine but I relaxed slightly when I thought I recognized it.

"It's me, Vivienne. It's Claude. I am so glad to see you escaped!"

"Where are you?"

I peered out into the club. Other than a heavy patch of darkness near the bar, I could see nothing.

"Here. I'm here. Hiding."

And out of the darkness, his face swam into view. I gave a huge sigh of relief. "You idiot, Claude, I am pleased to see you but you scared the hell out of me."

As he came closer, I got a better look at him. And yes, it was Claude, but . . . "*Sacre bleu, mon cher,* what has happened to you?"

One side of his body was badly burned, the skin peeling away in thick layers from those areas that were not covered by clothing. "I went outside in the sun." Barking out a harsh laugh, he shrugged, causing the glass of liquid he held in one hand to slosh over onto his burned skin. "Damn!" He dropped the glass and it broke into pieces at his feet. "It was a shame, I know, to take such a risk and ruin my otherwise rugged good looks. But"—and he lifted the bottle of whiskey he had grasped in his other hand and took a quick hard swallow—"this is preferable to what happened to the rest of them."

"The rest of them? Claude? What on earth are you talking about?"

He peered at me through squinted eyes. "You don't know?" he asked.

"Don't know what?"

"Ah." He took another swig off his bottle and looked at me. "Have some."

"No, thank you anyway. It is not my choice of drink—"

"It was not really a question. Have some. It will help dull the pain."

"Pain? I am not in pain."

"Not yet, in any event. Can we go back to your office? I'd like to sit down."

I gestured with my hand that he was to proceed me and he did. I followed his huge, hulking form down the hallway and back into my office. It was not politeness to let him go ahead of me; he was acting so strange I did not want to turn my back on him.

When we entered, he headed straight for the couch, settled in on the couch, and drained the last half of his bottle in what seemed one long gulp.

"Another?" I went to the bar without waiting for his answer, opened a new one of the brand he had been drinking, and poured myself a glass of red wine from the carafe that I kept filled.

I pushed the bottle at him and watched him drink, while I took the towel from my head and shook out my damp hair. When he seemed calmer I spoke again. "So? Can you tell me now, Claude? I think I need to know."

He sighed and pulled a handkerchief out of his pocket to wipe his face. Then he winced as he pulled the fabric away and saw that a long strip of skin had attached to it. He gave another harsh laugh. "Victor would have said it served me right. I always annoyed him with the gesture."

"Claude?"

"It will heal, don't you think?"

I walked over to him and took his chin in my hand, turning his head so that I could assess the damage. Even now I could see that the skin beneath the blackened burnt areas was pale and healthy. "Yes, it will heal. Your rugged good looks, as you say, will return in a day or two. Unless you do not tell me right now what happened and I am forced to scorch the rest of your skin off of your body."

He sighed. "I am sorry, Vivienne. It's just that if I don't say the words, then it might still not be true." He took a long drink.

"Cadre headquarters is gone."

Chapter 29

" Gone? How do you mean gone?"

"An explosion, around noon. News reports say that it was a terrorist attack. Or an inside job. Depending on which station you are watching. Basically no one really knows yet what happened, except that it did. The carnage was terrible." He licked his cracked lips and dabbed at his face again with his handkerchief. "Like one of those horribly graphic war movies. Smoldering body parts everywhere." He gave his head a violent quick shake as if to dispel the visions. "And those who survived the blast and hadn't the sense or the wits to seek shelter elsewhere burst into flames."

His voice trailed off and his eyes teared up.

I reached over and patted his hand. "How many others besides you survived?"

He shook his head. "I don't know, Vivienne, I just don't know. And there's no way to tell, really. Some of the bodies didn't necessarily have to be one of us. Even a human caught in that explosion would burn and shatter. I do not want to think that I'm the only one who made it. But it's been almost five hours since the blast, the sun's been down for at least half an hour, and I would think that the survivors would make their way here. It was the only place I could think of to run to."

He gave me a look out of the corner of his eyes. "I really thought that I had lost everyone, even you. But you were not there. So maybe others were not there as well. And maybe they have not yet heard the news."

"Claude?" A horrible thought struck me, one I did not want to give voice to.

"Yes?"

"Did you see Monique?"

"Yes."

"And so she is safe? Why didn't she come here with you?"

His face twisted up and he began to cry. Red-tinged tears streamed down his face and he made no effort to pat them off. "She's gone, Vivienne."

"No."

"She's gone, Vivienne. I saw her. She ran out of the wreckage ahead of me, burst into flames, and fell to the pavement. I wanted to get to her, to save her, but when my own skin began to smolder, my self-preservation instincts must've kicked in. All I could think of was to run and hide from the sun."

"Not Monique." If I said it long enough and strong enough, then it would be true. And she would not be dead. "Oh, please, oh, please, not Monique." The words were a wail of anguish and a prayer. "Not Monique."

"I'm sorry, Vivienne. There was nothing that could be done. She's gone." A great torrent of anger rose up within me and I could find no words with which to express it. Instead I found myself transforming into my white lioness form; no words were needed for this aspect of myself to show her rage.

I do not know how others of my kind see their transformations, as they are extremely private experiences rarely shared with anyone. But I visualized the events, as if standing outside of them and watching, in my human form, while still a part of my consciousness lingered in the creature into which I had changed. As if seeing through two sets of eyes, I both saw and acted upon my anger, slashing furniture, draperies, gouging out huge sections of the desk, the bar. Claude sat on what was left of the sofa not moving, not speaking, barely daring to draw a breath. He was smart in this. It did not pay to interfere.

When I had finished, I gave a great leap across the room and landed on top of my desk. I opened my mouth and a huge howling roar came out. Claude covered his ears and shivered.

And then the rage passed. Or more correctly the need to express it was gone. Deep within me, the anger still burned on and I intended to feed my enemies to its ravaging, deadly flames.

The lioness stretched, shaking off the tattered remains of my clothing. A shudder ran under her pale fur. And in just a split second I found myself crouched on the top of my desk, naked and shivering. Claude remained where he was, staring straight ahead, not moving a muscle.

I gave a bitter laugh as I went into the back room for more clothes. "I am done, Claude, you can breathe now."

I turned on the television as I dressed. "You can come in, Claude, if you'd like," I called out to him. "I want to see the news."

He squeezed his way through the narrow entrance, looking around. "Nice," he said, "much nicer than my hole in the Westwood."

"This place was just a cell when Max had it. Took a little bit of work to make it livable. It's serviceable; I just wish there'd been room for a bath." I couldn't believe we were making small talk about the decorating of my room at such a time. But it filled the empty spaces and made the tragedy seem less real.

He nodded. "Yeah, I can see that. But still it's nice. I should try to do something to make mine homier. But I'd always had that room over at Cadre—"

"Hush," I said, not to stop talk of the event, but because the news was starting and I didn't want to miss a word.

"Good evening, this is Bob Smith with the news. Our breaking story tonight—the bombing of one of New York City's finest restaurants, the Imperial. Terri Hamilton is at the site of the emergency. Terri?"

The view on the screen switched to the night street outside the restaurant. "Thanks, Bob. As you can see around me"—and the camera panned on the still-smoking wreckage—"this was one of the most devastating explosions ever witnessed in this city. Police are still not sure about the cause of the explosion, but they are sure"—and she began walking across the street to where there was a huge hole blown out of the sidewalk—"that the highest concentration of explosives was buried four or five stories below street level And that when it went off at approximately twelve noon today it triggered a chain reaction from smaller devices hidden on different levels.

"At first it was thought to be a gas main explosion, but the possibilities now of this having been an accident are very remote."

"So this was a deliberate act?" Bob's voice sounded smug, as if he'd like to say that he knew it all the time.

"Yes, Bob. A previously unknown terrorist group calling themselves simply 'the Others' contacted police shortly after the blast to accept credit. We have a tape of their statement." She paused, looking at first confident and then confused, nodding to someone standing out of view of the camera and giving a nervous laugh to cover the silence. "We had a tape of their statement, but apparently we are experiencing technical difficulties with it."

"Damn." I whispered the word, then breathed a silent thanks to Max and his journals. At least we had a place to start.

"People of New York City." Terri was reading the terrorist statement now from a slip of paper she'd been given. Her hands trembled slightly. "In time you will thank us for this violence. We shall not rest until every last member of the Cadre is exterminated."

"Shit." I turned around and looked at Claude. He was now sitting on my bed, his hands pressed up against his damaged face.

"Who the hell are these people, Vivienne?"

I held up a hand; the story was still running. ". . . found out that the Cadre, on paper at least, is a group of entrepreneurs who have been operating in New York City since at least the turn of the last century. Very little is known of them. Now rumors and speculations are flying about what this group really is. And as crazy as it may sound, ladies and gentlemen, it seems now that this organization is actually an international group of . . ." Terri paused, giving the next word its full effect. "Vampires."

I turned off the television and stood for a while staring at the blank screen. "That cinches it. It's over, Claude. It was such a wonderful life while it lasted. Now we'll need to pack up and move on. No more relying on the disbelief of humans; they have proof now. The dead bodies of our kind that they hauled away will no doubt tell them all they need to know."

The phone rang in the next room. "Claude," I said calmly, "get that for me, will you? Tell them I'll be right there."

"Hello? Yes, Miss Griffin, she's here. Me? This is Claude. You remember me, don't you?" He paused. "So far as I know, just myself and Miss Courbet." He paused again. "Yes, it was as bad as the news reported, or worse. And no one really knows why this happened."

I walked out into the office and held my hand out for the phone.

"Here she is, Miss Griffin. Nice talking to you."

"Deirdre?"

"Hello, Vivienne. I see that Claude and his impeccable manners escaped the explosion. And I am so pleased that you are still alive. Mitch and I cannot believe this is happening; when we heard the reports we feared the worst. Who are these people and what do they have against the Cadre? It almost sounds as if they know who and what we are."

"They do, Deirdre." I heard her make a whispered comment to someone else, I presumed Mitch, there with her.

"Mitch says hang in there, Viv. We're catching a plane there as soon as we can arrange it. Where will you be?"

"Probably at the club. We're at least protected here from the crowd. Everything is still sealed off from the murder."

"Murder? Now that is something I had not heard of."

"You remember Jules?"

I could hear the smile in her voice. "Oh, yes, the ever so handsome Jules."

I sighed. "Yes. But not so handsome anymore, I fear. Someone drove a stake through his heart on the dance floor of the club last night."

"Jesus." Deirdre took in a deep breath and I heard low whispers from her end of the line. There was a pause then and the next voice I heard was Mitch's. "Viv? Are you okay? And do they know who did it?"

"At this point, I think it is safe to assume it is this group called 'the Others.' Have you heard of them? Has Deirdre?"

"No. But if that is who is responsible, it's a bigger group than we can know and their members must be everywhere. I killed someone just the other night who tried to kill us. And Lily called to say that they'd attempted the same thing with her and Victor." He gave a small chuckle. "That girl is something."

"Victor. Of course. Damn it. Victor." I hit my forehead with the palm of my hand. "Victor knows."

"What?"

"Victor knows about the Others, Mitch. Meet us in New Orleans."

Chapter 30

New Orleans, present day

The bar was dark. And empty.

"Are you sure this is the right place, Claude?"

Claude set our luggage on the floor. Looking around, he pulled out a pack of matches to read the cover and nodded. "The sign out front said the Blackened Orchid, didn't it?"

"Yes, I think so."

"Then it's the right place."

A voice called out from behind the swinging kitchen doors. "We're closed right now. And I hate to be rude." The figure came through into the bar section. "But I wish you'd leave anyway."

I stood amazed. So this was Lily. A small girl, just about an inch or so taller than I, and she was painfully thin, with her red hair cropped so short it was almost a crew cut. But despite all the differences, it was like looking into the face of Deirdre. I shook my head and looked her in the eye. "I did not really believe them when they said you looked exactly like her."

"Well, they were right," she said, combing her fingers through her hair. "Now get out."

"Lily? You can't . . ." Claude moved up to the bar.

She laughed. "I saw you there, Claude. How on earth could I miss you?" She gave a little cry and leaned over the bar, reaching out and softly touching his burned face. "That looks horrible, does it hurt?"

He shrugged. "It's healing quickly."

Lily smiled. "Cool, isn't it? How that happens?"

I gave a polite little cough and she glanced at me, then looked back at Claude. "And since you are here, then this must he Vivienne Courbet. And I'm very pleased to meet her and to see you again, but still you'll need to leave. Victor." As she said the name her voice softened and I felt an ache rise up in my throat. "Well, he's not doing so well right now. After that attack the other night. You heard about that, right?"

"Yes." I gave her a smile. "And that is why we are here."

She turned to me and bared her teeth. "Oh, yes, you smile and lie very prettily, Vivienne. And ordinarily, I'd let myself be convinced. But you see, I heard from my mother and Mitch. You are here because you need Victor's help. But he's not going to be able to help you, not tonight and not if he gets upset again."

"Lily, if you would only let us see—"

"No way, Claude. It's not going to happen. I'm sympathetic to your cause, of course, and I sure as hell don't want any more raving terrorist lunatics breaking in here and threatening Victor with a pointed stick. These Others, whoever the hell they are, need to be stopped. But in all honesty, Victor will be of no use to you now. So"—she crossed her arms in front of her black T-shirt and looked me dead in the eye—"I suggest you take your cute little French ass out of here for now and I'll call you when he's able to talk."

I stared at her for a whole minute in disbelief. How dare she? Didn't she know who I was? Didn't my over three hundred years of life experience mean anything to her?

And then she smiled. "Please," she said, "he's really bad tonight. But he'll get better, he always does. And then we'll help."

I started to giggle and when she joined me the tension in the air vanished. "I apologize, Lily, I hadn't realized Victor was that bad."

She looked suspiciously close to tears. "Ordinarily, he's good. You'd never know he wasn't quite right from looking at him. You know, maybe better than any, how he is. Weren't you the one"—now her eyes were angry—"who had him confined at that Cadre place?"

I sighed. "It wasn't really my choice. And he really wasn't confined. I knew that. I doubt he harbors any bad feeling toward me on that count."

"True. He seems very fond of you. But just last night I heard him talking to Max. Max? What's that all about?"

"Do you not know?" I looked at her and raised an eyebrow. "Max was Victor's—"

"Oh, I know the story." She interrupted me and started lining up the glasses and bottles behind the bar. "Believe me, Vivienne, I know the story. But I'm scared if he sees you, it'll set all of those memories off again. He's stored up an incredibly large amount of bad memories. And sometimes he's not sure what is real and what is memory."

Lily kept fussing with the glasses until she knocked two of them over. "Damn it." She took out a towel and swept the mess into a wastebasket. Then she set the towel down and stopped to meet my eyes. "Don't you see?" she whispered. "He's all I have. I can't let him go."

I wanted to cross over the bar and give her a hug. I wanted to take her into my arms and kiss her and soothe her and tell her that everything would be all right. But I knew that was a lie. Hadn't I said the same thing to Monique countless times?

"I'm sorry," I said, "I do understand. Do you know where we're staying?"

She nodded and gave me a small wry grin. "My mother made me write it down."

I nodded. "Good for her. Call me. But do not wait too long. I have the feeling the Others will not be quite so concerned with Victor's well-being."

Claude turned to me as we climbed into our taxi. "What now?"

"Now, we lie low and hope Victor gets better before the Others manage to kill him. You can help me read through Max's journals in the meantime, just in case." I gave him my most rehearsed innocent smile. "I brought the last couple of hundred years' worth with me."

He groaned and I laughed.

"Where to?" the driver said, pushing the little meter flag down. The time began ticking away.

"The Hotel of Souls, please."

The hotel staff was waiting for us when we arrived and checked us in like royalty. Not surprising, really, since I owned a 75 percent share of the operation. But it was more than that. Many of the night staff were also members of the Cadre and all were worried that a similar incident could happen here. A legitimate concern, but since I had told no one but Sam that I was leaving the city, I thought that the hotel would be safe enough. Anyone who cared to investigate it could easily find out that there was a connection between this place and the Cadre, though, and so it wouldn't be safe for all that long. And neither would any of the other thousands of places owned by the Cadre or Cadre members.

"No place to run and no place to hide," I said to Claude on the elevator. "We are going to have to start living by our wits and our instincts again."

He flashed me a sad smile. "Some of us always have."

"True, but in the past few years, we all have gotten fat and complacent."

Claude laughed. "That may be true. But some of us have always been fat."

I looked over at him and smiled. I do not think he had any

idea of the seriousness of this situation. Or perhaps he did and had the same attitude as I did. Whatever his feelings, I was grateful for his solid comfort. "I did better than I knew with you, Claude. Thank you."

He blushed and I laughed and the elevator door opened. The bellboy was waiting there for us with our luggage on a cart.

He checked Claude in first and then walked me through the adjoining door into the largest suite available. "This will do quite nicely," I said, giving him a twenty-dollar bill. "Thank you," and I hesitated on his name.

"Raoul."

What a fortunate omen, I thought, and smiled, liking him already. "Thank you, Raoul."

"It's an honor, Miss Courbet. You are aware, I'm sure, of the amenities of these rooms. But let me reacquaint you with the more pertinent features. The windows," and he pulled aside the drapes, "are fixed with heavy shutters so that the morning light will not disturb you." He opened the shutters now, showing me the clasps. "It's a lovely view," he said, "and many of our clientele prefer to keep them open at night, closing them only when they wish to sleep."

I nodded and he continued, gesturing toward the bathroom. "All of the water gauges are set to extra hot for your bathing pleasure. And"—he walked over to the foot of the bed, opening the large ornate chest—"should you require extra safeguarding, you will find this feature most acceptable."

"Everything is perfect, Raoul. *Merci.*"

"I'm happy you are pleased. And now let me get you settled in a little bit more comfortably."

I was perfectly capable, of course, of unpacking my own cases. But he was young and courteous and handsome and I liked the look of him in his red and black uniform.

I lounged on top of the bed and watched him unpack my case, neatly hanging up clothes on hangers and laying the rest into lavender-sacheted drawers. "So tell me, Raoul, do you like your job?"

He turned from where he was setting up the laptop computer I'd brought with me at Sam's suggestion. "Yes, I do. This place pays twice as much as every other hotel in the area. Which is, I suppose, why it's so hard to get a job here. But it was worth all the effort. Especially when one gets to serve beautiful ladies."

I smiled. "And do you work the nights exclusively or do you do day shifts as well?" My question was more than idle curiosity. If he worked days then he was human, serving here because he was what we called a donor. And I was hungry.

Never let it be said that Vivienne Courbet went to her doom on an empty stomach.

"I usually do the day shifts, Miss Courbet," he said with a sly smile, "but I switched with Louis for this week." He plugged in two of the cords from the laptop, one into the power switch and one into a phone jack. "And there, you are all set up and ready to go."

"Thank you, Raoul. You have been most helpful."

"Certainly." He started to open the door. "Oh, I almost forgot." He reached into his pocket and pulled out an envelope. "This fax came for you."

I glanced at it, from Sam most likely. *"Merci."*

Raoul put his hand to the doorknob, but turned around once again. "And should you wish to call for room service a little bit later on, don't hesitate to ask for me."

I watched him walk out of the room and close the door. "Delicious," I said as I got off the bed and went to the phone to dial Sam's number. As it rang, I looked in the mirror on the other side of the room. "Vivienne Courbet." I made a face at myself, rolling my eyes. "You are an evil, reprehensible woman."

Chapter 31

S am had wanted to accompany us, but had been called back into the psychiatric hospital on an emergency.

"There's just no way now, Vivienne. All of a sudden everyone here has gone completely berserk. I have never, in all my years of practice, seen anything quite like it. It's almost as if someone threw a switch inside these people's minds. We've called the entire staff in to deal with it and I daresay no one will be leaving the building until it's all under control."

I had filled him in on everything that I could before we left the city, including the involvement of the Others and how it was likely that they'd ordered assassinations on both Deirdre and Mitch as well as Lily and Victor. "They seem to know everything we do, Sam. I'm not entirely sure what any of us can do to stop them. Unless Victor can help."

"I hope he can, Vivienne. I don't want to lose you, not like this, at least. I know it's inevitable that . . ." His voice had trailed off. Had I been with him, I'd have kissed him and told him he was being silly. But there was no way I could do that through the phone. And he wasn't being silly; instead his assessment of our relationship was uncannily accurate and that made me sad.

"Take the laptop with you, okay? I'll fax instructions to you later on at the hotel and you can at least set yourself up an e-mail account. The phone service here is down—we think some of the patients cut the wires—and the battery on this cell phone is starting to fade. At least the computers are still working—since they're newer, they run off of different lines brought in to the building at a different place . . ."

His voice had faded away. I had no idea how to set up an e-mail account or even how to turn the stupid laptop on. And he was expecting hourly updates via e-mail? *"Merde!"* I had slammed the phone down and called for Claude to get us a taxi to the airport.

Not surprisingly, there was no answer at the hospital. I sighed and looked at the laptop in disgust. It had taken me many years to get accustomed to talking on the telephone. And now there was this.

I opened the envelope that Raoul had given me. And read the instructions Sam had sent. Twice. I usually did not like admitting to my ignorance, but I seemed to have no choice.

"Change, Vivienne," I said to myself quietly as I walked over to knock on the adjoining room door. "Change and adapt—it's what keeps you alive." I knocked again louder this time and called, "Claude?"

"Yes?" He opened the door, patting the burned side of his face with a towel. He was wearing his pants with the suspender straps down and had only his T-shirt to cover his chest. Another towel was wrapped around his neck. I had interrupted his toilette, apparently. But when he pulled the towel down from his face, I noticed that the burned strips of skin were gone.

I put a hand up and touched his cheek gently. "Oh, that looks so much better."

He smiled. "And you can only imagine how much better it feels." He got a wicked glint in his eye. "I must confess, though, that I'm surprised and just a little disappointed in you, Vivienne."

No more Miss Courbet, I noticed. Good. Since we were two, and perhaps the only, survivors of the explosion, formality was hardly needed. "Why would you be disappointed, Claude?"

"I'd have figured you'd be still busy with the lovely Raoul."

I gave him a little slap on the arm. "He's for later, of course. Now, I have an important question for you."

"Shoot."

"Are you . . ." I paused. "Damn, what is that phrase?" I thought for a minute, then snapped my fingers. "Literate. Yes, that is it. Are you computer literate?"

"These days, who isn't?"

I laughed. "I am not, for one. But I am pleased that you know something of it. Could you help me? Sam has faxed me instructions but it seems to be filled with nothing but initials. ISP? IRC? What is that?" I shrugged and opened my arms wide in a gesture of helplessness.

"No problem," he said and pulled the chair out from under the desk, sitting down. His large hands practically obliterated the keyboard, but he was as agile here as he was on the dance floor.

By the time he was done, I knew enough to turn on the computer, initiate the auto-dialer, and send e-mail to the one and only address in my book. Sam had already set up an e-mail account for me and my address was, simply enough, vivienne-courbet at vampmail.com.

"No, no," Claude said for perhaps the hundredth time. "You can't write the *at* out. You need to put in the little symbol." And he showed me.

"Thank you, Claude."

"Now," he said, getting up from the chair and gesturing for me to sit, "you can surf the Web all night. Or all day if you keep your shutters closed."

I laughed and sat down. "I do not think so, Claude. But should I choose to do such a thing, how would I go about it?"

He showed me how to open the browser and search for things I wanted to see.

I giggled. "But this is delightful. I could find out almost anything, couldn't I? Just by typing a few letters?"

He gave me an indulgent smile. "Don't forget to close the shutters, Vivienne. Good night." I nodded and waved a hand at him, barely hearing his laugh.

I clicked on the ADVANCED SEARCH button and typed the words *the Others* into the little box. There were literally millions of matches so I set about refining the search to a more manageable number. No matter how much I tried to cut the total down, it didn't matter. The words were too common and

any attempt to pinpoint anything but the most recent news stories was wasted effort. I wasn't sure what I expected. It wasn't
as if international terrorists would set up their own Web site.
But still I searched, becoming more and more frustrated.

Two hours later I threw my hands up in exasperation, when
yet another likely choice turned out to be irretrievable. I looked
at the clock by the bedside and turned off the computer, shaking
my head. "Ridiculous," I said, "one could sit and starve and
never realize it. And still never find what it is one is looking
for."

Raoul was off duty by the time I called, but he had been waiting for me. "I'll be right up," he said.

"No, actually"—I looked around the room—"I'd much rather
go out for a while. Would you be willing to serve as my escort?"

"Gladly. You don't need to ask me twice."

"Fine, I'll be right there."

I went into the bathroom and splashed hot water on my face,
brushed my teeth, and combed through my hair. Then I changed
into a skintight black catsuit, boots, and a fuzzy pink angora
bolero jacket. Checking in the mirror, I nodded first, then smiled
and blew myself a kiss. "Not bad for an old woman."

Raoul was waiting for me in the lobby. He'd changed into a
pair of black jeans, a T-shirt, and a black leather jacket. "I'd almost given up on you," he said, as I got off the elevator.

"Would you believe me if I told you I'd lost track of time on
the Internet?"

He held the front door open for me. "Sure. It happens all the
time. Where to?"

I laughed. "Since this seems to be a night for new things, take
me somewhere I have never been before, somewhere different."

We started walking down the street. Even in December, the
air was warm and lush with a deep floral scent.

"And just how am I supposed to know where you've been
and what you've done, Vivienne?"

The significance of his switch to my first name did not go unnoticed. He was in charge now. I reached over and tucked my arm around his. "Easily, Raoul. Assume I've seen it all and done it all and start from there."

"Perfect," he said, "I know just the place."

I peered inside the bar to which Raoul had brought me. It smelled of urine and vomit and whiskey. A hand-printed sign hung on the wall next to the door. EXOTIC DANCER WANTED. MUST BE WILLING TO WORK FOR TIPS. INQUIRE WITHIN.

"Perfect?" I gave him a dubious look.

He chuckled. "In that I'm almost a hundred percent certain you've never been here before, yeah, it is perfect. That was the criteria, as I remember."

"True. I should have been more careful in phrasing my request. But how was I to know you would take me so literally?" But I smiled to let him know that I was only joking.

We walked in and Raoul found us a corner booth, ordering a bottle of red wine as he walked past the bar.

"So," I said after we sat down, "what is special about this place?"

"For one thing, half of the women in here are really men."

I glanced around the room, then gave him a sharp look, unsure as to whether he was making a joke. "Really?" I asked cautiously.

"Really. Not a big deal, I'm sure, to someone like you." Apparently he mistook my tone, thinking I'd meant to be sarcastic when I was merely fascinated. I let it go.

"And?"

"And in about"—he looked at his watch—"oh, a half hour or so, the voodoo guy will show up."

"Voodoo guy?"

"Sure. This is New Orleans, remember. The home of voodoo. Although they call it different names now. It's fascinating, don't you think?"

A waiter approached our table, put down a little bowl filled with some sort of crunchy snack sticks. "Raoul." He nodded, setting the bottle of wine and two glasses on the table. "And a lovely little friend." He smiled at me. "New in town, honey? You don't look familiar. And somehow I don't think you're here to audition as a dancer. Too bad."

I laughed. "I'm not a dancer, I fear. And I'm not exactly new, Monsieur, but certainly not a resident. I'm only here for a few days and Raoul agreed to show me the sights."

"I'm sure he did." He winked at me. "And no wonder. Enjoy."

The wine was hideous and cheap. But I drank it, not wanting to hurt Raoul's feelings.

He, however, had no such problem telling the truth. "God, this stuff is horrible. I apologize, Vivienne. You must think I'm some sort of yokel or something bringing you here. But I assure you, the voodoo guy is worth it."

"I certainly hope so. For this I have given up an evening in my room all alone trying to find out how to make a million by selling e-mail addresses. Or searching for things that do not seem to exist."

He laughed and took another sip of his wine. "It sounds like you are finding New Orleans a little bit less than exciting. You should have been here a month ago."

"Oh? Why?"

"Halloween. This town may not be as sharp and modern as New York City, but we certainly know how to throw a masquerade."

I shivered, reminded of Jules. "Let us talk of something different."

"Sure thing. Or we could just leave and go back to the hotel."

"Later. I want to see this voodoo man you keep talking about. Is he any good? Or more importantly, is he for real?"

"He's good, yeah. Very good. But real?" He shrugged. "I'm not sure. Before I settled here, I'd have laughed at you for asking that question. I didn't believe in any of it. But now, ever since working at the hotel, I see things in a new light." He sat staring at the door for a minute. "It's a lot different than I ever thought.

You know what I mean? All the supernatural stuff, it's a lot different than what you read in books. Or"—and he smiled at me and winked—"what you see on the Internet."

He looked back at the door and then at his watch. "Right on time," he said. "Angelo is here."

Chapter 32

I turned in my chair and stared toward the man who just walked through the doorway. He was old and wizened, with a two or three days' growth of grizzled beard and the most pronounced bowlegs I had ever seen. As he walked into the bar and started to a table, I caught a whiff of his scent—cheap whiskey and smoke.

"He certainly looks the part," I said to Raoul. "What does he do?"

"Buy him a drink and he'll tell your fortune. And if you pay him well enough, I've heard that he has other tricks. Talk around here is his spell repertoire is the biggest in New Orleans. Just don't ask him about Greg. We've all heard that story more than enough times."

He smiled, though, and I could tell that he had great affection for this man.

"Let's buy him a drink, shall we?"

He stood up and waved to Angelo to catch his eye. The man chuckled and nodded, walking to our table.

"Raoul. An' a sweet little *fille*. What can I do for you, my boy? Seem to me you got everythin' you need here already."

"Vivienne would like to have her fortune told, 'Lo."

He slapped his knee and gave a huge guffaw. "Boy, you know nothin', that for sure. Woman got a face like this one, she don' need her fortune told. But for a glass of gin, I do it, you know I do it." He tapped Raoul on the shoulder. "Come on, Raoul, slide outta there, get goin', and get that gin while I make friendly with Miss Vivienne here."

Raoul looked at me questioningly.

"I am fine, Raoul. Go get the man his drink."

He moved out and Angelo sat down across from me. "Give me your hands, Miss Vivienne," He chuckled to himself about something. I held my hands out, palms up, and he took the left one into his hands. "You can put that other one down now," he said, "I got the one I need."

He stared at my palm for a while, then turned it over and looked at the back of it. "You don' really want your fortune told, do you?"

I shrugged. "You can do it if you wish. I won't believe what you have to tell me anyway." And I laughed to soften the words. "It is not that I don't believe in you, you see. It is that—"

He finished my sentence. "You prefer to make your own fortune. Very wise, Miss Vivienne. But one as old as you should be wise."

I jumped, pulling my hand back from him. "How can you know how old I am, Angelo?"

"In your case, pretty lady, the years are in your eyes. And"— he tapped himself on the side of the head—"this ol' bokor has ways to tell."

"Here you go, 'Lo." Raoul handed him a small glass filled with gin. "Just the way you like it."

He bolted it down. "Thank you, young Raoul. Now make yourself disappear for a while. I need to ask Miss Vivienne some questions."

I nodded to Raoul and he went back to the bar. I watched him for a second, then shrugged.

"Now," Angelo started, "I can see you had a long life so far; maybe more than you should have. And you keep on losin' those you care for."

He leaned a little bit closer to me. I could smell the gin on his breath. "But what you don' know is that these people ain' necessarily gone." He gave a wheezing laugh. "No, they ain' very far from you at all." Then he grew serious and grabbed my hands again, gripping them tightly. His voice grew softer, but as he continued to talk, it was all I could hear.

"There's one there as blond as you. I catch hisself' starin' at you over the long years. He not quite the same man he was, there somethin' diff'rent there in him. Somethin' powerful and evil—growin' and reachin' and graspin' for more than he should. Oh, this man, he want and he want and he never rest.

"And a dark-haired girl, she there too with him. Starin' at a dead baby and a glass full of blood. She love you if he let her, but don' you know, he won'. There be no love in this man. No love for you, no love for her, no love for that dead baby. A cold man. He not like me, Miss Vivienne. And no, not even like you. He somethin' diff'rent, somethin' new. Somethin' *other* than what he should be."

I gave a nervous laugh. "That is all very interesting, Angelo, and I did know a blond-haired man and a dark-haired girl, but they are dead."

"There's dead and then there's dead. And some don' rest as well as others. And I shouldn't have to tell such as you about such as that, should I?"

"So what should I do?" I didn't actually ask the question of him, but he answered anyway.

"For now, you can take that boy Raoul back to your room and each of you get what you need. Ain' love, but it do you for now. Then you can seek out trouble and look for the blond man and the dark-haired girl. Or you can do nothin' and they will seek you. One thing I know for sure, it be better if you find them first."

He slid out of the seat then and stood up, smiling at me. "No matter what you think, Miss Viv, you a good woman. A little like a diamond and a little like a rose. I wish you love and a life no longer than you can be happy in." He kissed my cheek, laughed, and walked away.

Raoul came back. "That was quite a fortune. What did he say?"

I shrugged. "You know how these people are, Raoul, they hit on a few specifics that apply to everyone and hint wildly at everything else." It was such a blatant lie that I couldn't look him in the eyes. But he accepted my answer.

"What would you like to do now?"

"Take me back to the hotel."

Raoul was as sweet as I had thought he would be—an ardent lover, confident and skilled, he explored my body with great enthusiasm, welcomed my bite at his neck, and did all the right things in the proper order. But I was out of sorts, distant and distracted. He rolled off of me finally with a sigh.

"You do know, Vivienne, that this exercise works better when both parties are present." He reached over and stroked my cheek with the back of his hand.

I gave him a twisted smile. "I have heard that. I'm sorry, Raoul, it was nothing you did. Or did not do. It is I who has the problem."

"We could try it again tomorrow," he said a little too eagerly. "Maybe after a good day's rest you'll feel differently."

"Perhaps. We shall see."

He laughed. "That was a no. I've heard that phrase before." He leaned over and kissed me full on the lips. "If you change your mind, call me."

After he dressed and left with another kiss, I got out of bed and locked all the doors and windows, fastening the shutters tightly. Then I took a long hot shower, put on my nightgown and lifted the lid on the coffin at the foot of the bed, looking inside. It looked comfortable enough, but I wondered how it would feel to sleep in the open, without those confining walls around me. Dropping the lid, I turned out the lights and crawled back into the bed. The sheets were still warm and smelled of Raoul, a comforting human scent. I fell asleep quickly, not even giving myself time to ponder what that Angelo had said.

Chapter 33

I woke up in a state of panic, completely unaware of where I was. The room was pitch-black, with the only exception being the glowing numerals of the bedside clock. Glancing at it, I relaxed and remembered. I was in my room in the Hotel of Souls, New Orleans. And it was past sundown.

Sleeping outside of the coffin seemed to have done me no particular harm. I felt well rested and relatively prepared for what the night might bring. Stretching, I rolled over a bit and smelled the pillow next to my head. The scent of Raoul was fainter now, but still there. But it wasn't as much of a comfort as it might once have been. I thought for a while about why this might be. Was I growing so old that I was losing my passion?

As I stretched again I put my hand under his pillow and touched something dried, something scratchy. I pulled it out and saw that it was a bundle of lavender and violets tied in a red satin ribbon. I smiled. I didn't remember him buying this; he must have snuck it in while I wasn't looking.

Across the room a little green light was flashing, indicating a voice mail waiting. I jumped out of bed, thinking it might be a message from Sam.

And I stopped, midway between the bed and the phone. Sam? Could it be that I was missing him more than I'd expected? Could it be that I cared for him more than I knew? It could very well explain my reaction to Raoul last night. Not a lost passion, then, but a directed one.

I picked up the phone and pressed the MESSAGE button. To my disappointment it was not from Sam. "Viv? It's Mitch. We're here, stupid bloody airlines lost Deirdre's bag and we almost had to spend the day hiding out in rest rooms in the airport. Fine thing, that." He laughed. "Nice hotel, by the way." There was a pause. "Oh, Deirdre says we'll meet you in the lobby bar around seven or so. She talked to Lily and . . ."

There was a beep and the message was over. And he hadn't called back to complete the thought. I gave a laugh; knowing the two of them, they were most likely in the middle of a romantic interlude when they remembered to call. *Finish the message? Maybe later.* I can hear his voice saying the words.

I opened up the laptop and turned it on. Amazingly enough, I managed to connect to the Internet and find my e-mail. I smiled. Sam had sent me a letter. I opened it and read it.

As my first e-mail, it really wasn't anything special; he said nothing that I hadn't heard him say in person. Seeing his words in print, though, made them seem more real. It was a short letter; I knew he was having a difficult time at the hospital, so when I imagined him sitting down at his desk and taking the time from his hellish job to write, it made me feel wanted.

> *Hi, Sweetness. Glad you got there safely and glad Claude was able to show you how to use your birthday present. I'll bet you are surfing the Web right now. :) Keep in touch and remember to be careful. Love, Sam.*

I put my hand up to the screen and ran my fingers over his words. Then I laughed at my folly and got dressed to meet Deirdre and Mitch.

It wasn't until I was walking out the door that I realized I should have sent him a reply. So I turned around and sat back at the desk. It took me longer than I would have thought to send the resulting message.

> *Mon Cher, I enjoyed your e-mail very much. They say a girl never forgets her first and you were mine. I am taking care and will be meeting Deirdre and Mitch in just a few minutes. I send you many many kisses and hugs. And I miss you. Yours, Viv*

"Sorry to be late, Deirdre," I said as I sat down at the booth in the bar. "I had to send an e-mail. Where's Mitch?"

She looked at me. "Getting us a drink, I think." She looked across the room and spotted him, her face softening into a smile. "Yes, there he is." Then she blinked. "Did you say you were sending an e-mail?"

"*Oui.* I was sending e-mail." I sounded smug and was pleased at how easily the words came from my mouth.

"Is this a new development?"

I smiled. "Yes, Sam gave me a laptop for my birthday."

"So you liked the surprise?" Mitch set three glasses of wine on the table, leaned over, and gave me a kiss. Then he sat down next to her, draping his arm lightly over the back of the seat. She leaned into him slightly, making sure to maintain body contact. I sighed and wondered if my sister knew how lucky she was to have such a partner.

"He was telling us about it on the way to the airport last month and I have to admit we both wondered what you would do with it."

"I'd not have known if it were not for Claude." Then I put my hand to my mouth. "Oh, dear, I had forgotten about him. We will want him with us, I think, for whatever we will be doing."

Mitch got up again. "I'll ring his room."

Deirdre and I both sipped our wine while he was gone. "Oh, and I wanted to thank you for the lovely necklace you gave me. I love it."

She gave me a warm smile. "I thought you might."

"Wherever did you find it?"

"I had it made special for you, of course. It's not as good a present as Sam gave you, of course, nor near as useful. How is he?"

"Sam?" I felt my mouth curve into a smile. "He is fine, he was the one to whom I was sending the e-mail."

She gave me a curious look, and I sensed that she wanted to ask me about our relationship. I did not know what to say so I turned the tables on her. "I see that you and Mitch are together again. I am glad you were able to work it out. You have no idea how lucky you are in him."

"Oh, but I do." Her eyes glowed with affection. "He is everything I ever dreamed of, everything I have ever wanted. And he seems to feel the same. So it is possible, Vivienne, for our kind to hold together."

I wanted to ask her how she managed, but Mitch returned at that moment, took his spot next to her again, and the opportunity for girl talk was gone. Instead she gave a small laugh and jumped back to our earlier topic. "E-mail. I can't even imagine it. You must be a quick learner."

I laughed, the high-pitched peals filling the room. "After I get over the initial culture shock, yes, I suppose I am. While you, on the other hand," and I reached across the table and touched Mitch's hand, "you do not seem to be able to leave a complete message."

They exchanged a look. "I told you," Deirdre said, "that you should have called back and left the end of the message."

"Yes, dear," Mitch said meekly and they both laughed as if at a private joke. I smiled weakly, feeling as I always did in their presence, totally superfluous.

"So," I said politely, waiting a second or two for them to finish with their laughter, "you spoke with Lily? Will she let us see Victor?"

Deirdre nodded, her voice growing tight. "Yes, I spoke with Lily. And it was not easy. She tried to keep us away as vehemently as I hear she did you. But fortunately Victor was in the room when I called and he recognized my voice. He wants to meet with us in about an hour at the Orchid." She sighed and leaned farther into Mitch, running a hand on his thigh, seeking comfort, I thought. "That girl has got a chip on her shoulder a mile wide. But Victor is her soft spot. It's good to know that there is at least one person to whom she doesn't delight in saying no."

I smiled. "I liked her. She has great spirit."

"More than anyone needs," Deirdre said and I stifled a laugh. *And it's good to know that there's someone in the world who doesn't think you're perfect, Sister.* "No one can have too much spirit, especially at times like these." That thought sobered me. "Now, before we meet with Victor would you like to tell me what happened in England?"

"Starting without me?" Claude loomed over us and I looked up and smiled.

"Not at all, *mon chou,* please," and I patted the leather seat next to me, "have a seat and join us."

He laughed. "Even if I were able to get into there, Vivienne, how on earth would you pry me out again? No, I'll need a . . . yeah, there's one." He looked around, spotted a suitable chair and grabbed it, turning it around so that he could straddle it while leaning his arms on the upper rail. "Much better."

Mitch nodded to Claude and began his story. "There's not much to tell, actually. We had been at the pub to close up. It'd been a long night and we were anxious to get home so we weren't paying all that much attention. He was waiting inside the door. We never had a clue that he was there. No scent, no sound. He jumped at Deirdre first and that was his mistake. I snapped his neck before he even reached her." He leaned over and kissed her on the tip of the nose. "To be honest it all happened so quickly that at first we didn't realize what his weapon of choice was and when we did it was disconcerting. We've kept a fairly low profile there, not taking our victims too close to home and maintaining as normal-seeming a life as possible. And we'd been gone for so long. The implication that he knew we had moved back is frightening. I'd have preferred he'd been a common thief; at least that sort of crime is understandable. But this—" He looked around to see if anyone was nearby, but with the exception of us, the bar was deserted. Regardless, he lowered his voice. "This was a deliberate and concerted effort to kill vampires specifically. I don't like it."

"What did you do with the body?" Claude spoke up from his backward perch.

"Dumped it in an alley in the rough part of town and made it look like someone had attempted to rob him. He had no identification on him at all. No passport, no driver's license, nothing to give me any hint at all why he wanted to kill us. He didn't speak, so I can't even tell you if he was local or imported."

"And then we heard your news, Vivienne. And Lily's." Mitch shook his head and took a drink of his Scotch. "All of these are very much carefully timed and engineered events. To hear that it all may be a plan executed by some sort of international terrorist group doesn't come as a surprise to me."

"But why?" I asked the question, knowing of course that he would not have an answer. "Why kill us? And why now? It makes no sense, Mitch. We have, most of us, been around for centuries and despite all the books and movies about hunting us, very little of that has ever gone on. We lead our lives side by side with the humans and they never know we are there."

Deirdre nodded. "That's true. I have been wondering the same thing myself. Why us? And why now?"

Claude shrugged. "Don't ask me, I'm the new kid on the block. Mitch? Any thoughts?"

"I don't know, Claude. There must be a reason, there always is. But I'll be damned if I can figure it out. And"—he looked at his watch—"we had better get a cab or we'll be late to meet Victor."

Chapter 34

Victor met us at the front door of the Blackened Orchid. He looked like his old self; his eyes were clear and he stood erect and confident. In fact, he was so very much changed from the last time I had seen him that I stared at him a little too long.

"What's the matter, Vivienne?" he said, laughing at me and gesturing all of us into the bar. "You look as if you've seen a ghost."

"Not a ghost, Victor," I said, kissing him lightly on both cheeks. "Just someone who hasn't been around for a while. And

I for one am glad to have you back." I looked over to Lily where she stood, arms folded, behind the bar. "If this is your doing, Lily, I thank you."

She shrugged. "He woke up like this. Stubborn old man," and she gave him a tender smile to soften the words, "he wouldn't listen to me when I said that seeing all of you might not be a great idea."

"But of course it's a great idea, girl." Victor brushed at his black suede jacket. "It's a party of sorts. And Vivienne just loves a good party. Don't you, my dear?"

I smiled, not quite sure where he was going with this. But I had no doubt that this was the old Victor, the one who was capable of making me faint at our first meeting, simply by looking at me.

"And for our party we have a wonderful guest list. Deirdre and Mitch, two of our finest rogues." He nodded in their direction and Mitch scowled at him. "Pour Mitch a Scotch on the rocks, Lily, my dear, and give your mother and Vivienne a glass of that nice red wine we bought the other day. As for Claude." Victor clapped a hand on Claude's shoulder. "My former jailer, words cannot express how pleased I am to see you again. And in such fine mettle." He looked Claude up and down, then turned again to Lily. "I believe Claude's poison of choice is port. And while you're at it, please pour one for me."

He watched us all as we went to the bar to claim our drinks. "What is this all about?" I whispered to Lily but she just shrugged.

"I have no idea, Vivienne." She did not bother to lower her voice. "This is what I warned you about. He's worse today, but I couldn't keep you from coming. He was determined to see you all."

I nodded. "Victor," I said, sipping my wine, "can you tell us anything about the Others?"

He laughed and his eyes shifted around. "But I just did, Vivienne. There's Deirdre and Mitch and . . ." He stopped and shook his head, losing just a bit of his confidence, and my hopes for an easy solution plummeted. "But that's not what you wanted to know, is it? You wanted to know about the Others."

"Yes, Victor, that's it. Can you please tell us everything you know about the Others?" I made my voice as calm as possible; I saw now what Lily meant about him being difficult. Getting any information from Victor was going to be quite a task. I motioned to the others to move away and they did so, collecting in the far corner of the bar where Victor couldn't see them and be distracted.

"Think back," I urged. "It wasn't all that long ago, only a little over two hundred years. Do you remember Paris? The revolution? Max's journals mention a group called the Others that existed at that time."

"Yes." A wide smile crossed his face and his eyes focused again. "Max was always scratching away in those ridiculous journals. 'It's not as if anyone is ever going to read these, Max,' I would say. And he would get angry with me. He was always angry with me. Much of the time he was angry with me about you, Vivienne. You were such a lovely young thing then. So sweet, so innocent—he struggled so to try to keep you that way. But you wouldn't let him."

I snorted. "I? Innocent? I hardly think so. You must be thinking of some other time, some other Vivienne, perhaps?"

"Oh, but you were. That silly swan's head you were wearing and the way you danced and sang, you were so full of joy and youth and laughter." He paused for a second. "Max came dressed as a monk and I was the grim reaper. And you were a dancing swan." He chuckled to himself. "What was his name?"

I had a difficult time following his reasoning. "Whose name?"

"That man you danced with at the party. You must remember him, Vivienne. He was a doctor, I think. A handsome bastard in any event. And you, ah, you were particularly entranced with him, as I remember. And Max was furious."

"Eduard."

"And his last name was?"

"DeRouchard."

He snapped his fingers. "Yes. That was it exactly." His eyes glowed in triumph over such a simple memory and I sighed.

Poor man, that he should be reduced to this state. And poor us, should we not be able to get the information we needed.

Then the glow faded. "And you remember that we talked about the Others, don't you, Vivienne?"

"No."

"Yes, you do."

"No." I paused a second.

Victor smiled encouragingly. "Go on. I know you remember this. It was important."

I bit my lip. "Wait, I do remember that you spoke of getting all the others together and forming an organization to safeguard our lives and goals. And I laughed at you. But that was just a phrase, wasn't it? The others had been drawn there, by all the blood and the death. Just like carrion crows, you said."

He gave me a keen look. "If I said the Others, that is what I meant. Do not blame me if you did not understand."

"And did you meet with the Others, Victor? While you were in Paris?"

"Yes, I did. The evening after that silly party of yours. Max and I and Eduard and the rest of the Others all sat down—"

"No, Victor. Eduard cannot have been there. You must be getting it confused with the party. Eduard was at the party, that is true. And that is where you saw him. He wouldn't have been at your meeting."

"You were so young, Vivienne, so innocent. Max was angry that you were so trusting. He said he thought he'd taught you better, that after Diego, you would have learned your lesson." Victor's voice was trembling and Lily came over next to him. She picked up his hand and put it to her mouth, kissing the palm, and he smiled at her.

"Let's go sit down, okay?" she said. "And then we can talk some more. But at least we'll all be more comfortable that way."

Victor looked at me and smiled. "You see the way it is, Vivienne? She orders me around. I should spank her like the young impertinent girl she is."

"Later, darling." She stuck her tongue out at him and he gave a loud laugh.

Deirdre gave a small cough and I looked over at her. Even in the dimness of the bar lights I could see that she was blushing and I chuckled to myself. What an interesting evening this was turning out to be.

Lily settled us in at a small round table. She set another glass of port in front of him and caught my eye. "Keep going." She mouthed the words to me over his head. "He's fine."

"I have to apologize, Victor. I do not remember what happened at this meeting. And I do not remember that Eduard was there."

"Of course you don't remember. You weren't at the meeting. But Eduard was. Of this I am quite sure. He had to be. He is the leader of the Others."

"Eduard? How could he have been? He was human."

Victor laughed. "You were so young, Vivienne, and so innocent. He is not a human. He is not a vampire, either. But a combination of both, a crossbreed, if you will. The Others are just exactly what their name implies, something other than what previously existed.

"Somehow they had learned how to prolong human life, but without having any of the bad aspects of the vampire, primarily that of the detrimental effects of sunlight. And they could go for much longer periods of time before they needed to feed.

"Unfortunately, the process only kept the mind alive indefinitely. Eventually the body would begin to deteriorate and they would need to transfer their life force into a human baby, preferably one fathered by themselves. The baby would then grow at an accelerated rate and within ten years become that same being." He shook his head. "I do not profess to understand how this was done; all I'd ever managed to learn was that the process was possible. They refused to share their knowledge."

"But Eduard can't have been one of them. His body showed no signs of deterioration."

"It would not necessarily show at first. But I remember that they all bore a scar."

My heart stopped. "A scar?"

"Yes, across their throat. From the transfer, you see. Eduard bears that scar even today, I'm sure. And I'm surprised that you never noticed it."

"But you speak of him as if he were still alive. He is dead, Victor, I saw his body. Executed."

"Yes, that was Max's idea, I fear. It seemed a simple solution at the time, eliminate the rival organization's leader and the rest would succumb. And Max hated him for the influence he had over you. But, we hadn't known at the time, that one of Eduard's breeders had given birth recently. Nor that she was skilled enough to effect the transfer with one who had been dead for some time. But she did and she was and in just a short time he was back. The breeder stayed with him, I believe. You knew her. What was her name?"

I sat for a while and stared at Victor. How could he have known all of this for as long as he did and not tell me? But I knew that at least some of what he was telling me was true. It explained so much I had never understood.

"Monique?" I had not meant to say her name. I did not want to know.

"Yes, that was the breeder's name."

"But she was with *me,* she was my friend. She loved me."

Victor laughed. "You were so young and so innocent, Vivienne."

I sighed. I was getting very weary of hearing that phrase.

"Don't you see?" Victor continued. "She gave you exactly what Eduard wanted her to, no less and no more. She was his creature from the first. And to the last. Everything that you did at that time and everything that you felt for both of them had been forced upon you by Eduard. Testing, I believe, whether his powers over us were developed enough to take control."

I closed my eyes and bit my lip. It was as if someone had torn down my life and left it in rubble on the ground. Everything that I thought I knew was wrong.

I thought Eduard had loved me and he had not. I thought Eduard had died, but he still lived. With the sole purpose of exterminating my kind. And Monique? I did not even want to think of the enormity of her betrayals.

"Oh, Victor," I whispered across the table to him, "why didn't you tell me? Don't you think I should have known?"

"There was no need for anyone to know. Max and I both feared that the Cadre would panic and overreact. I had control of the situation. And Monique seemed to have weaned herself away from Eduard's influence, so she was no danger to you or to us."

And what of Monique? When she had come back, it was at his command. She had stood by my side for the past ten years, watching, learning, and reporting, no doubt, on all of the Cadre's activities. And she had done it all for him.

Suddenly Angelo's words from last night came back to me.

"*. . . She love you if he let her, but don' you know, he won'. There be no love in this man. No love for you, no love for her, no love for that dead baby. A cold man. He not like me, Miss Vivienne. And no, not even like you. He somethin' diff'rent, somethin' new. Somethin' other than what he should be. . . .*"

"He knew all of this. How could he know?" My voice sounded small and frightened in the darkness.

"Who?"

"I met this man in a bar last evening—he called himself a bokor. He told me my future and he knew everything you just told me now. How is that possible?"

Lily and Victor exchanged glances. "Tell me," she said, her arms folded, "he wasn't named Angelo, was he?"

"Yes. Do you know him?"

"I swear, I'm going to wring his scrawny little neck. Rest easy, Vivienne," Lily said with a dry smile, "his story at least is nothing out of the ordinary. There's nothing supernatural about it; unless you consider eavesdropping a mystical talent."

Suddenly the tension in the room eased and we all laughed softly. I did not mind that the joke was on me. "He seemed so sincere, so knowledgeable."

Victor opened his mouth.

"Don't, Victor." I shot him a warning look. "I am neither young nor innocent. And I really do not want to hear you say it again." Mitch walked over to us, followed by Deirdre and Claude.

"Forget Angelo," he said to me, "forget the past and the future. Forget about youth and innocence. Or the lack thereof. What we need to know is how to get rid of this Eduard once and for all. Right now. Just exactly how powerful is he, Victor? Say on a scale of one to ten, with ten being the strongest?"

"Getting right to the heart of the matter, Mitch?" Victor smiled at him. "You were always very good at that." He thought for a while. "On a good day, he is probably a nine. It's hard to gauge, of course. And I can only base it on my own peak strength."

"And how would he compare to all of us?"

"If you were older, Mitch, and more experienced, I'd say that you would stand a chance. Claude is an unknown. Deirdre might be capable of defeating him with a little luck. Lily too." He looked over at me. "I fear, Vivienne, that you would be helpless before him. He has already demonstrated quite aptly that he can manipulate you."

I looked away from him, knowing that what he said was true. I could no more strike against Eduard or even Monique than I could against myself.

"What about you, Victor?" I said. "How do you rate?"

He shrugged. "I was always stronger than Eduard. And so was Max. But Max is dead. And I am not all here." He gave a bitter, humorless laugh. "As I know you have all so aptly observed at one time or another. Eduard, on the other hand, is unimpaired by any disability and has been waiting for hundreds of years for this opportunity. He hates us. And will not rest until we are all dead."

"So there's no hope of defeating him?" Deirdre sounded indignant. "I cannot believe that, Victor. There must be a way. There is always a way. Why did it take him so long to strike at us?"

"I held him off." Victor pounded his fist against his thigh. "Max and I, between the two of us, kept him at bay. But Max is dead. And I . . ." His voice trailed off, his face twisted up, and he put his head down on the table and began to cry.

Lily sighed. "Thanks, Mom," she said. She urged Victor up from his chair and wrapped an arm around his waist. "I'm going to take him home now. I was afraid this was going to happen. Still, you all have what you wanted from him and you can leave us in peace again so that I can patch him up. Until next time." She nodded to Claude. "Lock up the front door when you leave, please. The keys are hanging on a ring inside the kitchen door."

I reached out and touched her arm. "Lily, take care of him."

"Yes, by all means, Lily, take care of him. Or I will."

I turned. Eduard stood in the open door.

Chapter 35

He was as beautiful as ever. Even now that I knew him for the evil he truly was, it made no difference. Victor had been right, I was helpless before him. And what made it worse was that he knew it.

"Vivienne." He crossed the room with his typical grace, picked up my hand, and kissed it. "You have not changed a bit, my dear."

I wrenched my hand away from his grasp, lifted it up to his face, and attempted to slap him. The blow glanced off him as if he were made of air.

Eduard laughed. "Yes, you have not changed. You are as young and pretty as that night we first met. And, I fear, as stupid. You are such a simpleton; I never cease to be amazed that you manage to survive. Tell me, Vivienne, have you ever had an original thought in your life? Beyond your petty vanities and games, that is? Did you not bother to listen to what Victor told you? You can't touch me now, none of you can."

He turned to where the rest of them stood staring. "Just the same," and he motioned with his head, "I'd feel better if you all would kindly step over here, in front of the bar, where I can keep an eye on you."

Deirdre clenched her fists and Mitch snarled, but they both moved as he ordered, followed by Claude and Lily, still supporting the weeping Victor. "Such a lovely family grouping," he said. "You must be proud, Victor, of your children. Or rather Max's children and your grandchildren. That is how you vampires trace your lineage, isn't it?"

"But no, Victor is not himself today, is he? Poor Victor, he's lost so much over the years. And virtually none of it was my doing. But I rejoiced in it all the same."

Eduard walked over to Deirdre and took her chin into his hand. "You, my dear, did me the kindest favor in killing Max. I think I'll let you die quickly as a reward."

"Why are you doing this, Eduard?" I forced the words out of my mouth. His control over me was frightening, mind numbing in its intensity. And from the expressions on the other faces, I knew that they felt the same.

He ran his hand down Deirdre's face, then caressed her neck and breast, watching the expression in Mitch's eyes change from anger to uncontrollable rage to helplessness. "Because," he pulled his hand away from her and laughed, "I can. None of you can lift a finger to stop me. And because worthless creatures who possess powers they refuse to use deserve to die."

He shook his head. "That's not exactly it, of course. When I rid the world of vampires, I will be a hero. I have always wanted to be a hero. Yes, maybe it's just as simple as that. Just think how grateful the human race will be. I will have freed them from their main predator." He bared his teeth in a humorless smile. "When the vampires are gone, then my kind will be the superior species without question. And we have no qualms about using our powers."

He looked around at all of us. "Is no one going to say, 'You are crazy, Eduard'? Or 'You'll never get away with this'? I must confess that I'm disappointed."

"I will say it."

All eyes turned to a dark figure in the doorway. As it limped haltingly into the room, I recognized the ravaged and burnt body. "Monique!" Despite all that Victor had said about her, despite the fact that I knew the truth of her, I felt a rush of joy that she still lived.

She advanced on Eduard, clutching a large knife in her charred hand. "I worked for you, Eduard, for all those centuries. I lied for you, bore you the body you bear even now. I killed for you and," her eyes darted over to me, "betrayed ones that I love. But I will serve you no more."

Eduard laughed. "Not dead yet, Monique? I'd have thought that either the explosion or the sun would have finished you. Have you looked into a mirror lately, my dear? Such a disgusting sight. You have grown repulsive and now that your duplicity is revealed, you are useless as well."

She gave a low growl and raised the knife. "I gave you the life you now have, Eduard, I can take it away."

His face twisted into a half smile. "I don't think so, Monique. What you can do, though, is turn that knife on yourself. Just drive it into your heart and it will all be over." Her hand trembled and she licked her lips nervously.

"Now, Monique," Eduard commanded, "do it now. Turn the knife around," his voice sounded almost tender, and he nodded to encourage her. "Yes, that's right."

Her wrist twisted around and the blade of the knife was pointed at her heart. "No," she whimpered. "I do not want to die, not like this."

Her eyes caught mine, pleading.

"Do not do it, Monique, fight him," I whispered, but already the tip of the knife was entering her chest.

"I'm sorry, Vivienne," she said, "so very sorry."

"Enough of this foolishness." Eduard spun around and drove the knife into her heart. She looked down in disbelief as her blood spouted from the wound. Then she gave a single gasp and fell to the floor at his feet.

He kicked her body out of the way and it slid across the room, leaving a trail of blackened skin and red blood.

I held back a sob. *Poor little lamb,* I thought, *I am sorry too.*

Eduard wiped his bloody hands on the nearest tablecloth. "There," he said nodding, "That is better. She really was too ugly to live. But," he turned to face Lily now, "you ladies are quite lovely. And now that Monique is dead, I will need companionship. Should I take one of you or all three?"

Something inside me snapped. Eduard was going to kill us all, as he had Monique. Right here and soon. He had aptly demonstrated his powers and there was no way any of us would survive this encounter. One glance at the faces of the others confirmed this. We were all helpless before him and we would all die.

With that thought my fear of him faded away. If he was going to kill us all, then fear did not help. And if I was going to lose my life, I would at least lose it with as much style and panache as I lived it.

"*Je t'emmerde, espece de porc a la manque!*" The words came out through clenched teeth, but he heard them and spun around to face me with a snarl.

"You are a stupid cow, Vivienne. You can't hope to gain anything with trivial insults."

"No," I said, "I do not want to gain anything. And all I can see is that what you are doing is stupid, Eduard. Just kill us and be done with it." I rolled my eyes and shrugged. "None of us really wish to stand around and have you taunt us for hours before we die. It is trite and boring and I'd have expected better from you."

Lily looked at me and snickered. "Good one, Vivienne."

I saw a flash of anger and doubt enter his eyes; his thoughts were easy to read. I should not have been able to defy him. I smiled and Lily laughed again. He backhanded her without a second glance and she crumpled to the floor.

Victor's head snapped up. There were no tears in his eyes now, just anger and hatred. And I felt a surge of hope. *Yes, Victor,* I urged him silently, *get angry.*

Eduard did not notice that Victor had revived. His first mistake.

I pushed against his control, testing the limits. He seemed just a bit weaker now, perhaps the use of his power against Monique had tired him. Under the surface of his steely control, I felt the undercurrent of his anger. If I pushed him hard enough, if I goaded him into attacking me, he just might drop his guard.

I caught Mitch's eye and he gave a nod. He understood what I was attempting—it was a comfort to know that I wasn't risking my life on idle chance.

Yes, it was a simple ploy, but then I was, by his words, a simpleton. Stupid and trivial.

I smiled again, a broad grin that exposed my fangs. And step by step I inched up on him, still smiling.

"You can't frighten me, Vivienne. I know you too well for that."

"You know nothing, Eduard. And you are nothing. You feel superior because you can live forever?" I snapped my fingers and he jumped. "There is nothing difficult about living forever. Even someone as stupid as I can manage that. And I can do it without stooping to murdering my own babies, or the woman who birthed them."

I kept moving in on him, each step becoming more difficult than the last.

He was surrounded now by a dimly glowing cloud, his power concentrating and forming a shield around him. But I continued to force my way to him, gratified to see the shield waver and weaken in spots. He was not totally invincible.

Mitch gave a sharp intake of breath. Had he seen the shield? Did he see the weakened areas?

No matter. I could not worry about any of them. It was taking all my energy and all my will to continue to push against him.

I smiled, holding my eyes on Eduard's, advancing step by painful step into the shining sphere of his power. I barely noticed or cared that small rivulets of blood were now trailing down from my eyes and my mouth.

"Tell me, Eduard, *mon chou,* does the murder of innocents make you important? Does it make you smart? Does it make you a hero?"

I pushed. I moved forward. I smiled.

And Eduard was beginning to sweat. I could see the beads form on his forehead and his upper lip.

"You can't do this, Vivienne, you don't have the strength to fight me. I have held you in my arms and I have made you love me. You can't act against me."

There was the key. We were, despite the years between us, bound together. I kept smiling. "You are right, Eduard. I cannot act against you, I love you." I held my arms out to him, pitching my voice at its lowest and most persuasive. He had forgotten something quite important: the ties of blood and passion that bound me to him held him also. His second mistake.

He took an awkward step forward.

"Kiss me, Eduard," I whispered to him. "Kiss me like you used to on those long lovely nights we spent together." I moaned, breathing my words on his skin. "You remember them, Eduard, I know you do. You remember them as well as I do, I know you do. And you want them to return as much as I. Don't you?"

He gave a small nod, barely visible.

"Then kiss me, Eduard. Nothing else matters."

He stepped into my outstretched arms and I clasped him to me in an iron grip. "Kiss me." It was a command this time; one he could not disobey.

And then Eduard put his lips to mine. His third and final mistake.

Instantly, I opened my mouth and sank my fangs deep into his upper lip, then into his lower lip. He struggled to pull away, but the pain dragged him back to me. And I smiled as my mouth filled with his blood, as his eyes grew more pained and confused. *Now,* I thought, *I don't care which one of you takes him. But one of you must. Now!*

I pulled away from him just as Victor sprang up and knocked him to the floor. I stood back to give them room, picking the small bits of Eduard's flesh from my canines.

Victor and Eduard fought, neither of them able to fully overcome the other and neither of them able to let go. Eduard's glowing shield shot to life again and encompassed them both, locking them together in a deadly embrace.

"Do something," Lily whispered. "He can't keep this up." Mitch moved toward the struggling figures and was thrown back. "I can't, Lily. I'm sorry."

"If you can't, I will."

"No!" Victor's voice was heavy and deep. "Stay away!"

And as we watched, Victor began to dissolve into a mist. It curled around inside Eduard's shield and began to match its glow.

The expression on Eduard's face was triumphant at first. Then as he saw the mist curling around him, the smile on his face changed from the grin of victory to the wince of fear.

"Look," I whispered, "what is that? And which one of them is doing it?"

At first I thought it was a trick of the light, but no, there it was again. A tiny lick of flame, followed by another and another.

Soon, the mist that had been Victor became flames and then an inferno, burning violently within the walls Eduard had built around himself for protection. By the time he realized what was happening, his skin had scorched and blackened beyond repair. He turned to me, his eyes pleading, his lips moving, begging me to save him.

I smiled. And shook my head. "This, my dear Eduard, is for what you did to Monique. And to me."

By now the flesh seemed to be melting from his bones. A death's head turned to me again as if in disbelief.

Then Eduard gave one great agonized scream and lay still. The shield fluttered and faded out.

The flames that had been Victor flared up around the lifeless body of Eduard, looming over him in triumph. Their roar was deafening. Then they subsided and dropped back down, radiating out from the corpse like water rings, spreading across the floor, thinner and thinner, until they dissolved.

Everything was totally silent until Lily choked back a sob. "Victor," she whispered, "you stubborn old man. What will I do without you?"

Deirdre put an arm around her and the girl buried her head

against her mother's chest, sobbing quietly. "Hush," Deirdre said, her hands softly stroking Lily's back, the two of them slowly rocking back and forth.

Then Deirdre's head snapped up and she seemed to be listening. "Hush," she said again but with different meaning. "Wait," she said with a half smile, "do not mourn him yet, Lily. Open your eyes and look."

She pointed to the far corner of the room, where the smoke from the fire seemed to hang heavy and still in the air. Then it thickened and curled, moving across the room until it engulfed the girl and spun her about in a wild dance. And suddenly, so quickly that my eyes could not register the change, it was Victor, scorched and singed beyond all belief, but alive.

Mitch approached him and hooked an arm around his shoulders, carefully trying to avoid contact with his ravaged skin. "Good trick, Victor. Now let's get you home."

I walked over and nudged Eduard's remains with the tip of my shoe. The body shook just a little and I jumped back. Then as I watched, it lost its resemblance to a human body and dissolved into a pile of ashes.

I knelt down next to it, gathered a little of the ash in my hand, and held it to my face. "All in all, Eduard, it would have been better if you had accepted the hero's death there on Place du Carroussel. But as I loved you once, may you rest in peace."

Epilogue

It is not really over, of course. The Others still exist and I suspect that Eduard's death will only slow them down for a short while. We will never be able to rest again until we can be sure that they will not retaliate.

But we have time now. Victor bought us that at great cost, and we must not waste it. We need to plan and to safeguard those of our kind still remaining. Mitch has moved back into the leadership of the Cadre, to develop it into something different than it had been. He has assigned each of us posts of duty, where we can watch for signs of the Others. Victor and Lily will remain in New Orleans, at least until his scorched body heals. Claude will go back to New York City. And Mitch and Deirdre win return once again to England. If a new Cadre headquarters is established, it will be based in England. At Whitby, by the sea. A site so obvious that no one would ever suspect.

And I have been assigned to Paris.

Now that Eduard is gone, and his influence over me has been burned away, I feel purified. I realize that my inability to love was nothing but a pretense on my part. A defense against being hurt. I am three hundred years old. And suspect that I have not yet lived.

I have begun to know that life is pain as well as joy. And that you cannot embrace one without letting a little of the other in as well.

And as for love, well, I do not know. Sometimes, as I lie in Sam's arms and I feel the warmth of him flow through me, I think it may be close. And I take comfort from the fact that if we are capable of changing into fire and back again, then we must also be capable of love.

Sam has come to Paris with me, for a time, at least. He and I walk, hand in hand, through the rain-drenched streets, visiting places of history. I tell him stories of the life I led, sometimes ending with laughter and sometimes with tears.

I find that the city has changed in many ways and in many more has remained the same. And life is good.

Exactly as it should be.

RESURRECTION

In loving memory of Emily Taylor.
May your journey home be filled
with peace and joy.

Acknowledgments

Thanks go out as always to my family, Pete, Brian and Geoff, for their help and support during the writing process. Special thanks to Barbara for keeping a space at her kitchen table open for me when I most needed it, to Jim for his photographs and stories of Whitby and for the use of his scanner, to John and his evil alter-ego David for always being able to make me laugh, to Joyce and Tim for caring, to William and Phyllis for being there, to Kelly for her bathtub-battered copy of *Blood Secrets*, to Jack and the other sff.net regulars for their late-night virtual hand-holding, and to Cherry, my agent, and John, my editor, for their patience and understanding. Last, but not least, I wish to give heartfelt thanks to all the fans and readers of The Vampire Legacy—you make it all worthwhile.

Chapter 1

The ruined abbey hovered over the town; visible from almost any vantage point, it stood like a sentinel—cold, stony and vigilant. My eyes were constantly drawn to its massive arches, its empty windows and the solid rows of surrounding graves. I was never quite sure if the abbey served as a headstone for the past, a warning for the future or an example of what we had become.

Forcing my gaze away from the ruins and from the stones gently glowing in the moonlight, I sighed. The hour was late and hunger threatened. We would have to hunt soon even if it meant risking recognition or capture. I wondered, and not for the first time, how we had fallen from our once exalted state into nothing much more than cornered and frightened animals.

"I don't know, Mitch. Perhaps they're right after all. We serve no purpose in this world."

I spoke the words quietly, leaning on the railing of the small boardwalk, staring now into the dark water that flowed past us. If he heard, he gave no indication, made no response. It made no difference, we'd had this same discussion many times during the past three years.

Three years. A short time in comparison with the almost two centuries I had already lived. And yet those past three years weighed heavily on my mind and my soul. We had been running for too long, living in fear and anger among people who'd previously had no knowledge of our existence. We had spent three years looking over our shoulders, constantly waiting for the next attack, moving and hiding, but still being drawn deeper into a rapidly changing world.

I shivered and Mitch wrapped his arm around my waist, drawing me close to him, brushing his lips against my hair.

"No, Deirdre, you promised you wouldn't start again. Remember what I said when we settled here?"

I gave a small, sad smile for the memory and leaned forward again on the rail, pulling away from him slightly, "It stops here." I whispered his words to the river, understanding as I did that they meant something different to me than they did to him. Mitch, I knew, was making a stand. Whereas I was merely resting, too tired for the constant struggle, content to let the current wash over me and pull me under.

"Damned straight. We're going to win this, Deirdre. We're going to beat those bastard Others at their own game."

I nodded, took his hand and held it to my cheek. "The swans are gone," I said, changing the subject back to something safer, "I suppose they've gone someplace warmer for the winter. If so, I'll miss watching them; they seemed so peaceful, gliding out on the water."

Mitch laughed. "Hardly peaceful—they always remind me of Vivienne." Then he sobered. "Damn it. I wish I knew where she was. Not a word from her since May. I don't like it one bit."

"Nor do I, Mitch. But I feel sure she is safe. Or"—I shivered again—"we would have heard about it on the news. I am sure Real-Life Vampires would have no compunction about reporting her death. And the no-contact rule was yours, after all, so she is merely following instructions. As are they all."

"Following instructions?" He laughed again, his voice warm in the night air. "Rest assured, our Viv is merely doing what Viv wishes to do. Chances are she and Sam are holed up somewhere passing the time very pleasurably."

"What must it be like?" My voice wavered. "To live a life like hers? No guilt, no remorse, no conscience, no ghosts to haunt her?"

"Deirdre." All of Mitch's previous humor and warmth were gone. "We've been through this before too. And none of it is your fault."

My fists clenched tight around the railing and I shook my head. "No, Mitch. All of it is my fault. Eduard said as much; had I not killed Max he would not have been able to make his move."

"And if you hadn't killed Max, I'd be dead. Damn it, Deirdre"—his voice rose over the still night air—"Eduard was a lunatic. And so was Max. Regardless of all that has happened, the world is a better place without either one of them."

He turned to me, grabbing my shoulders. I could feel the tension and anger in his grip and I thought he might shake me. Instead, he pulled me close to him and rubbed his hands up and down my arms. "You can't bear the burden of all the deaths they caused, love, you just can't. I won't let you. At the very worst, you were manipulated into acting as you did."

I gave another little sad smile, knowing that I wouldn't win this argument either. Perhaps I did not want to. "You're right, Mitch. I'm just overreacting and internalizing the conflict."

"Sounds like you've been talking to Sam," Mitch said, laughing again. Before becoming Vivienne's newest lover, Sam had worked as a psychiatrist at the institution to which Mitch had been committed for expressing his belief in the existence of mythical creatures of the night. Now Sam lived in Paris with one of us and the whole world believed in vampires. The irony of life in general and our lives in particular never ceased to amaze me.

"No. No Sam. That would be against the rules, remember? But," and I sighed, "I wish I could. I wish none of this had ever happened and the world could return to normal."

"We're working on that, Deirdre."

"Are we?" My voice rose in anger. "These creatures have managed to kill so many of us, they've cut off our finances and our ties with the rest of our kind. We have become afraid to move, afraid even to feed for fear of discovery. And worse, they have taken away the one thing that kept us safe for all these years. Human disbelief. How are we to fix that? Wiping the memory of one human is easy, but the whole world?"

Mitch knew me well enough to realize that I was not angry with him, but with the futility of our situation. "Hush, love," he said, smoothing my hair. "We'll find a way. After all, we're not dead yet—"

His body tensed and without warning, he pulled me down to the ground. I heard a sharp crack and felt a painful tug on my left arm.

The scent of blood, my blood, blossomed in the night air along with an almost tangible scent of anger and rage. They had found us here and it would all start again.

Looking up with a snarl, I saw a young man, seemingly no more than eighteen years old. Dressed totally in black, he perched on the railing, an empty crossbow gripped in one hand. He peered down at us, eyes narrowed with his smug smile.

"Bastard." Almost from out of thin air, I heard Mitch's voice and knew that he was even now changing form to meet the threat.

The man ignored him, and jumping down onto the walk, he reached into a pack slung over his shoulder to fit another sharpened stake onto the bow, aiming once again for me.

Forgetting the pain and the blood, I gave a sharp, inhuman hiss and dissolved my body into a mist, rolling across the concrete toward him.

His smile quickly turned to a gasp of amazement, then to a grimace of fear as I slowly and tortuously curled up his body and hovered around his ear.

"You cannot kill what you cannot touch." My voice was a whisper, tenuous to match my form, as quiet as the sea and as insistent. He made no sound, but he flinched and I knew that he heard. Wrapping myself around his neck, I felt the scar that made him what he was. I tightened my hold and hissed again, rewarded by the small shiver of fear and doubt that overwhelmed him.

"Other," I said, half phasing into my human form. "But," and my voice grew softer, "he is so young." Despite his current attempt on my life, our lives, I pitied him. "Why do they send them out so young? So totally unprepared?"

Another clump of mist formed into a familiar figure behind the boy, knocking the crossbow from his hands. The weapon tumbled over the wall and fell with a splash into the river. Unarmed now, the Other was less of a threat and I fully resumed my human form. Mitch did the same, grasping our assailant's arms and twisting them behind his back.

"What shall we do with him, my love? Wipe his mind and let him go?"

Mitch looked over at me and shook his head, eyes hard and merciless. "That won't work. We can't let him go, Deirdre, or he'll he back, followed by a small army. He may be the first to find us here, but he'll definitely not be the last. And if we take pity and let him go, well, you do remember what happened in London?"

I sighed. "Yes, I remember. But he's only a boy, Mitch."

"Not a boy." The gravelly words slid over gritted teeth, sounding like the hesitant, first-learned words of a beast. "I am older than either of you, and stronger than you think. And I will see you dead and rotting before I die."

With the exception of Eduard, we had never heard one of them speak before. Always they came at us, silent and sullen; always before they had fought and died without a sound. In that split second of surprise, Mitch must have loosened his hold. The man wrestled an arm away and reached into his pack, pulling out a small revolver.

I had begun to shift form, but seeing his weapon of choice, I stayed upright and solid, knowing that he could not hurt me with this. "A gun? What do you hope to do with that?" I gave a mocking laugh. "Don't they teach you any better than that where you come from, Other? You should not come hunting vampires with guns. In fact you should not come hunting vampires at all. What have any of you gotten out of this war but death?"

He smiled at me and I noticed with shock then that all of his teeth had been ground down to sharp little points. "You talk bravely for one about to die, my dear," he said. Then he aimed the gun at my heart and laughed. "Wooden bullets."

I ducked away to one side, throwing myself down to the ground again. Biting my lip, I waited for the pain and for the burn of wood into my flesh. I listened for the click of the trigger. Instead of the firing of the gun, however, I heard a struggle and feet scuffling on the pavement. Then, with an agonized groan and a sickening crack, the laughter stopped.

Mitch pulled his hands away from the boy's neck and the Other fell, eyes lifeless and teeth permanently clenched in his jack-o'-lantern grin.

"Are you okay, love?" Mitch extended a hand and pulled me up from the pavement. "Fine," I said, dusting off my jeans and adjusting my sweater. "Thank you."

"I wish to hell he hadn't made that last try," Mitch said, kneeling next to the body and going through pockets and pack. "We might have found out more from him." He held up the wallet he found and rifled through it. "As always, no identification, no charge cards, nothing to say who he was and where he came from. Nice amount of cash, though, and that certainly never hurts." He slipped the wallet into the pack and handed it all to me. "We'll keep those this time, maybe we'll be able to find out something from the labels."

Mitch picked up the body, looking down at the anonymous face. "Funny that this one talked, don't you think? Do you suppose the other ones could speak and were simply choosing not to?"

I shrugged, ignoring the pain in my arm. "Who can tell? It all seems so pointless, so futile. They keep trying to kill us and we don't even know why."

Mitch gave a grim laugh. "Well, here's one who won't be trying again. Nor will he be reporting back. And just think of all the time he's saved us tonight—no need to go looking for prey when they come looking for you." He glanced over the railing. "Perfect timing, the tide's starting to go out. There's no one else around now and we've still got a little time to feed; he'll stay warm for a while." Then he smiled at me. "Ladies first."

I bent my head to the Other's neck, avoiding the heavy scar

tissue and placing my fangs in the soft, unresisting flesh just a few inches below his ear. He was still warm, as Mitch predicted, and I drew on him hungrily, taking his blood in large greedy swallows, enjoying the warmth of its flow down my throat, eagerly anticipating the renewed strength and life it would give.

Then my eyes, almost of their own volition, opened wide and I pulled my mouth away abruptly, spitting out what little blood remained in my mouth. Choking and gagging, I doubled over and fell to the pavement, vomiting out the blood I had just drunk.

"Poison," I managed to gasp, between gulps of air. "Do not drink from him. He's poisoned."

"Son of a bitch." Mitch dropped the body and leaned over me, laying a hand on my shoulder. "Deirdre?"

I halfheartedly waved him away. "Get rid of him, just dump him, he's no good to us now." I swallowed and wiped my mouth on the sleeve of my sweater. "I will be fine in a minute," I said, "but the sun will be up soon and we must get inside."

As I struggled to my feet again, he picked up the body and hefted it into the air, tossing it over the railing and into the swiftly flowing water. We both watched it drop and sink.

"It seems such a waste," he said, "all that blood and not one drop safe for us to drink. Nothing we can do about that, I suppose."

"What will happen to the body, Mitch?"

"It should stay under long enough for the tide to carry him fairly far away. If our luck holds, he'll surface out in the middle of the North Sea, in a week or two, completely unrecognizable." Mitch wiped his hands on the sides of his jeans. "Provided, of course, that Other flesh isn't poisonous for fish. Let's go home."

Chapter 2

We walked back to our new home, a small flat above a pub in the oldest section of town. The street was narrow, dark and paved with cobblestones; wonderfully atmospheric, it was usually deserted at this time of the night, especially now that the tourist season was drawing to a close.

The flat itself was more than adequate for our use, not a huge amount of space, but it had a bedroom and sitting area with a large fireplace, a kitchen with a long counter and a small alcove that held a table and two chairs, and an impossibly tiny bathroom. Once the front entrance was refitted with a steel door and the two windows with steel shutters, it was reasonably secure.

Home had been a foreign concept to me for most of my life as a vampire. Always, it seemed, I had been running and hiding, not really living but just existing—so very many cities, so many different houses and apartments and rooms. I remembered each and every one of them; if I closed my eyes I could recall the colors of the carpets or the patterns of the wallpaper. But they were all empty, cold and loveless. And none of them could be called home.

The longest consecutive period of my life had been spent in New York. I dwelled in a posh hotel, in an upper-floor penthouse suite, the living room of which would hold our entire flat here. Ten years spent there did not make it home. It was only when I met Mitch that I began to understand the concept.

I remembered fondly the cabin in Maine where we had dwelled together for a time, happy and safe, until events conspired to separate us once again. Even that retreat was gone now, burned to the ground as a result of my anger.

The truth of the matter was that I belonged nowhere, felt safe nowhere, except in the circle of Mitch's arms. My only home, I realized, was with him. So it did not matter how much we traveled or how many times we were forced to move as long as we were together.

We were here now, and here we planned to stay for as long as fate allowed. And in spite of the threats of Other attacks, we could still be happy in our cozy little flat.

The pub below us was called, in one of life's ironies, the Black Rose, an appellation my creator and nemesis, Max Hunter, had bestowed on me many years ago. I laughed to myself every time I passed under the sign.

My onetime business partner, Pete, had found the flat for us and negotiated the lease with no questions asked. When we arrived, we discovered with surprise and delight that he himself had bought the pub below, with the proceeds from the sale of our shared pub in London.

"I needed a change of scenery after the wife died and here seemed as good a change as any," he'd said on the night we moved in. "And it's half yours, Dottie, darlin'." He always called me the first name he'd known me as. I had been Dottie then, and Dottie I would remain. "Mind, you and Mitch want to lie low for a while, avoiding whatever trouble the two of you stirred up in the States." He gave a low chuckle, contemplating our imagined escapades. "There's no one who'll blame you. Then again," he said, winking at me, "if you're wanting to pour drinks every now and then, I won't be saying no."

For the most part, we did a little of both, staying in the flat some of the time, but putting in an appearance at the pub every so often, so as not to arouse curiosity.

We need not have worried; the people of the town took us at face value with hardly a second glance. In their eyes, we were eccentric Americans, and if we happened to look a bit like some of the people featured on the news, well, coincidences happened. And Pete had spent time here in his youth; all of the old-timers remembered him from those wild days. If Pete vouched for us, they reasoned, then we must be acceptable folk.

What Pete thought of us, whether he knew or wondered what we were and what we did, I could not bear to ask. The subject

224 Karen E. Taylor

was never discussed. The place seemed safe enough, safer than many places we'd lived. Pete occupied a small room off of the kitchen and seemed happy enough, especially after he had encouraged three stray dogs to make a home in the small grassy area behind the building.

Two of the dogs were of indeterminate breed, small and wiry with bristly tangled fur. The third, and obviously the leader, looked to be a pureblooded mastiff. He towered over the others, black, massive and threatening. Although Pete had lured this one with food and attention, the dog had decided that it belonged to me and would follow me around when permitted.

Pete had given them no names, but Mitch had christened the largest one Moe, which, he said, automatically made the other two Curly and Larry. As a trio, though, they were not Stooges. They were, instead, Hellhounds. I had come up with that title, laughing at Mitch as he had at me for not recognizing those first three names.

"Hellhounds, my love," I had said, feeling pleased that for once I knew something he did not, "the traditional guardians of vampires."

These guardians greeted us now as we unlocked the front door of the pub. Or, more properly, Moe greeted me and the other two paid their attention to Mitch. For some reason, the two smaller dogs avoided me when they could and ignored me when my presence was forced upon them. I ventured the guess that the scent of cat on me was too strong for them to feel comfortable. But they adored Mitch, fawning upon him, sensing his canine side and accepting him as their pack leader.

"So, how are you boys tonight?" Mitch said, bending down to scratch a few scraggly heads. "Want to come howl at the moon with me?" Moe yawned in response. "No? Well, that's okay, it's too close to dawn anyway. Maybe some other night."

He took the Other's bag from my hand and held it out to the dogs. As they sniffed it, the hackles on the backs of their necks rose and they all gave a low growl. "Good boys," Mitch said, giving them each a pat. "Yes, this is a bad person smell. Now"—

he shouldered the pack and we started up the stairs—"it's bedtime."

I went first, followed by Mitch, who was in turn trailed by the dogs. They did not usually sleep in our flat but one or the other of them always stood guard outside the door. This night, agitated perhaps by the scent of the bag, all three of them settled down there.

When we closed and bolted the door, Mitch pulled me to him in a tight embrace. "That was just too close a call for you out there tonight, Deirdre," he said, whispering the words into my hair. "I can't bear the thoughts of losing you." Then he pulled back and stared intently into my face. "What were you thinking? Why the hell didn't you change at the end? Is your overburdened conscience giving you a death wish?"

"He surprised me, Mitch." I moved away from him and went to fasten the shutters at the windows. "First by talking. And then with those wooden bullets."

When I raised my arm, I winced, registering with disbelief the pain in my left side. I turned around and peeled back the ripped sweater from my shoulder, inspecting the corresponding tear in my arm. "In addition, this distracted me. How odd," I said, noticing for the first time the still trickling blood, "this should have healed already."

Mitch gently dabbed a finger in the blood, brought it to his lips and grimaced in disgust. "Damn bastard poisoned the stake." He tasted it again, then spat it out into his hand. "Something new for them, it seems. Poison the weapons and poison the blood," he said, going to the bathroom and washing his hands.

He came out holding the towel. "I don't like the way their attacks get more complicated, more intricate every time. I wish we knew something more than what Victor told us."

"Victor told us only what Victor wanted us to know."

"Or what little he could remember."

Victor had, at one time, been the undisputed leader of the Cadre vampires, all powerful, all knowing. But lately it seemed that his many years and the deaths of so many of his loved ones had caused him to come unhinged. He resided now in New Orleans with my daughter, Lily. "He's not himself" was the favorite phrase used these days to describe him. On the other hand, he was the one who'd managed to kill Eduard DeRouchard, the Others' leader. I had my doubts about his mental instability.

"After all this time, Mitch," I said, sliding my sweater off over my head, "I am beginning to believe that Victor's tired old man act is just that. An act."

I ducked my head and examined my arm, tentatively exploring it with the fingers of my right hand, and all thoughts of Victor and the struggles of the Cadre faded in the face of the pain. The area around the wound felt hot to the touch and tiny streaks of red were already starting to color my abnormally pale skin.

"Damn it. This should not be happening. It should already be healed. We are going to have to treat this, Mitch. Which do you think would be best, alcohol or fire?"

He shook his head. "I don't know. Maybe both. Get comfortable and I'll start."

Lying down on the bed, I put my right arm behind my head and stared at the ceiling. "I'm as comfortable as I can be, Mitch," I called to him. He was starting a fire in the hearth first. "And I'll be ready when you are."

He came over to the bed and gave me a kiss on the tip of my nose. "Let me get the medical stuff together and I'll be right back."

He gathered the necessary items and lined them up on the nightstand: a scalpel, a pair of tweezers, towels, some cotton gauze and a bottle of rubbing alcohol. Kneeling beside the bed, he began to peel back the layer of skin torn away by the crossbow shot.

I started to talk, hoping to take my mind off of the searing pain that shot through my body at his touch.

"So, do you think those wooden bullets would work?"

Mitch grunted as he picked the first few splinters of wood from the wound. "Why are you asking me? You've been a vampire for over a century now; if anyone would know, it would be you."

I bit my lip and held back tears, feeling the icy stab of the scalpel as he probed deeper. "You must remember, my love, for most of those years I did not have armed assassins hunting me down. Just a few sheriffs here and there, and one or two nosy detectives."

"Two? And here I thought I was your only detective." His tone was light, but I could feel the tension in his hands. I closed my eyes and attempted a laugh.

"Fine. I should know better than to try to fool you. You caught me in the lie. There has only ever been one detective in my life. But as for the question at hand, I have this sinking feeling they know more about us than we know about them."

"In which case," he said, nodding, following my reasoning, "the answer is yes, wooden bullets can kill us; otherwise they wouldn't be employing them. Unfortunately, that means they no longer need to deal with us up close and personal. The killing can be done at a distance even farther away than the range of the crossbow."

I sighed. "Yes, so it would seem."

"Especially if they coat the bullets with whatever it is they hit you with." He fell silent for a minute or two, studying my arm. "I think that takes care of the splinters, at least. How are you doing?"

"I'm fine Mitch."

"Liar," he said, his voice trembling only slightly less than mine. "I hate having to hurt you, Deirdre. I'd rather cut off my own arm."

I reached up my right hand and touched his cheek. "I know, my love. But this has to be done and who else is there?"

"True," he said, "but that doesn't mean I have to like it, does it?" He wadded up one of the towels and gently lifted me to slide it under my arm. I looked away again when I smelled the strong scent of alcohol.

"Hold on," Mitch said, slowly trickling the liquid into the gaping wound. This new pain was almost welcome, a clean and cold shock to my burning flesh; still, I couldn't help letting out a small gasp. Mitch gingerly patted the area with some of the cotton gauze, then paused for a minute or two.

"It's still not healing, Deirdre. Damn, I wish Sam were here. I think," and he was silent for a second, trying to avoid the inevitable, "I think we're going to need to burn the poison out."

I understood his hesitancy. All I'd had to do was lie quietly and manage the pain. He'd had to inflict it. "Burn it out, Mitch." I touched my right hand to my lips and put it up to his. "Be relentless and I'll handle it. I've had worse, my love."

A small moan escaped his lips; then he squared his shoulders, stood up and went over to the fireplace. I didn't watch, but knew that he was heating the poker until it was red hot. And when he sighed, I knew the device was prepared.

"Deirdre?"

"Just do it. Now. Show no mercy."

I forced myself to lie still as he slid the heated poker over my bloodied skin. The smell of burning flesh permeated the flat and the pain was almost more than I could bear. Even in the midst of it, though, I thought I could feel the healing start.

"Enough," I gasped, opening my eyes when the heat subsided, watching the blackened patch begin to lighten and fill in the deep-chewed furrow of damaged flesh.

Mitch held his wrist next to my mouth then. "Drink," he said, "you need it more than I do right now."

"We haven't fed in weeks, Mitch. You cannot afford to give it." But even the mere thought of feeding brought a tingling response to my gums, my canines grew longer and sharper. He was right, fresh blood always sped the healing process.

"Just do it, Deirdre. Now. And show no mercy." He echoed my earlier words and I gave a low laugh.

"Thank you, my love." I breathed the words as my fangs came down on his wrist. The taste of that sweet blood, precious to me in more ways than one, blossomed in my mouth and surged through my body, eradicating the previous pain and the slow burn of poison. Three swallows, four, five—I could have taken it all and wanted more. But this was Mitch and I pulled my mouth away by force of will.

I smiled up at him as a huge wave of exhaustion overcame me. "Thank you," I murmured again as I fell into the dark abyss of sleep.

Chapter 3

Mitch watched over me that day, not sleeping himself, but sitting by the bed most of the time. Periodically he would get up and turn on the small color television set to watch for any events about the war that had been declared on our kind.

Usually, in any given day, there were one or two vampire-sighting and/or killing reports. Although we suspected most of these were false, it made no difference to the general public. In addition to the television, he would also check, via the computer, for Internet reports.

At one point, early in the afternoon, he woke me.

"Deirdre, sweetheart," he said, "I hate to disturb your rest since you need some healing time, but I think you need to watch this."

I opened my eyes and sat up in bed, groaning slightly when I heard the horribly melodramatic organ music theme song to the show *Real-Life Vampires*—the program that had made the names Terri Hamilton and Bob Smith synonymous with that of Van Helsing. Their coverage of the bombing of Cadre head-quarters and their startling revelation that vampires really did exist launched them almost instantly from their obscure jobs as local television reporters to national celebrity status. Over the past three years, I had grown to hate them on sight.

Terri seemed her usual perky self for this show, with her cropped, straight dark hair and simpering pasted-on smile. She wore white, as always, a statement of purity and innocence, while Bob wore his pinstriped Armani with dignity and authority.

"What you are about to see," he intoned, over the standard introductory shots of historical, literary and cinematic vampires, "is true. And none of the names have been changed, for there are no innocents to protect."

"Bullshit," Mitch said. "I wish to hell they'd get a new opening."

"I wish to hell they would drop back into obscurity." I shifted on the pillows, trying to get comfortable. My arm still ached slightly, but I said nothing about it, wanting to see whatever travesty our friends Terri and Bob had worked up this time. "I'm tired of having my name bandied about for public entertainment. This show is a good example of why I never went in for the watching of television."

"Tonight, Bob," Terri said, smirking into the camera, "we have some particularly vicious footage of a vampire attack on four of our heroes in London. The film you are about to see is for mature audiences only; it contains graphic and disturbing events and should not be viewed certainly by children under the age of sixteen."

"That's right, Terri. I want everyone to keep in mind that the footage we're about to show is not cut or edited in any way; these are not actors, folks, they are Real-Life human beings being callously murdered by Real-Life monsters." The real-life phrase was obviously capitalized in his script and Bob milked it for all it was worth. "Because *we* believe *you* have the right to know."

"He's a Real-Life Ass," Mitch said with a small harsh laugh, when the show moved to a commercial break. "Notice that he's not out there fighting for the integrity and the safety of the human race. And I can't believe they're starting to film these encounters."

I sighed. "This is going to look bad, Mitch, I know it is. If only we had known that one of them had a camera hidden on him."

"It was an ambush, four of them against the two of us, and we barely escaped. We didn't have enough time to think, Deirdre, we were too busy protecting ourselves from heroes. And we didn't have time to search for hidden cameras."

The show continued finally with a plea for donations to the Real-Life Vampires Freedom Fighters Fund. I often wondered how much money was being made from this show—more than enough, unfortunately, to keep them on the air for three years.

"And we're back." Terri managed to don her serious face for this segment. "Once again, we suggest that children under the age of sixteen not be present for the viewing of this film footage. Are they out of the room?" She paused for a second. "Good. We will let the films speak for themselves."

The quality of the film was poor, grainy and underdeveloped, adding to the myth of its veracity. The camera must have been hidden in the lapel of one of the Others' coats, as at first nothing was seen but a bouncing version of the street they were walking down.

It was night, of course, and as in all Other attacks, the area was deserted. Neither Mitch nor I understood this phenomenon but had seen it too many times to question its reality. When the Others attacked, they attacked without audience or witness. We speculated that it was an effect much like the force field Eduard DeRouchard had demonstrated for us in a bar in New Orleans before he died. However, we had no evidence to back this speculation, nor did the current show offer any explanation. In truth, it made little difference why or how this worked; often the phenomenon was to our advantage as well as to theirs.

Voices had been dubbed over the film. I remembered these particular "heroes" quite well and like all of them, until this most current assassin, they did not speak.

The dialogue was surprisingly badly written; their chatter of wives and children and the trivial events in their lives belonged more properly in one of the old war films Mitch enjoyed watching, ones where men would reveal their plans to return home and marry their sweethearts seconds before they were shot and killed. Though banal and stereotypical, however, the words served their purpose admirably, making the four seem like nothing more than good friends, taking an evening stroll in the cool London air, instantly engaging a potential viewer's sympathy.

"Wait," one of them said, interrupting the talk of "Scott's" new car, "what was that?"

Suddenly the camera jumped and focused on two other people. At first I would not have recognized the blurred figures that sprang out at the camera as being Mitch and me, but they were obviously meant to be. The man had gray hair and intense blue eyes and the woman, long auburn hair and eyes that glowed like the red fires of hell. The astonished cries of the men were drowned out by the pair's loud growling and a very unflattering close-up of what was meant to be my face revealed yellowed, protruding fangs, positively dripping with gore.

Mitch gave a grunting laugh. "I guess we'd just come from dinner. How many times have I told you, Deirdre? Use your napkin."

I looked over at him, shaking my head and smiling, before turning my attention back to the television set. The colors for this segment had obviously been intensified and from my own firsthand perspective, I knew that they had done a great deal more than a little editing to make it seem as if we were the attackers. In fact, the whole sequence from this point on was mostly fabrication, with a few actual shots tucked in here and there. Gone were the weapons the men had carried, airbrushed or edited away. Two, I remembered, had in reality been armed with crossbows and the others had carried long, sharp knives that had claimed more than a small amount of our blood.

"We will drain you dry," a deep voice that could never have been mistaken for Mitch's boomed out into the night.

"And steal your immortal souls." The female vampire who was not me gloated over her victims before pouncing on one of them, knocking him down to the ground with a sickening crack of broken bones. She clawed open his throat and buried her mouth in the exposed flesh, making loud and grotesque sucking noises.

"Oh dear God," I said in disgust. "How could anyone think that this was real footage?"

The camera bent over her as she fed on this poor unfortunate; the audience was given a gratuitous glimpse of a demonic, blood-spattered face, a view of a creature from hell, reveling in the basest of appetites. Then, as if just becoming aware of scrutiny, she rose to her feet with a low, vicious growl, her lethal fangs bared and her clawed fingers crooked menacingly.

As she advanced, the vantage of the camera slowly retreated until it finally stopped. The female vampire also stopped, hesitating about a foot or two away, no doubt so that the next victim could say his lines.

"Scott's dead," he shouted right on cue.

"What a shame," Mitch commented dryly, "now he'll never get to drive that new car."

"Hush," I said, stifling a laugh, "this is serious business."

"Scott's dead and we can't help him now." The desperation in the man's voice rose as he came to the awful realization that he would soon be joining his friend. "And I'm trapped here, up against this wall. Save yourself."

The soundtrack included background noises of growling and fighting as, apparently, the male vampire gave the other two men the same treatment. Labored breathing was heard as the camera rose and fell.

Suddenly the female vampire made her move. The shot showed her clawed hands coming in, closer and closer, until they gripped the fabric of the man's coat. Then the viewpoint slowly rose, as, presumably, she picked up the man and held him up in the air over her head. Another close-up of her evil, laughing face ensued, followed quickly by the view of rushing pavement. The man had been tossed through the air and landed with a thud on the ground, obscuring the camera until she rolled him over.

"Mercy," the man whimpered, as her face moved closer and drool dripped from her mouth, "for the love of God, have some mercy."

She gloated and laughed again. "I have no mercy for scum like you. Humans are my food."

Apparently, though, in the end she did have some mercy, at least for those of us forced to watch this trash. Her hand came down, crushing the camera and ending the video portion of the film. The screen now contained nothing but darkness, but the microphone must have been concealed elsewhere, because the pained and agonized cries of the men continued for a full minute. And in the ominous minute of silence that followed, the audience was left to draw the conclusion that the heroes had fallen and that the villains lived in triumph.

Then the male vampire's voice rolled through the night air like thunder. "Come, wife," he said, "finish your feasting and get ready to fly. The sun will soon rise."

The next shot was of Terri, wiping away tears from her eyes with a lace-trimmed handkerchief. Bob had an arm around her shoulder and was patting her gently. The bottom of the screen proclaimed the current and rapidly rising amount of money in the Freedom Fighters fund, and the 800 number for donations flashed in bright red digits. "We'll go to a commercial break now," Bob said, "but stay tuned for more news and developments."

Both Mitch and I sat, stunned, staring at the screen. "Unbelievable," he said finally. "I don't know whether to laugh or cry."

"It certainly won't be winning any awards at Cannes this year," I offered, shaking my head.

"But it's an effective piece of propaganda, anyway. Provided they can convince people that this whole thing is true. And based on the money they're collecting, I'd say that they've been successful."

"I don't understand. The whole thing was such a blatant lie. How can they say it was not edited or cut? Wouldn't such tampering be obvious?"

Mitch shrugged. "People believe what they want to believe. And they all know that Terri and Bob would never lie."

The commercials were now replaced with Terri's face; her attempt at covering her tears with a sad smile would have been heartbreaking in any other context. As it was, I wanted to reach my hand through the screen and . . .

"Those two murderers are still at large, Bob," she said, sniffing slightly and squaring her shoulders. "And as the quality of our film was so bad, we are now showing another photograph of the two of them on the right hand of your screen. The woman is Deirdre Griffin-Greer, aka Dorothy Grey. And the man is Mitchell Greer, former NYPD police officer."

Somehow they had acquired a photo of the two of us at our wedding; *I wonder,* I thought, *if I could get a reprint of that.* All of our personal belongings were gone now, stolen from the storage unit into which Lily had them deposited.

"It is believed," Bob said, continuing the pitch, "that they are still residing somewhere in the United Kingdom. If seen, we advise you to approach them with extreme caution or not at all. And as always, donations can be made and sightings can be reported by calling 1-800-555-VAMPS or contact us at our e-mail address—tips@reallifevampires.com."

"I have a good idea," Mitch said, turning off the television as the theme music came back on. "Let's send them an e-mail that says we moved to Iceland."

"If only it were that simple, my love. I wonder what the repercussions of this show will be."

He glanced at the clock. "No way to tell now and there's not much we can do about it in any event. Can you get back to sleep?"

I smiled at him, "I don't know, that was pretty frightening stuff. I might have nightmares."

He turned off the overhead light and the room darkened completely. "Come, wife," he said, lowering his voice to match the one on the show, "finish your speaking and get ready to sleep. The sun will set soon."

Giving a little giggle, I turned over onto my right side, adjusted the blankets and rolled myself into a little ball. Mitch slid into bed next to me and, avoiding my sore arm, wrapped his arms around my waist.

"I love you," he murmured, "even if your table manners are atrocious."

"Very funny, Mitch." I snuggled back into him, enjoying the feel of his solid body against mine. Sleep came quickly.

Chapter 4

When I woke at sundown I was alone in the bed and my arm was still sore. Not surprising, I supposed, it had been a particularly deep and brutal wound, but already a thin layer of new flesh was growing over the damaged area. I stretched, yawned and got out of bed, crossing the room and putting my arms around Mitch's neck while he sat at the desk, dressed only in a pair of jeans and reading something from the screen. "Couldn't sleep?" I asked, depositing a kiss on his dyed-black hair.

He shrugged his shoulders. "I wasn't all that tired. And I was restless. You, on the other hand, slept beautifully. I know, I watched."

I felt a huge rush of emotion for this man and hugged his neck tighter. "Have I told you lately how much I love you? In spite of everything that has happened and will keep happening, I wouldn't change a thing if this were the only way I could be with you. But"—I kissed his head again—"I think I liked you better with gray hair."

He gave a small grunt, reaching a hand up and running it

over my hair, also dyed and cut shorter than his. "And I liked you better with long hair that wasn't bleached. But it will grow and your natural color reappear as will mine. The disguises are important. In the light of what we saw earlier, they turned out to be an excellent idea and just in time."

"Yes, you're right." Resting my chin on his shoulder I glanced at the screen. "Any more news?"

"No," he said, his voice sounding puzzled. "Not since this afternoon's show, which may well have been a repeat. No reaction to any of it—on the television or anywhere else."

"After that show, perhaps Terri and Bob have finally managed to stun the public with their appalling taste. No reaction is good, is it not?"

"Not necessarily. I'd prefer to hear their posturing; at least it gives me an idea of what they're up to. Silence is not always golden. Reminds me of when Chris was a boy—as long as he was making noise, I knew where he was and what he was doing. But when he got quiet, look out." He gave a small chuckle, then stopped and swallowed hard, sitting silent for a few seconds, his fingers resting motionless on the keyboard.

I had no words of comfort for him. Mitch's son had died a little over four years ago and anything I said or did now would not bring Chris back. So I kneaded Mitch's shoulders, trying to ease the tight muscles there, encouraging him to relax. Talking about it could only be beneficial; thus far he had managed to avoid the subject.

Finally he swiveled his chair around and pulled me down to sit on his lap. "So how's my patient this evening?"

Sorry that he had changed the subject, I still smiled and held my arm out so he could admire the newly grown pale skin. "Much better; you did a wonderful job."

"Gave me a hell of a scare, though. You could have died. And then where would I be?"

I wanted to say that he'd have had a good life without me, one that made more sense and that caused less grief. A life in which he was not a criminal, one in which he could face the

light of day, one in which his son would still be alive. I knew
better, however, than to broach that subject. Instead I leaned
over and kissed him, hard on the lips. "I am not dead right
now," I purred into his ear.

He returned the kiss, his tongue lightly flicking over my lips.
"So I see," he said, his voice hoarse. "You certainly feel right to
me. But I don't know, in the excitement last night, there may be
some wounds I missed examining."

"Oh," I breathed as he rose from the chair, holding me still in
his arms, "I certainly hope so."

Mitch carried me over to the rug in front of the fireplace and
gently set me down, unzipping and stepping out of his jeans. He
straddled my legs, pounded his chest a bit and flexed his muscles.

I gave a small laugh. "Come here, you," I said, holding my
arms out to him. He lay down next to me, not saying a word,
his eyes burning into mine. He unfastened the bra that I'd slept
in and threw it across the room, then slowly pulled my panties
down.

I shivered from the feel of his hands brushing my thighs, my
legs, my feet. "Everything looks fine from down here," he said
with a long slow smile, "but I think I'd better keep on checking."

"Oh, yes." I moaned as his mouth touched my toes and he
slowly kissed, licked and nibbled his way up my body. By the
time he reached my mouth, I managed a gasping laugh. "So, will
I survive?"

His voice was unsteady. "Unless you die from the loving I'm
going to give you, yeah."

He entered me, thrusting deep inside, and I drifted away,
abandoning my mind and my senses to our appetites.

Afterward, we lay quiet, breathing heavily.

"Mmmmm. That was worth getting hurt for, my love."

"Maybe," Mitch said, "but don't try it again, okay?"

I nodded, closing my eyes, basking in the warmth of the fire
and his love. "I feel like I could stay here like this forever, Mitch.
Not quite awake, not quite asleep. Floating."

He grunted, lightly gliding his fingertips over my arm. "Forever," I said again, drifting into a delightful waking dream.

The languor, however, vanished with a loud knock on the pub door. The dogs outside the door began to growl, bark and then we heard them tear down the stairs.

"Damn it." Mitch jumped up and grabbed for his discarded clothing, hurriedly putting it on. "I completely forgot; we were supposed to open the pub tonight for Pete. He was heading out for some sort of event at the church." He slipped a black T-shirt over his head and stepped into his shoes. "I guess the regulars are getting restless."

He came back to the fire, and leaned over me, caressing my naked skin and giving me a long kiss. "Lock the door after me, sweetheart. And come down when you can."

I leaned back, closed my eyes again and sighed. We could not make love often enough to suit me. Every time was like the first time with Mitch. I wiggled my toes and gave a low laugh. "And tonight was even better than then," I said. "Must be something about living on the edge."

I might have drifted off to sleep again, but felt a touch of hot breath on my face and opened my eyes to a furry head and a cold nose.

"Which one are you?" I asked the dog, sitting up and holding my knees to my chest. "I know you're not Moe. So which is it? Curly or Larry?" He cocked his head at that last name so I repeated the word. "Larry?" The wag of his tail confirmed it. "And exactly what are you doing in here, Larry?"

The animal looked around a bit nervously, then walked over to the door and settled down in front of it. "Oh, I see." I laughed as I got up from the floor and walked over to throw the bolt. "Mitch let you in for a little more protection. That's a pretty funny little coincidence, you know." I looked down at him and smiled. "Not all that many years ago I needed protection from a Larry." The dog wagged his tail when I said his name, his eyes darting to my face and then back down to the floor. "And now here you are. He was not a nice man, that

Larry. No, he was someone like Mitch's bad people. He smelled a lot better than you, though."

The animal sighed and I laughed. "Sorry, no offense meant. You be a good dog now and watch the door. I'm going to take a shower."

While I was upstairs, the pub had filled with more customers than normal for a weeknight and I felt guilty for the extra time I had taken for a shower. But Mitch seemed to be enjoying himself, talking up a young tourist couple. He winked at me as I came behind the bar and as I tied my apron around my waist he motioned for me to come over to him.

"Elise and Mark, meet my wife, Dottie."

I held out a hand and smiled at them. "Wonderful to see you here. Just visiting the town?"

Elise returned the smile, nodded and hugged Mark's arm closer to her. "It's our honeymoon," she gushed, "and we just got here this afternoon. Mark loved the name of this place so we had to come in."

Mitch came by and replaced their empty stout glasses with two full ones. "In fact, Dottie, Mark and Elise were the ones knocking on the door."

She gave a pretty little frown. "I know. And I'm sorry I interrupted your nap. We didn't see the sign that said you were closed."

A flash of suspicion ran through me. Both of them wore turtleneck sweaters and Mark had not said a word. Could they be Others?

"It doesn't matter, my dear." I kept my smile cordial and welcoming. "So tell me, how are you enjoying Whitby? And do you like dogs?"

Mitch laughed. "Moe has already greeted the two of them and pronounced them acceptable people."

"Moe is adorable." She stopped midsentence and blinked when the absurdity of the remark hit her. Then she laughed. "Okay, maybe not adorable. But he's a sweet animal."

I nodded. "Smart, too. You would never know that he was a stray."

"Sometimes they make the best dogs," Mark said with little effort, and I relaxed fully. These two were just what they seemed: human tourists on their honeymoon. Perfect.

I caught Mitch's eye from where he stood at the other side of the bar. He gave a slight nod. Yes, perfect.

"Stay for a while." I turned back to them, staring first into her eyes, then into his. "And after we close up we'll take you for a walk in the abbey ruins. You can see them better, I suppose, in the daylight, but at night they're breathtaking."

Mitch agreed. "I guarantee you won't want to miss this sightseeing opportunity. And afterward, Dottie, Moe and I will see you safely back to your hotel."

Elise giggled, reminding me briefly of Vivienne. "That'd be cool. Thanks." She hesitated a second, then continued. "So long as we don't see any ghosts or vampires or things like that."

"Well," I said with a low laugh, looking deeply into her eyes again and holding her attention, "there are more than a few ghosts, but they're shy and probably will not reveal themselves. As for the other, you can be sure there are no vampires in Whitby. Moe wouldn't permit it, for one thing. And for another, this would be rather an obvious place for them, don't you think?"

She giggled and nodded. "Yeah, but it's so perfect for them, too. All the old buildings and the ocean and all. I'd think a vampire would feel right at home here."

"Do you? I hadn't really thought of it in those terms, Elise, but I think you're right. If, that is, there were such things. But either way, this is a lovely little town."

She agreed and I smiled and moved over to the other end of the bar, putting a couple of stouts in front of some of our regulars.

Throughout the night, I saw Mitch continue to fill their glasses. He did not want to take the chance that they would leave; it had been a long time since we last fed.

Pete returned shortly before closing time, bursting with good news. You could almost read his excitement on his face, and the dogs milled around under his feet, catching the feeling.

"Hey, now, you mangy curs, give a man a little room, will you?" He took off his jacket and hung it on a post to one side of the bar. Picking up an apron, he fastened it around his waist, then stopped and looked around, hands on his hips and a grin so broad it threatened to split his head in two.

"So what's the news, Pete? I know you have some; it shows on every inch of you."

"I won, Mitch, my boy. A raffle at the church, can you believe it, Dottie darlin'? I won."

I smiled at his enthusiasm. For all of his years, he was still a child at heart. "And what did you win, Pete?"

"An all-expense-paid cruise. You should remember, I forced you to buy a few of the tickets. I leave in two weeks."

How would we manage to keep the pub open during the day with Pete gone? We needed this place for more than protection; it was also our only source of income since the Others had appropriated Cadre accounts. Pete's presence here was critical. I wanted to be happy for him, he was so very excited about the whole thing. But my face must have registered my distress.

He reached over and patted my cheek. "Not to worry, Dottie. I thought of you two and was going to turn it down, but then remembered I had a replacement. Not two weeks ago, I'd received a letter from my niece. She wanted to move out of London, she said, and wondered if I could find her employment here in Whitby. I told her to come on ahead and I'd find something for her. And so, I have."

He nodded his head, pleased over how neatly the universe had expanded to meet his demands. "She and her son arrive in a day or two." He grinned broadly at me. "Must've slipped my mind, or I'd have been telling you before."

Mitch clapped him on the back. "Congratulations, Pete. And don't worry about us, we'll be fine."

"Maggie'll take good care of you and the pub. She's not ex-

actly my niece, you see, but the daughter of a distant relative."
Pete moved behind the bar and began washing glassware. He
looked around and nodded. "Now our Maggie's a nice girl. Pretty
as a princess. Two boys, she has, but the one is staying somewhere with his father's kin. She'll be bringing the little one with
her. Can't be more than four or five years old. Haven't seen him
since he was tiny. Cute little bug, he was, all blue-eyed and
fuzzy-haired."

He pulled a few drafts and carried them down to the other
end of the bar, greeting some of the customers by name. Then he
returned to us and continued where he left off. "Had a spot of
trouble right after he was born, though. A shame, it was. I'm remembering it was a tumor or such; they cut it out and he came
through right as rain. He's a regular tiger now, or so she tells
me, and being as I haven't seen him since, I'll have to take her
word on it."

"Maggie Richards." Pete nodded again, happy in his good
fortune and ours. "She's a fine girl and will do right by you both.
Now why don't you run out for a little air? I'll manage things
here."

Chapter 5

"Not much farther now." Mitch turned around from
where he was leading the abbey expedition up the steep
and narrow cobblestoned street. A very drunk and giggling Elise
clung to him. Mark, equally as drunk, walked next to me, weaving from side to side every so often. The air blew cold and crisp
in from the sea and our visitors shivered. Moe had declined the
walk and stayed behind.

"Don't worry," I said, with a mock stumble, giving me a good reason to grab Mark's arm and pull him closer to me. "We can get out of the wind just as soon as we get there."

"That would be good," he said. "But," and he gave me a curious look, "you don't seem to mind the cold."

I shrugged, leaning farther into him, savoring his warm human scent. "I may have gotten used to it. And in any event"— we rounded the top of the hill—"here we are."

Elise gave a gasp of wonder. "Oh, you were right, Dottie. This is really cool. Can we go in?"

"You can dance on the grass, if you'd like, Elise," I said, "but stick close to Mitch if you want to do some exploring. He knows the place pretty well. We wouldn't want you to stumble into an open crypt, would we?"

She gave a practiced moan of delighted horror, tugged on his arm and off they went. I turned to Mark. "You don't mind, I trust. She'll be quite safe."

"Funny," he said, staring off in the direction they'd gone, "you'd think I would. But no, I feel okay with it all."

"Good. So what would you like to do? Explore? Dance?"

He laughed. "What I'd really like to do is find a quiet place to sit and maybe watch the ocean. I had way too much to drink to go staggering off into the ruins."

"A quiet place to sit? This whole place is about as quiet as you could ever ask for." I took his hand and led him through the cemetery to where a bench rested, overlooking the ocean.

He glanced back over his shoulder only once. "Kind of spooky, isn't it? All those dead people just behind us."

I laughed. "I suppose it is. But somehow I don't think they'll be bothering us."

Mark chuckled. "Nope. I gather you and Mitch are both Americans. What brings you to this area?"

I looked him in the eye. "It's a very long and unbelievable story, Mark. I doubt that it would be of interest to you. Tell me," I said, curious about the contemporary American's view of the Other situation, "does Elise really believe in vampires?"

He thought for a minute. "We've seen all the shows, of course. And used to watch the one with those two newscasters, you know the ones I mean?"

"Terri and Bob." My voice tightened with disapproval.

"Yeah, them. What's it called?"

"Real-Life Vampires."

"Yeah, that's it. We used to watch it all the time, but, you know, eventually it seemed like the whole deal was just a great big scam. They would rant and rave about this horrible threat to humanity and the American way of life, but never offered any proof, never gave anyone reason to believe it was a real danger. Lack of evidence sure didn't stop them from taking contributions from anyone with an open wallet, though. The show got boring and we stopped watching. Although I heard they had a real kick-ass one on not too long ago; we didn't see it, of course, being busy with the wedding and all."

"I saw it. The entire thing had to be faked."

"Probably was. You can do anything these days on film and make it look real. Anyway, I never knew anyone who's been killed or even threatened by a vampire. Have you?"

"No."

He tilted his head to one side. "It's a shame, really. I mean, it would be kind of neat to think that they existed, you know?"

I nodded. "Yes, it would be interesting, I suppose. As would meeting Santa Claus on Christmas Eve, but I don't think that's any more likely."

He laughed then. "It's a lot like that." He rubbed his hands up and down his arms. "It's really getting cold here, you want to move someplace warmer?"

I turned to him, catching and holding his gaze. "No, I like it here. As do you."

"Yeah," he said reluctantly as my stare bored into him. "It's nice."

"Besides"—I pitched my voice lower, so that it was no more than a persuasive throb—"you're tired, I'm sure. Such a long flight here, and dealing with the airport lines and the customs checks, to say nothing of all the previous excitement of the wedding. Why don't you just close your eyes and rest for a while? You'll be safe, warm and I'll stay here with you. When Elise and Mitch are done exploring, you can go back to the hotel. Does that sound like a good idea to you?"

He muttered something and his eyes fluttered.

"Sleep, Mark."

He nodded once and gave a moan. His head rolled to rest on my shoulder and I hesitated. Putting him to sleep and then feeding on him felt unsporting, but I was so very hungry and the thoughts of the normal seduction that ordinarily preceded a feeding tired me more than I wanted to admit.

Somewhere from inside the ruins I could hear the echo of Mitch's voice and I smiled. Had Mark been awake, he would no doubt have been alarmed by the moon glinting off my fangs and there might have been a struggle. Instead, I gently pushed his head to one side and rolled his turtleneck down, making small comforting noises. Easing my teeth into his neck, I drew on his blood slowly, delicately, holding him easily in my arms as if he were a child. He sighed in his sleep and his lips curled up in a half smile.

Time hung suspended as I drank, pulling in the richness of him, feeling it race through my body and warm me totally. *This*, I thought as I finally let go of him and swallowed the last precious mouthful, *this wonderful experience is worth all the danger, all the sorrow.*

I pulled his turtleneck back to its original position, folded it over neatly. "There you go, Mark," I murmured, smoothing back a lock of his dark hair, "good as new."

We sat for some time on the bench, Mark sleeping while I watched the sea roll under the light of the moon. Somewhere out there was the body of the young man who attacked us last night, somewhere out there were the answers we sought. But how would we recognize the answers, when even the questions evaded us? The only one I knew to ask was "why?" and I might as well have asked that of the ocean.

I heard Mitch's step behind me, and turned around on the

bench. He was carrying Elise and she was still giggling softly to herself. "Ready to go?" he asked, nodding toward Mark.

I stood up and smoothed my sweater down over my jeans. "Absolutely. We'll just need to wake him up."

Elise scrambled down out of Mitch's arms and stood unsteadily on her feet. "Markie passed out already." She laughed, swaying. "We've only been married for two days. I guess the honeymoon is over."

"Not at all, my dear," I said, smiling up at Mitch. "Sometimes it can last forever. Now, let's get him up and walking; I don't want to carry him back down that hill."

It took us close to an hour to get them back to their hotel, Mitch supporting Mark with Elise and me walking behind, arm in arm.

After Mark stumbled and almost brought Mitch down with him, I expressed some worry. "Is he all right, do you think? He seems so unsteady."

Elise shook her head. "No, he's just like this. Once he falls asleep, you might as well forget him for a full seven hours. Chances are he won't remember a thing about this night when we get up tomorrow morning. Probably just as well, really, I don't know what I was thinking, going off with a total stranger." She gave me a glance out of the corner of her eyes. "No offense, Dottie."

"None taken. But you were always perfectly safe with either one of us."

"Yeah, well, I know that now." She rolled her eyes. "But what if you'd been, I don't know, psychos or something? Mark always says I'm too trusting. Was he mad?"

I laughed. "That you went off into the ruins with a total stranger, a potential psycho?"

She nodded, biting her lip. "Yeah."

"No, he's not angry. In fact, I think he was relieved he didn't have to go running through the abbey with you."

"Thanks. I'm glad to hear that. And I'm glad we met you

guys. It was fun. Or at least I think it was fun." She put a hand up to her neck and sighed. "I guess I kind of passed out, too. But don't tell Mark, okay?"

I smiled. "Your secret is safe with me."

We walked the rest of the way in a comfortable silence, watching as Mitch half dragged, half carried Mark. Knowing that we were getting closer, Mitch picked up the pace. Finally, we escorted them into the lobby, waved as the elevator doors closed and practically ran out the door and into the night.

I paused and looked at the cabs waiting at the curb. "Should we take a cab back?" I asked.

He shook his head. "Can't really afford it. Besides, I didn't bring any cash with me."

I sighed, not so much for the lost cab ride, but for the state of our life. I'd once had millions stashed away before the Others appropriated it, and although money was not really necessary for our survival it certainly made everything much simpler.

On the other hand, it was a lovely night. Recent experience had taught us that it usually took one or two weeks to have another assassin dispatched, so it seemed unlikely we would run into anything more dangerous than a petty thief. Some nights we would welcome such trouble; on many occasions we sought it, leading an unsuspecting mugger into a blind alley. A human assailant could easily provide necessary sustenance, with little worry of the attack being reported. Especially now, when vampiric encounters with normal people might end up as front page news, the criminal element proved a mainstay of our diet and helped us hone survival skills.

We had, however, already fed well this evening, so there was no need to lure prey. Instead, we found ourselves free to simply exist in the moment, not driven by fear or hunger. We walked, arms twined around each other's waist, silent and secure in our relationship. Rarely did such moments exist and I savored them.

As we came within a block of the Black Rose, a large dark form ran out of the shadows heading straight into our path. I tensed, preparing myself for combat until I recognized the creature as it barreled toward us and flung himself at us.

"You missed a good walk, Moe, old man," Mitch said, "and a good dinner although we didn't save any leftover scraps for you."

I shook my head and laughed. "He far prefers solid food, Mitch." Eying the dog's size and bulk, I added to the thought. "And we certainly don't want him ever to get a taste for blood. None of us would be safe."

"Not fair," Mitch said, scratching the dog's ears. "Moe's nothing but a pussy cat." At that statement the animal turned his head to me. With his tongue lolling out of his mouth, and Mitch's vigorous attention, the dog looked as if he were nodding and smiling in agreement.

I shook my head again and grinned in response. "Fine. I give up. No one should ever try to come between a vampire and his hellhound."

"A good theory, Mrs. Greer. But in reality, he's more yours than mine, although I don't know why. I pay him more attention."

"Perhaps he's just a ladies' man."

"Or maybe he's got a thing for cats. We should take him out for a run some night and find out."

"I think not, Mitch, thank you very much." I eyed the dog. "He's friendly enough when we are in human form, but I don't think I would care to tangle with him. Cat or no."

We started walking back toward the pub, the dog between us, my hand resting gently on his head. I found his presence reassuring, somehow, if only for his value as a warning device. Or perhaps it was more than that. The addition of another living creature into our lives made us into a family.

Mitch unlocked the door to the pub and the dog walked right in, bounding up the stairs to lie by our door. I hesitated outside, not wishing to confine myself again, within the pub or even within our cozy lair. There were hours remaining before dawn; the feeding rejuvenated me and I had energy to spare.

Mitch looked at me questioningly.

"Now that you've mentioned it, Mitch, I think a run would be a wonderful idea. Without the dog, of course."

"Do you think that's wise after last night?"

"No. Probably not. Although we're not likely to meet an-other assassin so soon after that last." I paused. "And if we do, so be it. We manage their attacks well enough."

"Brave words from a woman who could have been killed last night."

I touched his arm. "But I was not killed. And don't you see, Mitch? That's an even better reason for going. If life is short, then let us enjoy what pleasures we can."

"Deirdre?" He put his hand on my forehead as if taking my temperature. "Are you sure you're okay?" Then he laughed. "Maybe a better question is, are you sure you're you? Normally you're the one who wants to play it safe."

"Of course I am myself. I have never felt better. And we are never safe, not now. So the hell with all of it, I say." I touched his face, enjoying the roughness of his cheek on my hand. "Let's run, my love. It will be just you and I and the night."

He shrugged and smiled. "You know, now that you mention it, it does sound like a good idea. Back to the abbey?"

I pulled the pub door shut and he locked it up again. "Yes, back to the abbey."

Chapter 6

The walk to the abbey was much quicker with just the two of us. Once there, we went into the inside of the building and into an area we knew was sheltered from watching eyes. We stripped off our clothing and hid it in a niche we'd discovered on a previous trip.

Then we began to change, Mitch to a large silver-gray wolf

and I to a tawny-haired lynx. As always, Mitch completed his metamorphosis quicker and more effortlessly than I ever had been able to. For years, I had fought against the trappings and powers of vampiric life, staying as close to my human origins as was possible, considering the way I had to live. That was why I refused to sleep in a coffin and why I was still considered a rogue by the rest of the Cadre.

With time, though, I had learned to accept the Cat and had finally come to terms with her appetites and instincts. Yet, even with that acceptance, I still felt reticent about forsaking my human form. To be trapped in that body or any body, living merely on instincts and appetites, without emotions or memories, was one of my worst fears.

The Wolf nudged at my still human-formed hand and nipped gently at my fingers. His eyes glowed with the thrill of transformation and I gave a low laugh. "Yes, I know, Mitch, this was my idea, so I should just get on with it."

Shivering slightly in the night air, I curled up on myself and summoned the image and the soul of the creature that lurked beneath my human surface, the creature that begged constantly fix release. My limbs stretched and reshaped themselves, the fine hairs on my body coarsened and lengthened. There was pain, yes, but it was a familiar pain, and one that was almost instantly paid for by the absolute freedom that followed.

And then it was completed and I was the Cat. As always she roared defiance to the being that kept her caged. *Free,* she cried, *we are free.*

Mitch gave a howl, I gave a rumbling growl and we began to run, loping off into the night, no destination and no purpose, just the sheer exhilaration of perfect bodies and powerful muscles, leaping through the barren and empty countryside.

Behind the abbey were miles and miles of nothing but sparse grass and hills and rocks—the perfect hunting ground for us, or would have been, had there been anything out here large enough on which to feed. But we had fed well enough earlier to satisfy even the Cat's appetite.

I glanced over at the Wolf, running next to me, his mouth open to catch the wind, his eyes still the eyes of the one I loved. The Cat had learned to accept his presence in our lives just as I had learned to accept hers. He pulled ahead of us and the Cat growled.

Come, she said, *give up these foreign thoughts and just run. The door of the night is opened for us.*

Abandoning the human emotions that had been holding me back in this race, I allowed the Cat to take full control. With a burst of speed we drew up next to the Wolf and matched him, step for step.

When we had run for about a mile, we slowed and stopped, taking shelter in a spotty clump of shrubs. Not another soul, human or animal, was in sight; we shifted back into our natural form and made love, quickly and violently—a human response to the sheer excitement of the night. It was different than the love we had made earlier in the flat, dictated by animal instincts and the beauty of the night sky rolling overhead. Different, but no less better.

When we had finished, he rolled from me and we lay in silence for a while, side by side, both staring up at the clear night sky. "About an hour to dawn," I whispered, tugging teasingly on his earlobe with my teeth. "We should probably be going back soon."

He grunted his agreement and I closed my eyes, leaned over to kiss him and ended up kissing the cold wet end of the Wolf's nose.

He smiled at me, tongue lolling, eyes glowing, looking so much like Moe that I laughed, shaking my head. "I think you and that dog must be brothers under the skin," I said, starting my own transformation.

We were about five hundred yards from the abbey when the Wolf stopped short, sniffed the air and began to growl. The hackles on the back of his neck rose. I moved forward a step or two and stopped, pacing, catching the scent as well. My tail twitched wildly.

The scent of man, the scent of Other. The Cat gave a low rumbling sound.

And yes, there, up against one of the crumbling walls near the niche where we'd hidden our clothes, stood a man. Dressed all in black as he was, we might have missed him had we been in our human forms, but we were still Wolf and Cat and the Other reek of him was strong.

He held my shirt in one hand and was idly slashing it with the large knife he held in the other, looking more bored than alert. But that was just an act, I knew, for when he looked up and in our direction, I saw the glint in his eye.

I began to advance on him, my tail still whipping in the air. Slowly and cautiously, I padded toward him, my quiet paws making no noise on the grass. The Wolf circled back to come up behind him.

Foolish man, the Cat growled, *you should have chosen a better place to hunt.*

One step and then another I took, moving like a shadow in the night. He stood, still looking unconcerned. He dropped my ripped shirt on the ground and began to clean his nails with the tip of his knife.

Seeing that the Wolf was in position, I gave a loud roar and the man looked up at me, smiled and nodded.

Bare your teeth all you like, Man, it will do you no good. For you are the hunted now and soon you will be dead.

I do not think he knew that there were two of us. Perhaps he had not burrowed deep enough into our hiding spot to find the other set of human clothing, perhaps he thought that we ran separately.

Or perhaps, the Cat interjected, *he is just a stupid man. The scar on the neck grants long life, not cunning.*

In a blur of motion the Wolf struck, hitting him from behind and knocking him to the ground. The man, however, managed to retain his grip on the knife and he slashed at the Wolf. The scent of blood splashed into the air, the Wolf growled in pain and anger and I sprang forward, fangs bared, biting deeply into the wrist of the hand that held the knife.

The man made no sound, neither of pain, nor of surprise. He did, however, drop the knife and within seconds the Wolf had ripped his throat wide open.

The man is dead.

I loosened my grip on his wrist and licked the blood from my mouth, then transformed back into my human shape. I knelt next to where Mitch crouched over the dead body, still in wolf form. His breathing was quick and the silver fur on his right shoulder was tinged with red as was his muzzle and neck.

I touched a finger in the Wolf's blood and brought it to my lips, tasting and testing.

"Not poisoned," I said, "so it should heal." I licked my lips. "And the man's blood itself tastes pure. I wonder what this means. Was it possible that last night's poison was a onetime attempt?"

Mitch began to pull back into his human self. As the fur covering his body disappeared, the cut on his shoulder became more obvious. It did not look deep and the bleeding had already ceased.

He looked up at the sky. "I don't know, but we have no time to discuss it. And no time to dispose of the body. I'll go through his pockets and you gather up our clothes. Make sure you don't leave anything behind. We're going to have to just leave him here and run for home. No doubt he was waiting, hoping to detain us until dawn."

I did as Mitch instructed and we hastily dressed and hurried down the dark streets to the pub. Mitch unlocked the door, and we ascended the stairs and made it inside with just minutes to spare, stopping for one second to reopen the door to let Moe inside.

Mitch closed and bolted the door then, turning to me and giving me a twisted smile. "Is this living close enough on the edge for you?"

"Oh, love, I am so sorry. You were right, we should not have gone. I never wanted you to get hurt."

He slipped off his shirt and I saw that the place where he'd been stabbed was completely healed. "No harm done," he said. "And I'm not at all sorry we went. In fact"—he gave me a mischievous smile—"until we met up with our friend, the evening was perfect. Running free and making love—nothing wrong with that at all."

I nodded and he continued.

"But this incident makes me wonder what the Others are up to, even more than I normally wonder. It can't have escaped their notice that none of their assassins ever come back."

He crossed the room and sat down at the computer desk, turned the machine on and swiveled his chair around to face me while waiting for it to warm up.

"Early on, that may not have been true," I said, "but at this time, yes, you're right. Terri and Bob proved that the other day; this was the first show they didn't brag about the vampire kill statistics."

Mitch typed a few commands into the computer, then spun back around. "The whole situation is damned odd. This most recent one didn't even put up a fight. He could have slit my throat easily and instead chose to stab me in the shoulder. Had the knife been poisoned, that kind of action would have been understandable. But a clean blade? It makes no sense. Do they all have a death wish? Who is in charge and why does he keep sending them after us, knowing they'll never return?"

"Perhaps he thinks that eventually one of them will get through."

"And what does he do to demand such dedication? The fact that their souls can be transferred doesn't do some of them much good. Our friend floating in the North Sea, for example, will get no rebirth. He is truly dead. They've got to know the risks and still they come."

I shook my head. "It all begins when they are babies, so perhaps they are trained from childhood to hate us. To believe that the extermination of the vampire menace is greater than individual purpose. And maybe they are told that their success will be rewarded with renewed life."

"Who knows? It's utterly futile to try to second-guess an organization filled with murderers and maniacs." He turned back to the computer and began his regular news search.

I took off my clothes, examining my shredded shirt. "This is one for the garbage now," I said, not expecting Mitch to hear or to answer. "Too bad, it was one of my favorites."

"I'll buy you a new one. While you were gathering the clothes I found a couple thousand pounds in his pockets. No identification and no credit cards, but plenty of cold, hard cash."

I chuckled as I put on my nightgown and crawled into bed. "Nice of them to subsidize us, isn't it?"

He nodded and turned back to the computer. "Sleep well; I won't be too much longer."

I smiled and turned off the light, so that the room was illuminated only by the glow of the computer screen. I knew he would be at least another hour or two, longer if he found something of interest.

I fell asleep, feeling safe and secure with the sound of the keyboard tapping and the quiet snore of the dog guarding the door.

To sleep, perchance to dream. The tapping sound follows me as I run along, run along, run along. The Cat knows nothing of poetry, of human fears. She is tireless and so am I. Immortal and free. We do not run to, nor do we run from. We have nowhere to go, no goal in mind. The running is the goal. The running and the sweet freedom. Our feet and our paws carry us far away, far away, over hills and rocks, out of the concrete and hard stone of the cities.

But we cannot go fast or far enough to please ourselves. We race up another hill, panting slightly, and stop at the top of it. Gazing up at the sky, thinking, yes, that would be a good place to run.

And we wish for wings. Silken and feathered, strong enough to kiss the fiercest wind. Yes, wings.

We curl down into ourselves and pull up that winged creature that has been lurking, that has been held captive, hooded and jessed—waiting and longing for so many years. Waiting for this night. Longing for this dream to give it release.

She bursts free, free of Cat, free of human form; this great and magnificent bird with feathers of velvet, brown and white and red. Pushing off from the ground, she spreads her wings, leaving the earth for the first time with a cry of triumph and defiance.

And we fly. Far and fast and free with no boundaries and no limits. Others now fly with us, we see. An eagle with silvered head, his strong wings carving out pieces of the sky. A swan with feathers black as midnight, her neck graceful and elegant even in flight. They call to us, swooping in lazy circles, but we push our new wings to their limits and fly beyond them, above them, higher now and faster than we would ever have imagined.

And then I see a black shadow, flying right next to us, pacing us, watching us, matching each of our movements. The Cat takes no notice of the shadow, nor does the Hawk, glorifying the use of her wings for the first time.

But I see him, he who is the shadow, and the form causes some spark of recognition deep inside me. I know him.

How did he find me, I wonder, *from so far away?*

And with the human thought, I falter. The Cat disappears and the Hawk is gone. My wings fail me and I drop to the earth.

Chapter 7

I woke with a quiet gasp. Mitch lay next to me, sound asleep as was the dog by the door. I slid out of bed, walked across the room and built up a fire, then sat down on one of the small sofas in our sitting area, curling my legs up underneath me and watching the flames rise. Moe woke with my movements, he yawned and stretched, then came over to me, laying his massive head on my knee.

Idly stroking his ears, I remembered the dream and wondered why I had never attempted to transform to a winged creature. That the possibility existed was certain: I knew that Mitch and Vivienne had mastered the form, presumed that other vampires also had winged counterparts. Often difficult to know, since many kept their animal forms secret. And no wonder, they seemed to be a reflection of our inner selves—not something one wishes to share with the world at large.

Max, I felt sure, would have been a raven or a crow, black, glossy, beautiful and totally evil. Larry Martin had been a vulture, ugly and vile. And Victor? I pictured him with a soft chuckle; Victor could be nothing other than a giant bat.

I had been a hawk in the dream. Could I change into one in reality? Glancing at the clock, I saw that it was almost sunset.

After last night, of course, it would be folly to go out, especially alone. But I felt different now than I had before. My flesh had been pierced with poisoned wood and it was not healing. This small taste of mortality and pain made me restless, as if the very blood in my veins had been set on fire. I grew more foolhardy, perhaps, but also more free, more willing to take a risk.

What the hell, I thought, *there's no benefit in living forever, if one must hide away to continue such a life.*

I got up from the couch, signaled the dog to stay. Keeping an eye on Mitch's sleeping form, I dressed quickly and slipped out the door.

"Dottie!" Pete spotted me at the bottom of the stairs. "You're up and about early. Going out?"

"Yes, for a little bit, Pete. If Mitch comes looking for me, tell him I am fine and that I will be right back. I just have an errand to run."

He nodded. "Did a bit of that myself this afternoon. Don't you be stayin' out too late, now; I'll have a hard time holding that husband of yours back if you're late."

"I'll only be gone for an hour or so, Pete, no more than that." I smiled at him. "See if you can manage to hold him back at least that long."

That what I was doing was a mistake, I had no doubt. I lectured myself about it all the way to the abbey. And turned away several times, starting back for home. But something drove me onward, some longing that I did not fully understand. I should not have been out here by myself, I knew this more certainly with each and every step I took. I should have stayed in the flat with Mitch where I was safe.

At least by the time I arrived at the ruins, I had managed to talk myself out of attempting the transformation this evening. Instead, I walked through the graveyard and sat on the same bench Mark and I had sat on the other night, listening to the sea and the sounds of the night, watching dark clouds roll across the sky.

As it was early after sunset, there were a few other people around. Their presence reassured me; if humans were about, then there probably would not be Others. And while it was true that humans represented a different sort of threat, I felt capable of handling the situation, even when, after hearing a step behind me, I turned to see an unknown man approaching me through the graveyard. He was dressed in a pair of dark slacks, a white shirt and a brown corduroy blazer.

"Excuse me, miss," he said in a voice that sounded calm and harmless. "I don't want to disturb you, but I wondered if I could share your view."

I gave a low laugh. "Help yourself. The view is free."

He did not attempt to share the bench with me; instead he sat down on the ground, his knees cracked as he lowered himself and he gave a small grunt of pain as he settled himself in, legs stretched out in front of him and arms straight behind him, propping him up, hands resting in clear view on the ground. I gave him a glance out of the side of my eyes. Definitely not an Other. He spoke too easily for one thing and for the second, he looked to be in his late fifties to mid-sixties. Others tended to opt out of a body before it became damaged with wrinkles and the approach of old age. *Not much of a threat,* I decided, *at least not at this very moment,* and relaxed slightly.

"Nice night, isn't it?" His accent was not local, he sounded more urban, more sophisticated, upperclass. Most likely a tourist, out of season, searching for peace and solitude. Whitby provided both beautifully, as long as you were not being pursued by immortal assassins.

"Yes, lovely. But then it always is here. The ocean and the ruins so close by make for a peaceful combination."

"American?"

"Pardon me?"

He laughed. "I was commenting on your accent. You're American, aren't you?"

"Yes." The caution in my voice was apparent. I did not like people asking questions.

"Just making an observation, miss, no need to be defensive about it. I suppose it would be totally inappropriate if I asked what brought you to this part of the world."

"Yes, it would be." But I smiled to soften my words. "Would the same be true of asking you?"

"No." He smiled and turned his body slightly so that he was facing me. "I don't mind at all. But I fear that I am here for nothing more exciting than business. I would hope that a woman as attractive as you would have a more interesting tale to tell."

I looked at him and began to laugh. Having been chased for years by predators who desired my life, I had apparently forgotten that there were other kinds.

"I seem to have missed part of this conversation," he said. "Was my last comment that humorous?"

"Yes."

"Oh." He paused for a bit, staring at my face. "May I ask why?"

"No, you may not."

"Then what shall we talk about?"

"Is there a need to talk at all? Why can't we just sit here in perfect silence and watch the ocean?"

He laughed. "I fear that talking is a prerequisite with me. I've been cooped up in a stuffy hotel room all this week, with nothing but a computer and a half-written article to keep me company. A nice young couple, American also as a matter of fact, recommended that I visit this site at night. I must say that they are right in their assessment; it is most interesting."

I tensed. "Article?"

"Yes, I'm a reporter. Which, of course, explains my need to talk." He gave a self-deprecating laugh. "As well as the half-written article. I've been meeting more dead ends than deadlines, I fear. None of the locals are particularly chatty, you see, at least not about what I wish to discuss. They'll discuss the weather and the latest football match, but on some subjects, they are as quiet as the locals represented here." He waved a hand at the gravestones and I smiled despite my tension.

"Perhaps you're not listening closely enough."

"Perhaps," he said, narrowing his eyes and focusing on my face, "but I have an odd feeling that my luck is changing, even as we speak. And that I will soon be blinded by a flash of inspiration."

He chuckled and stood up, grunting just a bit from the effort and brushing off the seat and legs of his trousers. "Hopefully it won't strike me dead in the process. However, I believe in playing hunches." He took a deep breath. "So here goes. Your name wouldn't happen to be Deirdre, would it?"

In the split second of indecision on how to answer this question, my eyes darted up to his. And that was all the confirmation he needed.

"So it is true. Despite the hair, I thought the face looked familiar."

With a quick movement I sprang up off the bench and into a defensive position. "I didn't say that it was."

"You didn't have to. But listen to me." He held his hands up in front of him, palms facing me. "I mean you no harm. Truly, I don't. Would I have come here, alone and unarmed, to face you if I were a threat?"

"You would be surprised, I think, at how many come alone. And as far as unarmed, I only have your word on that." I spun around behind him and grabbed his arms roughly, stretching them behind his back. "Put your head up," I said.

"So that you can rip my throat out? I think not."

"Well," I said with a laugh, "I believe that statement is obvious. Think, man, think. If your death had been my intention, I would have killed you already and your lifeless body would be on the ground." I pulled on his arms to emphasize the threat. "Now, do as I say and put your head up."

He complied and I stared at his neck. No visible scar. I reached a hand up to touch the area. He flinched as my finger ran over the whole length of his throat, but he stood stock-still and made no further move. I breathed a sigh of relief—no traces of a scar—his skin was smooth and unmarred.

"For what are you searching?"

I let go of his arms. "If you truly do not know, then perhaps you have a chance of leaving here alive."

"And then again," a familiar voice sounded through the cemetery, accompanied by a deep-seated growl, "maybe not. None of your kind can stand up to both of us together."

The reporter showed an admirable and surprising courage. The giant black dog skirted past him, still snarling, on his way to my side, but the man remained calm and stood still. When it appeared Moe was not going to attack or kill, the man straightened out his suit jacket and stepped forward slowly, his hand extended.

"I presume you are Mitchell Greer," he said. "Pleased to make your acquaintance. I'm with the *London Profile*." He paused for a second to see if we recognized the name. We did not. "And the name's George Montgomery."

"What's it to me who the hell you work for or what your name is?" Mitch's eyes glowed with anger. "When I find you up here threatening my wife, your name is more likely to be dog meat."

Moe growled and Mr. Montgomery gave him a glance out of the side of his eyes. "Please, Mr. Greer, I'm not threatening anyone, least of all your lovely wife. And while I understand your hesitancy to speak and your paranoia, I promise you I mean no harm. All I wish to do is set the story straight."

"There is no story," Mitch said, "and there never will be. Anything that is printed from this encounter will be dealt with swiftly."

"You'll sue me?"

Mitch threw his head back and laughed unpleasantly. "The correct response from a civilized man. Too bad for you that I'm not a civilized man, Mr. Montgomery, not now. Maybe I never was. I don't know anymore. But I do know that if you know who we are, then you know more than is safe for you. And there'll be no story."

"I don't understand, Mr. Greer. After that hideous television show, one would think that you'd be grateful to have your side known. It's a travesty of the worst kind, sensational and instigating; they don't even attempt to make it appear real now. It's all blood and guts and murder and, most importantly, contributions." George's eyes darted back and forth between the two of us, pleading. "If you trust me, I can help you; it's perfectly obvious to me that the two of you, indeed, all of the other 'vampires' featured"—he implied the quotes with a raised eyebrow—"are being unjustly persecuted. Isn't that the sort of thing for which you Americans fight?"

I caught Mitch's eye and he nodded. This man was telling the truth; in his mind I suppose he really did mean us no harm. But any publicity was bad publicity and must be stopped.

I moved in front of him this time, reaching up and holding his face between my hands, staring deeply into his eyes.

"We do not need your help, Mr. Montgomery. We merely wish to be left alone. There will be no story. And no blinding flash of inspiration either, I fear." I smiled and he gasped slightly at the sight of my fangs.

"So," he said, squaring his shoulders against the fear that entered his eyes. "I see. It's like that, is it? Everything they say is true. And now you're going to kill me."

"Kill you? No. We are just going to relieve you of the burden of this memory. It may be slightly painful, but I assure you that you will awaken tomorrow morning with no lasting harm. Relax now and it will hurt less."

I twisted his head down and bit his neck, sinking my fangs in deeply and taking his blood swiftly and effortlessly. After I estimated that I had taken enough, I pulled my mouth away. His eyes glazed over and he stared at me vacantly.

"You do not know me. You do not remember meeting me here." I led him back to the bench on which I'd been sitting and sat him down. "You met no one here. No one."

"No one," he murmured back to me.

"Yes," my voice low and soothing, "that's right. You met no one here. And you fell asleep, watching the ocean. The ocean is very peaceful, is it not? So calm. So soothing. You are tired, are you not, Mr. Montgomery? And sleep would be good, so good, would it not?"

He nodded and closed his eyes. I stood over him for a while to make sure that he actually was sleeping. Then I looked up at Mitch. "He's out." I mouthed the words.

Mitch came over to me and took my arm. "Let's go home," he said in an angry whisper, "and then you can explain to me what the hell you were doing out here all by yourself."

I shook my head. "I don't actually know, Mitch. And I don't want to explain, nor am I sure if I could. It all seemed the continuation of a dream. I dreamt that I could fly and I wanted to see if it was true."

"A dream? You came out here tonight and put your life in danger for the sake of a dream?"

"Mitch." I stopped in the middle of the street and looked over at him. "My only love, you know I adore you. And I love the way you protect me and care for me."

"But?"

I sighed. "There are times when I feel that I am suffocating in this stuffy little town, in that tiny little apartment. I don't know why. Cabin fever, perhaps. Or just the stress of dealing night after night with a death sentence. All I know is that when I feel that way, I must go out. And you must learn to accept that fact."

"I can understand that, Deirdre. Just let me know next time, okay?"

"You were sleeping."

"Well, wake me up next time. You might have been able to sneak past Pete without too much notice, but the dog went crazy almost as soon as you walked out the door. He woke me up and he led me here. Not that I couldn't have guessed where you'd gone."

He pulled me close to him, whistling for the dog, and we continued walking.

After a while he chuckled. "At least you got an extra meal out of the encounter. And Mr. Montgomery is none the wiser, I hope. But I really do wish you'd quit picking up strange men in cemeteries."

Chapter 8

We arrived back at the Black Rose with no new incidents. Outside, at least, all was peaceful and calm. From a block away, however, we could hear belligerent voices and hurried to see what was happening.

"I'll not be servin' you more, mister." Pete's voice carried out into the street. "You've had more than enough for one night, more than enough for two. And it may just be the drink talkin', but I'll thank you to keep a civil tongue in your head when discussin' friends of mine."

"Yeah," a voice from the end of the bar chimed in. "Nothing wrong with Dottie and Mitch. In spite of their being from the States and all."

"Is 'at so?"

We walked into the pub as the man in question stood up from

his bar stool, swaying slightly on his feet. Moving up behind him, we stood there, silent. Moe kept next to my side, whining quietly.

Too drunk to notice us or even to sense our presence, the man continued. "Nothing wrong with 'em, eh? Well, I'm tellin' you I saw 'em on telly t' other day and they seemed all wrong to me. We don't need their kind here in Whitby. Never have and never will."

A snicker ran through the regular customers. There was nothing they liked better than a confrontation, provided they were not directly involved. How we handled this would be talked about in many a home tomorrow.

"Wha?" The man leaned on the stool for support with one hand while banging the other down on the bar. "You think this is funny, don't you? Damn stupid twits. You think lettin' their kind in our town is a joke? Nah, I'm dead serious. I saw 'em on that Terri and Bob show and I'm tellin' you it's the truth."

With that comment, Mitch cleared his throat and tapped the man on the shoulder. "Excuse me, sir. I believe it's time for you to leave."

"I ain' goin' nowhere until I get another drink. Nowhere near closin' time." He staggered and turned around to face us.

The pub fell silent. The man looked at Mitch and gulped. He looked away and saw me with over two hundred pounds of dog by my side. I smiled pleasantly, but touched Moe on the back of his neck, giving him the signal to bare his impressive teeth.

The blood drained out of the man's face. But he kept up his aggressive actions, putting up his fists and jabbing them at Mitch, giving the dog wary glances every now and then. "You think you can take me? Come on, I'm ready for you."

Mitch did not move, did not say a word.

"See?" the man said, dancing around a bit. "He's not that scary, all you need to do is stand up to him." He pulled his right arm back and aimed a punch right for Mitch's jaw.

It never connected. Mitch caught his fist in midair, held on to it tightly and squeezed. The man's eyes rolled and seemed about ready to pop out of his head. He whimpered and the regulars at the bar laughed out loud.

"That'll show him who's a damned stupid twit, Greer," one of them shouted encouragingly. "You go get him."

Mitch caught Pete's eye. "Is this guy paid up," he asked, "or do I need to collect on his tab?"

Pete laughed. "You know better than that, Mitch, my boy. I don't run tabs for the likes of him."

"Ah, too bad," Mitch said, hustling the drunk toward the door. "I'd have liked to make him pay."

The bell on the front door jangled as Mitch escorted the man outside. Once there, I knew, he would send him on his way with the suggestion that he forget all about what just happened. Drunk as the man was, the suggestion would work fine even without the taking of blood. He would wake up tomorrow morning with a bad hangover, a sore right arm and hand and a few missing minutes.

"Last call," Pete announced, and the regulars turned back to the bar and their own drinking.

After closing, we washed up, Pete still chuckling over the drunk. "The look on his face, Dottie, when he saw that dog standin' next to you—he must've turned a hundred shades of white. And Mitch, catching that punch and dragging the idiot out of the pub? I guess that'll teach him to mouth off in the Black Rose."

"Or anywhere else for that matter, Pete," I said, with a smile, stowing away the clean glassware. "I wonder what brought it on."

"Too much drink in his gullet and too much time on his hands." He reached over and patted my cheek. "Don't you be worryin' yourself about it, Dot. He won't be comin' in here again any time soon, if I have anything to say about it. And I do, bein' the owner and all." He chuckled again as he took off his apron. "And that'll be it for me tonight. Have a lovely evenin', the both of you."

He headed back to his room and Mitch came up next to me,

wrapping an arm around my neck. "Never a dull moment," he said, kissing my shoulder.

"Not lately, at least. I rather miss them, to be honest."

Mitch laughed. "Pardon me, but aren't you the woman who was craving excitement so much earlier this evening that she snuck off all alone and worried her husband half to death?"

"Guilty as charged, Detective. I think what bothers me the most is them finding us and naming us, Mitch. Outside, we are on their turf. But it should not be that way here, not in our home."

"You're not still worried about that jerk from the pub, are you, sweetheart?"

I nodded.

"He wasn't a threat, Deirdre," Mitch said, tightening his hold on my shoulders. "He wasn't anything more than a belligerent drunk. And I took care of him. So come on, let's go upstairs. And I'll teach you to fly if you want."

I smiled. "There's not much room up there to soar, is there?"

"You forget," he said with a playful grin, "the windows do open. And maybe it's time to let a little fresh air in."

He whistled for Moe and the other dogs and they came, padding out from the kitchen, licking their lips. "Okay, you lazy mutts," he said to them, pointing his arm to the stairs, "get upstairs now. For once you hellhounds are going to earn your keep."

They ran up the stairs and we followed. Mitch unlocked the door and let all three of them enter.

He answered my questioning look. "If we're going to leave the windows open, and go outside flying around, we'll need a guard posted. I don't much want to return and find an unwanted visitor. And I doubt anyone is going to break in here with all of them raising the alarm."

Locking and bolting the door, Mitch turned to the dogs. "Stay," he said, staring into the eyes of each of them in turn. "Lie down and stay." Curly and Larry obeyed instantly, but Moe gave a little whine and looked to me.

"Stay, Moe." I chuckled as Mitch gave him a dirty look. The dog sat at my command and then lay down, his eyes never leaving mine. "What a good boy," I said, then smiled. "Well, he is my dog, after all."

Mitch snorted. "I guess I hadn't realized how much. No problem. Are you ready?"

With my nod, he started to take off his clothes and I did the same as he began his tutorial. "I'll be honest, Deirdre, this form may be a problem for you. True, the transformation is not really all that much different from taking on the Cat. And it's much simpler than mist. The biggest problem with flying is that the process is completely foreign to us at first."

I nodded, understanding completely. Running as a cat or a wolf was similar to running as a human; one merely needed to get accustomed to the two extra legs. Flying, on the other hand, would involve a whole new set of rules.

"It's too easy," Mitch continued, "to get yourself lost in the experience. In fact, it's necessary. You must bury your true self deep in the instincts of the bird. It's dangerous if you think too much and it's dangerous if you abandon yourself completely. In short, it's a highly complicated balancing act. But," and his eyes glowed, "if you think the freedom of the Cat is exhilarating, you will love this. And I'll fly close if you get into trouble."

I remembered the dream and how I fell at the end of it, remembered the pain of transformation and the difficulty I'd initially had in adjusting to it all. "You know," I started, "none of this seems like such a good idea right now."

Mitch looked at me. "Are you sure? This was something you said you wanted."

I bit my lip. "And I think I've changed my mind. There will be plenty of time for the experience later. Right at this particular moment, I find I have no desire to lose myself. But," and my voice acquired a wistful note, "we could still turn out all the lights and open the windows, couldn't we?"

He smiled. "But of course, Mrs. Greer. Your wish is my command."

We spent the rest of the night sitting together on one of the sofas, watching the night sky rush past our open windows. When the sky began to lighten with the dawn, though, we closed them again, bolted the shutters closed and went to bed.

"Son of a bitch. I don't believe this."

I woke up to Mitch's voice, swearing. I sat up in bed and looked over to where he was sitting at the computer.

"What is it, love?"

"An e-mail from George Montgomery."

"Really? I erased his memory of us."

"Yeah, you did. But like any good reporter, he keeps notes. Somehow, he found our names again. And figured out how to contact us."

I got up out of bed and read the e-mail over Mitch's shoulder.

> *Dear Mr. Greer,*
>
> *You don't know me. My name is George Mont-gomery and I have been a reporter for the* London Profile *for over thirty years.*
>
> *I have reason to believe that you and your wife are being unjustly persecuted by an international group known as the Others. If this is the case, I would most sincerely like to help clear your names of the ridicu-lous charges being leveled against you by the show* Real-Life Vampires.
>
> *While I can certainly understand hesitation on your part to meet with any reporter, no matter what his credentials, I'd like you to know that I have your best interests at heart and plan to write an article that once and for all sets the record, put forth by the most exploitative show of this century, straight.*
>
> *I am most eager to arrange an interview with you and/or your wife at your earliest convenience. A meeting would prove beneficial to all of us and I would be honored if you would grant me one.*

Please, Mr. Greer, let me help you. You may contact me by replying to this e-mail or by calling me at the Hotel Whitby Arms. Thank you for your time and consideration.
Sincerely,
George Montgomery
The London Profile
http://www.londonprofile. co. uk

"This is the same story he gave us at the abbey last night. Are you sure he sent this after we met him?"

"Positive," Mitch said. "The e-mail is date-stamped as having been sent today, not yesterday."

"So what should we do? Ignore him and hope that he'll go away?"

Mitch laughed and picked up the phone. "We can ignore him all we like, but I suspect it won't make any difference. He has a lead and he seems determined to follow it, at least for now. So we meet with him tonight and erase his memory again. And we do that every time we run across him. Eventually, he'll have to leave the area; he can't stay here indefinitely, following a lead that goes nowhere." He dialed the operator.

"Yes," he said when he received an answer, "I'd like the phone number for the Hotel Whitby Arms."

Mr. Montgomery was waiting for us by the hotel's front door right on time, in compliance with Mitch's telephoned instructions. From there we shook hands and exchanged pleasantries, a vast improvement over last night's hostile and threatening proceedings. We walked for a time, chatting about nothing in particular, until he cleared his throat and began his spiel.

"I hope you've had a chance, Mr. Greer, to check out my credentials and verify that I am, indeed, who and what I say I am. As I mentioned in my e-mail, I believe a great wrong has been done to you, your wife and many other people who have been branded as vampires, for what reason I cannot even fathom. But an article stating your side of the story could go a long way to dispelling these rumors and allegations."

I nearly laughed out loud, having now heard these same sentiments three times, twice in person and once in writing. After sneaking a glance at Mitch and receiving his slight nod of agreement, I turned to him.

"Mr. Montgomery," I said, with a sympathetic smile, "this is all well and good. If the rumors and allegations, as you put it, were not true, we would be most happy to provide you with the information you seek. However," and I put a hand on his arm and looked into his eyes, "we really are vampires. I do not think that is a story you wish to print."

"Excuse me?" His eyes, still held captive in my gaze, showed surprise and confusion. "I must not have heard you correctly. I thought I heard you say you were vampires. And what you must have meant, of course, was that you were not."

"No, Mr. Montgomery. The former is true."

"But I don't understand—" he started and I interrupted him.

"Yes, I know you don't. But it is all quite simple and just a moment of your time will suffice to explain."

I gripped him in my arms and my mouth came down on his neck for the second night in a row. He struggled for just a minute, then relaxed, permitting me to draw the blood I needed. Then I pulled away and planted the same suggestion as I had last night.

"You do not know us, Mr. Montgomery. You will forget everything about this meeting, you will only remember that pursuing this particular subject is futile. Futile, do you understand?"

He nodded and murmured something vague.

"Mr. Montgomery?"

"Hmmm?"

"You do not know me, you do not know Mitch Greer, you have never met us and you have no need to contact us in the future. No need, Mr. Montgomery, because vampires do not exist. There are no vampires, not in Whitby, not anywhere else. No vampires, Mr. Montgomery. Do you understand?"

"Yes."

"Good. Now go back to your hotel room, Mr. Montgomery, pack your bags and arrange to leave Whitby as soon as possible."

I turned him around and gave him a small push in the general direction of his hotel. He walked slowly at first, and then with more purpose, not once turning back.

Shaking my head, I turned to Mitch and sighed. "Let us hope that suggestion takes hold and stays with him. He seems so sincere that he almost had me persuaded to give him that interview this time."

"Yeah," Mitch said with a glance at his retreating figure, "he seems a decent sort. Too bad he's as persistent as he is; if he doesn't leave Whitby soon, he's going to suffer from an inexplicable case of anemia."

I laughed and linked my arm in his and we headed back home.

Chapter 9

When we arrived, we saw Moe, waiting outside the pub for us, pacing back and forth in agitation. That he was happy to see us was an unmistakable fact, as he bounded over to us, tail wagging and tongue lolling. "Sorry to have left you behind, big fellow," I said to him, placing a hand on his head, "but we didn't need to intimidate Mr. Montgomery that much."

Mitch opened the front door and gestured for the dog to go inside, but the animal hesitated slightly and whined, lowering his head submissively and tucking his tail between his legs.

"It's okay, boy," Mitch encouraged him. "What's wrong with you? We're home. Come on, get in." Reluctantly the dog entered ahead of us.

"Oh, so you're back?" An unfamiliar female voice asked the question and I tensed. We'd had more than our share of unwelcome visitors and surprises these past few days; I did not feel up to dealing with another.

So, I put a hand on Mitch's arm, holding him back, wanting to ascertain who this new person was before entering.

The voice was low and sultry, containing just enough of an edge to make you stop and listen, pleasant in tone, but mildly threatening overall. *A potent combination,* I thought, and one that I had used myself many times in the past. *Very effective. Sex and power.*

The woman stepped into our view and I saw that she matched the voice perfectly. At least as tall as Mitch, she stood slender but solid, glaring down at the animal. Thick curly jet-black hair fell down to her waist, her black jeans were skintight, her white cotton blouse had ruffles around the neck and dropped over one shoulder, exposing a lacy bra strap and a provocative glimpse of flawless skin. The hands resting on her hips looked strong and purposeful.

Then she smiled, exposing even, startlingly white teeth and a pair of dimples. With the dim bar lights shining behind her she looked like an angel. One who was, perhaps, not above a bit of vengeance.

"You may stay, dog," she said, a touch of laughter in the words, "but mind your manners."

Mitch stepped out of the shadowed doorway. "Thanks for the welcome. But I assure you, I always mind my manners."

The woman jumped slightly and it seemed that every muscle in her body tensed for just a second. "Oh," she said, relaxing and flashing him that sweet angelic smile. "It's you."

"That it is, my girl." Pete came up behind her. "This would be the very same Mitch and Dottie I'm always telling you about."

I did not need Pete's subsequent introduction to realize with a sinking of my heart that this woman must be our new guardian, our female Renfield, the one who would, in Pete's words, do right by us and manage the daytime pub business in his absence.

Maggie Richards had arrived.

*   *   *

We spent the rest of the night in the pub, lingering long after the private members left. Maggie's son, who went by the improbable nickname of Phoenix and who had turned out to be substantially older than Pete remembered, had been put to sleep in Pete's bed as soon as they'd arrived.

"Poor little tyke," Pete had said, after the pub had closed and we were seated around one of the tables. "The train ride just tired him out."

"No so little, Uncle Pete." Maggie gave him a fond smile. "I can't believe you thought he was only four."

Mitch laughed, got up and brought a bottle of wine to the table. He moved around and poured us each a glass, pausing by Pete and putting a hand on his shoulder. "And I can't believe you don't know this old man better than that. He's rarely gotten a year or a name right since I've known him."

"Old?" Pete took a mock punch at him. "I'll give you an old man, Greer. You should be knowin' that most folks my age are already dead." Then he stopped and a broad grin crossed his face. "Oh. I don't imagine that makes my case any better, does it?"

They all laughed, Mitch sat down between Maggie and me, and raised his glass. "To family," he said, reaching down with his free hand and clasping mine, "old and new."

"Cheers." I clicked my glass with theirs and took a sip. As I set the wine down on the table my elbow rubbed on something warm and furry and I looked down to see Moe, sitting by my side. I looked at him, making full eye contact, expecting him to look away, but instead he sighed and whined quietly, eventually resting his head on my knee.

"Mitch?" I interrupted the story he was starting to tell Maggie, something about a particularly funny case he'd solved before we met. "I think something is wrong with the dog."

Mitch looked around the barroom. "I don't see him."

"That's because he's here, sitting next to me."

Mitch leaned over and the dog looked up at him nervously. "So he is. And what's wrong with him?"

"Well, for one thing, he's shaking like a leaf and whining."

Maggie laughed and I felt the dog tremble again. I put a hand on his head and he calmed. "I can explain that, at least, Dottie," she said. "He carried on so much when we came in, I had to chase him out with the broom. Cracked him right on the nose, I did."

"You did that?" Mitch turned to Maggie, astonished. "He might have ripped you to shreds, you know."

Maggie gave another laugh, but it had a heavy sound as if filled with darkness, not mirth. She tossed her head and the action caused her thick black hair to sweep in ripples across her back. "Not me. No dog will ever get the better of Maggie Richards."

I took another swallow of my wine, nodded, then drained the glass. "This is nice, Mitch," I said, getting up from my seat, and walking toward the bar, trailed by the dejected dog, "but I think I would like something a bit stronger. Port? Or whiskey?"

"Whiskey for me, Dot." Pete sounded tired and old. I looked at him and saw new signs of aging I was sure had not been there before. Feeling a flash of anger for the shortness of human life, and realizing with a twist of my heart that I truly cared for him, I gave him a broad smile. Then I poured a shot of whiskey, set it on the table before him and deposited a quick kiss on his cheek.

Even in the dim light of the bar, I saw him blush. "Thanks, Dottie. What say you and me take that cruise together? You can leave that Greer fellow behind."

"I doubt that, Pete. He's probably a very good swimmer." I walked back to the bar. "Mitch?"

"Damn straight."

"No, I wanted to know if you would like something else to drink. Maggie, how about you?"

"Whiskey," she said, giving Mitch a confident glance. "For both of us."

Mitch shrugged. "Sure, why not?" He turned around in his chair, his back to me, and started into the telling of his story. Why not, indeed.

I poured two glasses for them and carried them over. "Here you are," I said. "Can I get you anything else?"

"Thank you, Dottie," Maggie said. "Aren't you nice?"

"No," I said, my voice flat, "not particularly."

She sat there, drinking her whiskey and looking so absolutely beautiful that I felt, for a second, small and homely and totally undesirable.

Mitch gave me an odd look. "Are you okay, sweetheart?"

I leaned over and gave him a kiss, full on the lips, felt his arms rise up around me, felt the wave of his passion, knew that I could not doubt his love for me. I pulled away and smiled. "I'm fine, my love. Just tired. I think I need some air."

Mitch started to get up from his chair. "No, absolutely not. We were just out."

I shot him a warning look. "And I plan to go out again." I pitched my voice low enough so that only he could hear. "You are not my jailor, Mitch."

Pete leaned over drunkenly and put a restraining hand on Mitch's arm. "If the lady wants to be goin', she'll go. No one in the town would harm our Dottie, no, not even one hair on her funny yellow head."

"Thanks, Pete."

"No problem, Dottie darlin'."

Mitch twisted his mouth in a grimace. "Fine. Then I'll go with you."

"No." I kissed him again, a short one this time. "Don't be silly, you should stay and talk. I may not go any farther than the back of the pub. But I'm sure it's a lovely night and I cannot bear the walls around me."

He nodded reluctantly, understanding. "Just out back shouldn't be a problem. But take the dog with you. And if you do go somewhere, don't go too far."

I kissed him again. "Thanks, love." Then I turned to the dog. "Come on, you." Moe jumped up from where he'd been cowering and instantly came to my side anxious to leave the room and the strange woman.

We went out through the door in the little kitchen, leaving it unlatched so we could return. Pete had equipped the small porch outside with two wrought-iron chairs and a small table on which rested a pack of Players, a pack of matches and an ashtray. I laughed to myself, remembering that when Pete's wife was alive, she wouldn't allow him to smoke in the house. Apparently he still followed that restriction. "Old habits do die hard," I said and the dog wagged his tail briefly, then lay down with a sigh, facing the door.

I took one of the cigarettes, lit it and inhaled deeply. "Speaking of old habits," I said softly, "here is one of the oldest. Did you know, Moe, I began smoking when it was something that helped one fit in? Now it only ostracizes one and I'm still doing it."

He wiggled and whined, still staring at the door. "Yes, I know. I don't like her much either and she didn't even hit me with a broom. I wonder what her sons are like. Or more importantly, what Phoenix is like. What sort of name is that for a little boy? And why on earth am I asking you? Your name is Moe." I laughed then and the dog sat up. "Come on," I said, crushing the half-smoked cigarette into the ashtray. "Let's walk for a bit."

We crossed some of the other backyards and ducked through a narrow alley to the main street, joined there by the other two dogs. At first, they shied away from me, but since it seemed that I had their leader's endorsement, they followed as I made my way down to the river.

"I feel like the Pied Piper, somehow. I hope you boys can put up a fight if we run into any of Mitch's bad people."

The night, palely lit by a cloud-enshrouded moon, was peaceful and quiet. I'd found I never tired of watching the water, seeing the ships bobbing and weaving in the harbor, listening to the waves lap up against the stone walls. Off in the distance, I thought I saw the dim shape of a swan, an early riser, apparently, gliding like a feathered ghost over the water's surface.

"I suppose," I said softly, smiling to myself, "that life is not all that bad. If it were not for someone trying to kill us every so often, I might be able to adopt Vivienne's positive attitude."

One of the dogs gave a quick low growl and I heard the

sound of footsteps on the pavement behind me. Much too late to change form, I gripped the railing as I braced myself for the sound of a gun or crossbow, held my breath, waiting for the burning pain of the poisoned wood.

When it didn't come, I spun around to face the intruder, with a growl of my own. A boy stood there, staring. Dressed in pajamas and barefooted, he was not much of a threat.

"Hello there," I said, and relaxed and smiled, hoping that my fangs would not show. "Should you be out of bed? Should you be out here at all?"

He did not answer me. His eyes, shining blue in the moonlight, stared off into the distance, unfocused and vague.

"Sleepwalking?" No response. "And what am I to do with you? Leave you here? Find your house? Call the police?"

I walked over and knelt in front of him. "Hello? Boy? Can you hear me?"

His eyes never wavered, never moved to my face. The child unnerved me, his hair so blond it was almost silver in the moonlight, his body so slight and so thin that a strong wind could have knocked him over.

I touched his shoulders and he shivered violently. His small hands came up, gripping my arms tightly. A sudden pain shot through my left side, then subsided as quickly as it came. As I looked down at his quiet little face, I saw that his eyes were still unfocused, but his mouth had stretched into a tight-lipped grin. He shivered again and I moved my hands away.

The dogs came over and sniffed at him, warily at first, then with more enthusiasm, wagging their tails and putting their noses against his hands. But nothing they did seemed to register with the boy and eventually the dogs moved off in confusion at his lack of response.

I sighed and stood, gently removing myself from his hold, wincing from the pain his touch had caused. "Well, I certainly cannot leave you out here dressed like this. And on such a chilly night. What must your mother be thinking?"

I hesitated and permitted myself a twisted smile. Maternal instinct was hardly one of my better virtues. My own daughter, Lily, had walked the earth for over a century before I even knew of her existence; I was most certainly not a good one to make judgments in matters of children. I decided to take the boy back to the pub with me; Mitch would know what to do.

"Come with me," I said, reaching down and taking his cold hand in mine. Except for one tremor that seemed to shake his whole body, he gave no resistance and walked beside me, silent and grim.

When we arrived at the Black Rose, I opened the front door. "Look what I found by the river," I said.

Maggie turned away from where she and Mitch were still deep in conversation.

All of the blood washed out of her face; she rushed over and gathered up the boy, tearing his hand away from mine and holding him tightly to her.

"He's cold as death," she said, glaring at me, then looked back at the boy, her eyes searching. Her voice rose and contained a note of panic. "What the hell did you do to him?"

"I did nothing to him, Maggie, but bring him back here with me when I found him. I don't even know who he is."

She crooned something to the boy and smoothed back his short blond hair. His eyes were closed now and his face peaceful, innocent. It was almost a scene from some medieval mural, the beautiful woman, the lovely child. A mother's love. Why did I not know the boy instantly?

She looked up from her examination. "No harm done." She smiled, then said quite unnecessarily, "This is my son Phoenix."

Chapter 10

M aggie tucked Phoenix back into bed and came out of the room with a rueful smile. "I'm so sorry, Dot. I didn't mean to jump all over you like that. I got a scare, is all, seeing him there with you when I thought he was safe in bed. Thank you for bringing him back."

"I trust he's all right?"

"Oh," she said, with a bit of a shrug, cavalier now that the shock had worn off, "you know how kids are. I'm sure he'll be fine after a few more hours of sleep. But he was chilled to the bone, going out as he did in just his pajamas, no coat or shoes. You wouldn't happen to have an extra blanket or two lying around that we could use, would you? That would seem to be all that Phoenix needs right now."

"Absolutely," Mitch said, "I'll go up and get some."

As he started up the stairs, Maggie came over and put a hand on my arm, gentle but firm.

I tried to suppress the slight shiver her contact caused and must have succeeded, or else she was too polite to mention the fact.

"You and I haven't exactly gotten off to a great start," Maggie said, her voice hushed and urgent, "have we? First I terrorize your dog; then I monopolize your husband, and finally I completely lose my cool and scream at you for no reason at all. When I should have been thanking you." She glanced down at her feet, seemingly embarrassed, and a slight blush rose to her cheeks.

I had a difficult time focusing on her words, distracted by the heat of her skin through my heavy sweater—so lovely, so human.

I cleared my throat. "Thanks are not necessary, Maggie. I found the boy and brought him back, without even knowing who he was."

"But you're wrong," she insisted. "Thanks are necessary."

She gave me a shy glance. "You know, before I arrived I had this picture in my mind that we would become friends. Because Uncle Pete thinks of you as his daughter, and that makes us family in a way. And because I'd heard so much about you and Mitch from him that I felt I already knew the both of you. Then I go and ruin everything with my quick temper."

"Nothing has been ruined."

"Good," she said, smiling, hitting me with the full impact of her beautiful face. "I hope you'll forgive me, Dot. Please say that you can."

I studied her; she seemed totally sincere and open, even down to the tears collecting in the corner of her eyes. I wanted to believe her, I wanted a friend, but over the years I had discovered that friendship was as great a risk as love. And something did not ring true about Maggie Richards; underneath that angelic exterior lay something dark, something she may not have known existed.

She inspired emotions in me that I did not understand and she frightened me. As did her son.

On the other hand, it was more than possible that three years of being hunted by seemingly innocuous killers had made me paranoid and untrusting. Perhaps the darkness I feared in her was merely a reflection of myself, a reflection of the fear and desperation that had driven me for so long.

I could not say any of this to her, however, so instead I gave her a slow, reluctant smile and nodded. "I can certainly try, Maggie."

"Fair enough," she nodded, smiling, pleased with my answer. She removed her hand from my arm and I breathed a silent sigh of relief.

"I guess," she continued, "we'll start here and see where it goes." Before I could protest or back away, she reached her arms out and enveloped me in a hug. "Thank you."

Her warmth and vibrance took me by surprise, and the musky scent of her hair and her flesh made me hunger as if I had not fed for centuries. My gums tingled, my fangs grew and I gave a low moan, struggling against her, trying to push her away from me, to a safe distance.

Her arms, though, held me tightly. It was almost a lover's embrace and awakened in me an instant and overwhelming desire. A desire for her blood, yes. But it was more than that. So much more.

I wanted to possess her in every way possible. I wanted to drink her deep into my soul and keep her captive there forever. I wanted to utterly consume her, remake her and consume her once more.

At that moment nothing else mattered. No one else existed; the entire universe consisted only of Maggie, this intoxicating morsel of flesh and blood.

My mind filled and overflowed with images of this woman: Maggie, smiling a welcome in the darkness of the bar, a halo of light surrounding her. Maggie, with her flawless skin, her perfect teeth, her full lips pressed to me in an eternal kiss. I could taste her sharp tongue darting against mine. I could taste her flesh, strong and vibrant, every inch alive and vital.

Time stopped. I could not breathe. Each gasping breath only served to pull in more of her heady fragrance, dropping me deeper into my fantasies.

I envisioned her naked, now, and the sight flooded my senses. Her beautiful ripe body lay before me, exposed for tasting and exploring, opened for my tongue and my teeth and my hands. Her sultry laugh rang in my ears, her deep and lovely voice whispered in my mind, and my desire for her quickened.

I moaned softly. Oh, the heat of her and the feel of her body pressed up against mine—this was surely heaven. My skin tingled from our contact, from the inner fires burning unbridled inside her. She enveloped me with those flames, searing my skin more surely than sunlight. And burn I did, delightfully, unquenchably, longing for more.

Somewhere, far in the recesses of my mind, a thousand warnings flashed. This union was forbidden, I knew with certainty. This union was fatal One taste of her blood and I surely would be lost forever. She was tainted in some way I could not understand, she was a trap, she was the lure on the hook.

Still, fully knowing this, I took the bait offered. I could not resist, though all of my soul and all of my self denied the urge, though all of the people I loved cried out for me. Her presence drowned out their calls, her voice silenced the alarms, and the air around me hung heavy with the scent of her, soft and wild.

I hovered on the edge, it seemed, teetering between the safe ground of past life and the abyss of hidden passion and fires that opened invitingly before me.

I cannot resist, I thought, as I swayed and shook under her touch. *God help me, I cannot resist.*

And the thought became action. With blessed release, my mouth opened and my teeth pierced her skin. I drew her essence into me and her blood, so sweet and so spicy, exploded deep inside me. No other blood had ever been as rich, as fulfilling; the red flood of it raged through my veins, setting my entire being on fire. It fed my darkest hunger and filled the empty recesses of my soul.

There could never be enough of this, never be enough of her. I could drink forever, hold her forever and still be left unsatisfied and desiring more.

Swallow after swallow, I drained her. Her pulse slowed against my lips and still her hot rich blood flowed into my mouth.

How long, I thought, *can this ecstasy continue? How much more blood can she have, can she give? How much more can I drink?*

As if the thought broke a spell, my world suddenly spun back into motion; the split second of time that had held me frozen and rapt in her embrace began to move once more. I heard her laugh echoing through my mind, found myself in her arms again as if nothing had happened. Finding the strength this time to deny my appetites, I managed to push her away.

"Have I offended you again, Dot?" Was there just a small note of laughter in her voice? Was she taunting me, teasing me? Had my instant attraction been a deliberate attempt on her part? Had it been real? I could not tell, my senses were still reeling. I was dazed, confused.

Had I imagined all of it? I must have imagined it, I decided; she would be a bloodless husk otherwise, I had taken that much from her. But the taste of blood lingered on my tongue. The taste of her blood, for it could be from no other.

I shook my head, fighting the dizziness, attempting to calm the tremors that shook me.

"No, you have not offended me, Maggie," I said, turning away so that she could not see my growing bewilderment, "not one bit. It is nothing you have done. I find myself out of sorts this evening, I fear. It has been a busy evening for all of us and I am so very tired."

I had meant it for an excuse only, but when the words crossed my lips, I realized it was true. I was bone weary and felt ready to drop. "Once you get Phoenix settled in and we lock the doors, I believe I will retire for the night."

She peered out the front window of the pub. "Retire for the day, is more like it." She laughed. "The sun will be up soon."

"Even so."

Mitch came back down the stairs. For one small panicked moment I did not recognize him, he had been gone from my mind for so long.

"Here we go," he said, "extra blankets, as requested." He handed them over to Maggie and looked at me as I stared at him.

"Mitch?"

"Deirdre? Sweetheart, are you okay?"

I opened my mouth to speak but no words came.

Maggie answered for me. "She's completely done in, Mitch. All this business with my arrival and Phoenix's sleepwalking." She turned to me then and I stepped back. An amused knowledge bloomed in her eyes. "Dot, why don't you go upstairs and sleep now? Mitch and I will take care of the boy and lock up. Can't be too much left to do and there's no time like the present to start learning my new job."

I nodded and started up the stairs, hearing their quiet voices as they walked down the hall and into Pete's room. I wondered where Pete would be sleeping this evening, I wondered if Maggie would have the same effect on Mitch as she did on me, but I suddenly found myself too exhausted to care about any of the answers.

My arm ached and I felt the approaching dawn weigh me down with each step. Finally, after what seemed ages, I reached the top of the stairs. I opened our door, vaguely registering the fact that one of the dogs came inside with me, while the other two settled down outside. Not even bothering to slip out of my clothes or under the covers, I fell on the bed and slept.

I wander through the ruined abbey, happy in my solitude, enjoying the gleam of the moon reflecting in the fallen stones. I have no worries, no fears. The night is beautiful, sacred and silent.

Running underneath the silence, though, I notice now the sound of breathing. I stop and hold my own breath. As I listen the noise grows louder and louder, until it seems that the very walls surrounding me echo the sound. Louder and faster the breathing progresses and I catch low moans of pain mixed in with the steady inhaling and exhaling.

Following the sound, I see movement in the cemetery, a rising and falling of the earth itself, it seems. But as I draw closer, I see that it is a woman. Naked, she lies on the cold ground, her pregnant stomach heaving with each contraction. Her eyes catch my movement and she holds a hand out to me.

"Help me," she gasps, "help me."

I take her hand and look down at her. I know her, know the scent of her flesh and the taste of her blood. She cries out from the pain and I drop to my knees next to her, brushing her long dark hair out of her eyes.

"Hush," I whisper to her, a comforting lullaby. "I am here now and I will help you."

I put my free hand down gently on her rolling stomach. Her

skin is stretched so taut and thin that I can see the movement of the child in her womb. More than that, I realize, I can see the face of the child, pushing out against the skin, fighting for its release.

It must be a trick of the moonlight, I think, that causes me to see the face of her unborn child in her skin. But I can also feel the face beneath my fingers, his eyes, nose and chin, the opening of his mouth in a silent scream of pain. Not the face of a child anymore, but that of a full-grown man. It smiles at me through the skin of her belly and the lips move, saying my name.

I try to jump up, but her hand still clasps mine. She gives a great cry of pain and the child is born. *See?* I say to myself. *It is only a child and nothing to fear.* I pick up the boy and hold him close to me, wrapping my shirt around him for warmth.

"It is a boy," I say to her, "a fine healthy boy."

"There is another," she gasps, still caught in the grips of birth contractions. I look at her stomach and see that she is right, there is another face, a different face, trying to find its way through her flesh. She gives another call of pain and another push and the second child is born. I put him into her arms and she begins to cry. Thinking she wants her other son, I hold him out to her, but she shakes her head. "No," she says between her tears and labored breathing, "that one is for you."

Well, I think, *why not? I helped him to be born, after all.*

The baby moves underneath my shirt, squirming over my naked flesh until it finds my nipple. It's mouth closes around my breast and its teeth dig deep into the skin. The woman laughs and I scream.

Chapter 11

"Evening, sweetheart. Did you sleep well?"
The dream faded into nothingness as soon as I opened
my eyes to Mitch's face. He gave me a kiss and I smiled at him.
"I think so," I said, faintly puzzled. "I can barely remember getting into bed at all."

"I'm not surprised, you were completely out of it last night. I
tried to talk to you a little when I came up, but you were dead to
the world. Worried me, so I tucked you in, all nice and cozy, and
Moe and I sat watch all day."

I reached up and touched his cheek. "That wasn't necessary,
Mitch, my love. I was tired, true, but nothing more than that.
You should have slept."

He ran his fingers through his hair. "I wasn't really tired. And
you shouldn't have been either. We had just fed. Was it the
arm?"

I thought for a moment. "It did ache some as I came up the
stairs."

"And now?"

"Fine." It was a lie, of course, one I did not even know why I
would want to tell. "Perhaps it took a while for the poison to
work its way out?"

He shook his head. "I don't like this, not one bit. There should
be no pain, no aches and no aftereffects." He sat down on the
edge of the bed. "Let me see it, sweetheart. Roll up your sleeve."

Reluctantly, I did so.

The skin in the area had completely regenerated; only a faint
tinge of darker red tissue underneath indicated that I'd even
been hurt. As we looked at it, though, there seemed to be a fluttering under the surface.

"What was that?" Mitch jumped slightly and reached out to
touch the spot.

"A twinge?" I suggested. "My cells moving around trying to

repair the deeper damage? I have never sustained a wound of this sort, so I'm just as confused as you. But it doesn't burn anymore and it doesn't really hurt at this moment. There are no striations and it hasn't swelled. Honestly, Mitch, I feel sure it will heal, given enough time. Can we not obsess about it anymore?"

"I'm sorry my concern for you has fallen into the obsession category." He sounded hurt.

"Oh no, Mitch, my love, I don't mean it that way." I wrapped my arms around his neck and kissed him long and hard on the lips. "But I'm not used to having something physically wrong with me. And I think I would feel better not talking about it."

"But—"

I let go of his neck and laid a finger over his lips. "Moe listens better than you, did you know that?"

He laughed at that, as I had intended him to do. Rolling my sleeve down, I stretched and sat up in bed. "What time is it?"

"About an hour before sunset. We'll need to be down in the pub soon to get Maggie acclimatized."

"Maggie?" My voice sounded unsure. There was something about Maggie that I needed to remember. Something vital. Something that caused my pulse to race and a flush to rise in my cheeks.

Mitch laughed. "Yes, Maggie. I know you weren't yourself last night, but you can't possibly have forgotten her. She's much too overwhelming to forget." He tilted his head to one side. "So, tell me, what do you think of our newest addition to the family?"

"Family is probably stretching the concept, Mitch. She seems capable, I suppose, but I'm not sure I trust her." *Or trust myself in her presence,* I added mentally.

"She'll only be here for two weeks, Deirdre. We can manage that long. And"—he gave me a mischievous smile—"you have to admit, she's easy on the eyes."

I shook my head. "Handsome is as handsome does. She is easy on your eyes, perhaps, but she makes me nervous."

"Ridiculous. I think she makes you jealous."

I thought about that for a moment. "No," I said finally, shaking my head, "not really jealous per se, although she does make me feel small and plain. In the same way that Victor always makes me feel uncouth. She is so vibrant and warm and so very much alive. Her smell alone . . ." My voice trailed off. Her scent had been bewitching, mesmerizing, confusing. And her blood and the taste of her skin . . .

Mitch laughed. "Now you're saying she doesn't smell good? Deirdre, I think you just got off on the wrong foot with her last night. She seemed perfectly fine to me; maybe you just need to give her a chance."

I did not want to talk about how I felt about Maggie; I did not know how I felt about her. So I shrugged and moved to a different subject. "And the son? He frightens me. If you could have seen him last night, Mitch, standing there in the dark. Silent and staring. He doesn't seem right."

"He's just a kid, Deirdre," Mitch said. "I remember Chris at that age, walking in his sleep. It's something they do and while, yeah, it can be creepy, it's nothing to get upset about. Believe me on this, you're not used to kids."

"I do have to admit that you're right about that, Mitch." My own daughter could barely stand to be in the same room with me. What did I know of children?

"Then quit worrying. And prepare yourself. There's a repeat of the very first *Real-Life Vampires* show airing in a few minutes and I thought we should both see it, if only to compare then and now."

I groaned and pulled the covers up over my head. "Not another Terri and Bob show, Mitch, please. Anything but that."

"Sorry, babe." He yanked the covers off the bed. "If I'm going to watch it, you have to too."

The introduction was the same, the same melodramatic organ theme and the still photos of vampires. Bob made his remark about there being no names changed and no innocents. But they both seemed inordinately nervous, which, since this was their first national broadcast, should not have been unusual. Except that their level of anxiety was so high and so obvious, I started feeling nervous myself.

Perhaps that was the effect they were after. If so, they succeeded admirably: a paranoid edge sharpened every word. Terri's eyes kept darting off camera, and flitting back and forth. She had not worn virginal white for the first show, I was surprised to see. Instead she dressed in a suit of pale variegated coral that under the cameras ended up looking as if it had been dipped in blood and then hurriedly bleached. Her hair was a bit long, also, and her smile seemed less practiced.

Their lead story was the bombing of Cadre headquarters, with a repeat of the original footage that shockingly revealed the existence of vampires to the general public. Following that was a lengthy obituary on Eduard DeRouchard, lauding him as a praiseworthy man of business and philanthropy.

"Doctor DeRouchard," Terri said, while behind her rolled collected films of Eduard, "was a pillar of the community and a prince among men, as well as a devoted family man." The photo behind her changed now to a casual family shot, the proud father with his two young sons. "Brutally murdered, incinerated alive by vampires of the Cadre, he will be sorely missed by the world in general and this reporter in particular."

Mitch scoffed. "Not a surprise, Terri, considering he single-handedly jump-started your dead-end career."

"Good-looking boys, although neither of them look like him," I said. "I wonder who the mother was."

Mitch shrugged. "Could have been any of his various breeders, I suppose. Victor never said anything specific about the process, but I always got the impression that they bred these children like prize cattle, with the high-ranking Other officials serving as studs."

"That is a particularly nasty interpretation, Mitch."

He laughed. "These are particularly nasty people, Deirdre."

"Yes, I know that, but what an awful life for the children and their mothers."

"I'm sure there must be compensations. Don't get all soft on me, sweetheart. We're not watching this to acquire sympathy for the bastards."

I shrugged and the show returned from a commercial break. Bob introduced their newly opened Web site and the toll-free telephone number for contributions. At the bottom of the screen the dollars were already accumulating at an amazing rate.

"And now," Terri said, smugly now, as if she was over her stage fright and had warmed to the show, "it's time for *Real-Life Vampires'* frequently asked questions. Each week we'll be taking one question each from three of our viewers and if we use your question on the air we will send you a free *Real-Life Vampires* coffee mug."

"That's right, Terri," Bob said. "Our first question today comes from a viewer in Laurel, Maryland. Brian asks: 'How do I spot a real-life vampire?' "

Terri smirked. "That's an excellent question, Brian, and one that is often difficult to answer. Some signs to look for are abnormally pale skin, sharpened canine teeth and discomfort when exposed to sunlight."

"That's useful information, Terri," Mitch said, tossing a pair of his dirty socks at the television. "Thanks so much."

"Our second question," Bob continued, "comes from a viewer in Pittsburgh, Pennsylvania. Will writes: 'I think I've been bitten by a vampire. What do I do now?' "

"I can understand your distress, Will." Terri smiled reassuringly at the camera. "First of all, don't panic. Just one bite will not have any harmful effects. But be sure to call our toll-free number at 1-800-555-VAMP to report this attack. Or contact us from our Website at reallifevampires.com. It is true that a vampire living in your neighborhood can drastically reduce property values and the quality of your life."

I groaned. "Did she really say that?"

"I'm afraid so."

"Our final question," Bob intoned, "comes from Sue in Burbank, California. Sue asks: 'Is it true that vampires don't have reflections in mirrors?' "

"Thank you for writing, Sue. And the answer to your question is sadly, no, that particular myth is not true. Vampires have reflections in mirrors just the same as you and I. Another popular myth that vampires are unable to cross a stream of flowing water has also been proven as untrue."

"And that's all the time we have tonight, Terri," Bob said, "so until next week, we urge you to be vigilant and be strong. We will be here to give you the truth, because *we* believe *you* have the right to know."

"So much for that," Mitch said, turning off the television set. "That's probably got to be the biggest load of misdirected bullshit I've ever seen. It's hard to believe that even Terri and Bob could have been that melodramatic or that they've actually improved over the years." He leaned over and gave me a kiss on the tip of my nose. "I'm going to go downstairs now and get the evening started. Get up when you feel like it, then get dressed and meet me down at the bar. But don't be too long, or I might have to get friendly with our new guardian angel."

Even that threat was not enough to hurry me through the shower. The water was as hot as it could be and I stood for a very long time just letting it cascade over my cold skin. I laughed to myself, thinking how glad I was that Terri was right at least about one thing. Certain mythical restrictions of vampiric life *were* wrong. Life would not be worth living without flowing water.

When the water finally cooled, I turned it off, took a towel from the rack and dried myself. Looking in the mirror was still a shock for me; I had cut my long auburn hair very short and bleached it blond shortly before moving here to Whitby. And while I was glad now that I had, I still felt that the woman looking out from the mirror at me was someone different.

I finished up with a little bit of makeup, a few passes of a towel over my hair and walked out into the bedroom to get my clothes from a small wooden dresser. *At least,* I thought as I pulled on my last pair of clean jeans and a heavy black sweatshirt, *I don't have to worry about wardrobe choices these days.* Every article of clothing I currently owned was made of dark material to better blend into the night. In addition, everything could also be rolled up and crammed into a small backpack. When we traveled now, we traveled light and in a hurry.

I began to gather all of the clothing strewn around the apartment and stuffed it all into a large canvas bag, except for the black sweater I'd worn the night of the attack.

Inspecting the tear in the sleeve, I determined that I might be able to fix it, and set it aside for repair. It was a favorite of mine and I did not want to discard it. Carefully folding it, I put it back into one of the dresser drawers. Then I topped off the bag with the wet towels from the bathroom and sat down on the bed to lace up my black hiking boots.

"A fine thing, Moe," I said to the dog by the door when I stood up. At the mention of his name, he jumped to his feet and wagged his tail; I lifted the bag and settled it over my right shoulder. "Who ever heard of a vampire having to do her own laundry? Picking up dirty underwear? Buying fabric softener? I know. Perhaps Terri and Bob could do a special show on that topic. 'Real-Life Vampire Laundry: How to Tell if Those Dirty Clothes Have Been Worn by a Bloodsucking Creature of the Night.' " I laughed at the ridiculousness of the thought as I opened the door.

I had to set the bag down to turn the key in both locks, and then slipped the key into the back pocket of my jeans. Shifting around, I started forward and almost ran right into the boy standing there.

I jumped, surprised at his presence. Then I smiled. "Hello," I said. "You frightened me. I'm Dottie."

He nodded sullenly.

"And you must be Phoenix. I met you last night but I feel sure you don't remember. You should not be up here, I think."

He reached up to touch my left arm, shook his head, then pointed down to the laundry bag.

"It's our laundry."

He nodded more enthusiastically this time, gave me a small

grin that lit up his entire face. Then he picked up the bag and started down the stairs, dragging our dirty clothes behind him.

I watched him struggle with the load and shook my head. Mitch was right, I did not understand children.

"Come on, Moe," I said to the dog, hesitating at the top of the stairs, "let's go down."

Chapter 12

Mitch stood behind the bar with Maggie; my entrance interrupted their quiet conversation and he looked up and smiled.

"Did you," I said, walking over to him and giving him a kiss, "happen to see a boy come through carrying our dirty laundry? And would you happen to know where he went with it? I won't even ask why."

Maggie laughed. "Isn't that lovely? He's such a good boy. You see, that's always been his chore, Dot, carrying the laundry for me. It's nice that he did it for you. It means he likes you. I think he must have heard us talking about your sore arm and decided you needed help."

"My sore arm? Why were you talking about my arm?" I gave Mitch a sharp glance.

"Yes, your arm, Deirdre. You do remember that, don't you?" Mitch looked at me, faintly puzzled.

"Yes. But my arm is fine."

Maggie's eyes swept over my face and I felt myself blush, remembering what had transpired between us the previous evening. She gave no sign of embarrassment. "That's not what Mitch says. Maybe you should see a doctor?"

"My arm is fine," I repeated and headed toward the small

laundry area located off the kitchen. The boy was already there, sitting in a little chair next to the washing machine, kicking his feet against the bag of laundry.

"Hello again," I said to him, offering him a smile as I pulled out clothes and put them into the washer. "Thank you for carrying the laundry down the stairs and into here for me. That was a very nice thing to do."

He shrugged his shoulders and kept staring at me with his pale blue eyes.

"Your mother says that you help her a lot. It's a good thing for a child to help his parents, don't you think?" I spun the dial to the proper setting, added detergent and glanced at him again. "You don't talk much, do you, Phoenix?"

I waited for a response. When none came, I sighed, closed the lid and started the machine. Turning and leaning back against the washer, I met his direct stare. "Do you even talk at all?"

Phoenix gave his head a violent shake, jumped up from the chair and ran out of the room.

"No, I suppose not," I said. "Or at least you don't seem to want to speak to me."

I heard laughter come from the bar: Pete's deep rumble, Mitch's hearty bass and Maggie's sexy contralto. Suddenly I felt very much an outsider—a feeling I knew all too well.

It didn't help knowing that there was no need to feel this way. All I needed to do was enter into the bar and I would be included into the group. Pete treated me as his daughter. Maggie wanted me to be her friend and sister. And Mitch loved me and only me; all I had to do was look into his eyes to know that truth.

Knowing all of this did not help. At that moment in time, as they laughed and talked, I felt desperately alone, more than I had ever been, more than I had ever expected to be again.

Quietly, I opened the back door and slipped outside into the night. I stopped by the wrought-iron table, picked up a cigarette and lit it, staring off into the darkness. Moe came up beside me, eagerly anticipating another walk, perhaps. "You cannot come with me tonight, old boy," I said softly, shaking my head and motioning for him to sit and stay. "You would not be able to keep up."

Crushing the cigarette out, I moved away quickly, heading back out an alleyway and onto the steep street that led to the abbey. The sky was cloudy, overcast with more than enough moisture in the air to bring a fog up from the water. A perfect night for a run.

Ordinarily, Mitch would be by my side. And although I knew he would be angry again at my going off alone, I needed solitude for reasons I could not put into words.

All I knew was that something was wrong. With me. With the world around me. With Maggie and with her son. With how I reacted to her. All of it was wrong, dead wrong. The situation's evilness hit me in the pit of my stomach and turned me inside out. And I did not know why.

My mind was as hazy as the sky, my thoughts as restless as the sea. A run would clear this, it always had before.

I stumbled over something as I entered the ruins. Looking down at my feet, I saw that it was a dead swan. "Oh, you poor thing," I whispered and reached down to touch its feathers. The lifeless body was still warm and its neck had been broken and crushed. It rested in a little pool of its own blood, coming from, I thought, the abrasions on its neck. It bore no other marks of violence. *How strange,* I thought, *that whatever animal killed it didn't carry it off somewhere to finish its feast.*

Perhaps my arrival had spooked the killer. And it didn't matter, the poor swan was beyond any help I could have given it. I left it lying there, thinking that I would bury it when I returned.

Finding a sheltered corner in the ruins, I removed my clothes and folded them neatly, tucking them into the niche we always used. Then I stood and took in a deep breath, preparing myself for what awaited.

I knew that the Cat would run the restlessness out of my bones, the uneasiness out of my heart, and that I would return from my run refreshed and released of fear and doubt.

A growl started deep within the center of my body, and I felt the transformation begin, the exhilaration of the Cat being released.

Free, she rejoiced, *I will be free.*

Suddenly, though, the normal pain of change became worse: an excruciating burning that started in what I thought was the fully healed wound on my left arm, a torture that spread to every inch of my body.

"No," I screamed out in the darkness, my need for secrecy supplanted by the severe pain. My voice sounded both human and bestial, my body caught between the human form and the feline.

"No!" I screamed again. "I cannot." The Cat howled in frustration and pain at being denied its freedom and retreated once again.

I fell to the ground, panting and sweating and shivering. The pain was more severe than any I had ever experienced or imagined. I longed to just close my eyes and drift away from it, but I knew that I must return to my natural form. With a tremendous effort of will, I kept my mind focused on the change back to human.

Finally, when my limbs returned to frail-seeming humanity, I curled up upon myself again and closed my eyes. The pain subsided as quickly as it had arrived, but I wanted to rest, just for a little bit of time, before returning to the pub. Something large and warm nestled down next to me, whining softly and offering comfort as it could. I wrapped my arms around him and smiled. "I thought I told you to stay," I said to Moe. "But you are a good dog for finding me. We'll go back home in a moment." My eyes closed and I slept.

I rise up from the cozy little nest I'd made for myself, laughing at how the pain was gone. I dress in the clothes I'd left stashed away: black leather jeans and a red silk shirt; slip my feet into black high-heeled pumps. I brush my hair out of my eyes, throwing it back over my shoulders, and look around. The city streets are quiet and empty. That does not matter. Nothing matters now. Although I do not know where I am or why I am here, I know that I am home.

My feet find their own way and I arrive outside the door of a building—a club, it seems. A young and handsome blond-haired doorman with insane eyes smiles and lets me enter. Inside, everything is strange but comfortably familiar. A band is playing and I watch the people on the dance floor. A tan gray-haired man dances with an equally tall black-haired woman; his eyes meet mine as he turns in the dance and I gasp. They are beautiful, blue and glowing. I know him. My heart aches with love for him and the knowledge of him. Why is he here? Why is he dancing? His name is—

He turns away and the thought is gone. Another dancing couple catches my eye. In this one the woman is small, frail and impossibly blond with keen gray eyes and an impish smile. The man she is with is young, much younger than she, with eyes similar to the gray-haired man's, but not as piercing or as familiar. He bends his mouth to her and drinks from her, draining her until her long slender neck falls limp and her feet falter in the dance. Like a swan, I think, a dead swan I saw somewhere, not here, but far away and so very long ago.

The crowd closes around them and they are gone, replaced by a woman, no, a girl, with short red hair. I feel as if I know her better than any of the rest and yet at the same time, I do not know her at all. Her partner seems to flicker in and out of existence. He is dark and elegant and carries the weight of many years in his body. I know him too.

There are more, dancing there. I know them all. But I cannot remember the names. I cannot remember how I met them or what importance they held in my life prior to this moment. And I realize it does not matter.

For, now, in the center of the dance floor, a lone man stands, beckoning to me. The knowledge of this man runs deep in my veins. I fear him. I hate him.

I love him.

He reaches his hand out to take mine and I marvel at his finely chiseled features, his dark hair streaked with gray, his twisted smile. I had thought never to see him again.

"Welcome home, little one," he says. "It has been a long time." Pulled into his arms, I cannot resist. I relax in his embrace. His mouth brushes my ear and he whispers a name—

"Deirdre?" I opened my eyes to an angry male face leaning over me. Disoriented as I was from the aborted transformation and the dream, it took more than a few seconds to recognize him.

"Mitch?" My voice sounded small and frightened.

"What the hell are you doing here? Naked and sleeping in the ruins? Have you lost your mind? What if one of the Others had come across you?"

"Oh, Mitch." I held back a sob. "I have never . . . changing into the Cat hurt so badly that I couldn't do it . . . and then I dreamt that . . ." But the dream escaped me, as if it had swirled off, dancing into the fog. Perhaps it had.

"Well," he said, looking down at me, still angry, "get dressed and let's go home. We can talk about it later. At least you had the good sense to bring Moe with you this time. He was standing over you, growling and snarling, when I arrived. He didn't even want to let me near you, until I convinced him otherwise."

I stood up unsteadily and began to dress myself. "Really? I didn't hear him. What time is it?"

"Almost dawn, love."

"Ah. Almost dawn." The dream languor continued; somewhere in the back of my mind I remembered the importance of dawn. I slipped into my sweatshirt, pulled up the jeans and zipped them, tucking my panties and bra into the back pocket. I picked up one of my heavy hiking boots and leaned against the wall trying to support myself and put on the boot at the same time.

"Forget this." His voice now held more laughter than anger and he walked over to me quickly, picking me up, cradling me in his arms. "We don't have time to struggle with your boots. I'll carry you home."

Home? But I was home, in the dream. And I no longer dreamed. "Home?" I said, my voice bouncing from the ruined stones and returning to my ears as if from faraway. "I have no home."

His blue eyes stared down at me. "Why would you say that, Deirdre? You know that your home is with me and it will always be."

I took in a deep breath of air, shivering slightly. "I'm frightened, Mitch. What's happening to me?"

He did not give me an answer, just held me close to him and started out of the ruins. I clung to him and cried.

Chapter 13

"Good." Maggie's brisk voice greeted us at the back door of the pub. "You found her. Two lost people in two nights are two too many."

"Lost?" From the shelter of Mitch's arms, I looked up at her in confusion. "I wasn't lost."

Maggie shook her head. "I'm not sure what else you'd call it, Dot. When Phoenix told us you'd gone out, we figured you'd be back in a little bit. But you've been out all night. If that's not lost, I don't know what is."

"Phoenix told you I went out? But he doesn't speak, as far as I can tell. How did he know? And how could he have told you anything?"

A mixture of sadness and anger entered her eyes. She moved in toward me, opened her mouth to speak, but Mitch shifted his weight, pulling me in closer to him, away from her, and interrupted. "Look, Maggie, I need to get her to bed now, I think. And try to get some rest myself. We can continue the discussion tomorrow sometime. I can explain to Deirdre about Phoenix, if you'd like."

"Yes, of course," she said, her expression softening. She patted me on the arm, surprising me once again with the heat of her touch. "I wasn't thinking. It's been another bad night, hasn't it? This keeps up and before you know it you'll begin to think it's all my fault."

He leaned over and gave her a quick kiss on the cheek. "I promise you, Maggie, no one thinks that. And don't worry; it's nothing we won't survive. Thanks, though, for caring. We'll both see you tomorrow night."

Once we had entered the apartment and locked the door, Mitch set me down gently on the bed. "Take your shirt off."

Something in the peremptory tone of his voice angered me. "Do not treat me as if I were your child, Mitch. I am perfectly capable of taking care of myself."

"Are you? I'd have said so until just recently. Now? I wonder. What the hell were you thinking? Going off alone like that again, without a word to me that you were going? You promised not to do that."

I shrugged. "I knew what I was doing. And I didn't think you would notice since I only planned to be out for a short run. Besides, you were completely preoccupied with Maggie."

His eyes narrowed and his mouth drew into a frown. "Exactly what's that supposed to mean?"

"Nothing. Just that you were busy." I could have stopped with that statement, but I was frightened and hurt and angry. "Apparently," I continued, the words spilling out, "you were so busy that you didn't even realize I was missing until it was almost dawn."

Mitch sighed, still frowning. "The pub was crowded, Deirdre, someone had to tend to business. We need this money, you know that as well as I do. We need to make a success of this place."

"And after the pub closed? What were you doing then?"

He ran his hand through his hair and shook his head, his eyes glinting at me. "Jesus, I can't win. You complain when I look after you and now you're complaining because I didn't." His eyes shifted away from mine. "As far as what I was doing, well, you know, I don't like what you're implying."

"And I don't like implying it. But it is an interesting question, don't you think?" I stopped for a minute and heard the words I had just spoken, seeing their meaning clearly as if they hovered in the air above us.

What was I doing? I loved this man more than life itself and I knew he felt the same about me. If I could trust no one else in the world, still I knew I could trust Mitch. Pain was only pain and the dream was only a dream and both could be ignored. But this moment was real and words could be said that we both would regret. I sighed and swallowed my anger. Smiling up at him, I touched a hand to his cheek.

"What am I saying? I'm so sorry, Mitch. I don't mean to imply anything about you. And I don't want to fight with you. Not about this, not about anything. Not for as long as I live. I love you."

"And I love you, even if you are an idiot at times. Now be a good girl and take off your shirt so that I can see your arm."

I nodded and pulled off the sweatshirt, wincing slightly, more from anticipation of what I might see than from the brushing of the fabric against my skin. I squeezed my eyes shut; I did not want to look.

"Interesting." Mitch gingerly touched the flesh. "Does this hurt?"

"No. It should, I suppose, considering how badly it did earlier. But no," I said in amazement, "it doesn't hurt."

He gave a low whistle. "And it's completely healed. Look for yourself."

I turned my head, opened my eyes and saw that Mitch was right. There was no mark, no scar remaining to show that I had ever been wounded there. Just as it should be.

"Then what's wrong with me?"

"Maybe nothing." He touched my skin again. "Unless . . ."

"Unless?" I bit my lip. "What are you thinking?"

"It doesn't necessarily have to be something bad, sweetheart. Why do you always think the worst? Maybe the poison has been dispersed through your body or maybe it's been neutralized by your metabolism. That process may just have taken longer than normal. I wish Sam were here. He could take a blood sample and find out for sure."

"Or you could sample my blood yourself."

"True enough." He smiled at me. "I know the taste of you better than anything else in the world."

"Do me a favor, my love?"

"Anything for you."

"Make love to me first."

"Why, Mrs. Greer." His eyes glinted at me as he turned out the light. "I thought you'd never ask."

His arms went around me, his mouth came down on top of mine, and all thoughts of the world outside disappeared. There, in the total darkness of our room, in the ruins of our life, we made love. Slowly and delicately, Mitch covered every inch of my body with his hands and his mouth until I grew wild with hunger and desire for him. He coaxed me to climax twice and I cried out with passion, thrashing and moaning.

"There," he said, when I had quieted and lay breathing heavily, "isn't that better than fighting?"

"Oh, yes, absolutely." I inhaled deeply. "Much better. Now I want you to lie still and let me love you."

He gave a little laugh, which turned to a low moan as I began kissing him, starting with his eyelids and his cheekbones and his bristly chin. Playfully I bit at his earlobes and his lips, nibbling my way down his body, hands trailing in the wake of my mouth. I loved the feel of him, loved the scent of him, loved the taste of him.

He gasped when I took him into my mouth completely, gave another moan and began to rise and fall with me in perfect rhythm. His hands touched my head and he laughed when he could not grasp my hair. It didn't matter, nothing mattered but my mouth and his body and the love between us. My teeth grazed the taut skin of his penis, drawing off a drop of his precious blood.

His muscles tensed and he growled, thrusting himself deeper into my mouth. I sucked on him deeply, savoring this fluid as much as I savored his blood, swallowing each and every drop.

Then it was over and he gave a loud sigh, reaching down and pulling me up to lie next to him. I smiled and snuggled into his side, my hand lazily brushing over his chest.

When his breathing returned to normal, he bent his head down and sank his fangs into the tender flesh over my right nipple. I felt the soft suction of his mouth on my skin. He took no more than a small taste before he stopped, his body going totally still. He choked and pulled his mouth away from me.

"I'm sorry, love." His voice was filled with anger, not directed at me this time. "The poison is still there. Those damn bastards; they'll pay for this. But first . . ." he gave me a quick kiss, got up from the bed, turned on the light and walked to the phone. "First, I'm going to call Sam. There's no way we can treat this ourselves. And you're more important than—"

"No, Mitch," I interrupted, my voice small and frightened, yet determined. "I am not more important than the continuation of our friends and our family. This must be what they've been planning: to force us out of hiding, to cause us to reveal the locations of those remaining. They know you apparently and they know how you think. How are they able to know so much about us when we know nothing about them?"

"You're right, of course." He set the receiver down. "But what am I supposed to do, Deirdre? Just stand around and watch you die?"

I forced a laugh. "I don't think I will die any time soon, my love. For one thing, you won't permit it. So," and I stretched my arms out to him, "come back to bed. You have had no sleep for two days now while I seem to have done nothing but."

He hesitated.

"Mitch, my love, there is nothing you can do right now. Come. Sleep. I'll watch and wake you if there is any change. Things may seem different after a good sleep."

He nodded, crossed the room and lay down next to me. I stroked his hair; he relaxed and slept.

The day passed slowly for me, with nothing to do but lie still, stare at the ceiling and think. My thoughts, however, were disturbing and always came to the same dead end. We did not know who and we did not know why.

I concentrated for a while on the feel of poisoned blood rushing through my veins. By filtering out all outside noise and distractions, I could hear the thrum of movement, the pounding of my heart and I could feel the slow burn spreading; not particularly unpleasant or painful, the feeling was just different.

I wondered if there was a cure, wondered what sort of progression the poisoning would follow, wondered why they had arranged it this way. I was not an important person in Cadre politics; Mitch would have been a more obvious target. Even had they chosen to poison Victor, that would have made more sense than inflicting it upon me.

To keep away from the dead ends, I began to run through my life, replaying important memories, calling to mind faces of those I had loved and lost.

They were not that many, especially considering the many years I had lived. I had always structured my life to avoid involvement whenever possible, but there were still a few dear ones who managed entrance.

Gwen, my sometimes silly but always endearing secretary when I owned Griffin Designs—dead at the hands of Larry Martin. Chris, Mitch's son, murdered also by Larry. Elly, our next-door neighbor when we lived in our cabin in Maine—not dead, perhaps, but certainly lost to me. There would be no return to that place.

One by one, I worked my way through the list, replaying important events, summoning up very real emotions until I made it down through the past and into the years of my humanity.

There I stopped with a shock as if I'd hit a brick wall. And try as I might, I could not get beyond it. Objectively, of course, I knew that something existed on the other side of that wall. But I could not even summon up the barest trace of what had been.

Gone were the memories of that time: the rich emotional warmth of recollection, the love I must have felt with people that I knew then, the laughter and the tears, even the process of becoming what I was now—all of this was gone, all of this that helped to make me who I was, violently ripped from me with no notice and no purpose.

"Bastards." I whispered the word so that I would not wake Mitch. "Goddamned bastards." Would it continue, I wondered, this loss of memory, until I became nothing more than a shell of the creature I was now? An undead machine, emotionless and cold. Was this the cost of the poison that even now I could feel filtering through my body?

I crawled out of bed carefully, and, finding the laundry that I had started earlier, now dried, folded neatly and stacked on the sofa, I dressed in black jeans, a black tank top under a red plaid flannel shirt and a pair of thick black socks. *Quite a change from the elegant costume of the dream,* I thought, and gave a small bitter laugh.

Not distracted by thoughts of clothes, though, I felt my mind still reeling with the implications of the memory loss and I sat down at the small computer desk, staring at the blank screen. "Is that what you want, you bastards? To drain me of everything that makes me what I am now? What possible use does that serve?"

"Deirdre?" The sleepy voice from the bed startled me. I had forgotten how lightly Mitch slept these past few years. "What time is it?"

I checked the clock on the mantelpiece. "About an hour to sunset, my love, go back to sleep."

"No." He yawned loudly and sat up. "I can't now, I'm awake. I'll make some coffee." He came over to me, looked at the blank screen and laughed. "I should have known you weren't using that," he said, "but you really should learn."

"Yes, I suppose I should." My voice sounded flat and emotionless.

"Something's wrong. Is it the arm?"

I laughed. "No, nothing that simple, Mitch, or that easily observable. I cannot remember."

He shook his head. "Maybe I'm just fuzzy from sleep, but I don't understand what you're talking about. Did you say that you can't remember what's wrong?"

"No." I sighed, leaned my head against the back of the chair, closed my eyes and tested the memories again. "Yes, they are gone, not even a trace. And although I know those times happened and I know I must have lived them, I cannot remember my human years."

Chapter 14

"So what do you think, Sam?"

I could not stop Mitch from making the call. In all honesty, I didn't try very hard. I was more shaken than I had ever been; the prospect of death was not nearly as frightening as the thoughts of having to live eternally yet without memory.

I could hear Sam's response, I could have guessed what he would say.

"I don't know, Mitch, there's no way I can tell anything over the phone. I'll need to see her. And soon. Should I come there?"

"If you would, yeah. Consider this our scheduled meeting, just a little bit earlier than intended. This is something we all should know. And I think it's time we fought back."

"I'll be there as soon as I can make travel arrangements." Sam's voice, even from such a long distance, was calm and reassuring. "Should I bring Viv along?"

I smiled, hearing her frantic answer in the background.

"Try to keep me away, Sam, *mon cher,* and you will find an angry vampire in your bed."

Mitch laughed. "God forbid, Sam. As someone who speaks from experience, an angry vampire in one's bed should be avoided at all costs." He sobered. "Look, the two of you be careful when you're traveling, okay? These guys aren't pulling their punches. They're using wooden bullets, apparently, tipped with the same poison."

"What is this all about, Mitch? Eduard is dead." Sam was still talking, but in the background I heard a few vehement words from Vivienne. I did not need to speak the language to get their meaning and I smiled again. "And if he's dead," Sam continued, "his resentments should have died with him."

"We'll find out, Sam. We have to." Mitch paused and ran his fingers through his hair in the tired gesture I knew too well. "You do know where we're located, right?"

"I'll find you. Are we contacting the others? Cadre members, I mean. Damn, I wish these bastards had used another name for themselves. It gets too confusing."

"Yeah," Mitch agreed. "And yeah, I'm officially activating the call list. Get as many of them together as you can; this sort of situation doesn't just affect one of us. It's something they should all be aware of, whether they can attend the meeting or not."

"Okay. I'll start the calls. You tell Deirdre to hold on for me. We'll be there as soon as we can. Wait, Viv wants to talk to Deirdre."

Mitch handed me the phone and I put the receiver to my ear. "I just wanted to ask, *mon chou,* what sort of clothes I should bring." She laughed, realizing the frivolity of her question. "And you are by the sea, are you not? Should I bring a bathing costume?"

I smiled. "You never change, do you, Vivienne? Even when the whole world is falling down around our ears, you are the same and you are wonderful, precisely the way you are. Thank God for that."

Her high-pitched metallic giggle warmed my heart, even through the phone lines. If I closed my eyes, I could picture her face, the dimples forming with her smile, the glint of innocent mischief in her eyes.

"I fear, Deirdre," she said, "that God has very little to do with it. But you must know that I love you, *ma chere*. And do not worry, sweet sister. Even if my Sam cannot work his normal miracle, I have the perfect solution to your problems. If you lose any more memories, I will simply share with you some of mine. I certainly have more than my share, and some of them? Oh la, yes, they are very interesting."

"I can believe that. And thank you, Vivienne. Walk softly this night and stay well." I hung up the phone before she could hear the tears in my voice.

"Feel better?"

I wrapped my arms around Mitch's waist and buried my head in his chest. "Yes. But I hope they get here before I forget who they are."

"It's not going to get that bad, Deirdre. I promise."

Grateful for his confidence where I had none of my own, I nevertheless changed the subject. "I think I'll make us some coffee."

"Oh, yeah, I'm sorry, I was going to do that, wasn't I?"

I laughed on the way to the kitchen. "Until I dropped this bomb on you, yes, you were." I measured the water, put the coffee into the filter and set the machine to start. Reaching up into the cupboard for two mugs, I called out to him. "Did I tell you that I found the body of a dead swan in the ruins last night?"

"We didn't talk about last night at all." He came over and leaned on the door frame. "So tell me."

I set out the sugar and the creamer, along with a spoon. "I wanted to go for a run—you know how it always calms me down. I was feeling left out. Alone. And I knew the Cat would help."

"Left out? You're jealous of Maggie, aren't you?"

"No. Not jealous. She and her son make me nervous. There is something that does not ring true about the two of them. Does the boy talk?"

Mitch shook his head. "No. But it's not what you think. He can't talk. That tumor Pete was telling us about had grown around Phoenix's vocal cords and when they removed it, well, something went wrong."

"Surely they could do something to remedy that now?" I poured two mugs of coffee and slid one over to him.

Mitch shrugged as he spooned sugar and creamer into his cup, taking less of both now than he did when he was human. "I get the impression that Maggie distrusts the whole medical profession. She clams up completely when the situation is mentioned. And maybe there *is* nothing they can do. The boy seems healthy enough otherwise. But we were talking about you and the abbey."

"Yes, we were. Although, there's not that much more to tell, actually. I attempted to change into the Cat, but the pain of transformation was so severe she refused to come out. For a while I seemed caught midway between human form and animal, but I forced the change back. Moe found me then, he had not been with me initially, and I just wanted to close my eyes and rest for a minute before returning home. I dreamed, I think, but I don't recall about what. And then you were there and you carried me home."

"Did you try any other transformations? To mist, maybe. Or did you try your winged form?"

Shaking my head, I took a long drink of my own black coffee, savoring as always the warmth of it filtering through my body. When I opened my mouth to reply, I managed only a gasp, as a sudden wave of nausea overwhelmed me.

Quickly, I leaned over the sink and vomited up the little bit of coffee I had just drunk along with a small residue of blood. The sour smell from the sink wafted up to me and I vomited again and again until nothing was left.

"Deirdre?"

I held up a hand to hold him off, turned on the water and washed the vileness down the drain. Then I splashed my face with some cool water and dried myself with a paper towel.

I looked up.

"Deirdre, are you okay? What's wrong?"

He had never seen me sick before. *Hell,* I thought, *I should not be sick. I am a vampire, eternal health and youth are supposed to be my birthright.* I had never before been sick, except perhaps during my human years, and those now I did not remember.

"Are you okay?"

My teeth began to chatter as I realized that I was cold, deathly cold. "No, I am not, Mitch." I groaned a bit and shivered. "I don't think I will ever be right again."

He came over to me and wrapped his arms around me. "Jesus, Deirdre," he said, "you're burning up. It's like you have a fever. But how the hell can you have a fever?"

I gave him a confused look, but could not find the words to say. My mind was hazy, my whole body shook and I felt waves of hot and cold along with the continued nausea.

"Never mind that," he said briskly, "let's get you into bed and warmed up. Or cooled down. Damn it, I wish Sam were here."

Mitch undressed me like a child, his hands gentle and strong. He helped me into a nightgown and settled me into bed, piling blankets over me. Laying a cool hand onto my hot forehead, he shook his head. "It's hard for me to tell, love, but your body temperature is certainly higher than our normal, maybe even higher than human normal." Then he pulled all the blankets from me and I shivered violently in the open air.

"Mitch?" I asked, my teeth chattering together. "No blankets? But I'm so very cold."

"Best not to be covered, I think. I'll start up a fire, though, and that should help. I'd go downstairs and find some aspirin for you, but I have no idea what they would do to you. We'll just have to wait this out."

I curled up on my side as he stacked wood in the fireplace. "Perhaps," I said, my words muffled by the pillow and by my shivers, "the poison is working its way out of my system."

"Maybe," he said, his voice grim and dark. "Or maybe it's working its way deeper."

I felt a flash of heat as he got the fire started, heard the warm crackle of flames. But I experienced it all as if from a distance. Nothing outside of me seemed important. Pain was the only reality. My head ached, my limbs ached and pain shot through every portion of my body. Nothing in my previous vampiric life had caused such distress.

Over the long years, I'd been beaten, stabbed, shot. I'd had a bullet cut out of my shoulder with no anesthetic. I'd suffered horrible pangs of hunger, burns from careless exposure to the sun, my skin had been slit open with glass and metal and wood. Through it all, though, I managed to completely ignore the ravages of pain, knowing that they were only temporary conditions. But this pain was different in that it seemed endless. And ultimately, fatal.

"What is happening?" I whispered the tearful words and fell into a state of unconsciousness.

The fever and the pain are gone, as quickly as they came. I get up from the bed quietly so as not to disturb the man sleeping in the chair next to the bed. I look at him fondly, wishing that I did not have to leave him behind, but knowing that I must. My desire for flight is a compulsion I cannot deny.

The windows open onto the night air and the crisp ocean breeze energizes me. I slip out of my nightgown and perch briefly on the windowsill, listening to the call of the night.

With a sudden forward movement, I launch myself out of the window, sprouting feathers and wings before I hit the ground, catching a wind current and soaring high into the sky.

My wings are strong and my heart is free and I fly tirelessly and quickly, crossing the ocean in just a matter of seconds, eventually touching down in a city of concrete, steel and glass. Home.

I search the streets for the place I want, for the place I need. Everything looks different from the air, even the scents of the city have changed. But still I know this place and know that this is my destination. I have been called, summoned to this place and I must obey.

There, I say to myself, as I dip lower and spot a familiar building, *there is where I am going.*

His window is open and I fly in. He is waiting, I recognize him from the other dreams. He is the man from the dance floor, he is the black shadow that paced me while I flew.

Laughing, he holds out his arm and I go to him, perching on his wrist, digging in with my talons.

But he does not seem to notice the pain. No, more than that, it is as if he welcomes it. He smiles and strokes my head, smoothing my feathers and whispering words of calm. Drops of blood, like crimson beads, roll from the wounds I have made and fall hissing onto the floor.

"Here, little one," he says, dabbing his finger in the blood and putting it up to my beak so that I can drink. "Remember this. Here is where you belong. Look around you and engrave it on your soul. You must remember this place, you must remember me, for when all else is gone from you, I will still remain."

I do as he commands. I will remember.

As if he had heard my thoughts, he nods. "Good. And now sleep." He fits a leather hood over my eyes and tenderly places me into a small silver cage.

"You will stay safe here, little one. Remember."

Chapter 15

The dream ended abruptly, long before I could grasp the significance of the man's words. And soon, after waking, they melted away into nothing as dreams often do. Like the memories I had lost.

I tested the edges of my mind, but try as I might, I could not bring back the past. More of it now was gone, but the pain of the loss seemed lessened, softened somehow by dream words of comfort that I could not recall.

I did, however, remember the sickness. Unfortunately it had not disappeared with the other portions of my mind. I moaned softly, slowly becoming aware of the activity around me: a soft knock on the door, and a whispered exchange between Mitch and Maggie.

"I've brought this for her," Maggie said, "nothing much, just some herbal tea and a bowl of broth. She might feel better if you could get her to drink some of it."

"Thanks, Maggie. I appreciate your help."

"And don't worry about the pub, Mitch. We're having a slow night anyway and it's nothing I can't handle."

There was a pause and then Maggie's voice again, still pitched low but with that threatening edge. "Hey, you dog, you can't come in here." I heard a low rumbling growl that ended in a whine.

"He'll be fine in here, Maggie. Go ahead, Moe, find a place to sit." I heard the clack of his nails on the floor, felt his heavy body lie down on the floor next to my side of the bed, heard his sigh. *Not such a bad protector,* I thought, and reached down and weakly patted his head, grateful for his presence.

"Now," Mitch said, "since you are here, why don't you come in too? And please, set the tray down." There was a pause and I could hear him clearing things from the computer desk. "Here will be fine."

I opened my eyes and looked around. Maggie stood in the small sitting room and surveyed the flat; she looked beautiful as usual, wearing a lacy white blouse and a full denim skirt, with a wide black leather belt cinched around her tiny waist.

Even in my weakened state, I could scent her strong human aroma from across the room. Licking my dry lips, I realized that I was famished, longing for another drink, another taste of her richness.

"Very cozy," she said, "just like a little love nest." Then she laughed and pointed to the windows. "Steel shutters? Are you expecting to be bombed?"

Mitch shrugged. "Keeps the sun out, mostly. Deirdre is very sensitive to sunlight."

"As she should be, most people of her kind are."

"Her kind?" I heard the threat in Mitch's voice, felt the tensing of the dog next to me.

"Of course, she's a redhead, isn't she? The bad bleach job doesn't really fool anyone, especially another woman. She has a redhead's complexion. Why, what did you think I meant?" Her voice shook with hidden laughter.

"Nothing. I'm just worried about her. She's never been sick before."

"Never? Imagine that, never been sick before. Poor baby." Maggie looked over at me and our eyes met. "She's awake now, though." She picked up the cup of tea from the tray and brought it over to me. "Here, Dot, drink this."

"What is it?" I leaned into her, sniffing, feeling my mouth begin to water and not for the tea. I licked my lips again, then wiped my mouth with my hand.

"Chamomile, mostly. It will help calm your stomach."

I had drunk chamomile tea before; it was something Elly always served me. I had not appreciated the taste then and probably would not now. *But hell,* I thought, *I am already poisoned. What harm can a little tea do?*

I nodded, and Maggie put an arm behind my back and lifted me up, pulling me close to her and holding the cup to my lips. My fangs clicked on the ceramic mug. "Careful now, don't want to chip a tooth."

She laughed as I sipped at the tea. "That's right," she said in the condescending exchange usually reserved for nurses and their patients, "just take a little bit at a time. We don't want it coming right back up, now, do we? I'll put it down on the nightstand here and you can have more when you feel up to it."

She laid me back down on the bed. "You're such a little thing, Dot. A strong wind could blow you away." Maggie laughed briefly, then put a cool hand on my forehead. "Still feverish, I see."

There was an awkward pause. I closed my eyes and settled back into the pillows.

Maggie pulled a blanket up over me, brushed my forehead

briefly and stood up. "Well," she said, "I need to get back down-stairs. I left Phoenix to watch the cash drawer. Get better soon, Dot. We need to get better acquainted and we can't do that with you sequestered up here, cozy though it is."

Mitch escorted her to the door. "Thanks again, Maggie."

"No problem," she said, "we're almost family. You've taken me and my son in, and that's reason enough for me to want to help."

I heard the door close, heard Mitch set the locks and relaxed. "Deirdre?" He sat down on the bed next to me. "Are you feel-ing better?"

"Some," I said softly. "I think now I just need rest. And blood. I am so very hungry. Had I not been so weak, Maggie would have found out what my kind is capable of."

Mitch laughed. "Probably not a good idea, although she is tempting."

"Yes. Very tempting." It did not seem a good time to reveal to Mitch that I may already have drunk from Maggie. And that if what I remembered was true, her blood was as intoxicating as she was herself. I was uneasy about the incident, feeling guilty about that transgression and for not being able to confess to Mitch what had happened. That is, if it had actually occurred. Maggie herself seemed oblivious of that particular interaction between us and she had never given me any indication that what I remembered was true.

"As your waiter, madam, I fear I must warn you that the din-ner specials are scarce this evening. You only have the choice of me"—he made a broad flourish of his arm and bowed, causing me to giggle a bit, as he had intended—"or"—he pointed down to the side of the bed—"the dog. And in this case," and Mitch grew serious, "I would advise you to choose me. You need the extra strength."

"Mitch, you cannot keep offering yourself like this to me. You need your strength just as much as I do."

"No, Deirdre," he said, "no protests. After I get you taken care of, I can always go out and find something. Here."

Once again he offered me his wrist, and once again I accepted, sinking my fangs into him and pulling on his rich blood. I felt it rush through my body, a comfortable warmth, unlike the progression of the poison. I started to pull away when I felt I'd taken enough. "No," he said, his voice stern, "take more. I'll be fine."

I drank fully then, abandoning myself to the sensations, to the sweet wild taste of him. He stroked my hair as I drank, until finally he pushed me away. "We won't tell Maggie," he said with a glint in his eye, "but I'll bet that'll help more than a thousand cups of chamomile tea."

I looked up at him and smiled. "Thank you, love." Then I closed my eyes and slept.

At some point during the day, I heard Mitch turn the television on. He turned the sound down quite low, but still I managed to make out what he was watching, another repeat of the *Real-Life Vampires* show. I listened for a while, without bothering to open my eyes to watch, drifting in and out of sleep.

"That's right, Bob," Terri was saying. "And this next question comes from Meg in Madison, Wisconsin. Meg writes: 'Dear Terri and Bob, is it true that vampires can change shape?' "

I answered for Terri on this one. "Provided they are not poisoned by the helpful *Real-Life Vampires* team, Meg, yes, they most certainly can."

Mitch looked over at me and smiled. "Sorry, Deirdre, I'll turn it down a bit more if you'd like."

"Just turn it off instead." I groaned, pulled a pillow over my head and fell back to sleep.

When I woke with the next sunset, I felt fine. No traces of pain or fever. Mitch was sleeping in a chair next to the bed where he'd kept vigil during the long-seeming day. I sat up, the bed creaked slightly and he woke.

I smiled at him. "All better," I said. "Thank you for taking such good care of me."

"What else could I do, sweetheart? You are my life."

"Did you manage to feed last night?"

He nodded. "Yeah; I did, indeed. You and Moe were all snuggled up safe and sound, so I took a little walk on the bad side of town looking for trouble. Fortunately, I found some. So I feel good about that. And then when I came back, Moe and I switched places." He gave a little laugh. "Took some convincing to get him to leave the room, but I managed. That creature is devoted to you, Deirdre. You seem to have that effect on us canine types. So tell me, do you feel like getting up?"

He turned grim and seemed anxious about something. "Yes, I would like to get up. What are you suggesting?"

He looked away from me. "I'd like to do something for Phoenix, maybe get Sam to look at him while he's here. I can't believe that his situation is irreversible. But Maggie doesn't seem to want to talk about it much. Maybe she would with you."

"Why get involved, Mitch?"

"Because, damn it, I like having the boy around. I don't think you've ever understood what Chris's death meant to me."

"How could I," I said softly, "when you won't talk about it?"

"How can I talk about it with you? Do you think I don't know that you blame yourself for his death? Guilt gets us nowhere on this, Deirdre, and it solves nothing. Chris is dead and although I'd give my right arm to get him back again, it's not going to happen. But this boy? He reminds me of Chris, not so much in looks, but in the way his eyes follow me, the way his face seems to light up when he sees me. It's like life has given me a second chance. If it weren't for you, I'd marry Maggie Richards just to have responsibility for the child."

"Oh." I could not hide the hurt in my voice.

"Shit." He ran his fingers through his hair. "That didn't come out quite the way I'd intended. I don't want Maggie, not like that, not ever like that. In fact, I can't imagine being with anyone other than you. An eternity with you is more than I'd ever hoped for. But the boy has gotten under my skin, somehow. I think about him all the time, even though the time we've spent together has been brief."

While he talked, I got out of bed, slipped off the nightgown he had dressed me in last night and put on the clothes I'd worn before.

"I don't understand any of this," Mitch continued. "I used to feel like I could rule the world. But now I feel so helpless, what with you, sick as you are, with that bloody poison eating its way through you and your memories. And I can't do a damn thing to stop it. But maybe I can do something for Phoenix. He's lost in a nightmare of silence."

"And you want me to talk Maggie into letting Sam examine him?"

"Exactly." He smiled at me and put his hand out. I went to him where he sat in the chair and kissed the top of his head.

"Done."

"I've been thinking anyway that I should stay up here for the night, check around a bit on the Internet for news and be available for any Cadre members who call. So this is a perfect opportunity for the two of you to get better acquainted."

"I can hardly wait."

"Be nice, Deirdre. She means no harm. If you gave her a chance, you might even find that you like her. You could use a friend, I think. Maybe the two of you could—"

I interrupted him with a laugh. "Go shopping together? Or maybe pub crawling? I know, we could exchange recipes. That would certainly be amusing. However," I said quickly when I saw that I had angered him, "you are right. I haven't given her a chance. I'll try to make amends this evening."

"Good." He stood up and gave me a brief hug. "Now what's this about a dead swan?"

"Dead swan?"

"Back before you got sick, remember? You said you found a dead swan in the ruins."

"Oh. Yes. There was a dead swan there. Didn't you see it?"

"I was looking for you, sweetheart. I doubt if I'd have seen a swan if it jumped up and bit me."

"Its neck had been broken, Mitch. Twisted and gnawed; then whatever did that just left it there."

"Maybe one of the dogs did it. It needn't be any more sinister than that."

I nodded and bit my lip. "Yes, I realize that. But it was just so sad. And I dreamt about it, I think." The whole incident seemed to me to be a long time ago. "But I don't remember for sure. And it was only a dream, after all. So for now, I'll follow your instructions and go down to help Maggie."

"Deirdre?"

"Yes, my love?"

"How are the memories?"

I sighed. "I was hoping you wouldn't ask. As far as I can tell, another twenty years are gone." I laughed humorlessly. "It is rather difficult to keep track of what is gone."

His blue eyes narrowed with worry. "Do me another favor?"

"Anything for you, Mitch."

"No matter what happens, don't ever forget me."

I smiled and taking his face between my hands, kissed him again, full on the lips. "You foolish man. As if I could."

I walked to the door and opened it, stepped over the dogs sleeping in front of it and went downstairs.

Chapter 16

Maggie and I worked side by side until the pub closed. She proved Mitch right; she was more than competent and certainly as friendly as one might ever want. I watched her interaction with the customers; her easy confidence and ready smile won their hearts and their attention. She seemed larger than life, somehow. Her laugh was infectious and overflowing with humor, her eyes flirtatious and flattering. Man or woman, it made no difference, Maggie Richards charmed them all.

By the time we had shown the door to the last of the regulars, she had charmed me as well and I found myself almost ready to admit she was nothing more than she seemed: a beautiful, good-natured and high-spirited woman with a flair for pleasing others. Pete chose well when he picked his temporary replacement.

As for what had transpired between the two of us on her first night here, I was by now more than half convinced that the whole incident was imagined, a by-product of my sickness and the poison.

After we cleaned the tables and swept the floor I started for the stairs, but she laid a hand on my arm.

"Don't go yet, Dot. Please. We need to have a heart-to-heart. Sit." She pointed to a chair. "And I will wait on you."

I hesitated, giving her a doubtful look.

"Please," she repeated. "You seem to be feeling better now, and I thought, or rather hoped, you might enjoy my company a little while longer." She walked over to the bar. "Port?"

I sighed and settled into the chair she had indicated. "Yes, thank you, that would be fine."

"And I'll join you." She grabbed two glasses and a bottle of our best tawny port. "The good stuff," she said with a flourish as she sat next to me, "not the stuff we serve the customers."

I laughed. "Mitch has been teaching you well."

She looked up at me briefly as she poured, her eyes glittered. "He's a good man, Dot. You should be proud."

"I am." I took a drink of the wine. "You do know that my name is not Dot or Dottie, don't you?"

She chuckled. "Dot is what Uncle Pete has always called you and I'm not sure I can do otherwise. But yes, I do know it's not your real name. And I know that the two of you're in some sort of trouble."

I started to protest, but she reached over and touched a finger to my lips. "It's okay. Life is trouble, most of the time. And when it catches up to us, sometimes we just need to take a break from it all. No one in these parts cares in the least who you are or why you are here. And Uncle Pete would defend you to the death."

"There should be no need for that." I looked around. "Where is Pete?" I asked, suddenly realizing I had not seen him since the night Maggie arrived.

"He left a bit early for the cruise," she said, "so that he could visit with his daughter in London for a day or two. He wanted to say good-bye last night but didn't want to disturb you. Nothing will suffer for his absence, though. I'm here and I'll take good care of the both of you and the pub."

"And would you defend me to the death?"

"Of course." Maggie gave a delightful laugh. "I'm quite the fighter with a broom. Just ask Moe."

"And where is he? I tripped over Larry and Curly to get down here, but don't see him around. He's been constantly at my side for days, now."

"Moe? He's sleeping with Phoenix right now," she said with a sigh. "I'm sure you gathered that I don't particularly like dogs. But I've never been able to deny either of my sons anything."

She gave me a hard, cold look. "Can you understand that? Loving someone that much? Of course you do," she continued, giving me no opportunity to answer. "It's that way with you and Mitch, isn't it? Anyone with eyes to see can tell that. Watching the two of you together is just lovely; you are so in tune with each other."

I reached for the bottle of port. "Oh, no," Maggie said, pushing my hand out of the way, "tonight I said I was going to wait on you. And so I will." She filled my glass and sighed.

"Yes, you and Mitch are quite the couple," Maggie continued. "I can well imagine that you'll stay together forever. I wish it had been that way with me and the boys' father. For a while, I thought it might be. And then . . ." Her voice trailed away.

"He died. I mean, he was a lot older than me, but I never expected him to die." She gave me a twisted little smile, "Funny, that. I mean, everyone dies, don't they? But he, oh, I don't know, he seemed too grand to die. Too large and too powerful to ever be subjected to death. Still, he gave me the children, my boys. And now that Eddie is gone, they make all the difference. Mitch says you have a grown daughter?"

"Yes, I do." I was unable to control the stiff tone of my voice. "Lily. She lives in New Orleans. She's a beautiful girl, but I don't hear from her much."

"Like that, is it?"

I gave Maggie a questioning look. "Excuse me?"

"The two of you don't get along, is all I meant. It happens. Take my oldest, for instance. He's living with his father's kin now. And seems more than pleased with the arrangement. I hardly ever hear from him either, not a word for months sometimes, and then when he does contact me, it's only because he wants something." She lifted her glass to her lips and drained it, scowling briefly.

"Well," I started, "perhaps he's just busy."

Maggie nodded. "He is that, yes. He's learning a trade, though, and that's something. They own a chain of funeral homes in the States, you see."

"Ah." I took a sip of my wine.

"What do your people do?"

I stifled a laugh. "For the most part, they run bars and clubs and restaurants." I could hardly tell her the full truth; that the only people I had were vampires, related to me by breed and blood.

She nodded and poured us each another glass of wine. "It's a good business. People always need food and drink. The way they always need burial. What did your father do? The same thing?"

"My father? Why, he—" I hesitated, sipping the wine to stall for time. What *did* my father do? I searched my memory frantically and came up with nothing. "He owned a bar." I smiled to smooth over the lie. "Family tradition, I suppose." For some strange reason, I felt driven to say more—something interesting, something that might impress her. "Before that, though, he was a priest." It could have been true; it was true of Max and he was almost a father to me.

"No, go on. A priest?"

"Really. I could never see it, myself. But that's what he said."

She chuckled a bit. "I guess he wanted to serve them wine, one way or another."

"Yes, I suppose that's true."

"We have much more in common than you'd think, Dottie. Take my oldest, he once wanted to be a priest, but life had different plans for him. Now, I fear, he is too solidly ensconced in the world of flesh." She laughed her low, charming laugh. "Both dead and alive."

"And what about Phoenix? What does he want to be?"

"Grown up." Maggie smiled sadly. "It seems to me that if I look hard enough I can see him grow a little bit every day. His brother was the same. They stay little for such a short time."

I thought of Lily's extended childhood, a childhood that, even though it had been spread out over a century, I had missed completely. I knew nothing of children or motherhood, as my own daughter constantly reminded me. I sighed and nodded as if in agreement. "So, why do you call him Phoenix? I assume that's not his real name."

She laughed. "Might as well be—it's the only one he'll answer to. When he was born, you see, he had a tumor and they all said that he would die. But the doctors operated anyway and miraculously he lived and thrived. Rising from the ashes, so to speak."

"And he can't talk at all?"

She dropped her eyes, her sooty black lashes covering any expression they might have held. "He makes sounds, sometimes. Grunts, moans, that sort of thing. And I have heard him laugh, once or twice."

"Mitch and I have a friend. A psychiatrist, really, but still a medical doctor. He will be visiting us in the next day or two. Would you like him to examine Phoenix? Perhaps he could help?"

Maggie gave me a curious look. "Somehow I suspect that it's really Mitch doing the asking on this." She laughed. "If it makes him feel better, yes, certainly. I just don't think it will do much good. We've seen more doctors than I care to remember. Some of them think that eventually the vocal cords will heal. I'd like to hope that, for his sake. He never learned sign language but he's smart as a whip. Reads and writes years beyond his age. I've taught him myself. I was a teacher at a private boys' school before I met his father."

I smiled. "I'm sure all the students were in love with you."

"What a lovely thing to say, Dot." She reached over and touched my hand. I stiffened as, once again, I felt that surge of warmth wash over me. *Damn it,* I thought, *why does she have to be so attractive? So alive? So human?*

Her voice continued, droning on and on, spinning its tale, until it became nothing more than an insistent, seductive whisper. I was not listening to her words; all I could concentrate on was the burning of her flesh against mine. She loomed very close to me, so close that I could scent the aroma of her skin, her hair, her blood. I wanted to taste her again, wanted to explore and pierce that perfect body with fang and claw, to drink in her incredible life force. Slowly. Savoring her flavor, basking in her heat.

"Yes." Her answer was not communicated by voice, she was still telling me stories about the school at which she'd met Phoenix's father. Instead the unspoken word seemed to fly through my veins and shout in my head, "Yes, please, let's do that again."

I leaned in close to her; her hair, soft as a cloud, brushed my cheek. My fangs began to grow and I licked my lips in anticipation of the feast. Luscious and ripe, Maggie's neck loomed in front of my eyes. I felt hypnotized by the faint beat of her pulse visible through her skin. *Lovely, she is so lovely,* I thought. And *I must have her again.*

Once more I bent my mouth to her neck, once more I drew in her blood and vitality. Before I could completely abandon myself to the experience, though, I caught a glimpse of Phoenix, standing as I'd first seen him, barefooted and dressed in pajamas. But this time his eyes were focused and on me. He smiled, nodded and his frail body shook with silent laughter. One hand pointed at me and in the other he held a long white feather tinged bloodred.

I blinked and when I looked again, he was gone. Had he ever been there? What was happening to me?

I swallowed hard and shivered, pulling away from Maggie and forcing myself to concentrate. I needed to remember that I had come down to the pub to learn what I could of this woman. Not to feed, and certainly not to abandon myself to instincts and emotions that normally I kept under better control.

You are not hungry, I told myself, *and you do not want this woman, sexually or any other way.*

Biting my lip so hard it drew my own blood, I roughly removed my hand from her grasp.

"Oh," she said, her voice shaking. *With laughter,* I wondered, *or a sense of shared passion?* "I'm sorry."

"What?" In my dazed state it was all I could say.

"I forgot, you don't like to be touched, dear, do you? I could tell that, the first night I was here, by the way you instantly drew back when I hugged you." From across the table, Maggie inspected the hand she had touched. "No harm done, though. And I will try not to remember not to invade your personal space, Deirdre. It won't be easy; I'm a naturally demonstrative person, I fear."

"No, no, it's not that. Or rather, it is. But the fault is not yours, it is mine." She smiled at me, baring her teeth in the perfect example of angelic innocence.

I glanced at the clock over the bar, then gave it a second look. "How did it get to be so late?" I could not believe I had spent the entire evening talking to Maggie without realizing the time that passed. Was this why Mitch didn't come to find me that night? Did she have the same effect on him as she did on me?

Maggie nodded, rather smugly, I thought. "Yes, you're right, it's late. Near dawn. But you know, I have this strange desire to go out and watch the sunrise over the abbey. Care to join me?"

"The abbey? It must be beautiful at sunrise."

"Yes, it is. Join me?"

For one small second of time I almost agreed, even knowing that such an expedition would mean certain death for me. What power this woman had to exert such a strong pull. Our evening together did nothing to make me her friend; it merely made me fear and desire her more. *And still, the abbey would be beautiful,* I thought, *I should go with her.*

"No." With great reluctance and greater resistance, I shook my head. "No, thank you, Maggie. Some other time perhaps. For now, I think I had better go upstairs now and see how Mitch is doing."

"Suit yourself. And good night, Dot. Pleasant dreams. Give my regards to that handsome dog of a husband and tell him I hope to see him again soon."

The sound of Maggie's laughter lingered in my ears as I mounted the stairs. The remembrance of her touch burned, very much like the poison in my blood. And I felt wearier than I had ever felt in my life.

Chapter 17

"Maggie must leave. Both she and her son. Soon. I don't care about the pub or who takes care of it during daylight hours. We could just close it until Pete returns. But, no matter what else we might do, one thing is quite certain in my mind. They have to go."

I had not even greeted Mitch on entering, but closed the door and leaned up against it, out of breath as if I had been running for miles.

"Leave?" Mitch looked up at me from where he sat at the computer, wearing only a pair of jeans. "Why the hell would we want her to leave? She's here to help us, remember?"

"Help? She is dangerous and I want her out. Jesus, Mitch, she almost talked me into going for a sunrise walk with her in the abbey ruins."

He laughed. "She did? She's quite a persuasive person, isn't she?"

"No, Mitch, you don't understand. There is something not right about that woman. And Phoenix? I know you like him, Mitch, and that you feel drawn to him, because he reminds you of Chris and gives you a second chance to be a father. But I'm sorry, I cannot agree. I think he is the one who killed that swan. The boy is a monster."

"A monster? That sweet child? You must be joking, Deirdre. One only needs to look in his eyes to realize what kind of boy he is."

"I am not joking, Mitch. Phoenix is an evil boy. Disturbed. And frightening."

Mitch laughed again and I grew angry.

"You may find it all amusing, Mitchell Greer, but I still say that he is not quite right."

He sobered. "I'm sorry, I'm just having a little fun with you. God knows we get precious little opportunity for that. And I'm in a good mood; I'm rested, you're obviously feeling better, I didn't have to deal with Maggie or the pub and I had a remarkably good night of research on the computer. Amazing what one can find out with just a little bit of information and a lot of time."

Didn't have to deal with Maggie? "I thought you liked Maggie."

"I did. And on the record, of course, I still do. Or at least I want everyone to think I do. Nothing like a little good cop/bad cop to throw someone off guard."

"You *don't* like her?" I felt as if I had walked into the middle of a story.

"I might still like her, Deirdre, her charm is irrepressible. But after what I've found out about her today, I wouldn't trust her any farther than I could throw her. I'm ashamed to admit that I was taken in by her act at first and completely charmed by the son."

"I don't understand, Mitch, what could you have found out tonight to make you change your mind so completely?"

"I found out the name of Maggie Richards's husband."

"And?"

"And if you are right about Phoenix being a little monster, and I still can't agree with that, it's hardly his fault. Heredity and environment play a huge role in forming the personality of a child. And with his parents? I'm surprised he turned out as well as he did." He smiled at me, drawing out the news.

"You have been around Pete entirely too much, Mitch," I said, giving him a fond smile. "Now, quit dancing around the subject and tell me what you've learned."

He laughed again. "Evil, like beauty, is in the eye of the beholder. If, as you say, the boy is evil, then it's for a good reason. I suspect that's just the way he is. What else would one expect of a DeRouchard?"

I took a deep breath. "DeRouchard? Eduard? But Eduard is dead. They could not have transferred his soul or his consciousness. We saw him die. Burned beyond belief, beyond revival or resurrection."

"But his sons live on, Deirdre. And his deep hatred of vampires continues in them. We needn't look any further for our persecutors."

I felt my legs weaken and I slid down the door, landing on the floor in front of it. "His sons." My voice was flat as the realization sunk in. His sons. "And Maggie's. Oh, dear God. And two of them are living here? Protecting us? Do you suppose they know who we are?"

Mitch looked at me and raised an eyebrow. "What do you think?"

"Then she knows we had a part in killing her husband?" I stopped for a moment. "Of course she does. Hell, even Terri and Bob knew that he was dead and knew who killed him."

Mitch tensed for a second. "Come to think of it, how *did* they know about his death? Or how he died? That show can't have been taped much more than a week after he died. Unlike bloody *Real-Life Vampires,* we don't gloat over our kills. We don't publicize them. And in Eduard's case, there wasn't even a body to discover and identify. All that was left of him was a pile of ashes."

"What difference does that make, Mitch?"

"It makes a difference, Deirdre. A big difference. It means that either someone observed that confrontation or that one of those present for the occasion talked. Neither is a good alternative, but you're right, it has no relevance to the matter at hand. Which is, what do we do with his widow and son?"

"Sons, Mitch, don't forget that there is another one out there. Living with Eduard's relatives. And still, I'm not sure. If neither of these children is carrying Eduard's soul, then why has the persecution continued? It should have died out when he did."

"Deirdre, sweetheart, I think that fever must have addled your brain. Revenge for a beloved husband's murder? Or for a father's life? Vendettas have been waged for far less important reasons."

"So what are we to do? Stay here and accept their presence as if we had no idea who and what they are?"

"Well, not hardly, considering that we know what they are now. But that seemed to have been their plan. Gain our trust and our friendship. And then hit us when we least suspect it."

"But now that we know, we can get rid of them." He looked over at me. "Right?"

"A good plan, Deirdre. But exactly how do you propose to do that?"

I shrugged, sighed and got up from the floor, brushing dog hair from my pants. "I don't know, Mitch. Kill them both and drop them into the North Sea?"

"Could you? Could you kill that beautiful woman and her angelic son?"

I thought for a moment. I feared her, mistrusted her, while at the same time desiring her more than I'd ever have thought possible. And her son made me shiver, arousing both disgust and sympathy. I thought of how I might kill them. Would I slit their throats, suffocate them as they slept, rip open their chests and tear our their still-beating hearts? Just the thoughts alone brought tears to my eyes and made my stomach roll over inside me.

"Could you?" Mitch repeated.

"No," I said, a defeated tone to my voice, "I don't think I could."

He shook his head and ran his fingers through his hair. He smiled at me, his blue eyes shining with love. "That's not saying much, though. You're not the murdering kind, we both know that. God, woman, you've got more humanity than most humans. That's not the issue, really. We're talking about Maggie Richards and her bloody little mute son—hell, I don't think I could kill either of them. And we both know it's not because I'm incapable of murder. I'd gladly wipe anybody off the face of the earth if he threatened a hair on your head, or," and he winked at me, "even Viv's head. In the abstract.

"But the reality of the situation, I suspect, is that none of us are going to prove capable of killing our Maggie. She's good, damned good. In fact I suspect she is one of the best breeders those bastard Others have ever had. She has layer upon layer of protective covering and she's the perfect vampire bait. Remember what Vivienne told us about Monique? How she could not forsake her or abandon her no matter what the circumstances were?"

I nodded.

"Maggie," he continued, "seems to have developed that quality a hundred times over. Have you noticed that the scent of her skin alone can put you into a feeding frenzy? I'm a happily married man and I love you more than I'd ever dreamed possible, but the touch of her hand makes me forget all of that. She arouses emotions in me I've never felt before."

"You're not the only one, Mitch. But I attributed it to my poisoned condition. And I think I may have fed on her." I looked down at the floor and began to cry softly. "Twice. But I don't quite remember, since I have been sick it feels as if everything now is a dream. I don't know what is real and what is remembered."

"Oh, baby." He pulled me into a tight embrace and stood there for a long time, holding me and rocking slightly from side to side. I pressed my head against the smooth skin of his chest. "It'll be okay, Deirdre. I promise you," he whispered into my hair, "I'll make it right."

"Then we will have to kill them somehow, all of them."

"No." He pushed back so he could look into my face. "Don't you see? There's no value in their deaths right now. Alive, though, they provide a nice little bargaining chip. We will trade Eduard DeRouchard's son for the poison antidote."

"What if there is no antidote? We don't really know what this poison is supposed to be doing."

"Sam and Viv will be here soon, possibly even tonight." He moved away from me and headed back to the computer desk. "You and Sam can work together on analyzing and, I hope, counteracting the poison. Vivienne and I will keep an eye on Maggie and Phoenix. And the rest of the Cadre will begin arriving in a week." He sat back down in the chair. "Damn. We'll have to give some thought on where to put them all, since they'll all be arriving now too early for the Goth Festival. I'd counted on that to help camouflage all of them."

I nodded and began to strip off my clothes. "How many have you heard from, Mitch?"

"Forty-three have been accounted for. Not that many will be coming, though. I suspect we won't have more than fifteen or twenty once they all get here. But that number includes Vivienne and Victor, the two oldest surviving house leaders, so we're likely to get agreement in whatever we decide to do." He shrugged. "Not that it really matters at this point, the Cadre has outlived its usefulness. Hell, let's be honest—the organization was outdated years ago and has just sort of been running out of habit. And personally, I don't give a damn whether they approve of my actions or not."

I gave a grim little laugh, wiping away the rest of my tears. "Most of them will never agree on anything, except that none of them have ever liked either one of us. There are still some major grudges being held because I killed Max. So if you can get fifteen to come, that is a major accomplishment."

"If it were just for you, Deirdre, that would be true. We need to face the facts. This may be our last stand before total extinction. You have been poisoned and although we don't know what that will eventually do to you, I'm sure it won't be good. At the very least, the remaining Cadre members must be warned. And at the very worst, who's to say that you aren't just one of many?"

"On that cheerful note, my love, I think I will take a shower. Would you like to join me?"

"You start without me; I'll catch up later. I still have a few e-mails to answer and reservations to tend to."

"Suit yourself, but if you wait too long I'll use all the hot water."

"You wouldn't do that to me, Deirdre, would you? You wouldn't use up all the hot water and make the man who loves you more than life itself take a cold shower, would you?"

I smiled at him and shrugged. "I might," I said. "It could be that a cold shower would do you some good."

"Is that what you think?" Mitch got up from the desk and slowly removed his jeans and advanced on me in a mock-threatening pose, backing me into the tiny bathroom and closing the door behind us.

I put my arms around his neck and whispered in his ear, "So now I'm to understand that you want to take a shower?"

"Not exactly." He reached around me and through the curtain, turning on the water. "I want to take you, in the shower."

I laughed softly as he picked me up and I wrapped my legs around his waist. "Here is a question for that stupid show. 'Mitch from Whitby, England, asks: Why do vampires engage in sexual intercourse as often as they do?' "

"That's an easy one," Mitch said in his best Bob Smith imitation. "Because they can. And because they never know if this time will be their last. Now quit asking these silly questions, Deirdre, and kiss me."

Chapter 18

I hummed a little song to myself in the shower, loving the feel of the water on my body, amazed at how well I felt, compared to that one period of being ill. "You know," I said to Mitch as he soaped my back, "I don't think we fully appreciate the perfection of our bodies."

He laughed. "Funny," he said, "I vaguely remember doing just that not all that long ago."

"No, you know what I mean. After being sick, I realize what a gift it is to be immune to human illnesses, to be ageless and immortal. I used to hate what I was; every waking moment was spent in self-loathing for the monster I was. But now, I feel enriched, enlightened."

"That's good, sweetheart. But I feel cold. Is the hot water running out?"

"No, I turned it down a touch."

"You what?" He sounded shocked. "Since when did you start taking cold showers?"

"It's a far cry from cold, Mitch." Turning around to let the water rinse my back, I gave him a quick kiss. "However"—I shrugged, stepped out of the shower, and reached back in, turning up the hot water to full force—"I was finished anyway. Enjoy."

I dried myself, still humming the song I had been singing in the shower. I wrapped another towel around my body, tucking the top of it in above my breasts, and wiped the steam off of the mirror with my hand. I turned my head from side to side, looking at my hair. "Now that they've managed to find us, and plant their agents in our home, there's probably no good reason for me to stay a blonde. What do you think? Should I dye it back to the original color, or just let it grow out on its own?"

"It's up to you, Deirdre," he called to me over the running

water. "It looks fine now the way it is, and it looked fine before."

I made a face at him. "Some help you are. I think the color is horrible with my complexion, makes me look even paler than I am." I leaned farther in toward the mirror. "And shows up the dark circles under my eyes. I should not have dark circles."

Mitch made some noncommittal grunt when I heard a crash in the apartment. I ran out into the hallway.

"Mitch!"

In the time we had been in the shower, what Maggie had called our cozy little nest had been vandalized. The computer had been knocked off the table, the television overturned, the phone had been ripped out of the wall and tossed into the fireplace. The cushions on the furniture had been torn off and one had been shredded, bits of fluff and stuffing were spread across the floor.

And from underneath one of the cushions, I saw the tip of a dog's nose, a large black nose. My first thought was that Moe had done this damage and then had tried to hide.

Then I realized that he was not moving, that there was no way his massive body could have been hidden under the pillow. I held my breath and walked slowly to the middle of the room. A large butcher knife, one I recognized from the pub's kitchen, was driven down into the floor next to the dog's lifeless and bodiless head. The open eyes stared up at me, a sad parody of his attentiveness in life.

I knelt down and patted it. "Poor thing," I said, starting to cry, "you were such a good dog. Who did this to you?" Tears were now streaming down my face and I made no attempt to stop them. "Oh, God, Moe, you certainly did not deserve this. I am so sorry."

"Deirdre?" Mitch came out of the shower, a towel wrapped around his waist. "What the hell happened?"

I stood up, holding a hand over my mouth while my other arm cradled my stomach. I sniffed, choking back a hysterical sob. "Someone broke in, the goddamned bastards. And left me a little present."

"Broke in? That's a solid steel door, how the hell can some-body just break in? A present? What do you mean, a present?" Then his eyes focused. "Oh, bloody fucking hell. Why on earth would anyone do such a thing?"

With that statement, the door swung inward slowly and both Mitch and I turned with a growl.

"Mitch? Dottie? Are you okay?" Maggie stood on the thresh-old, staring in shock. "I just came back from the market"—she held up a bag filled with groceries to illustrate her alibi—"and noticed that the door was open."

"We had a small intruder problem, Maggie," I said.

"Someone's broken in? Who would do such a thing?"

"I wish I knew," Mitch said, "and I'm sure we'll eventually find out. But for now . . ." He shrugged.

"We should call the police and report this." Maggie's eyes widened as she saw the dog's head. "What is that? Is that . . ." Her voice trailed off and her eyes seemed to glaze over, frozen to the sight. "Oh, dear sweet heavens, yes, it is. Have you called the police?" Not waiting for an answer, she continued. "We should call the police, you know. They'll take care of it."

"No," Mitch said, "no police. We'll deal with this ourselves. Just close the door, Maggie, and go about your business. There's nothing you can do in this situation. Please leave us alone."

"But the dog." She stared at the mess on the floor. "He's dead. And where's—" Maggie gulped. "Where's the rest of him?"

"I'll find him. And bury him myself." Mitch's voice was cold and hard. "Tonight. It's no concern of yours."

"Phoenix will be heartbroken, though. I won't let him up here until it's all over."

"That would be a good idea, Maggie." I walked over to her, adjusting my wrap, noticing that my hands were shaking and that there was a smear of blood across the towel. "Now, you should go back downstairs."

She looked into my eyes and backed away from me, and for the first time since we met I noticed a trace of fear in her face.

Good, I thought, *you should be afraid, you god-damned*

bitch. Hold on to that fear, remember it. Perhaps it will make you think twice about doing something like this.

But I said nothing; instead, I closed the door on her stunned expression and set the locks.

"No one broke in that door," Mitch said, "not without major explosives. We may have been preoccupied when it happened, but we'd have heard something. No, that door had to be opened with a key."

I agreed. "And we know that there are only two other people besides us with access to that key."

He knelt down next to the dog's head. "Maggie does seem like the obvious suspect, doesn't she? Even so, I think we need to look elsewhere. She certainly seemed genuinely shocked, more than enough to give me reasonable doubt. For what it's worth, my gut feeling is that she would never have killed the dog, no matter how much she disliked him. And she's not here to kill us, I'm sure of that. She's had ample opportunity to finish off either one of us."

"Perhaps it wasn't her. I don't remember if I locked the door when I came upstairs. If I didn't lock it and you didn't, then this could have been done by anybody."

Mitch gave a short laugh. "I don't know which is worse—to think that Maggie did this, or to think that a total stranger was here. Either way, they've left us quite a mess to clean up."

I sighed, dropped the towel from me and tossed it over to Mitch. "We might as well start there," I said, pointing and choking back a sob. "Poor dog."

"Yeah." He mopped up the small sticky pool of blood as I pulled on a heavy flannel nightgown. "I wonder how anyone managed to do this to him. I'd think he'd have put up more of a fight."

I had a sudden vision of the boy, bending over the dog he'd befriended, sitting down next to him. The dog would look up and wag his tail and the boy would hug him around the neck before quietly and happily slitting his throat and carving off the head. It was a particularly revolting image and kept replaying itself over and over in my mind.

My stomach rolled. I swallowed to keep down the bile that rose in my throat, but it did no good. Clapping a hand over my mouth, I quickly turned and ran for the bathroom.

When I had finished vomiting up the remains of what I had drunk earlier, I washed my face and hands. "Fine vampire I make these days," I said with a small laugh. "Apparently I can no longer stand the sight of blood."

"Are you okay?" Mitch had finished mopping up the blood and had wrapped the head up in one of the blankets from our bed. He picked up the bundle now and gently carried it to the front door, laying it down to one side.

"Fine." I pulled the phone out of the fireplace and set it back on the small computer desk. "At least the fire had gone out," I said, bending down to plug the cord back in. "This might still work—wait. "What is this?"

The computer was still operating, apparently, resting on its side. The screen had not broken and the machine was turned on. A message ran across the screen in big black letters.

NOT HIS SON.

I tilted my head to read it. "This says *Not his son.* Is this something you were working on earlier, Mitch?"

"No. Before I was so rudely interrupted by my overly amorous wife, the screen was displaying the marriage data I'd found for Maggie and Eduard." He dropped the towel from his waist and pulled on a pair of briefs, then his jeans. "I may not have logged off and I may not have closed down the screen; I was distracted, as you should well recall."

"We're getting careless, Mitch. First, I don't lock the door and second, you leave the computer running. "What do you think it means?"

He picked up the television and put it back on its stand. "It means we're letting ourselves get overwhelmed with all of it. It means that I can't think straight for worry over you, wondering if I'm the memory you'll lose next. Worried that no one will be able to stop the progression of whatever goddamned poison these bastards put into you, sick to death at the thoughts of you being left only a hollow shell."

I went over to him and held him close to me. "I know, my love, I worry about the same things. Promise me." I reached up and touched his cheek gently, enjoying the rough texture of his beard against my skin, inhaling deeply, savoring the scent of him. "If the worst happens, if I become a mindless creature with no memory of who I really am, promise me, Mitch, that you will let me go."

"Deirdre." His voice was almost a moan. "It's not going to get to that point."

"But if it does, you must promise me."

His eyes did not meet mine. "I can't."

I sighed. "But you must, Mitch. And you will, my love. You will remember this discussion and you will let me go. It would be a blessing then, Mitch. And a sweet relief. But that isn't what I wanted to ask, really. I wanted to know what you thought the message on the computer meant."

"I assume it means that despite the marriage certificate, Phoenix is not Eduard's son."

"But that makes no sense. Even if it were true, why would whoever did this want to tell us? Maggie certainly wouldn't admit to that, she loved Eduard. I could feel it when she spoke of him last night. And if Phoenix did this," and once again I flashed on the image of the boy with the knife and shivered, "why would he deny his own father?"

Mitch shook his head. "I don't know, Deirdre. And with the exception of the dog, who wasn't even killed here, there's been no real damage done."

I sighed. "Then this was just malicious mischief for no reason at all?"

"There's a reason, there always is. Why they killed the dog, of course, is obvious. You have been specifically targeted by these people, singled out for some purpose. And now you have lost your protector. Moe"—his eyes darted to the door—"had been your constant companion pretty much ever since we've been here. He was a good deterrent for humans and Others alike. That night in the abbey, when he was guarding your sleeping body?"

I nodded.

"Well, he was acting up so much, snarling and growling, that even I was afraid to approach him. God only knows what might have happened to you already if it hadn't been for him."

"He was a good dog," I said, starting to cry again.

Mitch came over and held me in his arms. "Yeah, he was. And we'll find the person responsible and he will pay for it. But you know, I can't seem to think clearly right now. It's all too close, too immediate. But we'll find out. We have to."

He moved away from me, walked over and checked the locks on the door one more time, stepping around the blanket and its contents with a sigh. "Let's try to get some sleep. I have a feeling we'll need to be fully rested for what happens next."

Chapter 19

I would not have thought that I could sleep after all that had happened. But when I lay down next to Mitch, the scent of his skin and the solidness of his body comforted and relaxed me. I curled up next to him, wrapped an arm around his waist and a leg around his leg, rested my head on his shoulder and fell asleep almost immediately.

I walk in the ruins, naked, the moonlight gleaming on my white skin, giving it an eerie glow. On either side of me are two women. They are naked also, but none of us are ashamed. These are our true bodies, I sense. Beautiful and real.

One of the women is small and blond, her hand is light, cool in mine, her laugh is like the sound of wind chimes.

The other is tall and dark, her hand burns mine, and her laugh is like the low rumbling of a cat's purr. I love them both. I have no choice, I must love them both. And although I do not know them, I recognize that they are indeed my sisters.

The blond woman tugs on my hand. "Come, sister," she says, her voice high-pitched and melodic, "the night and everything in it is ours. It is our legacy."

I hear her words and sense the truth in them. The night is mine. I veer over in her direction.

Now, however, the other woman, the dark one, pulls on my hand, exerting a pressure equal to the blond sister. "You are changing, even now," she says and I feel the lure of her voice. "You can feel your body adapting, evolving. Turn your back on the legacy and come with me to watch the sunrise."

Ah, the sun. I have not seen the sun for so long and I crave its warmth, its light. I head in the dark sister's direction.

But I find I cannot choose between the two of them. So I stand still and lock my feet together. They each retain their holds on my hands and they pull, harder now with each passing second, both of them urging me to join them. Night and day they are and I cannot decide.

My sisters pull on my hands harder still, and I feel a small ache begin in the center of my forehead. From there it spreads, crackling down my body like a fracture in ice.

I tell them to stop, but they continue pulling, until my skin is divided down the center. Blood trickles and then gushes as they rip the skin from my body, half for one and half for the other. Each sister takes the piece of me she wanted and moves off in her own direction.

And I am left, skinless and crying, alone in the ruins and the dust.

I woke with a gasp. My heart pounded in my chest and I breathed deeply, attempting to calm myself. *Only a dream*, I thought, and ran my hands over my still intact skin and body. Only a dream.

Stealing a glance at the clock on the mantelpiece—only another hour to go until sunset—I lay back into the pillows and tested the edges of my memory. My oldest memory now seemed to be my arrival on the East Coast soon after the opening of the Empire State building. The year was 1931. So almost a hundred years of my life had already vanished, surrounded by a seemingly impenetrable wall. And although I knew that something existed on the other side of that obstacle, it was engulfed in a thick fog that obscured reality.

I could live with all of that, if only the wall were not slowly but surely encroaching on my present. Unless a way could be found to stop the progression, soon everything I remembered would be forgotten.

And then, I thought, *who would I be? What portions, if any, of me would be left?*

My thoughts were interrupted by a soft knock on the door. I checked the clock again. At least another fifteen minutes remained until sundown, but this upper part of the building had no windows except for the ones in our apartment. I could open the door safely without exposing myself to any stray rays of sunlight.

But why would I want to open it? It was too early for Vivienne and Sam to arrive; it most certainly would be Maggie or Phoenix and I did not wish to see either of them. Ever again, if the truth be known.

Whoever was there knocked again. Paused and then knocked for a third time. *What the hell,* I thought, got out of bed and opened the door.

The boy stood there, arms at his sides, fists clenching and unclenching. Tears streamed down his face, silent tears he made no attempt to hide or wipe away. His clear blue eyes met mine seeming to plead for admittance to the room. He gave a sad smile and put a hand out to me.

I hesitated and he pushed his hand at me again. This time I grasped it and he entered the room, falling down on his knees next to the wrapped bundle by the door. Shaking his head violently, he pulled the blanket back, picked up the head of the dog and hugged it to him.

"Oh, Phoenix." Despite the knowledge of who this boy was, my heart went out to him. There could be no questioning of the truth of his reaction and I found now I could not believe that he had done this deed. But somehow, he knew it had been done. And he may have known why and by whom.

"I wish you could speak," I said quietly. "But your mother says that you can read and write. Could you tell me like that? Do you know who did this?"

He gave me a sidelong glance, then set the dog's head down reverently on the floor, tenderly tucking the blanket back around it.

No, in spite of the clearness of my earlier vision, I now could not believe that this child, no matter whose son he was, had killed the dog. He wiped his eyes and nose with his sleeve, then touched my hand again and pulled me over to the small desk on which the computer sat. I noticed as we passed the bed that Mitch was awake and silently watching, his eyes glowing with interest.

Phoenix sat down in front of the computer, his fingers poised over the keyboard. He looked up at me, expectantly, his expression saying as plain as day, "Well?"

"Do you know how to use a computer?" I asked him. In answer he rolled his eyes and pressed a few keys, bringing up a blank screen in which he typed: *of course. dont you?*

I laughed. "No, actually I don't. But I am old-fashioned. Where did you learn?"

special school.

"I thought your mother taught you at home?"

He shrugged and typed. *used to go to school, then we moved. i liked school, but she didnt want me there. they made fun of me.*

"Because you don't speak?"

He nodded. *other children are cruel she said. and get used to it.*

I nodded my agreement. "She is right about that. Perhaps not about the getting used to it. But it is a cruel world, Phoenix. Do you know who killed Moe?"

He sniffled a bit. *not me, i didnt do it. i know you probably think i did, but i didn't.*

"I do not think you would kill Moe. It's all right, Phoenix. Just tell me the best way you can what you think might have happened."

He started sobbing and his fingers flew on the keys. *i woke up and got dressed and saw that the door was open and i heard the water running and i knew something was wrong. she was at the market, she left a note telling me so and i know i shouldnt have come upstairs but the door was open. the door should not be open, should never be open, Uncle Pete told her so the first night we came. and i came up to close the door and looked inside and saw the head. i got scared and mad.*

"Because of the dog," I said, brushing back his fair hair, "because you loved him too?"

He nodded and began typing again, crying as his fingers talked. *you killed the dog, i thought, i dont know why i thought that but i did. so i knocked down the tv and threw the phone into the fire.*

He stopped for a moment and sniffed, wiping his nose on his sleeve again. I grimaced slightly and walked across the room, bringing back a box of tissues for him. He ducked his head and grabbed one, wiping his eyes and blowing his nose.

thank you, he typed, *im not a baby but the dog . . . he was my friend.*

"I know." I hoped my voice was soothing and comforting. "Sometimes it's a good thing to cry."

He rolled his eyes. *only babies cry.*

"Fine, if you say so."

He nodded.

"And then, after you threw the phone into the fire and knocked down the television, what happened then, Phoenix?"

and then i saw what was on the computer and i got scared again and typed the note but i heard someone coming out of the shower and i jumped up and knocked the monitor down while i was trying to get away. but its not broken, nothing is broken and if you didnt kill the dog then you wont kill me and maybe you wont be mad and youll let me stay.

I stared at the words he had typed. It all made perfect sense, I supposed. "Of course I didn't kill the dog. Why would you think that?"

she said you might have. dottie just might have done it herself, she said, because she is mad at us.

"Well, Phoenix, I am not angry with you. Even if I were, I am not in the habit of killing children. Or dogs, for that matter."

He seemed to relax a little bit in his chair, then tensed up again and typed: *she said you might kill me. you might kill us both. will he kill me?*

"Who? Will who kill you?"

mitch. he will be mad that i made a mess. will he kill me?

I managed to suppress a laugh, he was so concerned that someone would kill him. When I thought about it more, though, I no longer found it comical; instead I found his worries heartbreaking. What sort of upbringing, what sort of damage did Eduard and Maggie do to this child?

I smiled down at him tenderly and brushed his fine hair away from his forehead. "I hardly think so, Phoenix. And I promise that Mitch will not kill you."

He seemed satisfied by my answer.

"Now, tell me one last thing, if you typed that note, what did you mean? Not his son?"

something he used to say to her. he was not a nice man, he was mean and cruel. not my son, he would say, not really, neither of them are mine. and she would cry. i dont belong, i never have. and he never liked me because of that. he only wanted me because i might be useful. the boy might be useful one day, he would say. he never liked that i can remember things that never happened.

"What sort of things, Phoenix?" I asked softly.

Before he could answer, Maggie's voice called from outside the door. "Phoenix? Phoenix! Answer me right this minute! Are you here, baby?"

He jumped and before I could stop him, hit a key that erased everything he had written.

"He's in here, Maggie," I called.

"Oh, thank heaven," she said, rushing over to him. "I worried that maybe he'd wandered off again. I hope he wasn't bothering you." Her eyes darted to the bundle by the door. "Or that he wasn't getting into something he shouldn't have." She gave him a little push. "Haven't I told you not to come up here? Didn't I tell you that just this morning?"

He nodded sullenly.

I flew to his defense. "He was fine, Maggie. He was showing me how to play a computer game. No harm was done. He was not doing anything wrong. And"—I looked down and met his eyes—"he's welcome to come back and play some other time. So long as he is polite and knocks first."

I was rewarded with a small smile from the boy. As he raised his head, I saw for the first time the scar across his neck. I reached out and touched it, thick and heavy like all of the Others.

"From the operation," Maggie said quickly, her eyes darting away from mine quickly, "when he was a baby. It never healed properly, those damned doctors. We usually try to keep it covered or people stare." She grabbed his hand roughly and practically dragged him out of the room. "Come on, boy. You have bothered Dot long enough and we have work to do downstairs."

I followed them to the door and watched her hurry him down the stairs. When they reached the bottom landing, she let go of him and he turned around and gave me a small wave. He mouthed the words "I'll come back."

I nodded and gave him a little smile. Then I closed the door and locked it, walked back across the room and sat in front of the computer again, gently running my fingers over the blank screen.

Chapter 20

"What the hell was that all about?" Mitch came up behind me, as I peered at the now blank screen, wrapped an arm around my neck and kissed me on the shoulder. "You and Phoenix were playing a game?"

"You know we weren't, Mitch. He told me a lot of interesting things, though. He wasn't particularly thrilled with having Eduard as his father, which easily explains the 'not his son' message. He didn't kill the dog, but he admitted to the rest of the pranks. He was frightened, he said, and angry because of Moe. He wrote it all out, but then deleted it when Maggie showed up."

"Here." He pulled the chair back. "You get up and let me sit down. Maybe I can find the file." He pushed a few keys. "Yes, here it is. Give me a second to read it over."

At one point he chuckled while reading. "Poor kid. Do you think he really thought we were going to kill him?"

"Yes, I think he really did expect that we would, for a little while at least. I gather he has not had the most pleasant of childhoods up until now."

"Do you believe him about all of this?"

"I do, indeed, Mitch. Most especially about how he didn't kill Moe. No child, no matter what his background, could be that good an actor. Nor am I that bad a judge of character. Most of the time."

Mitch smiled briefly. "And now you think he's not a monster?"

I sighed and rubbed my hands over my eyes. "I don't know what he is, Mitch. There's no question about one thing: he does bear the mark of the Others. Maggie can deny it all she likes, but I know what I saw and I know what I felt."

Shivering slightly, I hugged my arms to myself. "That scar is not the mark of an incompetent doctor's scalpel. So he cannot be what he seems. Physically, he may be the son of Maggie and Eduard, and he may seem a child, but he carries another soul, a mature soul, the soul of one transferred at birth. He could be anyone." I shook my head. "I feel sorry for him, Mitch. He seems so lost and frightened. He remembers things that never happened."

"What sorts of things?"

"I asked him, but Maggie came looking for him before he could answer."

"Interesting. And speaking of memories, dare I ask?"

I gave a small humorless laugh. "I still remember you, my love, you need not worry about that." The unspoken "yet" hung in the air. "But other periods of my life are not as vivid." My voice softened. "I seem to be missing about one hundred years so far."

He fell silent, most likely calculating, as I had, how many more days until my forgotten past would catch up to the present. The answer to that equation was not favorable. When he spoke again, his voice was low and husky. "Other than that, sweetheart, how do you feel?"

I thought for a moment. "Not bad at all," I said, surprised as I said it to find it was true. "But I am famished. I feel as if I haven't eaten for months."

"Then get dressed. We'll bury poor Moe somewhere and go out and find you food. Shouldn't be too difficult, it's Saturday night and all of the other pubs will be crowded. We'll want to get back early, though, because Sam and Viv should be here no later than two or three o'clock. They're catching the nine o'clock flight from Paris, then renting a car and driving up from Manchester. The train left too early in the day for Viv to board it safely."

I nodded. "Travel arrangements were certainly easier in the Cadre days. All we ever had to do was grab a private jet. I wonder how the others are getting here."

"Lily and Victor are taking the trip in stages. They'll fly to New York and stay with Claude overnight. Then the three of them fly to London and stay in a hotel, driving up here the following evening. Lily was quite outspoken about what a pain it was to get here."

I gave a rueful smile. "I'm sure she was. I have always been an inconvenience to her, to say the least."

"Stop it. She's gotten over all of her revenge issues, years ago. And she was only joking and sends her love along to you until she can be here. It sounded like she was actually looking forward to the trip, pain or no. And Victor sounded like Victor, inscrutable as ever."

Neither one of us had to say what we were thinking: unless Sam was able to perform a miracle, I might not remember who either of them were by the time they arrived.

"I've decided not to open the pub tonight," Mitch said. "Maggie's not capable of handling a Saturday night crowd all by herself."

"I feel fine for the moment, Mitch. We shouldn't lose a night's income because of me. We need the money."

"Money be damned. All I want is to be with you. In fact, I may close down indefinitely, or at least until Pete returns. We've more than enough cash from the last two assassins to keep us and the pub going for a while."

"I suppose you know best, Mitch. To be honest, I don't much want to spend my next couple of evenings pouring out stout and whiskey."

He nodded. "Then it's settled. And after we feed, all I really want to do is settle in with you on the couch and watch the fire until Vivienne and Sam show up. I will not leave you alone again. Not until this matter is settled. And you, young lady, are not allowed to sneak off anywhere by yourself. As I said earlier, I'm sure that Moe was killed to leave you unprotected."

He turned back to the computer again. "Here's yet another e-mail from George Montgomery. He's a persistent bastard, isn't he?"

I peered over Mitch's shoulder and read the letter; it was exactly the same as the previous one, with a paragraph tacked onto the top that said *I fear my previous communication (quoted below) may not have arrived. If this is not the case, I apologize for the duplication of mail. Please answer at your earliest convenience.*

"Persistent, yes, but he seems sincerely interested in helping." I laughed. "Even after I drank his blood and left him wandering around aimlessly not one time but twice. Fortunately he doesn't seem to have remembered either of those encounters, despite the fact that he keeps coming back for more. I almost wish I had given him his interview; at least that way some of my memories would remain, if only in print. I wonder . . ."

"Hmmm?"

"If we talk to him and he publishes his article, do you suppose somebody else might read it and know a solution to my situation?"

"We don't need Montgomery's article. Once Sam gets here—"

"Mitch," I interrupted before he could begin his hopeful speech, "we need to face the facts. Sam is a fine doctor and a wonderful friend, but this whole thing is probably out of his league. Don't put too much responsibility on him for finding a cure."

He sat silent for a while. "You're right, Deirdre. Do you want to talk to Montgomery?"

"I don't see that it can hurt our situation much. And it may even help."

"Okay." He typed in a few lines and hit the return key with a flourish. "I've asked him to meet us at his hotel, tomorrow night around seven."

After we dressed, we headed down the stairs. The first thing Mitch did was make sure the sign on the pub door read closed. Then he locked and bolted that door and turned off all the outside lights.

"Mitch?" Maggie came around the corner, wearing an apron over her tight jeans. "You locked the door?" Her voice trembled and she cleared her throat. She looked genuinely frightened. "Why?"

"We're not going to be opening tonight, Maggie. And possibly not for another day or two. Neither one of us is going to be here and we both thought you could use a night off. You've been working so hard and we've all been keeping crazy hours. A night of rest won't hurt any of us one bit."

"Well, that's true," she said, visibly relaxing, "but is it a good idea just to close down?"

Mitch shrugged. "We'll manage."

"Besides," I added, "we have friends coming in from Paris later on this evening."

At my mention of Paris, her eyes acquired a hard and angry edge. With good cause, I realized. Talk of Paris would most likely bring back sad memories of Eduard. Quickly following that thought was the certainty that she knew exactly who these friends were and that she might well have reason to hate Vivienne. Or all of us, for that matter.

I wanted to laugh. What an interesting experiment in tightrope walking we had unfolding before us. Mitch and I knew what sort of creature she was and she most certainly knew what we were. And none of us were willing to reveal our knowledge. Yet. Instead we danced a complicated pattern around the issues, ensuring that every word said could be interpreted two different ways.

"We can entertain them in our apartment, if you'd like," I said, "so that we don't disturb your rest."

She smiled, and the expression seemed effortless, guileless. "There's no need for that. Once Phoenix falls asleep he stays asleep. Even if he does get up and walk around every so often. As far as the pub goes, well, I don't mind a little time off, I'll admit that, even though I haven't been here all that long. Maybe after Phoenix gets to sleep, we could all meet here for a drink of something."

"We'll see," Mitch said. "They may be too tired following their trip. But I'm sure," and he gave her a twisted smile, "you'll meet up with them eventually."

Maggie nodded again. "That would be lovely; any friends of yours are likely to be friends of mine."

I glanced at her and she gave me an angelic smile. "Really, I mean that," she said, and then she hesitated for a moment. "And why that reminds me of this next, I've no idea." Giving a short laugh, she shrugged and continued, "Maybe I'm more like Pete than I'd ever have imagined. In any event, Phoenix tells me that he found Moe," and she frowned, suppressing a shiver, "or at least the rest of him, hidden away up near the abbey. He was most anxious that we reclaim him and give the poor creature a decent burial. And I was hoping that the two of you would take him. I don't think I have the stomach for it, poor creature."

"Not a problem," Mitch said, "but I'd like to get an early start on all of it. Is Phoenix around?"

"Always." Maggie smiled. "At least until you want him for something. But isn't that always the way?" She turned her head and called to the back of the pub, "Phoenix? Honey? Did you want to go with Mitch and Dottie now?"

Phoenix appeared next to us and touched Mitch's hand shyly. In turn, Mitch looked down at him and gave him a warm smile. "Come on, then, boy," he said, his voice much softer than the words. "Why don't you go behind the bar and get me the flashlight? You know," he said when the boy looked at him, confused, "the torch?"

Phoenix nodded and fetched the object, holding it proudly in front of him. "Good job," Mitch said. "Now let's get moving."

The dog's body had been hidden away outside the abbey, just as Maggie said, surrounded by a clump of sparse but thorny shrubs.

Mitch walked around the site for a while after Phoenix pointed it out, checking the ground and searching, I assumed, for any evidence that might help determine the identity of the culprit.

"The dog was definitely killed in this spot," he said after a few moments, "but there's not much else in the way of clues. Now if this were a human corpse, it would all be different. The local police would be involved and a crime laboratory would be able to find out a lot more. Unfortunately, we're the only ones likely to care about this murder. And all we've got to go on is a puddle of dried blood and one shoe print with no way to analyze any of it."

He directed the flashlight beam at the ground again and shook his head. "There's absolutely no sign of a struggle, which leads me to believe that our perpetrator must have sedated or drugged the dog before killing him. No way would Moe have just lain down and let someone do this to him. Friend or stranger, it wouldn't have mattered."

He knelt down next to the body, licked his finger, ran it over the severed neck and put it to his mouth to taste. After a second he grimaced, then nodded. "Not the most sophisticated of methods, I'll grant you, but there is a slight medicinal taste to the blood."

He got up, and brushed his hand on his jeans, looking over at Phoenix, who stood about five yards away, refusing to come any nearer. "If it's any consolation, son," Mitch said with a nod in his direction, "I'd be willing to bet that the dog didn't feel anything at all. He most likely went to sleep and just didn't wake up again. Think of it that way, if you can. And thank you for finding him for us; you've been a regular trooper and I appreciate your help."

The boy nodded and gave Mitch a tentative smile, his eyes wide with admiration and gratitude.

"Okay then," Mitch said, "I'm finished here. Think fast, son," he said and tossed the flashlight to Phoenix, who managed to catch it. "You take that for me. And I'll bring the poor old boy home." He knelt down next to the dog again, wrapped up the body in his jacket and without a word carried him back, Phoenix and me trailing along behind like a gruesome and dismal parade.

We buried Moe in the small yard behind the pub. As Mitch was digging the grave, Phoenix crept up next to me, his small fingers working their way into mine. We both stood solemnly, brushing away our tears and watching as Mitch finished the job. He reverently laid the dog in the hole, filled it all back in and patted the dirt down.

"Poor dog," Mitch said by way of a eulogy. "He was a great protector and a good friend." The boy next to me sniffled and nodded, his hand still gripping mine tightly.

He did not let go as we went back into the pub, determined, apparently, to stay as close to me as possible. It almost seemed as if he was trying to take the place of the dog he'd always seen with me.

Chapter 21

Despite the desperateness of our situation and the sadness of having to say good-bye to a good friend, that night stood out in my mind as being a near perfect evening. *Of course*, I reminded myself wryly, *you have far fewer nights against which to compare it than you did a week ago.* Even so, I enjoyed the time. Every small detail grew to be important, more poignant with the knowledge that this too could and probably would disappear without warning.

We did not go out after all, but rather ended up sitting in the closed pub. Maggie and I worked behind the bar, rearranging bottles, washing glassware and polishing the mirror. With the recognition of what she was, a breeder for the Others and as such an enemy, she had lost most of her appeal for me. She seemed more subdued than usual, moody and morose. It was as if she had an inner switch and could turn her charm and magnetism on or off at will.

Oddly enough, through it all we managed to reach a kind of mutual admiration. We worked well together and talked of commonplace things, avoiding all the important issues. I was grateful for her presence, actually. Had it been just Mitch and I, we'd most likely have spent the evening running through the same old circles of thought that had, thus far, gotten us nowhere.

"Looks like we need more port, Dot." Maggie looked up at

me from where she knelt on the floor taking inventory of our stock.

"Which kind?" I asked, making the list.

"Both, I think. And some more of that merlot that you like. Plus a bottle of Irish whisky."

I glanced over to where Mitch and Phoenix were playing a game of darts. "How's our supply of scotch?"

"Quite good, actually."

"I'll write it down anyway; I have a feeling that we'll need to have a lot on hand fairly soon."

"Oh? Is it something your friends from France drink?"

"No," I said, without thinking to whom I was talking, "it would be for Mitch. He drinks it when he gets angry."

She laughed. "Is he planning on being angry any time soon? Is it something he schedules on the calendar? No wonder the two of you get along so well."

I laughed along with her.

She stood up and dusted off the knees of her jeans, then leaned both of her elbows on the bar, staring at Mitch and her son. "They're quite the pair, aren't they? Funny, because he doesn't usually take well to men. His father was a strict man."

They had moved away from the dartboard and Mitch was now patiently explaining the fine art of shooting pool to the boy. Phoenix, it turned out, had a natural ability for the game, in spite of the fact that the pool cue he insisted on using was almost twice his size.

I watched the scene in front of me for some time, marveling how to anyone looking in the pub windows at us, we would have looked like a normal human family.

Finally, Maggie looked up at the clock, slipped off her apron and laid it over the bar. "Bedtime, Phoenix."

He looked up at her and bit at his lower lip.

"Don't give me that look, young man, we're actually hours past bedtime. So say your good nights and off we'll go. I'm rather tired myself, so I'll tuck you in and stay with you."

He nodded reluctantly, touched my hand in farewell, then walked back over to Mitch and hugged him, tightly.

The shocked look on Mitch's face gave way to an expression of happiness and he hugged the boy back, then ruffled the top of his hair. I wondered if Mitch had any idea that he'd just thrown away any credibility he might have had with his hostage idea. Anyone seeing the interaction of the two of them would know he had no intention of ever hurting Phoenix.

And when I saw the love on Mitch's face, as Phoenix walked dejectedly down the hallway to his little cot in the room off the kitchen, I felt a huge responsibility leave my shoulders. When the poison ran its course and the person that I was disappeared into nothingness, Mitch would have someone to carry him through.

"Good night to the both of you," Maggie said. "I'll be seeing you tomorrow evening some time."

We heard the two of them moving around back in their room, and then there was silence.

"Have you noticed," I said quietly, all too aware of the presence in the other room, "that there have been no attacks on us since Maggie arrived?"

Mitch looked over at me. "Now that you mention it, yeah. They came on pretty hot and heavy for a while there, but now, other than Moe's accident, there's been nothing."

"A coincidence?"

Mitch laughed. "I told you when we first met that I didn't believe in coincidences. I may have had to add a lot of beliefs to my original short list, but coincidence is still not one of them. I have also noticed that you only became sick after Maggie arrived."

"Obviously, then, she is connected." I stopped for a second, then shook my head and gave a wry laugh. "Hell, of course she is connected. About as connected as one can get, without being in charge of the whole operation. But," and my voice grew wistful, "it's easy to forget all of that when she's present. I do not want to believe she's an assassin of any sort."

"Protective covering," Mitch said with a nod.

At that point, there was a knock on the front pub door. I got up to answer it and opened it to the hurricane that was Vivienne.

"Oh, *ma chere.*" She pulled me into her arms and held me close. Then, drawing back a little, she deposited a long kiss on my lips. "It is so good to see you, my sister. And good to be out of that car. Four hours of English countryside? *Merde,* I do not know how you stand it."

She studied my face, her easy smile turning into an angry frown. "But I see that the bastards have done their dirty work to you, Deirdre. We will not speak of the hair, since it seems you have done that on purpose. Otherwise, though, you look positively green, *mon chou;* like a walking case of *mal-de-mer.*"

I laughed. "It does feel like that sometimes, Vivienne. And I am glad to see you too. Where is Sam?"

"Here." He appeared in the doorway, his black doctor's bag in hand. "Just getting some stuff out of the car. Viv's right, it was too long a trip from the airport. But unlike Viv, I kind of enjoyed the scenery."

Sam came into the room, gave me one quick worried glance and set his bag on the table. "Mitch." He nodded, extending his hand. "Good to see you as always. You, at least, are looking well."

Mitch clapped him on the shoulder. "I can't even begin to tell you how welcome you are. Can I offer you a drink of something?"

"Coffee would be wonderful at this point. About an hour outside of Whitby I suddenly got very tired and I'm still a little groggy."

Vivienne laughed. "It was most exciting. We veered all over the road before he woke up just in time to avoid hitting some silly cow."

"There was no cow, Viv."

She stuck her tongue out at him. "And exactly how would you know that, *mon beau morsel,* you were asleep at the time."

I walked around behind the bar and poured Sam a cup of coffee. "Mitch, do you want coffee?"

"Sure," he said, "that will be fine." I fixed Mitch's coffee and stirred it, handing it over to him. Looking at the second mug, though, I frowned. "I fear I don't remember how you drink this, Sam."

He took it from me. "This will be fine, as is." He took a sip, then stopped. "You don't remember? Has it progressed that far already, Deirdre?"

"No," I said quickly, "it's not that." Pouring two glasses of red wine, I walked back out from behind the bar and handed one glass to Vivienne. "I truly do not remember."

"Good." He sat down at one of the tables. "So here is what I propose we do. It's too late in the night to do anything now. But tomorrow, at sunset, you'll need to report to my clinic."

I sat down next to him, sipping my wine. "Your clinic?"

"Well, okay." Sam laughed. "Calling it a clinic is a bit of an overstatement. What I have set up is really just a couple of rooms with a few beds and some rented testing equipment. Nothing particularly fancy, but it was the best I could throw together on the short notice."

"How did you manage that?" Mitch joined us, followed by Vivienne.

Sam shrugged. "A few inquiries here or there, a couple of favors from European colleagues called in. And a whole stack of cash."

"Cash?"

Vivienne gave a giggle. "You do not think that I have lived so long, Mitch, by trusting in banks and society, do you? My little swan's nest is quite properly feathered."

"But you should not be spending your money on me, Vivienne," I said, secretly pleased that she cared. "You will need it to live on."

"Oh, foo," she said with a wave of her hand. "It is only money. And there are ways to get more, there are many ways. I have plenty, as it turns out, and even if I did not?" Vivienne gave a pretty little shrug. "It would still be well spent. I have only one sister in the whole world and we must stick together, *mon ami.*

Besides," and she laughed a bit, "this puts you firmly in my debt. And there is nothing wrong with that."

I touched her hand. "Thank you," I said, feeling tears begin to fill my eyes. "It means so much to me to have you here now."

She gave me a sharp glance and placed her other hand on top of mine. "How long has it been since you've fed, my sister?"

"A couple of days, I think, since our last big feed. To be honest, I've lost track of time. Why do you ask?"

"Because your skin feels warm, hot almost, as if you had just fed. Sam?"

"I'm on it," he said, rummaging around in his black bag and pulling out a strange instrument. "May I?"

I nodded.

Sam reached over and inserted the instrument in my ear. "A new kind of thermometer," he said, "much more sensitive than the older kinds." It beeped and he pulled it away. "Quicker, too."

He looked at the thermometer's display screen. "Hmmm, let's try that again, shall we?"

The second reading was no different from the first. "You, young lady," Sam said, "are running a fever. Not particularly high, really. And if you were human, I'd say it was nothing to worry about. A low-grade infection, maybe. Or the start of a cold or flu. But you are not human. Who the hell knows what sort of damage is being done to your system?" He looked over at Mitch, who had stayed remarkably silent, staring down into his coffee cup.

"I wish you had called me in sooner, Mitch."

He shook his head. "I wish I had too, Sam. But all of this came up out of nowhere. One day Deirdre was fine, the next she was sick and losing memories right and left. We'd never had any reason at all to believe that was even possible."

I gave a laugh. "That's true, Sam. Please don't scold us. Immortality makes one rather cavalier about all sorts of things."

"No more," Sam said, standing up. "We start tomorrow night. Sunset."

"How about two hours past sunset, Sam? I have an interview with a newspaper reporter scheduled for early tomorrow night."

"You have a what? What happened to the keep-a-low-profile rule?"

"The rules have changed," Mitch stated firmly.

Vivienne laughed. "But of course, *mon cher,* what else are rules for?" Then her eyes opened wide, staring beyond the table and down the hallway into the back of the pub. "*Bon soir, mon petit gamin.* Oh, Deirdre, what an adorable urchin. To whom does he belong?"

I turned in my chair and saw that Phoenix was standing there, looking lost and frail in the darkness. Even with his unfocused eyes, though, he managed to find Mitch and crawl into his lap.

"This is Phoenix," Mitch whispered. "He walks in his sleep. Be quiet and don't wake him. But take a look at this." Gently he grasped the boy's chin and raised his head, exposing the ugly scar.

"*Mon Dieu.* " Vivienne jumped up from her chair. "He carries their mark."

I nodded. "Yes, he does."

"Phoenix?" A sleepy voice carried down the hallway and a light turned on.

"He's in here, Maggie," Mitch called softly and she came out into the room, dressed in nothing but a white cotton nightgown, almost completely sheer in the backlit doorway. She looked every bit an angel.

Vivienne gave a small gasp. When I looked at her, I saw that she was biting her lip and staring at Maggie like a drowning man dreaming of dry land. Sam, too, seemed fascinated with the new arrival.

Completely unperturbed with the obvious hunger in Vivienne's eyes and stance, Maggie nodded to everyone and picked the boy up from Mitch's lap. "I'm sorry to interrupt." She gave a low laugh. "One would think that with all the occurrences of this boy walking in his sleep, I'd learn to lock the door. It would be lovely to meet your friends, but I am tired. And I'm sure"— she smiled at Vivienne, exposing her even white teeth—"you all have important things to talk about. So let's save the introductions for later, if that's okay. Good night."

We all stared after her until the light turned off and we heard the door close. "Interesting," Sam said, sinking slowly into his chair.

Vivienne shook her head and smiled, her dimples deepening. "So," she said, her eyes glowing as she looked to Mitch, to me, then back again to him, as if we had just done something incredibly clever, "you not only have one of their children here, you have a Breeder as well. And tamed, although just barely."

"There's more to it than you see, Viv." Mitch took a sip of his coffee. "And I hesitate to mention it for fear of bringing up bad blood."

She made a clicking sound with her tongue. "There is no such thing, Mitch, *mon gars,* and you know it. Tell me now, or I may burst. I do not care if we stay until after the sun rises—this is a story I simply have to hear."

"Indeed you do, Vivienne," I said, draining my glass of wine and setting it back down on the table. "Maggie Richards is none other than the widow of the late Eduard DeRouchard."

Chapter 22

Vivienne sat for a moment, staring off down the hall after Maggie and her son. "Eduard's widow? And here? Staying with the two of you?"

I had feared her reaction. Eduard was, after all, an ex-lover of hers. Beneath the soft and frivolous surface of my blood sister lurked wildfires and tempers, ordinarily kept banked and under control. But by her own admission, she had adored Eduard, even to his death.

Her face was totally still for a minute. I reached over and touched her hand in a gesture of support. She looked back at me, her expression unfathomable, until she began to laugh that delightful high-pitched giggle of hers.

"Were you afraid that I would crumble to pieces out of grief over Eduard's defection? Over hearing that he married another woman? My dear sister," she said, fanning herself with her hand, "it is sweet that you should be concerned with the state of my heart. But I assure you that I am free from the fascinating spell of Monsieur le Docteur."

I shrugged. "It was possible, I thought."

"No," she said, still laughing, reaching over to take Sam's arm and hugging it to her. "And no again. One doctor in my life is quite enough, *merci.*" Then she sobered just a bit. "But the boy? Surely you do not believe that he is Eduard, reborn? The last time we saw him he was nothing but smoking ash and cinders. There is no resurrection from that."

"We don't know who the boy is," Mitch said. "But we intend to find out."

Sam cleared his throat and glanced at the clock over the bar. "It's not an issue for me, folks, but I suggest we either tell this story quickly or save it for another time. Viv and I still need to find our house and unpack a few things from the car before dawn. And, Deirdre"—he gave me a discerning glance—"you look tired, if such a thing is possible."

I sighed. "You're right, Sam. Let's hold this discussion until tomorrow night sometime. I am weary and hungry."

"Oh, damn." He slapped himself lightly on the head. "That reminds me. I brought you a gift, of sorts." Sam got up and headed for the door. "Hold on just a second and I'll go get it."

On his return, he was carrying an ice chest. "My mother always taught me that every self-respecting guest comes bearing drink and food. And in this case, I've brought both."

I lifted the lid and smiled, seeing the rows of plastic blood bags lined up in the chest. "Thank you, Sam."

"Enjoy." An expression of disgust flitted over his handsome face for a second. Then he set the chest down on a table and smiled at me. "Keep it cold," he said, "and keep it safe." He gave me a small hug. "Keep yourself safe, as well."

Sam broke the embrace, touched my forehead briefly and frowned. "Get some rest, okay?" He turned away from me. "Ready to go, Viv?"

"Lead on, my darling, and I will follow," Vivienne replied as Sam and Mitch headed for the door. She leaned over, wrapping an arm around my waist. "For one thing," she whispered in my ear, "the view is so enchanting, don't you think?"

Laughing in response, I gave her a wry smile and a kiss on the cheek.

Mitch opened the door for both of them, shook Sam's hand, ruffled the top of Viv's hair. "Thanks for coming," he said. "If nothing else, the company will be good for her. Maybe with more people she knows around, she won't be as likely to forget."

He closed the door behind them and the room felt empty.

"That girl," Mitch said with a smile for the irony of the word, "is like a breath of fresh air. She sure hasn't changed in the last three years, has she?" Mitch picked up the ice chest and started for the stairs. Realizing I was not following, he turned back to me. "Deirdre? Are you coming to bed?"

"I suppose I should."

"But?"

"I don't want to sleep. Every time I wake up, I'm missing a piece of my past."

His eyes reflected his worry. "Well, we don't have to sleep. Come on, love, I'll serve you breakfast in bed."

I trudged up the stairs behind him, stepped over the two dogs at the door, looked around the room and sighed. "I'll build up a fire," I said, forcing a smile, "and slip into something more comfortable. You can fix breakfast."

Unfortunately, the something more comfortable turned out to be nothing more than an old plaid flannel nightgown. The wood Mitch had brought in earlier seemed damp, giving me no end of trouble with getting a fire started. It seemed the possibility of a picture-book romantic moment was lost. Not that it mattered. We had never needed the trappings of love.

When Mitch emerged from the kitchen, he bore a tray that held two of our best wineglasses and a small vase that held a single red rose. The glasses were filled with heated blood. In the cold air of the fireless apartment, I could see the steam rising from them.

"That is lovely, Mitch," I said, accepting my glass.

"Careful, it's hot," he warned. "I tried to warm it differently this time. Running hot water over the bags seems to take forever, but I let the fire get too high under the pan. Wasn't paying attention, I guess, because I was searching for the vase." He chuckled. "Which emphasizes what I've always thought: never let ambience get in the way of the food. But I think it's still drinkable, at least it hadn't reached the boiling point."

"And the rose? Where did that come from?"

He laughed. "A gift from Vivienne, I think. It was tucked into the ice chest."

I sipped and then drained the glass. "It's fine, Mitch. Thank you."

He drank his and set the empty glass on the nightstand next to mine. "No fire?" he asked.

"The wood was damp. And I hadn't the patience."

"Allow me," he said and in what seemed like no time at all he had a crackling fire going. "Turn out the lights, sweetheart, and join me."

We settled down in front of the fire. "While I was fixing the blood," he said, "I started thinking about the time I found you in your bathroom drinking from one of those stupid little plastic bags. Do you remember?"

I smiled at him, from where I was snuggled into his arm. "Yes, quite clearly. You thought I was crazy and couldn't get out of there fast enough."

He lean over and kissed me. "I came back, though, because I loved you so much that I didn't care. I fought so hard against believing the truth about you. The obvious answer was staring me straight in the face, and I chose not to see it. Human nature, I guess."

I gave a low laugh. "Vampire nature, too, I think we all deny what we don't want to accept."

We fell quiet for a second or two, watching the flames leap and fall. My sigh broke the silence. "That all seems so very long ago now. And although it is hard to believe, life was so much simpler then. How did it all get so complicated, Mitch? Was there a point in time when all of this could have been averted? A specific action taken that, if undone, could change everything?"

"Somehow, Deirdre, I can tell where this conversation is headed. And we've been there before."

"I know. And I did not bring it up to assume the blame this time. Rather, I'm just thinking out loud. I have been dreaming of Max, you see. And I wonder if my subconscious is trying to go back and change that one pivotal moment."

"That sounds like a question for Sam. I'm still just a dumb cop, struggling through the best I can."

"Do you miss it, Mitch? The police work?"

"Deirdre—" he started in a warning tone, but I interrupted him.

"Yes, I know what you're going to say because you have said it before—I am more important to you than the work."

"Damned straight."

"Even so," I said with a smile, "try to imagine life without me. Would you return to the force if you could?"

"In a New York minute," he said.

"There," I said, "that didn't hurt a bit, did it? Why have you never spoken of it before?"

"For the same reason I don't talk about Chris. Let it go, sweetheart, please just let it go."

I sighed, thinking that soon I would have no choice but to take his advice. We lay in silence again for a while.

"Mitch?" I shifted my position slightly, and traced my fingers down his chest.

"Hmmm?" He was more than half asleep already.

"We need to talk about this."

"About what?"

"About what we are going to do when Sam fails to find a cure."

"If." He sat up and looked into my eyes. "And notice that I said *if* Sam can't help, we'll use Maggie and Phoenix as hostages against the Others providing an antidote."

"And if that doesn't work? What then?"

"Hell, I don't know, Deirdre. Maybe I'll get them to poison me too and we can live together, both of us with no memory and rediscovering each other every day."

I laughed. "The way you say it makes it sound rather exciting."

"I hope so," he said, leaning over to kiss me. "I'd hate to think that I was getting boring in our old age."

"You? Boring? Never."

I responded to the kiss; he began to run his strong hands over my body. And with an inner smile I thought, *No, we definitely do not need to rely on romantic trappings.*

Afterward, I did not sleep; instead I occupied myself with cleaning up our small flat, washing dishes, changing the bedsheets, dusting. Then I sat on the sofa, with my legs curled under me. Watching Mitch sleep in front of the dying fire, I shed more than a few quiet tears.

Mitch had arranged to meet George Montgomery in his hotel room shortly after sunset. I wondered as we took the elevator up to his floor if he had any clue at all what he was about to hear.

George met us at the door, wearing jeans and the same suit jacket he'd worn when I first met him in the cemetery by the abbey, the occurrence of which he obviously had no recollection. As far as he was concerned this was our first meeting.

He shook hands with Mitch, then took my hand and gave it a kiss. "I'm so glad to meet you at last. And I can't thank you enough, both of you, for agreeing to talk to me."

I sniffed the air and noticed a tray with a half-eaten plate of food sitting on the desk. "Did we interrupt your dinner?"

"No, I was done. Hotel food is not the most appetizing thing in the world. But it's quick and easy."

"Smells like fettuccine Alfredo," Mitch said appreciatively. "I haven't had that for years. Deirdre, do you remember that little restaurant we went to on our first date?"

"Yes, my love, I still do." But for how long? I wondered.

George put the cover back on his plate. "The chef had a heavy hand with the garlic on this dish. I'll just set it out in the hallway and then we can start."

As he walked past me with the tray, an overwhelming wave of nausea washed over me. "Bathroom?" I managed to blurt the word, and ran for it when he pointed.

When I finished vomiting up the blood I had drunk that morning, I rested my feverish head against the cool porcelain until I felt strong enough to stand. I splashed water on my face and stared at myself in the mirror.

I looked like hell. And Viv was right, it was not just the hair. My eyes were heavy with dark circles and my skin was blotchy, discolored. Sighing, I dried my face and hands and went out to join George and Mitch.

"Deirdre?" Mitch got up from the chair he was sitting in and took my arm, guiding me to that same seat.

I smiled up at him. "I'm fine, Mitch. Must have been the smell of the food."

George nodded knowingly. "My ex-wife was like that when she was pregnant. When's the happy event?"

I looked at him in shock at first. "Pregnant? You think I'm pregnant?" Mitch caught my eye and we both burst out laughing.

George glanced back and forth at us, giving us a sheepish grin. "Well, it was just a hunch. A nice young couple, newly married, and she throws up at the scent of food. Made sense to me, but I guess I was wrong."

I wiped the tears of laughter away from my eyes. Poor man, he really did have no idea what we were. He had built up this image in his mind of a young American couple being persecuted by some sort of international conspiracy. He believed we were human, he believed we were innocent.

"You have no idea, Mr. Montgomery, how wrong you are. Now please sit down and I will tell you why."

"May I record this?"

I nodded. "That would be the best idea, I think. If for no other reason than that I would like to have a record of it."

He pulled out a handheld tape recorder, checked to see that there was a cassette loaded and ready to go, then clicked the button and set it down on the table next to me. "Fine, then," he said, "this one's for posterity."

Chapter 23

I told him everything I could recall of my life. A much shorter story than it would have been yesterday. But certainly longer than it would be tomorrow. At first, he kept interrupting with questions and exclamations, but as the telling progressed, he grew quieter and more thoughtful.

"So here we stand, Mr. Montgomery. My memories are being pared away with each passing day. We are a species being hounded to extinction with no understanding of why. Our lair has been discovered and infiltrated by members of the Others' organization. All we have to bargain with is a woman and her mute son, both of them with far more appeal than is conceivable, making it nearly impossible for us to take action."

He sat still, his hands folded in his lap, his eyes searching my face for confirmation that this story was all true.

"You have just handed me the story of the century," he said finally. "Unfortunately," and his mouth twisted into a reluctant grin, "I can't use any of this for my article. If it's not true, I'd be crucified. And if it is true"—he chuckled a bit—"I'd still be crucified. Printing anything you have told me, true or not, reduces me to the level of sensationalism of *Real-Life Vampires*. And, regardless of how you may feel about my profession based on Terri and Bob, I have some integrity."

Sighing, I got up from my chair and stretched. "I understand, Mr. Montgomery. I'm not sure what I had hoped to accomplish by talking to you. I'm not sure of anything at this point. Except that my time is running short."

He reached over for the tape recorder, removed the cassette and handed it to me. "A gesture of my good faith."

I took it, stared at it lying in my palm, then pushed it into the back pocket of my jeans.

"I am sorry," he continued. "If I could do more to help you both, I would. And for what it's worth, I do believe your story. However, as a detached bystander, I have an idea or two."

Mitch ran his fingers through his hair. "Whatever you have to offer is probably more than we already have. Go ahead."

"Should you discover that no others of your kind have been pursued as relentlessly as you, maybe you need to think 'Why us? Why me?' If you, Deirdre, are being specially targeted, and it seems that you are, then there must be a reason. There always is. It may not be a good reason, but still . . . So if all of this were happening to me, I'd go back and check the source. There are no coincidences in life. Just series of connected events."

Mitch chuckled a bit at that statement, but I sighed.

"Easy enough to say that, Mr. Montgomery, but all too soon my ability to think things through to their logical ends will be completely erased by my inability to remember. Thank you, however, for your time."

We walked almost as far as the address Sam had given us before I spoke again. "That was a complete and utter waste of what little time I have left. I sincerely hope that Sam will have more to offer."

"I don't know," Mitch said. "Montgomery was right about one thing. We do need to get to the source of all of this. And that won't be accomplished by hiding out here in Whitby. I'm going to leave you with Sam and Vivienne for the rest of the night and do some investigation of my own. Now that we have Maggie in hand, we might as well use her if we can."

He checked the paper on which Sam had written the address. "This seems to be the place."

I rang the bell and could hear Vivienne's excited call from inside the building. "Yes," I said with a smile, "it is indeed."

Mitch took me into his arms and held me in a long embrace, not moving away when the door opened, but tightening his hold on me. "I love you, Deirdre," he whispered into my hair, "and I don't want you ever to forget that."

"I will try, my love."

"Secrets?" Vivienne's light voice rang in the air. "I love secrets."

"Not a secret," Mitch said, his voice shaking. "I love this woman."

"Oh, foo," she said, with a pout and a little shake of her shoulders. "That is not a secret. We all know that. And of course you do. She is, of course, absolutely wonderful. Being, as she is, my sister. Now come in, both of you. Sam is fussing around in his lab, as happy as a child with a new toy. He'll be glad you are here finally so that he can try it all out."

Mitch shook his head. "I can't stay. I have some investigation to do." He kissed me, hard on the lips. "Do what Sam tells you to do, sweetheart. I'll be back long before dawn to see what's happening."

Watching him walk away, I tried to hold back my tears and almost succeeded until Vivienne put an arm around my shoulders. I broke down then and cried, as she held me there in the open front doorway; she stroked my short hair and whispered nonsense words of comfort. When my sobbing subsided, she held me out at arm's length, wiped away my tears and smiled.

"Feel better now?"

I sniffed and gave a small choked laugh. "Actually, I do."

Vivienne pulled me into the house, closing and locking the door behind us. "See, we are still more female than we are monsters. Sometimes a good cry is all we need. Come now, Sam is waiting for you."

The layout of their house was similar to the one of the pub, with the substitution of a waiting room for the bar area and a sterile-looking laboratory in place of the kitchen. Apparently, I would be secluded in the room beyond the lab.

I looked around. "This is amazing, Vivienne," I said. "I cannot believe you set this all up in just a few days. You must have spent a great deal of money."

She shrugged. "It is not as impressive a feat as you are thinking. This building had been used as a doctor's office before we bought it and so we changed it not at all. Mostly, we had it cleaned. Sam has been working all day to set up the equipment that was here waiting for us when we arrived. So," and she gave me a wicked little smile, "you are not so much in my debt after all. Which is a shame, *ma chere.* I like having people in my power."

Sam came out of the back, pulling on a pair of latex gloves. "How's my patient this evening?"

"Nauseated. Anxious. Frightened."

"Good." He smiled at me. "At least that gives us something to work with. Come on back. No, not you, Viv. I'll give you a call if I need you."

She flounced out to the waiting area. "I did not live for over three centuries, Doctor Samuels, so that I could wait here at your beck and call. Perhaps I will take a tour of the town."

"That's a good idea." Sam nodded absentmindedly. "Have fun, but be careful."

With a few choice words, in her native language, she flew out of the front door.

I waited until it closed, then gave him a stern look. "You have done a very bad thing, Sam."

He looked surprised and just a little guilty. "I have? And what have I done?"

I laughed. "You have unleashed Vivienne on this poor little unsuspecting town."

"Oh," he said, smiling, "is that all? I suspect if Whitby survived Dracula, it'll survive Vivienne." Then he laughed. "Maybe."

He had me take off my clothes, put on a hospital gown and then started with a basic physical exam. My weight, height, temperature and blood pressure were taken and recorded. He listened to my heart with a stethoscope and tested my reflexes with a little rubber hammer.

As he worked, he talked, keeping up a running stream of commentary to accompany his actions. "I ran all these same tests on Vivienne earlier, so that I'd have some sort of control results. There are no textbooks written on vampire physiognomy. In fact, there's probably only one doctor in the whole world capable of documenting the phenomenon." He laughed. "And Viv would kill me if I tried such a thing. Still, it's very tempting, especially when you consider that I started out in med school primarily to become a hematologist."

"Really? What moved you into psychiatry?"

"Contingencies. During my first year, a full scholarship became available; I fit all of the qualifications except for my medical concentration. And so, since I needed the money, I changed majors. But I've kept up as much as possible in the new advances of the field, even to the point of doing private research for interested individuals."

I smiled. "Such as I?"

"Exactly. Among others. In fact that's where I get the blood from—my other research assignments. I take two or three bags from each shipment and put them into storage. Vivienne says that I am a larcenous squirrel, hiding away acorns for the winter." He laughed. "Now," he said, getting back to business, "I am going to take some of your blood. I've never been able to draw blood from Viv's veins with a needle, so I've had to devise another method. She says it doesn't hurt much."

With a scalpel, he made a small incision in the crook of my right arm and inserted a tiny glass tube that ran into a larger glass cylinder. He pushed a button on the cylinder and I heard a rush of air. "This creates a vacuum," he explained. "Otherwise we'd be here all night waiting for a drop or two. Ah, there we go."

I felt the suction on my arm and watched as the cylinder filled with my blood. *Odd,* I thought, *it looks no different than any other blood.*

He pulled the tube from my arm when the cylinder was almost full and turned to move the blood out to the lab.

"Sam," I said, staring at my arm and trying not to panic, "am I still supposed to be bleeding?"

"What?" He turned and looked at me, watching for a moment as a small red flow trickled down my arm. "No, you are not supposed to be bleeding. Viv always dried up to the point of it being difficult to even get the tube out of her arm. Interesting."

He set the cylinder down and held a small wad of cotton to the spot. "Here," he said, bending my arm up, "hold that there for a bit while I get ready for the next test."

He wheeled in a small machine and began to attach small round disks to various portions of my head and body. Each disk was attached by a wire to the machine. "Before we start this," he said, "I want to see if I can draw blood from you the normal way. I should have done that first, without relying on the anomalies I'd previously discovered with Viv."

"More blood?" I said. "How much do you need?"

He shook his head. "This is not for the blood, actually. I just want to see if your blood behaves as Viv's does. So I won't take much."

I held out my left arm and he slid an empty hypodermic needle straight into the same general area as he had hit on the other arm and drew off about half a tube. "No problem," he said, sounding rather pleased with the result. "Interesting," he repeated.

"What does it mean?"

"For now, it merely means that your blood is different than Viv's. Not necessarily good or bad, just different. Relax, Deirdre."

I tried to do as he asked through all the prodding and poking. But after several hours, I grew restless.

"Will we be finished soon?" I asked. "What else can you possibly do to me, other than slit me open and take a good long look at what is inside?"

His mouth twisted up into a grin. "Now, there's an idea . . ." Then he laughed. "But no, on second thought, Mitch would skin me alive. And Viv would eat my liver or something equally as horrible. Actually, we're almost done. Only one more test, a polygraph. I'm just going to ask you some basic questions about things you should remember but don't. And then I'm going to hypnotize you and ask again. But before we do that you can take a break and walk around or something."

"In this gown?" I blushed. "I think I would prefer to get it over with, if you don't mind."

He laughed. "Whatever you say."

The questions he asked were simple enough, but for most of them I had no answer. Finally, I sighed. "Don't ask me anymore, Sam. The sheer volume of things that I have forgotten is depressing."

"It's okay," he said, "I've got enough to go on already. Do you remember how I hypnotized you during the Larry Martin situation?"

I nodded. "Yes, that time frame is more recent."

"Good," Sam said, holding up a pen, "now just stare at the pen and listen to me as I talk."

He used the same type of procedure as I did when hypnotizing my victims. And it was just as effective.

I opened my eyes to see Sam turning off the tape recorder he'd used during the session. "Well?"

"I'm not sure what it means, Deirdre, but I think it's probably good news. The memories are there—under hypnosis you can pull them up without hesitation. That tells me it's not a permanent block and not a physical problem."

"So you can fix it?"

"Theoretically? Yeah, I believe so. But you can't rush research, Deirdre, so this may take some time."

I sighed. There it was again, time I did not have. "That's wonderful news, Sam, thank you for all of your effort."

"Viv came in while you were under," he said. "She'll entertain you until Mitch shows up. I've got work to do."

When Mitch arrived, I was exhausted emotionally and physically. I had dressed and was sitting quietly talking to Vivienne in the outer rooms. The clatter of beakers and tubes and the clicking of the computer keyboard signaled Sam as being hard at work in the lab.

"So?" Mitch came over and gave me a kiss.

I shrugged. "He is working on it, right now. 'These things take time, Deirdre, you can't rush research.' " I mimicked his words and Vivienne laughed.

"Sam always says that and then, *voila!* He comes through." She reached over, took my hand and held it up to her cheek. "You will be fine, *ma chere,* I feel sure of it. Now you and Mitch should get home before the sun rises. Have a little something to drink—I swear, Sam takes more blood than any of us ever do. And they call us monsters."

Mitch laughed and I gave a weak smile.

"Ready, Deirdre?"

I kissed Vivienne. "Tell Sam I said good night and thank you. And that I will come back tomorrow night if he needs anything else."

Chapter 24

I could tell that Mitch had news for me, but did not want to speak about it in the open. The dogs greeted us at the door of the pub and for a second I looked around for Moe, then sighed when I remembered that he was gone.

"Poor fellow," I said. "I don't think I appreciated him enough."

"Who?" Mitch looked up from the attentions of the two mongrels, then seeing the expression on my face, nodded. "Yeah, he was sort of a fixture of the place. Doesn't quite seem the same without him. Kind of like Pete."

I smiled sadly. "Yes, but Pete will be coming back." It made no sense in saying that when he did, I would not know him.

We mounted the stairs and locked ourselves in.

"Hungry?" At my nod, he went into the kitchen, opened the refrigerator door and took out a bag of blood. "I'll warm it up for you. And then I'll tell you what I found out. It was all I could do not to come running over to tell you."

I gave a brief laugh. "Sam wouldn't have liked that; he wouldn't even let Vivienne into the room."

He called out to me, over the sound of running water. "So what did he do to you?"

"Besides draining all my blood, you mean?" I smiled when I said it, though, for hadn't Sam made amends with the gift to replace it? "He connected me to a lot of machines. It was all tests and little graphs on computer screens. None of it meant anything to me, but he seemed pleased and content that he had enough to work with. And he hypnotized me. He believed that the memories were not gone forever. Just blocked."

Mitch came out of the kitchen with a large glass tumbler filled with blood and handed it to me. "That's good. Now drink up."

I sniffed at it and took a long sip. "It's not quite the same thing as getting it fresh. But it will do, I suppose." I drained it and he reached for the empty glass.

"More?"

"No. That was more than enough. Now tell me your news."

He gave me a broad smile.

"Well?"

"I found out who is in charge of the Others. And it appears that we are holding a larger bargaining chip than we initially thought. Maggie Richards is more than the widow of their dead leader. Much more. She is also the mother of the current one.

Such a nice direct connection, don't you think? Blood ties run thick in their organization, apparently."

"I thought the eldest son was staying with his father's family, learning the funeral business. Oh." I shook my head. "Of course. Where better to take care of their transfers of souls? So who is this man? And how do we get in touch with him?"

"Steven DeRouchard currently resides in New York City. I have a phone number."

"Just like that? How could it be so simple? How did you find this out?"

"Phoenix paid me a visit." Mitch smiled in remembrance. "I'm getting to like that child more and more with each passing day. Which I should not, I guess, considering his origins. But we had a nice talk, until Maggie came to interrupt us. We'd already guessed that the boy hated his father, but apparently he's not particularly fond of his brother, either. He was more than willing to answer my questions and was able to find the DeRouchard Mortuary on-line listing for me."

The whole thing seemed too easy to me, too much of a coincidence, somehow. Then it hit me. "I don't like it, Mitch. It feels like a trap, as if he wanted us to find him."

"Yeah, of course he did. But we'll use the information to our advantage, not his. Besides, what else can they do to us now?"

To me, such a statement was challenging fate, but I said nothing, letting Mitch rattle on with his plans to contact the DeRouchards, how we would catch a flight to New York City with Maggie and Phoenix in tow, how he felt sure that they would cooperate fully, how he felt sure that the solution to my sickness was just a day or two away.

I loved him for many reasons, not the least one being his refusal to surrender. Unfortunately, I did not share the feeling, being frightened and totally weary. I had not slept at all the previous day, for fear of losing more of myself. Ultimately, though, I knew that I could not stay awake forever. Leaning my head on the back of the sofa, I closed my eyes for just a second. Nothing made sense. Nothing. And I was so tired.

*   *   *

I get off the plane in the city alone; I do not mind the solitude. It seems natural to me. The way it should be. And I know that somewhere, he is waiting. I will find him when it is time and then things will be made right.

I love being on these streets again, enjoy staring up at the tall buildings and the crowds of people rushing past me. Putting my head back, I inhale the city air. It smells of gasoline and car exhaust, it smells of flesh and blood and life and death. And home.

As if I were invisible, the people ignore me when I walk by, laughing. And when I hear the voice call, they must not, for they do not react, do not respond.

The voice is filled with pain and betrayal and it tears at my heart. I follow the voice, I have no choice, my feet move of their own volition and I follow.

I know the building. I have been there before, dreamt of it before. But now it is different; there is no one to greet me at the door. There is no music playing, for there is no one there to dance. The room is dark and silent and empty.

Except for the voice that calls.

It calls a name. And I follow, down a hallway. I push on a door that hangs heavy. Even with my full strength I can only open it halfway. Stepping into the room, I think that it is empty also.

But the voice calls me and I turn around.

He is here. There. On the door, held up and pinned by a long piece of splintered wood.

Here, I think, *is the answer I have sought in my waking life. I need only undo this act and all will be right.*

I put my hand to the wood and pull it away.

And the world seems to rise around me again. There is music playing somewhere, sounds of voices filter in to this room and the lights grow bright.

He moves away from the door and walks over to me. I am frightened, but he smiles.

"Have I done well?" I ask.

He nods and smiles and encircles me with his arms. His embrace is soft, comforting me like black-feathered wings. His grasp is as strong as steel and holds me captive.

"Once more, little one," he says as I stare into his eyes, "once more and all will be right."

I woke panicked and completely disoriented. The dream seemed so real, so natural. It hurt to be back here, submerged once again into a body that did not react as it should, into a mind that was failing.

Looking over at Mitch, sleeping, I breathed a sigh of relief that I still knew him. Testing the edges of my memory, though, I discovered that all of my years prior to my arrival in New York City as Deirdre Griffin were gone. As if I had been born the night I had arrived there.

Fewer than twenty years were left to me. And so much had happened to me during those years, so much of what made my life worth living. Mitch, of course, comprised the bulk of that worth. But there was Lily, the daughter I had never known, had never had a chance to know and now never would. And Vivienne and Sam and even Phoenix. Gwen, Victor, Claude, the memories of Larry Martin, of Chris, of the cabin in Maine, of Elly, who plied me with herbal tea and scented candles.

Also rising to my mind were the memories of all of the countless victims from the past twenty years, those from whom I had stolen a portion of their life, so that I might live to reach this point in time.

One more sleep, one more dream, and all of them would be gone.

I had not the optimism of Sam, nor the perpetual gaiety of Vivienne, nor the hardheaded stubbornness of Mitch, who refused to give up even in the face of truth. All I had was love and the past events that served to make me the creature I was; when that past no longer existed, there would only be love.

I feared that it would not be enough to weather this storm.

Inwardly I raged. These bastards would pay although I did not know how I would exact my revenge. Deep inside, I felt the anger of the Cat; she had not deserted me, I realized, but had only drawn further into my being. I visualized her, retreating as if into a dark cave from the pain and the sickness.

And although she'd retreated, she was not beaten or cowed; rather she stood facing the entrance of her lair, snarling her defiance. Biding her time. Her spirit and her inner fire still burned. As did mine.

Years ago, Sam had theorized that the Cat was merely my subconscious way of dealing with anger. Despite his then denial of the physical manifestation, he was, in a way, quite correct. She held on to feelings with which I could not deal, and it was with her that I kept my rage and my frustration, feeding her basest instincts.

I reached deep inside and walked into her lair. She came to me and I caressed her fur, searching for her mind, attempting to touch the mind of the Cat. When I did find her and touch her, I also filled her with my hatred and my anger, feeling it drain out of me and into her.

Soon, I whispered to her, *soon we will find a way. We have to find a way. Until then, my pet, sleep and heal. And do not forget to hold true to the anger as I will try to hold on to the love.*

The phone rang, startling me out of my meditation, and I jumped from the couch to answer it.

"Hello?"

There was a pause. "Mom? It's me. Lily."

"Yes, I know. Where are you?"

"London."

"Did you have a good flight?"

She laughed. "It's too goddamned long a trip. And we barely made it to the hotel. But we're here. And we'll be leaving shortly after sunset to drive up there."

"Is Claude driving?"

"Shit, no. I am. There's no way I'd trust this journey to anyone else."

"Well, please drive carefully, Lily. You do know that they drive on the other side of the road here, don't you?" I shook my head and rolled my eyes when I said the words. Apparently mothering was not an entirely foreign concept to me after all.

She sighed. "I wasn't born yesterday, Mom. And I'll manage fine. But why do you always have to pick these god-awful out-of-the-way places? Like that place in Maine? It was barely a dot on the map." She paused, remembering, as was I, that she had come to our cabin in Maine with the sole purpose of destroying my life. And remembering that she had almost succeeded. "Oh. I'm sorry. I probably shouldn't have brought that up, huh?"

"Lily," I said, trying to sound motherly and comforting, "don't worry about that time. It's over and done and"—I gave a harsh little laugh—"practically forgotten."

"Oh." She sounded like she understood. "That's okay, then. I need to go now, Mom, so that we can get started on time. See you in about five hours or so."

"Lily?"

"Yeah?"

"Vivienne says there are cows on the roads. So be careful."

She laughed again. "Come on, Mom, Viv wouldn't know a cow if it jumped up and bit her on her cute little French ass. Jesus. Cows."

I smiled to hear the sarcasm in her voice. "It was not your"—I hesitated—"ass that I was worried about, Lily. Rather it was the car and the occupants."

"Okay, okay," she continued, "I get the message. And I'll be careful, promise."

"Good. See you soon, then."

"Yeah. And, Mom?" I heard a trace of mischievous laughter in her voice.

"Yes?"

"I'll be bringing some good news when I come. Bye."

I hung up the phone, laughing at how she had to get the last word, while at the same time brushing away a few tears. No sense in crying over this relationship. I had no time in which to repair it.

Mitch came over and put an arm around my waist. "Was that Lily on the phone?"

"Yes, they will be leaving London soon."

"You knew who she was?"

"Yes, Mitch, I knew." I did not want to tell him that I had

lost more memories in my sleep. His worry and sorrow would not delay the inevitable. "Of course I knew her."

"Good. I'm going to take a shower now. Join me?"

I reached up and kissed him. "In a bit."

He went into the bathroom and I heard the water start. "In a bit," I repeated softly, "but I have something now that I need to do before it is too late."

Chapter 25

While Mitch was in the shower, I hurriedly dressed and went downstairs to the pub. The time for subtlety had come and gone. It was time, long past time, to confront the enemy. Before everything I'd ever known faded from my sight, it was important that there be honesty between the two of us, Maggie and me.

Phoenix was standing at the pool table, pushing the balls around with his hand and watching the caroms they made. The dogs we'd shut out of our room that morning flopped around his feet.

"Hello," I said to him with a smile when he looked up at me, "perfecting your game?"

He nodded.

"Well, how would you like to go upstairs and keep Mitch company for a while instead? I want to have a private talk with your mother."

He gave me a doubtful look and I smiled again. "It will be all right with her, I promise. I'll tell her where you are. Mitch is in the shower right now, but I know he won't care if you go in. You can even use the computer if you want. How does that sound?"

His eyes lit up and he nodded, starting for the stairs.

"Wait," I said, "take the dogs with you. And tell me where your mother is before you go."

He gestured with his head to the back of the pub. "Room." He mouthed the word and grinned at me, then whistled to the dogs and bounded up the stairs, opening the door I'd left unlocked.

Now, I thought as I headed to the small room that was Maggie's, *now I can say what needs to be said. And do what needs to be done.*

I knocked on the door but did not wait for her to answer; instead I tried the doorknob and found it unlocked.

"Maggie," I said, the tone of my voice low and controlled, "you really should be more careful. Almost anyone could have just walked in here."

She sat on the end of the narrow bed, slightly hunched over, but her profile showed clear in the light. "I don't care," she murmured, "I don't bloody care anymore." Her shoulders quivered.

"I have come to ask you an important question, Maggie."

"Go ahead." Her muffled voice sounded small and sad, but I did not allow the emotions it aroused to deter me.

"Tell me, Maggie, is there any particular reason why I should not kill you right now? Right here where you sit?"

"No." She turned to me and I saw that she had been crying. Her beautiful face looked old and ugly. For the first time since we'd met, she had no magnetism, no pull on me.

"Just get it over with." She wiped away her tears impatiently with the heel of her hand, a small photograph of a child clutched between her fingers.

I took a step closer to her and looked at the picture. It was not of Phoenix, that much I knew. And there was something odd about the eyes of this child.

"What are you waiting for? There is no reason for you not to kill me. I won't fight you, Dot. In fact, it would be a blessing."

"What?" This was not the answer I had expected to receive.

That she would call me on a threat I had no intention of carrying out shocked me beyond belief.

She rose up and dropped the photograph. I watched it as it fell, fluttering slightly and landing on the floor between us. She stepped over it and stood in front of me, her hands clasped in front of her and her eyes downcast.

I did nothing, said nothing. The silence grew between us and the moment seemed to stretch to years.

Eventually her eyes rose from the floor and met mine. She was not afraid, that much was plain. Not afraid, no, but I also saw she fully expected to die. I could almost taste the hopelessness and despair in the air.

"How do you propose to do it, Dot?" she asked. "Will you just drain me of every drop of my blood? I'd imagine that would be a painless way to die. In fact it might be downright pleasant, I'd probably just slowly drift away. Or you could take the quicker approach, I suppose, and simply rip my throat out. Leaves more of a mess behind, though, and"—she gave a small laugh—"I won't be around to help you clean it up."

"Or—" She unbuttoned her shirt, slowly slid it off her arms and dropped it to the floor where it lay crumpled next to the photo. She removed her bra next, exposing her white breasts, nipples slightly crinkled from the cold. "You can tear out my heart. Go ahead, take it. It's never done me much good anyway."

"Maggie," I said softly, "put your shirt back on. I am not going to tear out your heart."

"And you're not going to kill me either, are you?"

"No, I cannot kill you. I wanted to; I came down here to do exactly that, I think. But I was lying to myself. Even if your death at my hands would solve all my problems, I could not do it."

"Why not? I came here to spy on you and Mitch. I brought with me the ingredient needed to catalyze the poison in your veins."

"Catalyze?"

386 *Karen E. Taylor*

"Oh. You didn't know that part, did you? I thought maybe Sam would have figured it out. If I had never come here, if you had not taken my blood, you would have been fine. And so would your memory."

"You know about that?"

Maggie sighed and picked up her bra and shirt from the floor, sitting down on the bed to put them on again. "I know everything. About you and Mitch, at least. And I know who is calling the shots. I wish I didn't."

I nodded. "It's your oldest son, is it not? Steven DeRouchard?"

"No! My son would never do these things. He'd never call for the death of so many. He was loving and warm and entirely mine. Until . . ." Her voice trailed off and the expression in her eyes grew distant.

"Until?" I prompted her, picking up the picture from the floor and placing it once more into her hand.

Maggie looked at the picture and held back a sob. "Can you even understand what my life has been like? I was raised to be a Breeder; it takes a certain sort of woman, you see, a certain upbringing to enable you to birth children and give them up."

"Give them up?"

She gave me a sharp look. "Okay, you're right. And we should be honest, you and I. It is not giving them up, that would be pardonable. No, instead I've given birth to children only to put them willingly into the hands of murderers."

Maggie started to cry again, ugly tears streaming down her face. I did not know what to say; I moved toward her, my intentions unclear even to me.

"No," she said, "don't touch me. If you touch me, the lure will begin to work on you again. You won't want to kill me. And I very much want to die. I deserve to die."

"Why, Maggie? Why do you want to die?"

She pressed her fingers against her eyes. "When Steven was born, I was so happy. I loved Eduard, I loved my baby, I was doing what I had been raised to do. They took him away from me all in a hurry one day and when he was brought back he had the scar. But they didn't tell me the truth. Eduard explained that as a result of that night's work, the baby would have an incredibly long life span, he would never get sick, he would grow and thrive and be a powerful, influential man one day. Every mother's fondest dream.

"I believed him. Of course I did. To think otherwise . . ."

Once again her voice trailed off. But I made no move toward her, knowing that she would continue.

"Steven grew quickly. In the case of Other children, that growth is not just a trick of time, not just the perception of a mother who does not want to lose her children. They do grow at an accelerated pace. It's not a standard rate; it varies from child to child. Phoenix is growing much slower than his brother did. I asked Eduard about it once, noticing the phenomenon in our own two. 'A difference in the life force of the soul,' he told me, 'and their strivings. Some of them just want to be alive again more than the rest.' And still after that statement, I didn't understand what was really happening, what the awful truth was.

"Then, one day without warning, the soul that dwelled inside the boy I knew as Steven came to life. I watched it happen. We were sitting at the dinner table and I asked him to pass me something. Peas, I think it was."

She looked up at me with a twisted smile. "Isn't it funny how the commonplace things can acquire such importance? That bowl of peas changed my life. Changed the way I looked at the world and not for the better . . ."

I waited patiently.

"I asked him to pass me the peas, Dot, and between the second he turned his head to get the bowl and the second he handed it to me," Maggie continued, "he changed, completely transformed into someone I didn't know right there before my eyes. Suddenly, in the body of my son, the body that I bore and fed and bathed and comforted, there dwelled a stranger. He spoke then, I heard his voice for the first time since they'd taken him away from me as a baby. 'Mother,' he said, just that one word, and he smiled at me. The smile of a demon, it seemed to me, with an uncanny and unholy knowledge shining out of his eyes. No child can smile like that. I dropped the bowl of peas and Phoenix began to cry, silently."

She stopped suddenly and looked around. "Phoenix? Where is he?"

"He is safe, Maggie. I sent him upstairs to stay with Mitch."

She gave me her angelic smile then, turning on some of her near-fatal charm. "He likes Mitch. And you. More than one would think, considering the circumstances. It's almost as if he'd known you before." She shrugged and tossed back her hair. "Who knows? Maybe he did in some other lifetime."

"Whose lifetime, Maggie?"

She looked away from me and dropped her head again; this time, however, it seemed less a response than a deliberate gesture. "I don't know. Eduard never told me. And I never asked." She glanced up at me from under her black lashes. "Oh, I know what you're thinking. I should have asked. Once I knew the truth, how could I not have asked? It's possible that Eduard might even have told me. Maybe I just didn't want to know. I guess we'll find out soon enough, anyway, when the soul they put into him comes to life. But then he won't be Phoenix anymore, will he? He'll be as dead as Steven is."

She gave me a hard look. "I don't want to lose another child that way. Not him. They'll take him away, just like they took Steven. And I will be left with nothing."

"Why are you here, Maggie?"

"He sent me. That man who used to be Steven. God forgive me, he still holds enough of my heart and soul to move me. And I obey him as I always obeyed Eduard. It's the only life I've ever known."

"But why did he send you here? He had to have known he was putting you in danger, you and Phoenix both."

She gave a bitter laugh. "He's not human, you know. None of them are. You and Mitch are more human than they will ever be, regardless. So I doubt he cared, for either my safety or his brother's. My coming here served his purpose at the time."

"And other than the complete and total extermination of my kind, what is his purpose?"

Her face closed up completely and she would not answer.

I should have pushed her, I suppose, pressured her to answer my question, but she turned her eyes to me and I saw the pain that she bore. She was already broken. Nothing could be accomplished by hurting her more.

I sighed. "Thank you, Maggie. I'll bring Phoenix back down to you. And I would suggest that the two of you stay in your room tonight. Lock the door. There are some visitors arriving I do not think you should meet."

Chapter 26

M itch and Phoenix looked up from the computer in tandem when I opened the door to our flat.

"Have you two been having fun?" I asked, absently, thinking not of how they'd been spending their time. Instead I noticed for the first time how similar the two of them looked. There was something about the shape of their mouths and the way they both looked out of their eyes.

They smiled and Phoenix nodded, typing something out on the keyboard. Mitch read it and laughed. I walked up behind them and read the words on the screen.

hello, deirdre, how are you tonight? want to play some pool with me later on? i know youll beat me again but i dont mind. much.

"What is it with you and pool, Phoenix? Since Mitch first

taught you to play, you have done nothing but, every chance you get. And I don't believe that you and I have ever played together, although I would probably beat you."

we played, yeah, we played. it is one of those things i remember. you and me and

He stopped typing for a second and glanced over at Mitch.

mitch, he continued, *in the bar. we were drinking beer.*

I laughed. "If you were drinking beer, young man, that explains all of these false memories. Now you had better get downstairs and go to your mother."

He got up from his chair, but kept his fingers on the keyboard.

i want to stay here with the dogs. shes mad at me again. its not like i can help the memories coming, can i?

Mitch stood up and took the boy by the hand. "For now, son, I think it's best if you stay with your mother. She needs you."

Phoenix pulled his hand away and angrily typed something. Then, without a backward glance, he ran to the door and down the stairs.

Mitch stared off after him but I read what he had written.

you always say that. and its just not fair.

"Typical child," I said, as if I were an authority on the subject.

"Yeah," Mitch agreed, "he's quite a kid. I was surprised to find him here, but he'd typed out a note and slipped it under the bathroom door while I was showering. He told me you and Maggie were having a little talk. And he said you didn't seem too happy and that was okay because neither was she."

"That," I said with a sad smile, "is the understatement of the year. Poor Maggie. I cannot help but feel sorry for her."

"What did the two of you find to talk about?"

"I asked her to give me a good reason why I shouldn't kill her. We have all been dancing around this issue for too long, all three of us pretending that there wasn't some kind of crazy game going on. A game in which none of us, apparently, know the rules." I sighed, trying not to think about tomorrow night, when I might know nothing at all. "I don't have time for subtlety anymore, Mitch."

"Did you lose more memories, Deirdre?"

I walked over to the fireplace and built up the fire. "No," I lied, not wanting him to know that tonight might very well be our last together, "but it's bound to happen again. And so, in that light, I thought that honesty would be best."

"And what did Maggie say in response?"

"That she wanted to die, she deserved to die. For allowing the Others to murder her babies."

"Her children are still alive."

I shook my head. "No, Mitch. You forget, I think, what her children have become. Even Phoenix, as good a child as he seems, is an unknown. So while the bodies of her children are still alive, their souls, their personalities, their very life comes from somewhere, or rather, someone else.

"In a way, I suppose, it is the exact opposite of the situation with Lily. I gave birth, thought my child was dead and discovered years later she lived. Maggie gave birth, thought the child was alive and found out years later that *her* child really was dead. How can you not feel pity for her?"

His mouth tightened. "I'm trying not to. What else did she tell you?"

"Steven DeRouchard is in charge of the Others, as we already knew. He sent her here to act as a catalyst for the poison."

"Interesting," Mitch said, "considering that Sam called earlier with some initial reports and said that there seem to be two separate foreign elements in your blood, the poison and something else."

I gave a soft laugh. "He did? Then what Maggie said confirms his findings. He should be pleased."

Mitch nodded. "Very pleased, I'd say. He and Viv are on their way over here now and although he wouldn't say anything about it all on the phone, he sounded happy."

I gave a small snort. "Of course he's happy. He has a vampire

guinea pig at his disposal again. There is nothing else on the face
of the earth that he loves more."

"Except for Viv."

I shrugged. "Who knows? The possibility of research may be
what attracts him to her."

"Yeah, right. I'd believe that only if he were over the age of
seventy and maybe not even then."

"Any more news from Lily?" I was pleased to hear that the
note of desperation I felt did not show in my voice. "I hope she
will still be driving up tonight?"

"No news. So I assume she's on her way."

"Good,"

I walked over to the dresser and pulled open one of the drawers. "Damn."

"What's wrong?" Mitch hurried over and put an arm around
my shoulder. "Do you feel okay? What are you looking at?
There's nothing in there."

"Exactly. I wanted something nice to wear when Lily and the
rest of them showed up. Victor always makes me feel so shoddy;
if I had a pair of fresh jeans to put on, at least I would feel
clean."

"Why the hell should you care how Victor makes you feel?"

I shook my head. "You're right, of course. We have way more
important things to think about. But it would have been nice to
feel beautiful again, to feel like Deirdre Griffin for one"—I
paused—"night."

Mitch laughed, not understanding. "But you *are* Deirdre
Griffin, sweetheart. And you are always beautiful."

I kissed him. "Don't lie to me, Mitch. You never have before
and this is a bad time to start. It doesn't matter, really."

There was a light knocking at the door. "Let me in, let me
in," Vivienne's slightly muffled voice pleaded. "it's an emergency."

"Bloody hell," Mitch said, flinging the door open and expecting the worst. "I wonder what's wrong now."

There stood Viv, carrying a small cosmetic case and a large
garment bag.

I could not help the smile that crossed my face and quickly turned into a laugh. "Come in, Vivienne," I said. "You must have read my mind."

She looked beautiful, as always, and was dressed in a pink sheath dress that showed off her white arms and magnificent neck. Taking one look at Mitch, she shoved him out the door. "Go," she said, swinging the case at him. "Go downstairs and talk to Sam. He's been forced into playing a game with that boy. Deirdre has a party to attend this evening and I know she wants to look her best."

She closed the door behind him and leaned up against it. "Men." She giggled. "They just cannot understand that a girl needs to feel pretty. And that what we see in the mirror is not always what they see in their beds."

"You are a lifesaver, Vivienne."

"Foo," she said, "I am nothing like that. I just did not want my little sister looking, well," and she hesitated, rolling her eyes slightly, "looking like you. Now get out of those awful clothes and see what I have brought for you."

When Viv had finished, the woman in the mirror had little resemblance to the woman who had greeted her on her arrival. Makeup covered the dark circles under my eyes and the fever-blotched skin. She even managed to style my short dyed hair into something less marinelike.

"What did you do?" she'd said, clicking her tongue, "chop it all off with a razor? And then pour bleach on your head?"

I nodded. "Damn close to that, actually. We were in a hurry."

"When one's looks are involved, one must never be in such a hurry, *ma chere*. However, do not fear. I have fixed you, have I not?"

And she had, bringing a red velvet dress, matching heels and a short jacket made out of black fur.

I had looked at the dress, stroking the fabric between my fingers, and said, "I'm glad it's not green."

She cocked her head to one side. "But green would be lovely on you. Had I anything that color, I would have brought it."

"Green," I said with conviction, "is an unlucky color for me." Then I broke into tears.

"Bad memories, *mon chou?*" At her questioning look, I shook my head.

"No, no memories." I wiped the tears away. "I have no idea at all why I would even say such a thing."

"So," she said then, "are we done with crying? I will do your makeup."

Viv gave me one more appraising glance now, applied a little more mascara to my lashes and stood back. *"Voila!"* she said, giving a little wave of her hand. "And you are transformed!"

"Thank you," I said. "No one else will understand, but this has meant so very much to me."

She came up to me and held my hands. "I could not bear to think of you spending what might be your last night dressed in denim and flannel."

"My last night?"

Her gray eyes met mine and all trace of laughter and gaiety had disappeared. "Do not lie to me, sister. I may spend most of my time convincing the world around me that I am trivial and stupid, but I am not. And I know that you have one, maybe two nights, before your memory is gone. Sam is hopeful that he has found something to reverse the damage—"

My eyes flew open. "He has?"

She put a finger on my lips. "He will want to tell you all about that himself. And hopeful is not the same as sure. But he is sure that with time—"

"Time that I do not have."

Viv nodded sharply. *"Oui.* And Mitch, he would protect you with his very life if what threatened you came from outside. But he is powerless in this. I thought, the last time I looked in your eyes, that you knew exactly what was happening, better than either of them. And that you were going to fight this with all your might and heart. But how can you fight that which is flowing through your veins?"

I started to answer, but she continued. "You cannot, of course, not even you, my indomitable sister. So, I see my Sam trying to solve the problem with his brains, and you and Mitch, with your strength and your love. And I think, what have I to offer? Nothing." Viv giggled now, burying her emotion again under a frivolous gesture. "Nothing, except a new dress and some makeup to lighten your spirits."

"Hardly nothing," I said. "Now I can face Victor and the rest of them without feeling shopworn."

"I will make a confession, *ma chere*. He makes me feel just the same. Victor is very good at making one feel his inferior. He always reminds me without a word that I was nothing but a cheap whore when we met."

"Vivienne." I looked back into her eyes. "I will venture a guess that you have never been, nor will you ever be, cheap."

She gave a little flip of her shoulders and took my arm. "But of course, you are right. I was, and am, very, very expensive."

We laughed together as we walked down the stairs, arm in arm.

Mitch hovered around the entrance to the bar, alternating between watching Sam and Phoenix playing pool and waiting for me to come downstairs. He turned to see us and smiled at me, his eyes glowing with love.

Vivienne let go of my arm as we reached the landing and gave a small curtsy. "See, Monsieur Greer, I have delivered your wife, much improved."

"There was nothing wrong with her before, Viv." He laughed as she shrugged and sauntered past him. "You have just gilded her a bit. Her true beauty is not kept on the outside."

I gave him a sharp glance, wondering if he knew how painful those words were, but quickly realized that he'd meant no hurt to me. He still had hope, I knew.

I could not afford hope. But I smiled at him and we went into the room, joining Vivienne at the bar.

Chapter 27

I accepted a glass of wine from her and sipped it as we watched Sam with the boy.

Vivienne applauded when Sam sank a particularly difficult shot to win the game. He solemnly shook hands with Phoenix and walked over to us, holding out his cue to Mitch. "Your turn," he said, "and Vivienne will cheer you on, won't you? I want to have a private talk with Deirdre."

"Doctors," she said, with a pretty pout. "They are so fickle, no? But if you insist, Sam, *mon amour,* I will leave the two of you alone."

Sam gently cupped his hand on my elbow and led me over to a table in a far corner of the room, handling me so delicately that I laughed and pulled away from him. "Whatever else I may have forgotten, Sam, I have not forgotten how to walk."

"I'm sorry," he said sheepishly, sitting down across from me, "it's that bedside manner. It never goes away."

I nodded. "Vivienne says that you have news for me. And good news at that."

His eyes flicked over to her and then back to me. "She shouldn't have said anything. I may have found something in your blood, some element that can be isolated, that is responsible for blocking your memories. And if I've found it, then perhaps I can neutralize it. But it's going to take a lot more research and a lot more time."

I sighed. "Time? I have plenty of time. And I suppose if the memories are only blocked and not erased, that they can be brought back?"

"In theory, yes." He reached over and took my hand. "But there is nothing I can do for you now. Not even in a week or a month. And at the rate at which you are losing recall . . ."

"There will be nothing left of me by tomorrow night. I understand. I have seen this coming for a while, Sam, and I will survive it. I will beat it. I am holding on to what matters most. My love and my anger."

We fell silent for a while, watching Mitch and the boy. "They look like fast friends, don't they?" Sam said, and I nodded, giving the two of them a loving glance.

"Yes. Regardless of what and who he is, Phoenix has been good for Mitch. An ill wind, as they say."

"What will you do, Deirdre?"

I raised an eyebrow. "Do? About Mitch and the boy?"

"No, what will you do when it's all gone?"

"Stay here, I suppose." I gave a grim laugh and held out my arms, lurching from side to side in my chair and making a low growling sound. "Terrorize the townspeople with my zombie impression, perhaps."

"Well, that sounds like fun." He shook his head and gave me a full smile.

"Oh, yes. I can hardly wait."

"Excuse me." Maggie stood over us, an unopened bottle of wine in her hand, an extra glass and a small corkscrew, with which she proceeded first to peel the foil from the bottle's neck and then to remove the cork. She set the wine, the glass and the implement on the table.

"May I join you before the party starts? I won't interfere, I promise. But I can hear you talking and laughing from my room. I'm not good company for myself tonight. And now that we are no longer enemies, or," and she gave a sad smile, "at least now that I am a known evil, I can't hurt you anymore. Besides"—she smiled and a fraction of her previous charm came through—"you could always say that you let me join you so that you could keep an eye on me."

Her eyes, still red and moist from crying, were vacant and kept darting erratically over to her son and then back to us. Her smile seemed hesitant, not the full alluring expression that normally painted her face.

"Please, Maggie," I said, somewhat remorseful of my earlier treatment of her, "sit and join us."

She moved like an old woman and sat with a sigh, tearing her eyes away from Phoenix. "You must be Doctor Samuels," she said, holding her hand out to him, a little of her old charm surfacing. "I'm Maggie Richards. But you know that already. You know everything, I suppose."

He shook her hand and gave a small laugh, "Not everything, I'm afraid."

She gave him a searching look and stared at the hand clasping hers before breaking the grip. "But you are still human, aren't you? How strange that he would be wrong about that."

"Excuse me? I don't quite follow you."

"Steven. He felt sure that Vivienne would have transformed you by now. 'If they call in reinforcements,' he said, 'most likely you will need to deal with Samuels as well. I cannot believe that Vivienne would let him slip through her soft little fingers.' " She gave a short barking laugh. "Isn't it funny that he could be wrong? I thought he was invincible and omniscient. And he's not."

"Maggie, why are you telling us this?"

"It doesn't matter, don't you see? I've already done what he asked me to do. And you know all of it. Soon he will have everything he wants and this will all be over. And when Phoenix changes, there will be nothing left for me anyway."

I glanced over at Sam and he gave an almost imperceptible nod.

"Why do you say that, Maggie?" he prompted. "You're a young, beautiful and vibrant woman. You can have more children if you want—"

At that point there was a call of triumph from the pool table and she jumped visibly, for the voice was not Mitch's.

"I got it," Phoenix shouted. "Did you see it? I shot it right in and won the game." Silence fell on the room, deathly and grim, as the import of his being able to speak registered with all of us.

The change had begun.

Maggie stared at him, grief-stricken, holding a hand to her throat. "Too soon," she whispered, "this is too soon." She gazed around the room, looking at each of us in turn, drawing us into her sorrow, her grief. "He's too young and I'm not ready,

I'm not prepared for this, not now. I cannot stand the thoughts of losing another child."

Her hands shook on the table and she knocked over her glass, splashing herself with red wine. Taking no notice, she rose slowly from her seat, pulling herself to her full height and straightening her shoulders.

"Phoenix," she called, her voice clear and commanding despite the tears that streamed down her face, "look at me."

The boy turned and began to walk toward us. Even in that short span of time, he had changed. The host body conformed to the awakened soul within and brought about subtle changes in facial structure. I could plainly see the skin move, making room for the rearrangement of bones and muscles, transforming his face to match the original. But the eyes, the eyes stayed the same.

I gave a small gasp of recognition. I knew him, I should have known him all along. What had seemed a great puzzle was now so very simple. It was as I had told Mitch, we had actively fought to deny the obvious.

And although I could not fathom how or why it had happened, it appeared that Eduard DeRouchard had given Mitch a priceless gift. From the body of a boy named Phoenix, Christopher Greer had been reborn.

"Oh, my God."

Next to me, Sam also registered the transformation. "But how?"

Maggie sobbed quietly, still standing, staring at the creature who, not even five minutes ago, had masqueraded as her son. But her son was dead, he had died a little over four years ago on the same night that Christopher Greer had died.

"He was buried out of their funeral home." Her voice was emotionless now and deathly quiet, but we heard every word. "DeRouchard Brothers Mortuary, in New York. When Eduard saw the name on the death certificate he was very happy.

" 'Here's my chance,' he said, 'here's my leverage over the Cadre. I can hold Greer's son as hostage for their compliance.' "

Mitch gave a small intake of breath and stepped forward. He had not seen the change, I realized, for Chris had been standing with his back to him. Mitch was just now understanding who the boy was; I saw a great joy and relief leap into his eyes. He moved in his direction. I caught his eye and I shook my head slightly. Now, in the face of Maggie's great distress, was not the time for their reunion.

Mitch nodded his agreement and held back.

Maggie continued her story. "Eduard reached for my baby then and I protested.

" 'You told me that this one was to be mine, that if I gave Steven to you, I could keep any other children that followed. And you have Steven; he's not my child anymore. He is one of your Others now. But this one, Eduard, this one is mine. You promised.'

"Eduard looked into my eyes. His expression seemed cold and lifeless to me. There was no love in those eyes, no mercy, no regret for what he was about to do. 'I know, Maggie,' he said, 'and I am sorry, but this is too big an opportunity to ignore. And there are no other babies right now. I can't afford to pass this chance by. There will be others. Now, give the baby to me.' "

She looked around at us, her expression panicked and wild. "You knew him," she said, catching Vivienne's eye, "you know what he was like. I loved him. And I hated him. And I couldn't say no. God forgive me, I just couldn't say no."

She collapsed into her chair and Chris walked up to her, hesitantly. "Mum," he said, his voice cracking. "It's okay, Mum, it really is. I'm still here, the little boy you raised, your baby. Mum? It's Phoenix. I'm still here. And I won't be like Steven, I promise."

Maggie's shoulders shook convulsively and her sobs grew louder, more uncontrolled. "He promised, too. And then he broke them; all of his promises, one by one, proved worthless. And you, you're just the same as he was, just the same as your brother is. You're not human, not normal. I'm sorry I brought you into this world."

"Mum? Please don't say that, you don't mean it. I know you love me. And I love you."

I saw the glitter of her eyes through the dark curtain of her hair. "Love? Not that, Phoenix, don't talk to me about love. You are a DeRouchard, you know nothing of love."

Before I knew she had even moved, her hand shot up to the table, she grabbed the corkscrew and stabbed at the boy, aiming for his heart. He ducked to his right and the implement pierced his arm instead.

He gave a loud cry and Mitch flew across the room and knocked the object from Maggie's hand before she could strike again.

The smell of blood permeated the air. Sam rushed to Chris's side as he stood there, swaying slightly, blood spurting from between the fingers of the hand he had clasped to the wound, the corkscrew still protruding from his arm.

"Mum?" His voice was quiet and confused. "Mum?" Louder now, his voice reached her.

Maggie looked at him. Her face turned deathly white when she realized what she had attempted to do.

"Oh, Phoenix," she moaned, "I didn't mean it. Honest, baby, I didn't know what I was doing." She reached over and grabbed my hand. "You don't think I meant to kill him, do you, Dot? He's my baby, my little boy. I couldn't hurt him, not ever."

Sam looked up from tending to Chris's arm and over at Vivienne. "Get my bag," he said to her calmly, "and give Maggie a sedative. Valium should work just fine. You remember how to give a shot, right?"

"But, of course, *mon cher*." She fetched the bag, prepared a hypodermic needle and injected Maggie. Then Viv tugged on her arm and coaxed Maggie to her feet. "Come now, little lamb, and take a walk with Nurse Vivienne. She will tuck you into your bed, all safe and secure. Do not worry, your Phoenix will be fine and so will you."

Maggie teetered a bit and Viv looked over her shoulder. "Mitch, could you help, please?"

The look of love on Chris's face as he watched the three of them walk back to the room was heartbreakingly familiar. When they reached the room, he turned his attention back to Sam. "She'll be okay, won't she, Doctor Samuels? She really didn't mean to hurt me."

Sam shrugged. "If she'd actually hit your heart, Chris, she'd have done some real damage. But maybe she didn't mean to. We'll continue to think that, hmmm? Now keep still and let me get this bandaged."

Chapter 28

Mitch and Vivienne came out of the back bedroom. In answer to my questioning look, she smiled briefly. "Poor little lamb," she said, "she reminds me so of Monique. Not a huge surprise, I suppose. Eduard leaves his mark, does he not? Bastard that he was." Her eyes grew hard. "And I fear his malice will live on for years and years. But Maggie, she will sleep for a while yet. What she will be like when she awakens is, I believe, a question for our doctor."

Sam finished bandaging Chris's arm. "Hard to say," he admitted. "I've no idea what sort of trauma this situation could cause." He gave a shaky laugh. "I may need to tranquilize everyone."

Mitch stood for a minute, just looking at the boy who had been Phoenix. Then he crossed the room and clasped his newly reborn son in his arms. "Damn," he said, his voice thick with emotion, "you're alive. I can't believe it, you're actually alive."

Chris winced from the pain in his arm. "I don't know, Dad, not five minutes after I get back, the woman I thought of as my mother for so many years tried to kill me again. Maybe it's not such a good idea, after all." But he smiled as he said it to soften the words.

"What's it like?" Mitch asked him. "To be dead and then to return?"

"Confusing." Chris shook his head. "It's going to take me a lot of time to adjust. And to be a child again? I'm not sure if I'm ready to talk about it; I can barely remember being Phoenix now. As if it were a dream I had just woken up from. And at the same time I have all the old remembrances and emotions from my previous life, jumbled up inside me. I can't seem to sort any of it out in my mind. . . ."

Something about the mature words coming from the mouth of the child was disconcerting and I could well understand that Chris would be overwhelmed.

"Take your time," I said, "we are none of us going anywhere. But know that you are welcome. And"—I looked at Mitch—"much loved."

There was a knock at the pub door then and I went to answer it. Through the window I could see one of the largest men I'd ever seen with a slim redheaded girl at his side, a backpack slung across one shoulder. Lily and Claude had arrived.

I opened the door.

"Hi," Lily said, giving me a brief hug. "Sorry we're late. We had some trouble getting started in London." Then she pulled back and took a long look at me, her eyes searching my face.

"Hello, Lily," I said, totally at a loss for words. I never knew what to say to this girl, my daughter. Except for the truth. "I'm glad you're here."

"Are you okay? You look different." She reached over and touched my hair. "Might be the new style, I guess. Although, I don't think it suits you."

I shrugged. "Vivienne doesn't like it much either. But we thought at the time that a disguise was a good idea. Even Mitch dyed his hair. It didn't help much, they still found us. How they do it, I don't know, but they always find us."

"But no more." Lily reached into her backpack and pulled out a videotape. "I come bearing wonderful news. Amazing news. Terri and Bob have recanted. And the Others have called off their vendetta, because of a recent change in leadership. The silent assassins with sharp sticks won't be stopping at our doors anymore."

She peered into the pub. "No television? Shit, Mom, this is like living in the Dark Ages. Anyway, do you think we could come inside? Or are you going to leave us standing here all night?"

I laughed. "I'm sorry, please, come in." She walked past me, grabbing my hand as she did and giving it a quick squeeze.

"Hey, kiddo," I heard Mitch say as Lily entered into the lighted pub, "how've you been? You're looking good. And where's Victor?"

"Back in London," she said, her voice flat.

"Well, never mind about that. You've managed to come late for all of the good stuff. Come meet Chris."

Claude cleared his throat, pulling my attention away from Mitch and Lily. He smiled at me, took my hand and kissed it. "You're looking well, Deirdre."

"And you are a liar, Claude. I have never looked worse. However, you are welcome. And yes," I said to the question in his eyes, "I still remember you. For now."

I took his arm and led him into the pub. "Mitch?" I asked, "can we bring the television down here? I would very much like to see this tape that Lily brought us."

"Good idea," he said, "I was wondering where we would find room for everyone upstairs. I'll be right back. Chris? Do you want to help?"

The two of them headed up the steps and Sam began rearranging chairs for the viewing. Vivienne poured wine for everyone and Claude came back to my side after taking one.

"So who's the kid?" he asked. "He has the scent of an Other about him."

"With good cause. Four years ago, Eduard apparently thought he could use a hostage, and so he borrowed the soul of Mitch's son and planted it into the body of his newborn child. We are all still adjusting to the idea. Chris only came back to life tonight, forced out earlier than he should have been, I think, because of the presence of Mitch. Such a strange situation. And where's Victor? I had hoped he could shed some light on an of this."

Claude reached into his pocket and took out a handkerchief, dabbing at his face. "Victor decided he did not want to accompany us. He had other business, he said."

Lily walked up to us. "Yeah, he's a stubborn old man. That's why we're late. After we saw the tape last night, he refused to come. 'No need now,' he said. And 'He's making his move.' That's all he would say. He seemed inordinately pleased about the whole thing, though. Ecstatic, I'd say. And not so much because we were all safe now, but more because of the change in leadership. When it was time to go this evening, he told us to come ahead without him. No reason, no explanation. Just do this because he said so."

"Typical," Mitch said, walking down the stairs with the television in his arms. Chris trailed after him, followed by the two dogs. Lily coaxed them over to sniff at her fingers.

"Somehow," she said, laughing up at me, "I'd not have taken you for a dog person."

"I'm not. Curly and Larry belong to Mitch."

She laughed at the names. "So where's Moe?"

"Dead," I said. "Which reminds me. Chris?"

"Yeah?" He looked up from where he was attaching the video player to the television.

"Who killed Moe?"

"Moe?" Chris straightened up, a confused look on his face. He struggled for a minute; then recognition and sadness came over him. "Oh, yeah. Moe. Poor dog." For a moment he looked like the boy he had been, his eyes haunted and frightened. "I really don't know for sure, Deirdre, he was that way when I found him. I think Phoenix knew who did it, but I just can't remember."

"I suppose," I said, "given her recent penchant for violence, that it could have been Maggie."

"No." He shook his head vehemently. "It wasn't Mum. I know that for sure."

"Well, I'll have to take your word for that. Perhaps it was one last parting shot from the Others."

"Maybe." Chris reached down and turned on the television. "Okay, Lily," he said, "let's see this tape."

The opening was the same. The same overly dramatic organ music, the same beginning credits, the photos of famous and infamous vampires. But from there everything changed. The *Real-Life Vampires* logo appeared briefly, then was covered over in a wash of black. The theme music stopped midnote and all was silent.

The camera cut to Terri Hamilton, wearing a dark suit and an extremely somber expression, as if she had just come from a funeral. And perhaps, in her mind, she had.

"This," she said without one trace of her former smile, the smile we had all wanted to wipe off of her face, "will be our last show. And one that we taped with great trepidation and sadness. But it must be said that we have always been dedicated to the truth. We have dedicated ourselves, putting our careers and our lives on the line to expose things that had been kept hidden and secret. Things we felt you had a right to know."

Mitch gave a half laugh. "She still manages to say all the keywords, doesn't she?"

"And now, dear friends, we have received news of great import. News that affects both Bob and me personally. News that affects a great many of our listening audience.

"We have . . ." She paused, her eyes briefly darting to the script in front of her. ". . . been duped. All of us. There are no such things as vampires." At this point, her voice cracked and she looked over to Bob, who picked up the speech.

Vivienne giggled. "This is very good, Lily. Perhaps they can both be more humiliated?"

Lily snickered. "It gets better, Vivienne. Just wait."

"That's right, Terri." Bob looked authoritative as usual and about as comfortable as a man forced to eat his words on national television could be. "New evidence has been brought to our attention that completely discounts the vampire scare. Medical reports have been falsified, documentation and film footage that had been certified as genuine are now proven nothing more than the basest fabrications. Most especially," and on the screen behind him came the film we had viewed no more than a week ago, "this most recent report, depicting the murder of four men by supposed vampires, turned out to be nothing more than a prescripted staging, a fake."

"Oh," Viv sneered, "was that a sham? But it looked so real. *Merde.* I cannot believe that people would be so stupid as to believe their propaganda."

"Let us hope, Vivienne, that they are," I said with a half smile. "If they believed what they were told earlier, then those same people might just believe this as well."

"We are horrified," Terri continued, "that we played a part, no matter how innocent, in the persecution of certain people. In our defense, I can only say that we were expertly and deliberately misled by the leadership of the Others, the group responsible for this widespread hysteria."

"The Others," Bob continued, the screen behind him now changing to a large photo of an extremely handsome, blond-haired, green-eyed man, standing and waving at the door of an airplane, "an international group of supposed philanthropists, had previously been under the direction of this man. Eduard DeRouchard."

Chris gave a short gasp. "I do remember him," he said, his voice tight and angry. "I remember him quite clearly."

Terri spoke again. "The campaign against the Cadre, another international group, had been Mr. DeRouchard's brainchild. And although no one fully knows what he had hoped to achieve, since he died shortly after the initial attacks on his rival organization, his plans were continued for years by his seconds-in-command. Recently, though, his eldest son, Steven DeRouchard, took control of the group and the truth came out. Eduard DeRouchard, a wealthy and influential man, was in reality a delusional madman, who fully believed in the righteousness of his actions, wrong though they were."

"Here, here!" Vivienne raised her glass to the television set. "That is the most truth Miss Terri Hamilton has ever spoken in her life."

Bob cleared his throat and took a sip from the water glass sitting next to him. "Steven DeRouchard has declined to appear on camera or to have his words taped. But he has given us a statement to read."

" 'People of the world, esteemed colleagues and most especially my wronged and persecuted brothers and sisters of the Cadre, I know that the pain, sorrow and fear caused by our organization can never be fully repaired. But with Mr. Smith and Miss Hamilton's gracious assistance, I can at least set the record straight. I honor the memory of my father as a son should, but cannot allow the atrocities committed through his orders and in his name to go unrecompensed.

" 'Therefore, I have authorized the return of all monies and properties seized to their original owners. In addition, damages will be paid to those who lost loved ones in this unnecessary strife. The fallacy that vampires can exist, side by side with humans in our world, should be dismissed as nothing more than the ravings of a madman.

" 'Mostly I offer my sincerest apologies for the wrongs that have been done in my father's name. And I urge the alliance now of both of these organizations, the Others and the Cadre. Together we can rid the world of many woes and evils; together we can make this world a better place for us all.' "

The camera panned over to Terri. She was smiling now while dabbing at her eyes with a lace hankie. "Such beautiful and brave words, Bob. Thank you for sharing them with us and thank God for Steven DeRouchard. Somehow I think he will make the world a more wonderful place."

Mitch laughed, a rich hearty sound. "I think we're all supposed to join hands now and sing a song about the brotherhood of mankind."

Lily reached over and turned off the tape. "And that's it, except for a rather boring recap of it all. Now, I think a party is in order, don't you?"

"If you can trust him, that is," Chris said. "I have vague memories of him having a very cruel streak when he was younger. He seemed to enjoy making lesser creatures squirm. He was good at hiding it, though, and Phoenix's bruises and scars healed quickly, so Mum never suspected. But Eduard knew. And he encouraged the behavior."

"That does not surprise me," Vivienne said, "but still, if Terri and Bob have fallen, can the empire of DeRouchard be far behind?"

Chapter 29

Lily went behind the bar and motioned for Vivienne to join her. Within a few minutes, I heard the pop of a champagne cork and the splash of liquid hitting the bar.

"Listen, you two," Mitch called to them, "I don't mind you helping yourself to our inventory, but don't make a mess unless you plan on cleaning it up."

Vivienne giggled and stuck her tongue out at him. "We will clean it up, Monsieur Greer. But only after we celebrate. This is a very special evening for us all, is it not?"

Lily found the champagne glasses and began to pour one out for each of us. Then she hesitated, looking at Chris. "I'm not sure what the drinking age is here, Chris. But out of all of us, I'd say that you most deserve a glass of this."

"Just a small one, Lily, no more than half a glass. I sure don't need to face Mum tomorrow morning with a hangover. You've all forgotten that when everyone else retires for the day, I'll be left here alone with her."

"We could keep her sedated, if you're worried about your safety, Chris," Sam said. "Or I could come over and keep watch."

Chris's face reflected more sadness than fear. "I don't think you understand, Doctor Samuels. She's not going to attempt to kill me again. That was just the shock of the transition."

I looked at him. "I agree, Chris. Her violence was a mistake, similar to her dropping the bowl of peas with Steven's change."

Vivienne held back a giggle. "How could it be like a bowl of peas?"

"It's a long story, Vivienne," I said, half smiling, "and I suggest we hold off on it until another time. It's not really appropriate material for the party mood you're trying to establish."

Chris rubbed his right hand across his eyes. "Yeah, I think it was like that, Deirdre. Did she tell you that story?"

I nodded. "Yes."

"Maybe tomorrow night you could tell it back to me. I can barely picture it, and I think I'm going to need every trick in the book to pull her out of this. I'm hoping that once she discovers I am not going to turn into another like Steven, she will adapt."

Sam nodded. "That would be the ideal solution."

Chris gave a short laugh. "It's not as if she's lost anything, not recently, at least. It was always me, inside, in spite of the illusion that Phoenix and I were different people. She'll learn that with time."

I knew, of course, that what he said was not really true. Maggie *had* lost her baby and she would carry the guilt for that the rest of her life.

"We all hope that she adapts, Chris," I said. "I don't believe that any of us could wish her ill."

Lily came around then and distributed champagne to everyone. Finally we all stood with glasses in hand.

"In Victor's absence," Vivienne said, "I am the eldest, although"—she gave Sam a wink—"I will kill the first of you who suggest that I look it. Even so, I shall propose the toast." She paused for a moment, to catch our attention and to collect her thoughts.

"To life." She held up her glass. "May it always be good. To love, may it always be true. And to truth." Her eyes acquired a wicked glint. "May it never be delivered again into the hands of the likes of Terri and Bob."

"Cheers!" We all laughed and clinked our glasses together, moving back into the conversational groups we'd been in prior to the toast.

I did not participate fully in the party, although I sat at the same table with Sam, Vivienne, Claude and Lily, drinking with them, and producing a smile or a laugh at the appropriate times.

"So, Viv," Lily said, "Mom told me you ran into cows on the road on the way here."

Vivienne laughed and started telling her the story of Sam and the cow, embellishing the tale until it was so far removed from the truth that it was unrecognizable. Then she stood up and sang a song in her native language. "And that, *mes amis,* was the song of the earl and the milkmaid," she said when finished. "I used to sing it centuries ago. It is the cow's fault, of course."

"Viv," Sam said dryly, "there was never any cow on the road."

I watched them all as they laughed, and I put on the appearance of joining in the fun. In reality, though, I was doing nothing more than counting the minutes ticking by. I wondered how long I could manage to avoid sleep. Looking around at this small group of people that I loved, I knew that, no matter how long, it would not be enough.

Mitch and Chris sat away from us and talked quietly together for most of the night. The undisguised joy on my husband's face brought joy to me as well, and I found that I could not begrudge him the time spent with his son. Instead, I was content to watch, more than content to pore over my remaining memories as if they were jewels or golden coins.

The Others may have promised recompense, but I doubted that there was any cure for me that they would share. It was all too easy, the recanting of Terri and Bob, the brave words of Steven DeRouchard that sounded so noble, so uplifting. *No, I* thought, as I watched the celebration around me, *there is something else happening here. Something else to which all the hardship we have experienced is just a preamble. Something more terrible, perhaps, something more permanent.*

*   *   *

About an hour before dawn, Sam went back to check on Maggie and reported that she was still sleeping soundly. Chris got up from where he and Mitch had sat talking, stretched and yawned. "I need to get some sleep, too. I'm totally exhausted. Night, all."

He walked back to the bedroom he had been sharing with Maggie and once again I marveled at his reappearance and the intellect and experience of a man in the body of a boy. It's an ill wind that blows no good, I had told Sam earlier. And although that was certainly true, I could not help worrying about what the payment for this particular miracle would be. For payment would be required. Of that I was quite sure.

Lily left Vivienne and came over to sit next to me. "You're being awfully quiet, Mom, are you sure you're okay? Can I get you something else to drink maybe?"

"I am fine, Lily. Just a little tired and hungry. And that can easily be cured with sleep and blood. Tomorrow night I will be right as rain."

She gave me a sharp look. "If you say so. Anyway, Claude and I should be getting back to the hotel before dawn. Maybe some of the rest of the Cadre will be joining us tomorrow night, although I tend to doubt that now that the dogs have been called off. We are, as a group, very self-serving."

I gave her a weak smile. "True. If you should hear from Victor, please give him my regards. You are happy with him, are you not?"

"Yeah."

"That's good." My eyes went to Mitch and he sensed my gaze and smiled at me from across the room. "A strong relationship can make all the difference in the world."

"Well, about that, Mom. It's not really what you think. Our relationship is strictly platonic, we've never progressed to anything even remotely sexual."

I blushed and turned my head away. "Oh," I said, "I had rather thought it had."

"Well, to be honest, Mom, I wanted you to think that. Because I knew it bothered you." She laughed. "Hey, I'm a pain in the ass most of the time, Victor always says that. Why should I treat you any differently?"

"Why should you, indeed? I certainly have never done anything to deserve your love or your respect. Perhaps, in the future, we can change that." *If I have a future.*

"Sure." She kissed my cheek and patted my hand. "I'd like that."

"We could do some sight-seeing tomorrow night, if you would like," I lied to her, smiling. "You'd probably enjoy roaming around in the ruins. And the cemetery."

"It's a date. And now I'd better go, before sunup. Good night, Mom." She kissed me again and waved to the others. "Mitch, Sam, Viv, see you all tomorrow night."

She and Claude left, followed fairly quickly by Vivienne and Sam.

"I should know more on the test results, Deirdre. I'll call if there are any new developments. Failing that, we'll both see you tomorrow night as well." He shook Mitch's hand and moved to open the door for Vivienne.

"Bonsoir," she whispered in my ear, "and do not worry, sister. It will all be made right."

I shivered at her words. *That, my sister,* I thought, *is exactly what I fear.*

I stood for a while staring at the door after they left, wishing that I could make this particular moment in time stop and stay.

Mitch came over and draped an arm around my shoulders. "Quite an evening, wasn't it?"

"Yes," I said, "it was that. I think, though, that I might miss having Terri and Bob on the air. If it hadn't been so pointed an attack at us, they might have been amusing."

Mitch chuckled. "At the very least, their scripting was original. Now come, wife, it's almost dawn."

I reached up and kissed him. "I love you. You must know this, Mitch. That no matter what the future holds," *or does not,* I thought, "I will always hold that love for you deep inside me. It will never die as long as I live. Every time you see me or every time you look in the mirror I want you to think, 'Deirdre loves me.' "

He said nothing, he did not need to. Instead, he picked me up, carried me up the stairs and through the door as if we were newlyweds. He set me down on the bed gently, and checked the locks on the door and on the window shutters.

Then he turned on every light in the place and we made love. There was no darkness in which to hide and the love we felt surely must have shone from our eyes.

When it was over, I laughed and stretched. "That was wonderful, my love. Just like the first time and the last time and every other time rolled into one."

He smiled. "Glad you liked it, Mrs. Greer."

"I did not merely like it, Mitch. I loved it. As I love you."

He kissed me. "I love you, too."

We talked for a time about the events of the evening; Chris's return, the Others' abrupt and unexpected turnabout, even Vivienne and her nonexistent cow. Eventually, though, his responses came further apart and his voice grew sleepy.

"Get some rest, Mitch. We can always talk more when we wake up." I forced a cheerful tone to my voice, wanting to get through this last meeting without tears. I did not want his last memory of me to include red eyes and a sniffly nose.

"Yeah," he murmured, already dropping off. "Good night."

"Good night, Mitch." I kissed him and he rolled over and slept.

I lay awake for as long as I could, watching him sleep, capturing this feeling of love and hiding it away in my heart. I had promised him I would.

Then sleep overcame me, as I knew it would, and I fell into what seemed an endless dream.

Come home, it said, *and leave all of this behind.*

Chapter 30

And when I woke, it had been done. I opened my eyes to a strange place, to a stranger sleeping beside me, to a world that held no place for me. I quietly slid out of bed and looked at the man I had left behind. I knew what we must have meant to each other, but the memories were gone, along with the years— *had it been years?*—we had shared.

Instinctively, I knew that there must have been good times and bad times, tears and laughter. And love. I felt sure I would not have stayed with him if there were not love.

I sighed and looked at the clothes draped across the furniture and dropped on the floor. We had, I supposed, shared a time of passion, before we had slept. But if he had ever held me, had ever kissed me, the touch of him had been completely washed away.

Come home, the dream had said. And so, quietly, I put clothes on my body, not the ones that had been on the floor, but some others that I found: jeans and a sweater and a pair of heavy boots. As I sat down to put the latter on, I felt something in the back pocket of the pants, reached in and pulled it out. It was, I saw, a small cassette tape.

"Why it was there, I hadn't a clue. What it contained, music or voices or silence, was a mystery to me. Yet, it had obviously been important enough for me to save, so save it I would. I tucked it back into my pocket and finished lacing the boots.

I unlocked and opened the door, peering out into the hallway. Two dogs slept at the door. They opened their eyes as I stepped out and rose to their feet, stretching and yawning. They followed me down the stairs and then surged ahead of me, showing me the way to a back door. As I passed through a kitchen, I saw a woman with dark hair and sad eyes, sitting at the table. Just sitting and staring off into nothingness.

I should have known what sorrow she was nursing, should

have known why she sat here, like this, all alone and crying softly. And my heart broke that I could not remember.

She jumped as I stepped into the room, then relaxed. "Hello, Dot," she said, not smiling, "did you have a good sleep?"

Dot? I thought, *is that really my name? No, that does not seem quite right.* "Fine, thank you," I said, with what I hoped was an appropriate smile. "And you?"

She gave a small humorless laugh. "You should know well enough that I did. Vivienne gave me enough Valium to drop a cow, I think. But even at that, I feel better now."

"Good," I said, "I'm glad."

I stepped over to the door and put a hand on the knob.

"Going out?" she asked. "Shall I tell Mitch where you've gone?"

Mitch. That was his name, then. A good name, strong and confident. Perhaps it matched him, but I did not know, I could not remember.

However, the state of my mind and memory were none of this woman's concern, so I smiled and played along. "Yes, if you would please. Tell him that I am just going for a short walk and I should be back soon. He shouldn't worry; I'll be fine."

She nodded, seeming to understand much more of this conversation than I did. "That's right, your kind is safe again. The vendetta has been called off by Steven. Phoenix told me. Or Chris told me. We had a very long talk today, while the rest of you were sleeping. And I think, we think, everything will be fine."

"Good," I repeated, "I am so very glad for you and Chris." Reaching over, I opened the door, letting the dogs out into the night. "And I will see you later, then. Good night."

"Good night, Dot." Her eyes glinted up at me. "Enjoy your walk."

I closed the door and looked at the dogs. "Where to?" I asked them and then laughed at my own folly. They could not tell me.

I began walking, just walking. Admiring the rows of tidy little houses, sniffing the sea air appreciatively, I decided to move uphill, to get a better vantage point of this town. Perhaps a glimpse of it as a whole would trigger some glimmer of remembrance.

As I reached the top of the steep cobblestoned street, I was greeted with a glimpse of ruins, of moonlight shining through empty windows, of rows of graves. Somehow, it felt appropriate, it felt right that I should find my way here.

"Is this home then?" I asked the question.

"No," came an answer from behind me, "you are not home yet, Deirdre, but I promise you it will be soon."

And a hand clapped down on my mouth and I felt a needle slide into my skin. My mind dissolved and my eyes fluttered shut.

I did not know that I had slept, so little time seemed to have passed. I had closed my eyes in the old church ruins and opened them here. Where was here? Was it real or a dream? And now that there was nothing left of me, did it matter? Would it ever matter again?

The surface upon which I lay was smooth and soothingly cool. I rubbed a hand against it. It was leather. My hand dropped farther and my eyes began to focus. Black leather, I saw, and supported by chrome.

And I was dressed in different clothes. Instead of the jeans I had been wearing, I had on a black silk nightgown with a plunging neckline and a billowing skirt. Oddly enough, this garment seemed as familiar as the jeans, shirt and hiking boots. *Perhaps that was the dream,* I thought.

The room was dark but even as that thought crossed my mind, the shadows retreated somewhat giving me limited vision. A large room, it smelled of new leather and fresh paint.

I sat up on the couch and looked around me at this new place. *It must be a dream,* I thought, *since it seems familiar. And now only dreams are real.*

Feeling more comfortable in that assessment, I relaxed. No matter how terrible the dreams were, I knew, they never hurt me upon awakening. I studied the room again. A bar stood in one corner of the room, black and chrome and sparkling. On the bar top, stood a bottle of opened red wine and two clean glasses of delicate crystal.

"Why not?" I said with a quiet laugh. "I'm very thirsty."

I rose from the couch on unsteady legs; once standing I discovered that I felt dizzy and slightly nauseated. *Odd,* I thought, *I normally feel well in the dreams.* However, I managed to cross to the bar and pour myself a glass of wine.

The first sip brought tears to my eyes. It was not that the wine tasted bad; on the contrary it was wonderful, sharp and rich. No, the tears had nothing to do with the wine's quality. I cried because I knew I'd drunk this vintage before, in happier times, perhaps, although I could not remember.

Glancing at the empty glass, I wondered for whom it was meant. My head ached and I sighed, turning around with the wine in my hand and leaning my back against the bar. I faced a different view of the room now and saw across from me that there was one door, a heavy wooden one. And deeper in the shadows, back in a dark corner, there was a massive desk, so black it might have been carved of onyx. On the wall next to the desk, seeming horribly out of place in this sea of modern furniture, stood a huge ornate and antique armoire. And behind the desk sat a man, so completely engulfed in shadows that had it not been for the glitter of the eyes that watched me, I might never have seen him.

"So," I said unsteadily, trying to peer through the shadows to see the face of the man sitting at the desk, "you are Steven DeRouchard."

Attaching the name did me little good. I knew the name, recognized it the same way I knew the difference between my foot and my hand, but the recognition was academic. Cold and emotionless. The name represented a man, no more and no less. He meant nothing to me. Like all the rest of them, he meant nothing.

The voice laughed. "Truly, little one, you have named me. Or have you? The name DeRouchard is, perhaps, unimportant. I like to think of it and the body it represents as a vessel, or," and he paused, searching, I thought, for a word or perhaps only for dramatic effect, "a bottle, if you will. Its importance, its value does not lie in external trappings. Its true worth can only be determined by that which it holds. The essence of the vessel is all."

"Then I am nothing," I said, following his logic, "since I have no essence."

"Not necessarily, my dear. You have potential. A bottle that is empty can easily be filled."

Suddenly the peaceful feeling I had been enjoying exploded into anger.

"If I am empty, you bastard, it is your doing." I picked up the wine bottle and with all my strength threw it at his head. It came up short and struck the edge of the desk, splashing him with bits of broken glass and wine.

I opened my mouth to speak again but stopped, dead in the water and drifting. For one second, one very short second, I had a flash of memory. Something about the violence, the tinkling sound of shattered glass and my anger all blended into the vision of this man and he was . . .

No. The memory vanished, washed away in his laughter. The moment disappeared and was gone. "There," I said, moving forward a step, "why don't you see if you can fill *that* bottle? Bastard."

He brushed the slivers of glass from his coat. "See? You are not empty, little one, you still have your anger."

"I have held on to my anger. And I have saved it for you. I'm glad you are pleased."

"More than pleased, actually." He got up from behind the desk and began to move toward me.

Although I did not want to show my weakness to him, I could not help my reaction. I shrank back into the bar, fearing his approach.

"Why have you done this to me?" I whispered the words as he came closer to me. "What have I done to make you hate me, hate us, so much?"

"Hate?" He stopped about five feet away from me. "This has nothing to do with hate and everything to do with love. I saved your life, Deirdre."

At the mention of that name, I shivered. I had heard his voice say that name, my name I now knew, in dreams and in life.

"How did you save me?"

"If you could remember, you would know. I stopped the attacks on you. I brought you here. And you are alive."

I shook my head. "I do not think I am alive, not here, not in this time and place. I am dreaming, all of this. You have been in my dreams, since . . ."

"Always. I have always been in your dreams. That is where I belong." He moved toward me again and I saw him, clearly, and as if for the first time. His face with its finely sculpted lines, his mouth, his hair, the way he walked—all of it was real. This was no dream. Something deep inside me knew this man. Only one thing was different, only one detail seemed strange.

He stood in front of me now. Close enough so that I could reach out with a trembling hand and touch the scar that spread from one side of his neck to the other. "DeRouchard," I whispered. "It is the mark."

"Yet still, you've missed my true name. Try again, little one. The memory is there and you must find it if you are to survive. And once you do, I can save you. I alone hold the key; only I can fill you again and make you whole."

He gently grasped my chin in his hand and lifted my head to meet his gaze. I knew his touch. I knew his eyes. Straining for the memory, I stood on the tips of my toes and stared deeply at him.

And then I began to cry.

His arms pulled me into him. "It's been a long road, Deirdre, but now you are back home where you belong. The rest of it is much better forgotten. Now, say my name."

"Steven DeRouchard?"

"No, that is wrong." His mouth came down on mine and he kissed me, causing a thousand memories of him and him alone to stir and rush to the surface.

Oh, dear God. Somewhere deep inside I heard the roar of a caged animal. Somewhere deep inside me a woman was weeping over a lost love, a perfect love. And from somewhere far away I heard a voice, a well-loved voice, say "remember me . . ."

Gone. All gone. *I must get them back,* I thought, *the anger and the woman and the memories.*

But all I had left was here and now.

And I said his name.

"Max."